AN UNEXPECTED ANNOUNCEMENT...

Jaysus, God, he thought, steeling himself, trying not to get emotional, trying hard to keep his own tears at bay. What would he do without her? How would he go on?

"Siobhan?" His voice came out husky, a rough whisper as he took her hand and knelt in front of her, kissing her forehead as he reached a level with her eyes. "Darlin? Ye must tell me, whatever it is. I'm here for ye. I won't ever leave ye. Never." The last came out on a choked, half sob and Siobhan's eyes widened.

"Henry, why are ye cryin?"

"I'm not," he lied, feeling the tear leave his eye.

"Don't lie to me. I can see ye're tears plain as day. What's wrong?"

He couldn't believe it. Here she sat, teary-eyed in the window and she was asking him what was wrong? "Are ye daft, Siobhan? You, sitting here lookin' like a month of rainy weather and ye're askin' me what's wrong?"

He could tell she had to think about it as she opened her mouth, though nothing came out. Except a sigh. A very big, loud sigh.

"Ye'll find out eventually," she finally said.

Henry braced himself. This was it. This was when his life would change forever and it would be all downhill from here.

"The thing is, Henry, ye're goin' to be a father."

Lumau Publishing
C'mere To Me © 2019 by Sonia Gay
Cover image Celtic knot © Tata Donets/Shutterstock
Cover background image © Sonia Gay
Cover design © 2018 by Lois Hotte
and Lumau Publishing

ISBN: 978-0-9958376-9-0

Lumau Publishing
lumaupublishing@gmail.com

C'MERE TO ME

Book Five of
the O'Farrell Legacy

S. M. Cross

I dedicate this book, the last of the series, to all those who had a hand in making it possible; from the friends who read for me to the people who helped with the cover, and to my copy-editor. None of this would have been possible without your help. Of particular note, to M.D. Without you, the manuscripts would still be on my computer and going nowhere. Lastly, to my family, whose love and companionship have buoyed me up on many a day when I needed it.

You are all incredible people.

Celtic Dreams

By Sonia Gay

I'll tell a tale of Ireland's blood
Where love and turmoil grow
Where cupid's bow hath touch the hearts
And vanquished every foe
***

A tale of Hank, so strong and true
And of his love, fair Laura
Of broken hearts and broken dreams
Of mending lives with honour
***

'Twas Brandon, like a jester's son
To change his shattered past
Who Aine fed and nursed to health
To keep and hold him fast
***

Of Niall whose love for Michael
Was censured and love forbidden
But in the dark and in their hearts
That love was never hidden
***

Where Liam found his lovely lass
Though Sine, fair uncertain
Against them though the world contrived
His love she learned was certain

***

Young Ciara spanned three century's years
To find her love held fast
Within the arms of Cian
Whose love would always last

***

So hark ye now and learn the tale
Of Ireland's children free
Of lives and loves, of romance sure
And O'Farrell's Legacy

C'MERE TO ME

Chapter One

Siobhan looked at the strip on the pregnancy test stick and felt faint. The room spun and settled, as did the information on the stick. Positive. It said positive. Not only that, the notation confirmed the pregnancy was also much farther along than she thought, and no amount of repeating the test over the last two days had come up with anything else.

She was well and truly pregnant.

Sitting down heavily on the closed lid of the toilet seat, Siobhan didn't know if she felt like laughing or crying. They'd tried so hard over the years, she and Henry, to have a child of their own before giving up to the realization that it just wasn't going to happen for them—until now. Now, when Henry's half niece Emily, who had been living with them as their own since the age of ten, was planning on leaving home to get a job before heading off to university in another year. Emily, who had been the only child Siobhan had thought she would ever have.

Then there was Henry. When he and Siobhan had met, he had already taken over custody of Emily and had come to Killarney looking for his half brother, Hank, a man Henry had only recently learned existed. Instead, he'd run into Siobhan, or rather she had run into Henry thinking he was Hank, they looked so much alike.

She remembered that meeting on the street as if it were yesterday.

"Hank, oh my God, I haven't seen ye in ages. Didn't even think ye were still around," she'd exclaimed, seeing him standing there, big as life, tall, black-haired, and as handsome as ever. No, her mind amended. Handsomer, if that were possible.

He'd looked at her as she'd spoken. "What did ye call me?" he'd asked, and Siobhan had been taken aback.

"I do apologize," she'd said, flustered and feeling embarrassed. It wasn't Hank after all, but oh, how similar they looked. Like twins!

"No, it's alright, don't leave," he'd said. "I've actually been looking for someone named Hank. Could ye tell me a little more why ye think I'm him?"

He had looked at her with eyes like Hank's, deep blue, enough to drown in, and her heart had done a little somersault. She'd been so in love with Hank and he'd dumped her for that Canadian girl before leaving for Canada after a whirlwind marriage. It was only about a year after his mam had died and he'd left Killarney, left all his friends. Left her. Siobhan had been angry. Upset. She'd wanted to shake some sense into him but he would have none of it, telling her it was none of her business and they were through.

And then, on that last night before Hank took his Canadian girlfriend as a wife, Siobhan had convinced him to go to bed with her, thinking she could change his mind.

Instead, he'd enjoyed the tumble, said thanks-very-much, and left her before midnight. She'd lain awake the rest of the night, cursing him to the moon and back.

And crying. She'd done a lot of crying.

Then suddenly, so many years later when she'd finally

got over him but was still single because no one could ever take his place, she'd stumbled across his doppelganger on the street.

Peering into this man's eyes, eyes that made her melt, she recovered herself in time to see the weyan at his side.

"Oh, hello," she said to the young girl. "I almost didn't see ye there."

"Ah," said the man, his hand holding onto the little girl's, her eyes looking so similar to his; her hair, hanging in waves of raven black, curling of its own accord, just like Meara's used to do. She'd envied Meara, Hank's younger sister, that beautiful head of hair. "This is my niece, Emily. Say hello, Em."

The weyan turned her face shyly into the man's side and then, peeking out from beneath his arm, whispered, "Hello."

Siobhan couldn't help but feel drawn to the little girl. Her uncle seemed to be a person she was very attached to and could no doubt rely on if the girl's grip on his hand was anything to judge by.

"I'm Siobhan," she said to Emily. "And I'm very pleased to meet ye." She didn't take the little girl's hand in hers to shake; could tell that Emily wasn't ready to do that yet so she stood upright again, having crouched down to the girl's height in order to greet her.

"The name's Henry. Henry O'Farrell."

She met his eyes and told him her full name. "Siobhan. Siobhan O'Sullivan." Then, looking around at the crowded street, she said, "Perhaps there's a place we can talk where it's a little more private. Would ye care for some tea?"

Henry nodded, smiling at young Emily. "I'm sure Emily could use a quick bite. It's been a while since breakfast."

They strode down to the local chipper and ordered up

some burgers and chips, and while Emily had an orange fizzy drink, Siobhan and Henry ordered tea.

Finding their seats, Henry brought up Hank's name again, watching as Emily tucked into her food. "Why did ye call me Hank?"

"Ah, that. Well, if ye don't know, ye could be twins."

"That's interestin', that is."

When he didn't say more but instead lifted the burger to his mouth, Siobhan took note of his hands, his strong, lean fingers, and remembered that Hank had hands like that. Strange. He was so much like Hank. And this man had been looking for someone named Hank. "Why were ye lookin' for Hank? If it's the one I'm thinkin' on, he's not here anymore. Gone to Canada, I think," she said.

Henry shook his head and swallowed his mouthful. "That's unfortunate, that is. I just hoped I could meet him."

"If I knew where he was, I could tell ye. I might be able to find him, but it would take a while. Are ye stayin' in Killarney?"

"For now, yeah. I have some work to do here, and Emily needs a stable place for school. Seems the schools here are as good as any, and she likes it."

Emily smiled up at Siobhan, a mouthful of burger tucked into one cheek. "It's good craic," she said, almost losing her food.

"Don't talk with your mouth full," admonished Henry.

Again, Siobhan had to smile because it was something a father would say. "So, ye're takin' care of her?"

"It's a bit of a story, and if ye've time, I'd like to ask a few questions about Hank. But later, if ye get my drift." His head nodded ever so slightly toward Emily, whose burger now threatened to fall apart on her.

4

"I do."

"I've my sister visitin' just now. She'll gladly watch Em tonight if I can take ye to dinner."

Siobhan was gobsmacked. "Dinner? Oh, I…em, sure. That would be lovely. Where shall we meet?"

"Here," he pulled a pen from his pocket along with a small, ratty notebook that looked as if it had seen better days. "Here's my phone number, and if ye can write your address and phone number there, I can ring ye later, pick ye up, and we can decide. Would that be alright?"

"Oh, yeah, of course. That'd be grand."

* * *

Later that night, after they'd decided on a quiet dinner at a local restaurant, Henry began the story of how he came to have a ten-year-old niece in his care. "Her mam saw me one day, same as you, thinkin' I was Hank. If I ever get my hands on him I'd like to wring his neck, desertin' his family when they needed him the most."

"He was in love with a Canadian girl. Far as I know, they married and moved to Canada. I tried to stop him, to tell him it was a mistake, but he'd have none of it. He was determined, was Hank."

Henry shook his head, angry at Hank's desertion. "Meara was surprised to learn I wasn't Hank. But once we got to talkin', and me askin' a few questions, turns out we had the same da."

"What?" If Siobhan was gobsmacked earlier, she was now completely shocked at Henry's admission.

"I know. My sentiments exactly, especially at the time. I didn't want to believe what she was tellin' me, that our da's names were the same, that they worked at the same trade, and that he'd disappear for months at a time, and then show up in a hail of glory. Ye see, my da was killed in a rollover with his lorry some years back and we found some items he was carrying. Gifts, we thought. Perhaps for other weyans, and a lacy bit of somethin' that would not have fit me mam. Wouldn't have come up past her hips, if it went that far." He grinned, and Siobhan could imagine he was thinking of his mam, a portly woman, from the sound of it, trying to put on something much too small, if what Henry was saying was true.

She remembered Hank's mother, a frail-looking woman who always seemed on the brink of tears. "Hank's mam was a bit of a thing. Very tiny. Petite. A puff of wind would blow her over."

"That's what I learned from Meara. It all made sense. Hadn't before then but there was no denyin' the truth. Meara was stayin' with me at the time. Wee Emily hadn't had proper schoolin' and needed some stability. So I agreed that Meara could live with me since she was a half sister and needed lookin' after. And there was a school not far from where I was livin' at the time that Emily could attend."

"What brought ye to Killarney?"

"It was where Meara said they'd lived. She gave me the address and I looked it up when we got here. 'Course, someone else lives there now and if there was anythin' there that had belonged to our da, it was no longer there. But I kind of liked Killarney, and as me da did, had worked a lot of contracts here. I'm a stonemason by trade, and there's lots of work hereabouts. I figured it was as good a place as any to put down roots. Em seems to like it and she's made some friends. There's more for her to do here than Inishannon."

Siobhan swirled the wine around her tongue and swallowed, taking in all Henry was saying. Something seemed left out though, and so she asked, "How did ye come to have Emily? Did Meara not want her, or are ye just lookin' after her for a bit?"

His eyes immediately lost their luster, and he swallowed. Hard. "Meara's dead."

A gasp escaped Siobhan's lips before she could prevent it, and feeling at a loss for words, all she could summon up was, "I'm so sorry. So sorry to hear that." And then, "How?"

"Overdose. She had a drug problem and I was trying to get her to seek help, thought she was doin' okay. Then one night she went out, said she'd be back around ten, but ten came and went and finally I went to bed. About three in the morning there's a bangin' on me door and it's the shades, saying they'd found Meara's body and my address in her purse. To make a long story short, I went to me mam to tell her what happened. By that time, she already knew about Meara and Emily, so it wasn't a stretch, hearin' what mam intended to do about the weyan. She adopted her. But since Em was used to livin' with me, I said as I'd keep her, raise her as my own, and so I have. Mam's too busy with her own work anyway. She's a nurse at the Cork University Hospital and works all kinds of hours, none of which work when raisin' a child."

"How did she manage, raising ye without yer da?"

He laughed outright at her words. "I guess I'd best tell ye of my family. Ye see," he chuckled at his own words, "there was more than just me. I was the eldest at fourteen when Da was killed, so I helped raise the rest, kind of became the man of the family. Next to me is Brandon, then the twins, Niall and Liam, and then our wee sister Ciara. Ciara was four when Da was killed, the twins were eight, and Brandon was ten. I always thought it would've been Ciara who was most affected by his death but I think it was Brandon. That arsehole, pardon my expression, gives trouble a whole new meaning."

Siobhan had to join Henry in his laughter. "I'm not surprised. Sounds like he was the one in between. Ye know, not the eldest, and certainly nothing like being a twin with someone that is so much a part of yerself, nor a young girl that would've been special all on her own, just for bein' a girl in a family of boys."

"Sounds like ye know people quite well," he said, the lines at his eyes crinkling in laughter as he spoke. "I think ye've nailed us all."

"Well, human nature is human nature. It just makes sense." Sitting a little more forward in her seat, she continued. "So now ye've got Emily, and she's enrolled in school here." Henry nodded. "So now what?"

His shoulders lifted in a shrug and he sipped his coffee. "Don't know. Guess I'd best look for a mam for her. She's goin' to need one soon, ye know, girl stuff."

"She's ten, ye say?"

Henry nodded.

"Hmm. Well, I don't know what I can say to that, but if ye need someone, ye know, to talk to her, like, I can do that. Ye've only to call me."

They'd finished off the evening in the car outside her flat, with Henry's hands on her breasts and their lips locked together as they steamed up the inside of the car.

"Oh, God, Henry, I'm not usually into someone I've just met but Christ, ye make me want ye," she sighed into the dark interior.

"Aw, feckit, Siobhan. I've no rubber johnny, but I want ye, too."

"Come upstairs. I've maybe somethin' in the house."

They scrambled out of the car and ran quickly inside,

dodging fat raindrops that had begun to splat on the pavement and wet the grass. And as she opened the door to her flat and closed it behind them, all thought of looking for a rubber had gone out the window.

Henry had her up against the wall, his mouth attached to hers, his hands roaming her body as if seeking a way in.

She hadn't been innocent. She'd made her way inside his jacket, run her hands down his sides until they'd edged their way into the waistband of his trousers. Then, pulling up his shirt, she'd managed to slide one hand down farther, finding his lad stiff and erect as could be managed within the confines of his clothing.

Henry had moaned into her mouth, found the buttons of her coat, and was undoing them as rapidly as possible until finally Siobhan shrugged it off without releasing his lad until she had to. Her bedroom was just to the left of the door, and she walked backward, knowing the bed would be encountered soon enough. They'd stopped at its edge, leaving a trail of clothing littering the floor as they went.

Off went Henry's shirt as she spread her fingers across the broad expanse of his nearly hairless chest, with only a slight fuzz between the muscled mounds, topped by his erect nipples. Rubbing her fingertips across the nubs encouraged him, and he grasped the globes of her arse and pulled her close. So close she could feel his erection, hard against her belly.

"Ah, Henry," she murmured.

His response was to kiss her silent and undo the back of her dress, peeling the zip down until he could push it from her shoulders. And suddenly, as if by magic, her pantyhose followed, along with her knickers, until she was left before him wearing naught but the necklace she'd clasped about her throat before going out.

She could have sworn his eyes dilated at seeing her standing naked before him, but she didn't have time to ponder that. She was eyeing him as well, and never had she seen a man so finely wrought before, not even Hank, whose body she used to worship with her own.

"I've no rubber," Henry reminded her, pulling her close against him, kissing her hair, her eyes, her lips. "Didn't ye say ye might have somethin'?"

A fine time to remember, she thought, her mind working fast. Did she have anything? She'd known she hadn't when she invited him up. "It'll be okay. I'm due any day now," she said into his mouth, her hand rolling his nads between her fingers, knowing she was driving him wild.

"It's been a while for me. A long time," he said, and she instinctively knew he meant he wasn't carrying anything.

"Oh, right. That. Yeah, that's me, too." She hadn't lied about that little tidbit. Any man she'd dated had been nice but not interested in bedding her, at least not for anything more than what the moment might offer, and after a couple of those, she hadn't been interested anymore. She'd decided that until someone sent her into a tizzy, as Henry was doing with his mere presence, she'd avoid dating altogether.

Which brought her to the point in question…could she convince him it would be alright?

"Aw, feckit, Siobhan, I could pull out before I come," he offered.

"Right then," she managed, before grabbing at the bedcovers and throwing them back.

Seconds later, they were horizontal, and Henry had slid into her moist depths, feeling to her like he belonged there. It hadn't felt strange, hadn't felt as if they'd just met. It had felt right. True to his word, Henry had pulled out before he climaxed, and she hadn't become pregnant.

* * *

Well, there'd been a lot of water under the bridge, as the saying went, since that time. The extended family had grown, but although she and Henry had tried, she'd never become pregnant. Still, she loved Henry as if they could never be apart and remain whole, and was certain he felt the same. Yet for all that, she didn't know if he'd be pleased or pissed about this new turn of events.

They had talked of moving to some place smaller, to downsize the house because they wouldn't need a three-bedroom anymore, now that Emily was talking of moving into a flat with some friends. At nearly eighteen, she didn't need a mother and father hovering over her, as she seemed to think they were doing.

Siobhan was rethinking the downsizing bit. She had a good job as a school secretary and moving would mean that she would likely not be able to walk to work, but would instead have to rely on buses or a car. Single homes were farther outside the city center, and a flat wouldn't work, not now that she was pregnant. No, she'd have to convince Henry that they needed to stay where they were for a while. He'd figure it out eventually.

"Siobhan, are ye comin'?" Henry's voice reverberated up the stairwell and into the loo where she was still staring at the stick in her hand.

"Jaysus feckin' Christ," she said on a sigh, crossing herself, and sending a silent word of apology heavenward for her language. Then, shaking her head, she stood, wrapped the stick in toilet paper, and buried it at the bottom of the waste bin. She'd take it out with the rest of the trash later.

"Siobhan?"

"Comin'," she called out the door, and checking the mirror to make sure she hadn't suddenly changed during the few minutes she'd been in there, she turned and left the room.

Henry was waiting at the bottom of the stairs, looking up as she came down, smiling appreciatively at her dress. "That's very fine," he murmured, pulling her close to kiss her before she could fully interpret his words. "Lots of cleavage. It'll be good craic later," he grinned.

"Ah, leave off." She batted him away with a flick of her fingers but was secretly pleased that he'd noticed her dress.

And her cleavage. He seemed…distracted, lately. For a while, she'd thought maybe he was losing interest in her but quickly squashed that thought. He was always home, never away for long periods, not even overnight as his da used to be. Pushing aside thoughts of infidelity on her husband's part, she had chosen her dress with care. It had been a while since she'd last worn it, mostly because she'd gained a few pounds in the last couple of years. But suddenly, she hadn't been hungry. Or rather, she'd feel hungry but one look at food and her stomach would turn. Or she'd be famished, but if she couldn't eat something right now, it would be too late; five minutes later would be too late.

And then it had struck her that her period was overdue. But life had been busy what with Emily's graduation and two babies in the family due soon, and…life. Her once organized life had somehow turned upside down and even Henry, steadfast Henry, had seemed…uninterested.

With Henry's seeming disinterest in mind, she'd dressed with care for this graduation dinner of Emily's and pulled out all the stops. She'd somehow lost half a stone, enabling her to squeeze into her favorite dress, a wrap dress in shades of red and blue as if a painter's brush had gone a little wild, and gathered at the side, pressing burgeoning breasts together for a grand display of cleavage. One benefit of pregnancy, she mused when she'd gazed at herself in the cheval mirror in the bedroom.

Henry placed a possessive arm around her waist, heading her in the direction of the car where Emily was waiting in the back seat. The girl gasped in surprise at Siobhan's appearance. "Mam, ye look so fine," she exclaimed, and Siobhan couldn't help but smile back.

"Ah thanks, my sweet, and ye're lookin' quite fine yourself, ye are. I like what ye chose. Looks…" she faltered, felt the tears suddenly come.

"Mam?" Emily's expression had changed from happiness to one of concern.

"It's nothin'," Siobhan sniffed. "Just, ye were so little and then suddenly, ye weren't. And now look at ye. All grown up." She took the tissue Emily pulled from her purse.

"Here, I thought ye might need it. Ye've been a wee bit emotional lately, like."

"It's not like that at all, and don't ye be makin' things up," Siobhan sniffed.

"Into the car with ye, then," said Henry, climbing into the driver's seat. "We'll be late if we don't get a move on."

Siobhan slid into the seat. "Where are ye takin' us? Ye never did say, as if it was some great secret." Siobhan finished wiping her nose and looked askance at Henry as he pulled away from the curb.

"Ye'll see once we get there. It was Liam's doin', and I agreed."

"Oh, ye don't mean…"

"I do," he finished for her before she could say the name.

"So that's why ye were rushin' me. What time's dinner?"

"We've plenty of time, it's barely an hour away and I can do it in half that time."

"Don't ye dare. I'd rather get there in one piece."

From the back seat, Emily asked, "Where are we goin', like? Ye haven't yet said, though both of ye seem to know."

"Do ye really want to know?" asked Henry, glancing in the rearview mirror, teasing Emily.

"Cop on, ye know I do," she scolded.

Henry just laughed. "Ah well, ye'll know soon enough. We're goin' to Parknasilla. Liam says how he's arranged for a small get together in celebration of yer graduation."

In the back seat, Emily looked like a kid again, thought Siobhan, pumping her fist into the air, a broad grin across her face.

"I take it ye think it's fine?" he asked, and was joined in laughter by both Siobhan and Emily.

Less than an hour later they pulled into the parking lot and walked the path toward the hotel, watching its elderly spires and mullioned windows coming to life through the dense forest. They passed a tree with a faery door in it, and Emily laughed, pointing at it.

"I remember ye takin' me here when I was little and showing me that faery door. I was afraid to go any farther because I thought the faeries would get me."

"And how do ye know they aren't here waitin' for ye now?" Henry goaded.

She gave him that look, thought Siobhan, the look that all children give their parents at one time or another, accompanied by a rolling of her beautiful eyes.

When she was little, Siobhan had thought Emily's eyes like Hank's, but now, as a young woman, Emily was growing to resemble her true mam, more and more. Meara had been a beauty. Too bad all that beauty had gone to waste on the plonker who'd knocked her up and left her. If she ever found out who he was, she'd kill him, she thought. He deserved no less for leaving a mam and a child all on their own.

Very soon they were inside the hotel, walking its ancient hall toward the dining room and then stepping inside to a standing ovation at a very long table. A table that held absolutely every one of the family, including Emily's Uncle Hank and Auntie Laura from Canada and their two children, Ryan, two, and Meara, only a few months old and named for Em's mam.

As well, there were the twins, Niall and Liam, and their respective spouses, Michael and Sine, as well as Ciara and her new husband, Cian, who was Liam's actor friend from Denmark. That couple was expecting their first child in another three months, much to the delight of Cian's parents, who had visited earlier that month but had already left for home.

Brandon and his wife, Aine, also expecting their first child, were seated next to Kathleen, the matriarch of the family, the one who had legally adopted Emily and was now known to her as Gran. And next to them, Kathleen's parents, on a visit from Garrettstown, just off Old Head of Kinsale. They'd be staying the night, thought Siobhan, and secretly wondered if she and Henry would, too. It was grand to see the entire family here. She hadn't realized Henry could pull such a feat together, let alone keep it a secret.

Emily's squeal of delight caught the attention of the waiters in attendance, the rest of the diners in the restaurant grinning, having heard the applause on Em's entrance.

Tears choked Siobhan as she concentrated on smiling,

so happy for Emily. But she couldn't prevent them. They escaped to run down her cheeks faster than she could swipe them away.

Emily had rushed forth to hug everyone in turn, finishing up with her great-grandparents, no less incapacitated for all their nearly ninety years, and just as glad to see their entire family in attendance as Emily seemed to be to have them there.

"Oh, Mam, here," said Em, reaching into her purse for another tissue. "Ye're doin' it again."

Siobhan quickly took the tissue and dabbed at her eyes. "Thanks, and never mind the again part. It's just nearin' that time, I think," she hissed in defense of her emotions.

She hadn't hissed quietly enough.

"I've never known ye to be emotional," said Liam from his spot near the far end of the table. "Not even during Em's graduation ceremony and certainly not at any of the weddin's." His look encompassed his siblings and their spouses, and all the weyans in attendance as well.

"Yeah," agreed Niall, Liam's twin, seated beside his partner, Michael, "ye'd think ye were knocked up they way ye're carryin' on."

Siobhan blushed and Michael shushed his lover. "Whisht, now," he said to Niall, "you've made her blush so she not only has wet cheeks, she has wet cheeks that are bright pink."

Siobhan laughed. "If ye were closer I'd hit ye," she said through her tears.

And then Ciara's voice came through the gathering and everyone was suddenly quiet. "Ye are, aren't ye."

It wasn't a question, and Siobhan felt herself freeze on the spot.

Chapter Two

Whisht, all of ye. I'm fine. Nothin's goin' on, I'm just a bit overwhelmed, what with Em turnin' into such a beautiful young lady and suddenly seein' ye all here. Henry never said it was a gatherin' like this," she said, being completely truthful, at least about the last part. But then, she was fine. There was nothing wrong with her that a few more months wouldn't cure. About seven months, if she made her calculations right. Maybe six.

And then they were all seated at the table, the waiters began bringing out the food and it was like a Sunday brunch after church at Henry's grandparents' house, where everyone got together and tucked into the black pudding, the white pudding, the rashers, bangers, and fried spuds, and anything else they could think of cooking. It had been a while since they'd had one of those. They'd have to wait until Ciara's baby was born for the next great get-together. That couple had been married on St. Patrick's Day rather than wait for warmer weather to be wed at Ballycarbery Castle, because, as Ciara had said, she didn't want to be walking down the aisle looking like she was carrying a beach ball beneath her dress. Come to think of it, that was exactly what she looked like now, her face rounded in pregnancy, the baby she carried a very visible belly bump.

Taking the heat off herself, Siobhan turned to Niall and

Michael and asked, "So how's the adoption comin' along?"

"Grand," they both said at once, causing no amount of chuckles around the table.

"We've found a woman who is giving up her child and has agreed to allow us to adopt it," said Michael, his cultured English accent still noticeable though he'd been in Ireland for a few years now.

"The grand part about it," said Niall, "is that she has a background similar to Michael's. She's part Arab like him, says her parents don't know she's pregnant and so she's stayin' here until the weyan is born before goin' back to England."

"So what's she doin' while she's here, then?" asked Henry.

"Hiding," came Michael's reply. "Says she was having trouble hiding her increasing belly, so told her parents she was going to take an extended holiday. A three-month-long vacation with a girlfriend, touring Ireland. She figures she'll have the baby and then go home as if nothing has happened."

"Do ye think it'll turn out that way?" asked Kathleen.

Niall and Michael both shrugged. "We don't know, but we certainly hope so. We've found a place for her to stay and a way to continue the ruse of her traveling with a friend. We just hope it all continues to work out," explained Michael.

"And how far along is she?" Kathleen asked, ever the nurse, "And who's givin' her prenatal care and what midwife will deliver?"

"All taken care of, Mam," said Niall. "We're payin' for that, too. She's got good care in Dublin."

Kathleen agreed with their choice. "They're good there, they are, and I'm right happy for ye; but honestly, if her parents get wind of what she's done, it'll go badly for ye. Is she at least legal age?"

Niall nodded. "Twenty-three."

"Have ye seen some ID?" asked Henry, and again, his brothers nodded.

"She's legit," offered Michael. "I looked into her background myself."

"Ah, well then, that's settled it sounds like," said Kathleen, knowing that both Niall and Michael were computer experts. No, that was making light of it. They were geniuses, pure and simple. There wasn't a system they couldn't hack, a program they couldn't write, and if there was anything at all odd about the woman whose child they were going to adopt, those two would find it.

"So, all talk of babies aside, what are ye plannin' for the next phase of yer life, Em?" asked Liam. "I can get ye a job on my next film if ye've a mind."

"Don't ye dare," scolded Siobhan, knowing that Liam's films were often filled with nudity and not a little swearing and cursing. "She doesn't need ye to send her off on the wrong foot."

"What wrong foot?" asked Liam, looking hurt. "I'd watch out for her. Besides, she could stay with us. Sine would be glad of the company and maybe Em could watch the baby once Sine goes back to work."

"Thanks, Uncle Liam, I appreciate the offer but I don't know what I want to do yet, and as much as I like babies and weyans, I want to do more with my life than be a nanny." There had been no malice intended in her words, Siobhan knew. Emily was known to be frank and to speak her mind, much like Henry.

Yet Emily's feelings seemed to be quite mixed, and rightfully so, thought Siobhan, looking at her daughter

19

with a mother's eyes. Although she, herself, had never had the experience of minding babies, she thought it could be wonderful…hoped it would be wonderful, at least for herself. And still the question remained as to what Henry's reaction would be.

It was answered with Henry's next statement. "Well, I can't say as I blame ye. I'm glad that ye were already ten when ye came to us. Don't know if I could have handled a baby, all that screamin' and gettin' a body up in the wee hours. It's like to send someone off the deep end, that would."

"Ah, it's not that bad," Hank said in defense of fatherhood. "Look at me, I'm still sane. In fact, I think I'm saner now than I've ever been, and that's a fact!" To which the entire table gave a hearty, "Hear, hear!" No one had known Hank even existed for so long, but here he was, now an accepted part of the family, and adding on to it quite nicely. And even though Kathleen's parents were no relation to Hank—Hank being related to his siblings through their deceased father—his babies, Ryan and Meara, had been welcomed just the same.

"Well, I don't know as I could take it," Henry continued. "I'm not a young fella anymore. I'm kind of set in my ways and don't know if I could adjust to havin' a weyan underfoot."

"Ye'd get used to it, trust me, Henry, ye would. Ye have no idea how fatherhood changes a man," Kathleen said. She'd had five children and watched as her husband had gloried in the birth of each one.

"I'm not so sure. As I said, I'm ever so glad Em came to me as a ten-year-old, potty trained and all that!"

Emily blushed. "Thanks, Da. Everyone really needed to hear that at the supper table."

Henry grinned and leaned back in his chair, fully sated if the pat to his belly was any indication.

"Is there dessert?" asked Ciara. "I could sure use somethin' sweet."

"Of course there's dessert, oh, faithless one," chided Liam who, like Henry, was leaning back in his chair looking sated and rather pleased with himself as well.

With a nod to the waiter who'd been refilling water glasses, a moment passed and then a trolley was pushed toward the table carrying a large cake lit with a single sparkler to announce its presence. "Congratulations, Emily," Liam said, and accompanied his words with a wink.

Henry was watching everything with a detached eye. He'd been concentrating on Siobhan all evening, knew something was up and wondered at her appetite. It was there, and then it wasn't. She'd taken a few bites and then she'd pushed her plate away, only to go back to it when everyone was almost done, to have a bit more. Then she'd lain her cutlery across it and sat back, leaving most of the food still there. He was worried; she'd lost weight and now she wasn't hungry. Was she ill? Did she have something incurable? It didn't bode thinking about but he couldn't push the thought completely away.

And then the cake came out and she ate one entire piece. Siobhan never ate sweets. She was a woman who ate sensibly, watched that her weight didn't get out of hand, and never ate sweets. Never. But tonight, Henry had watched her polish off a large piece of cake and then not hesitate when offered a bit more. Hadn't his mam once said that cancer patients often craved sweets? He felt a cold dread settle into his bones and prayed he was wrong. Unable to keep quiet, he remarked, "Ye didn't eat all yer dinner and here y'are, fillin' up on cake," and expected her usual retort, the scolding she'd often give him in response to his words.

"I was savin' space," she said, but looked as if she couldn't get enough of the confection and was hoping to eat the entire cake on her own.

"Da's right. Ye never would have let me get away with that," laughed Emily.

But Henry noticed that Siobhan wasn't laughing. "Ah, that's enough of that, now, Em. Yer mam's old enough to know her own business. I was just havin' a bit of craic."

"So what would ye do, if suddenly Siobhan was to have a baby?" asked Kathleen.

Henry swallowed, feeling as if he were somehow treading in quicksand. One wrong step could put him in jeopardy, but of what, he wasn't certain. "Hmm, I suppose I'd get used to it, but it's not likely to happen now, is it. Hasn't in almost ten years so I don't expect things to change now."

"What do you make of it, Ciara?" Michael, sitting next to his sister-in-law, asked. "You looked fairly certain a little while ago."

"I don't know."

Everyone at the table stopped talking and fixed their gaze on her.

"Well, don't everyone look at me that way, I simply don't know."

"But Ciara, ye've always known," Kathleen observed, "ever since ye were a weyan, ye've always had insight into other people's lives."

"We haven't told everyone yet, Cian and I," she indicated her husband of three months seated on her other side. "After all the past experiences, well," she hesitated, and Henry could see that it was difficult for her to explain, "I can't see things anymore."

Cries of "What?" and exclamations of "No!" went round

the table, leaving another gap of silence at the end of it.

"It's true," Cian answered for her. "Since that last episode where we found out all about the castle, she hasn't had any inkling of anyone's future. It's as if everything up to then was leading her to the ultimate ending, with us together. It was the first time we could be together without her having… uh, memories," he stressed the word as if he didn't know how else to phrase his meaning, "you know, her visions. It was at the castle, the day we got back and announced our engagement. That was when we realized she wasn't having them anymore."

Henry was grateful the table was quiet so that Cian didn't have to raise his voice to be heard. It was a large family gathering, the table spread the length of the room. But there were still a few other diners left to overhear, although no one else in the room knew them. There would be no innuendos or whispered words behind her back now. No one calling her crazy or odd. Everyone at the table had known of Ciara's gift, had known that she could see everyone else's future but nothing of her own.

Until Cian. Her visions about herself had begun after they'd been together for about six months. They were tied together in this life, and if Ciara's visions were correct, had been in a past life as well.

But now it was over, and Ciara, on the verge of motherhood, seemed relieved, although it had been a part of her for so long.

A quick glance at Siobhan, and Henry could have sworn she seemed as relieved as Ciara, waving her hand in front of her face as if she had suddenly become too warm and saying, "Whew! Yeah, kind of glad that's all over but I have to admit, I do miss you not tellin' us what's comin' up."

Dinner over, they all stood, and since the evening was fair, decided to take a stroll outside. All except Hank and Laura, who were going to take their weyans up to bed. Wishing the rest of the family a goodnight, the couple left the gathering with Ryan chatting nonstop and Meara asleep in her mother's arms. They'd been so well behaved during dinner.

Everyone else filed out of the old hotel, down the steps toward the path. Just out of the light from the large dining room windows, Henry grasped Siobhan's hand, holding it tightly, stopping her from following everyone just then. "Wait," he said, and watched until there was some distance between themselves and the rest. Even Emily had run ahead, as if she were still ten instead of nearly eighteen.

"What?" asked Siobhan, looking unsure with the moonlight glancing off her cheeks and reflecting its light in her eyes.

Henry couldn't stop himself. He leaned over and kissed her, urged her mouth open with his. He wanted more than a peck on her lips. He wanted her to know how much he loved her, because suddenly he was scared. Scared he was going to lose her.

As her mouth opened for him, his tongue went inside and she came into his embrace to spear her fingers through his hair. He wanted more, wanted it now, but it would have to wait until later. He'd packed bags for them all, had booked rooms for themselves and Emily despite the close proximity to Killarney, but hadn't said anything yet. He wanted this night to be perfect. Not just as a celebration of Emily's graduation, but to show Siobhan how much he loved her. He'd already had flowers delivered to the room and asked for extra bottles of soda to be on hand. If ever there was a night he wanted to celebrate with a drink, this would be it; but he remembered that one time when it had become too much and Siobhan had given him the ultimatum: it was either a life with her and Emily or the drink. Because, as she'd told him, she wouldn't allow him to take the girl with him if he was just going to drink his life away.

It had been a wake-up call. Siobhan hadn't understood at the time why he'd got completely ossified that night, more than he'd ever been in his entire life. So dangerously flaming that had he not puked it all up, he would have landed in hospital with alcohol poisoning. But then he'd compounded the sin and driven home.

Siobhan had been livid. Had railed at him about driving drunk and the no forgiveness rule by the authorities if he'd been caught.

But he hadn't seemed to notice, and she'd taken away both the car and truck keys and made him sleep on the sofa. He woke in the morning to hear that his mam had already picked up Emily and taken her for the weekend. And then Siobhan went to town on him.

Henry hadn't had a drink since. Couldn't trust himself. But he'd never told Siobhan why. Had never said that he'd lost a good friend that day, had seen the stone fall from where they'd been placing it and crush the man. It had been Henry's fault. He was supposed to have been on that part of the job but he'd been late back from town with supplies and Jimmy had elected to go ahead. As he watched the stone totter, saw the crane operator misjudge the placement, he'd tried to call out a warning, but no one could hear over the sound of machinery.

And then it was too late. Henry had liked and respected Jimmy. His death reminded him all too well of how his da had been killed, of the truck rolling over and the stone shifting and crushing him, and it had brought home how quickly

25

things can go from bad to worse.

It should have been Henry who'd been killed.

It had been too real and he'd begun to shake. He was only going to have one drink, he told himself, just enough to steady his nerves. But one drink had become two, and two… well, he'd lost count after the fifth. Whiskey went down far too easily, he knew.

"What?" she asked again when he'd released her mouth but still held her close.

"Nothin'," he answered, his words a hoarse whisper on the warm night air, "I just had to do that." He grinned at her and chuckled to see her grinning back.

"Ye're a terror, ye are, Henry O'Farrell," she laughed quietly. "Let's catch up to the others."

"Why? Let them get ahead. I'd just as soon enjoy this bit of time with you. Ye know, alone, without the crowd. I love my family, I'm grateful for them, for all of them, but is it wrong to want ye to myself? We've never really been alone, ye know. We've had Emily right from the time we said our vows, and before. So I'm thinkin' how nice it'll be, just the two of us, if Em decides to move into that flat with her friends."

He'd been caressing her back, not just rubbing it, the urge to undress her here, now, beneath a full moon, so strong that he moved his hand down to cup the globes of her arse.

"Henry," she admonished, but he knew she felt it, too. That she could feel his chubby through his trousers, pushing against her body, there but for a few layers of clothing.

Her hands mimicked his and cupped his arse, pulling him closer as he thrust against her, as if there was no barrier at all, and Henry bent his head to stuff his face into her cleavage. His tongue tasted the side of her breast and he heard her intake of air, the warm night breeze being inhaled and then let out on a sigh. "Aw, feckit, Siobhan, we should just go upstairs," he chuckled.

"So ye did get us a room here. I'd wondered."

"Well, I couldn't very well drive all the way back to Killarney with a chubby," he joked.

Siobhan joined his laughter. "Come on, let's get walkin'. It'll take yer mind off yer lower half for a bit."

"Not likely," he said, but went along with her. He was glad she still had her sense of humor. It meant that whatever was wrong with her might be troubling but maybe not deadly. Maybe not the "c" word. He didn't even want to say it, not even in his mind, because they'd been blessed, his family had. No one had ever been touched with the disease.

But Siobhan's had. She'd lost her mam when she was a teenager and her da shortly after she and Henry had married. Both to cancer, and both gone quickly. What were the chances of Siobhan doing the same? She'd already outlived her mam's age. There was still the age her da was when he passed for her to reach. That was only a couple of years away. What if that was all the time they had left to each other? A couple of years. It scared the hell out of him.

* * *

Siobhan took Henry's arm and began to walk, knowing he'd follow. What else would he do? Stand there like a recalcitrant child, planting his feet and refusing to move? It was normally something he'd do, if he'd a mind.

But for all his suddenly amorous musings, she hadn't been immune. She wanted him as much as he wanted her, but that would come later. There was Em to think of. Emily wouldn't know they were staying, or where her room was. It wouldn't be fair to desert everyone without telling a soul.

Yet it would be so fine…she let the thought trail off, unable to help smiling.

Henry hadn't missed her smile. "What's that for?"

"What?"

"That smile. It's like the cat who got the cream, it is. Ye're hidin' somethin'."

Henry's words struck deep inside her. Did he know? Suspect? Ignoring the possibility of his guessing, she gave him a hip check and laughed. "I'm just thinkin' on later, like."

"Ah, then that's good. Not too late to turn around."

"Henry O'Farrell, don't ye dare. We'd best catch up or they'll come lookin' for us and I don't want anyone askin' questions."

"Only one askin' questions would be me, such as, why we don't turn around now?" he quipped. "Everyone else already knows."

They couldn't. No, he was just guessing, and so would they be. "What do they know?"

He stopped, bringing her round to face him. "Don't ye know?"

She shook her head.

"Ah, it's just that I love ye so."

"Ah, Henry." All kinds of relief flowed through her.

His lips came over hers and she gave herself up to him. It wasn't about the secret she carried, not at all. Still, it was there between them, in a very literal sense. How soon was too soon to tell him? And how late was too late?

A shrill whistle split the night and they both looked up to the flash of a camera going off. "Caught ye," yelled Liam, causing both Siobhan and Henry to laugh.

"Right then, we're comin," said Henry.

"And ye will later as well, if I'm not mistaken," laughed

28

Liam, a remark that had Sine give him a good punch to his shoulder. "Well, it's true," he said in his own defence.

"Don't be crass," she scolded, and then to Siobhan and Henry, said, "He's just jealous because we're fast approaching the time when he won't have me to himself anymore."

"How long?" asked Siobhan, because she'd forgotten. It was true what they said about baby brain. You really did forget the simplest things and yet she'd known for months when Sine was due.

"Any day now, actually," laughed Sine. "I just hope it isn't tonight."

"Sneem wouldn't be such a bad place to have a child, nor Killarney," said Liam.

"It's not Galway, not home," she argued.

"Ah, we'll be goin' back soon, never fear," said Liam.

"I'm glad everyone was able to make it tonight," commented Henry, "and very glad it's over. I had a helluva time keepin' it a secret."

"Come see the moon," came Ciara's voice through the trees, beckoning them to hurry, "it's just rising and it's magnificent."

They came around the bend to see where everyone else had been standing, near the edge of the water with the waves lapping gently at the shore and the clear night above them filled with stars.

And the most glorious moon she'd ever seen, thought Siobhan. If she had a daughter…but she'd got no farther in her thoughts because suddenly they were all chatting and Henry's arm came around her, pulling her close.

"It's beautiful," he whispered into her ear, "just like you."

His comment brought her to tears.

Chapter Three

Henry and Siobhan were finally alone. They'd left his mam and Emily outside, grandmother and granddaughter, still staring at the moon and engaged in girl talk.

He'd turned to Siobhan, taken her hand, and led her back up the path to the hotel, through the beautiful, grand entrance and up to their room. Ensuring the door was locked, he pulled Siobhan close, his hand sliding up her back to grab at the tiny zip that held the dress together, and pulled it down.

Standing before her, he thought he'd never loved her as much as he did just now. She stood still, looking like a virgin on her wedding night, eyes dark with desire, hiding her thoughts, yet letting Henry do whatever he wanted.

And Henry wanted so much! He peeled the dress from her shoulders, exposing her breasts barely contained within the confines of her lacey bra. As the dress fell to the floor, Henry once again pressed his face into her cleavage, laved the side of one globe with his tongue, and felt her giggles begin to erupt.

"That tickles," she complained, but Henry didn't care. He kept on and deftly flicked the bra clasp open, sliding the straps from her shoulders and freeing her large mounds that, despite her weight loss, didn't seem any smaller.

Pushing away his negative thoughts, he was determined

to give her the best night of her life. It was all about her tonight, from the flowers right down to the massage he'd planned, and of course, the loving. Always the loving.

She sighed in his arms as he tongued her nipple, felt her body rub up against his, knew when her hand dropped that she'd be dragging at his trousers, eager to get to his lad. He was so chubbed up he thought he'd poke a hole through the material.

As if reading his thoughts, she did just that and soon had his arse bared to the room and to her touch. Not to be outdone, he kissed his way down her belly, to the rounded softness there and stopped.

Round?

Ignoring the warning bells in his head, he tucked his thumbs into her knickers and drew them down, exposing her soft curls and the secrets beyond, to his touch, his gaze, and his taste. His mind was still working, though, and had gone back to the feeling of her belly so that he hadn't noticed how intensely he'd been concentrating on her fanny until she gasped.

"Henry, on the bed for God's sake," she said, as he felt her begin to tremble.

He still had his shirt on but he couldn't wait, didn't want to wait, and as soon as she hit the bed, he'd climbed on after her. And while she was frantic to touch him, to guide him, he'd got hold of himself and pressed into her, feeling her insides grip him through the abundant juices he'd encouraged with his tongue.

"More, harder," she encouraged, and Henry did just that. He could no more have held back the floodgates of a dam than he could ignore her urgings.

He didn't have time to think, to wonder anymore about

her illness, about her weight loss, about the fact that her breasts were so full and her belly round, and yet she was losing weight. His body climaxed and all he could think of was how good she felt, how well they fit together, and how much she seemed to be his perfect partner.

And then the climax erupted, exploded, and Henry was frozen into her body, still pulsing as her muscles convulsed around him. As her internal spasms subsided, so did his thrusts, and he lay atop her, sweating into his shirt, feeling her laughter build, the jiggling of her slightly plump body beneath his, and wondered all over again about her health.

"That was grand, Henry," Siobhan breathed, spearing her fingers through his wavy hair, then bringing them round to cup the sides of his face to bring his lips down to hers. "I haven't seen ye so eager for a long time. We need to do this more often," she grinned, kissing him lightly before pressing her lips harder against his, opening, inviting him in while she invaded his mouth.

Henry felt his lad slip from her depths and he rolled from her, despite her arms holding him, to remove his shirt. He felt her eyes on him, observing every move he made until he tossed the shirt aside and slid once more into the shelter of her embrace. Running his hands down her side, Henry thought if eyes could caress, hers were doing just that as she lay quietly beneath his gaze.

He slid his hand toward her flange, rubbing lightly, playfully, and noted one leg rise to fall sideways, allowing him greater access. "What are ye thinkin'?" he asked, still locked on her gaze with his own.

"How much I love ye."

He grinned. They didn't often say it, didn't often have the time when Emily was young, as if their words should not be heard by anyone but themselves. And now that Emily was grown, well, it seemed a little too personal to have her hear them.

"I love ye, too. So much that it fair takes my breath away. I see ye doin' everyday things, like dishes at the sink, and all I can think of is how much I want to be inside ye, lovin' ye, like."

"Ah, Henry, ever the romantic," she chuckled. "But that's okay. With Emily nearly out the door, we'll have some time to ourselves, to get to know each other like we didn't have the freedom to do before."

"All the time in the world," he agreed, but as he said so, he noted her suddenly downcast eyes and wondered if she, like he, was regretfully counting the days until they wouldn't have each other anymore.

Then the laughter was back in her eyes, in her smile, and he lay down beside her. "Get some kip. I need to recoup before I take ye again."

"You need to recoup? What about me? I don't think I've come that hard ever. It was like to knock me into next week," she laughed.

"Good then, that's grand. I'd hate to think I'd lost my touch."

They had shifted position, and she snuggled against him, breathing into his neck as he lay on his back, his arm around her. "Henry?"

"Hmm," he mumbled, almost asleep.

"The flowers are beautiful."

He began to chuckle. "It took ye that long to notice them, did it?"

"Yeah," she said, sighing out her pleasure, "I was a wee bit busy, don't ye know."

"Ah well, ye've time to enjoy them when ye wake. They'll still be there."

Now it was her turn. "Mm."

He kissed the top of her head, and she tilted her chin to meet his eyes and they kissed again.

"Good night, my love," she said softly, the endearment like a prayer to his ears.

"Night," he replied, holding her as close as he could.

They settled into sleep after that, Henry's arm pulling her into his embrace, breathing in her scent. He was going to miss this, he thought, choking back the sudden emotion in his throat and finally letting sleep overtake him.

* * *

In the next room, Emily and Kathleen had been watching the television while in bed.

"Anythin' else on?" asked Kathleen, yawning and stretching.

"No," answered Emily, turning off the set, glad Gran hadn't seemed interested in what was on. She was curious about the man her gran seemed to fancy, but more than that, she'd been meaning to find out if they had any plans of moving in together. "Gran, are ye keen on that fella ye're seein?"

Kathleen's head quickly followed the direction her eyes took, focusing in on Emily. "What?"

"Don't look so surprised. I know ye're seein' him quite regular, like. In fact, even Da says as how he's not seen ye this keen on any other fella."

"He says, does he? I don't know that it's any of his business. Besides," she added, "I haven't decided how I feel about him. And why would ye ask, anyway?"

Emily bit her lower lip in thought, hesitating, even though

she was very certain what Gran's answer would be. "Well, ye know I'm thinkin' on movin' out, like?" She stopped only to note Kathleen's nod. "I was wonderin' if…would it be okay, or, would ye mind, if I was to go to Inishannon, maybe move in with you for a bit? Just 'til I get a job and settled, like."

"Inishannon? There's more in Killarney than Inishannon. There's naught there for ye to do, let alone find a place to work. What would ye do?"

If the look on Gran's face was anything to go by, this talk was not going as Emily planned. She'd figured that Gran would be only too happy to have her there. Maybe she'd been wrong. Maybe Gran was very sweet on this man.

"I don't know. Ye see, that's it. I don't know, but I'm sure whatever I'm lookin' for isn't in Killarney. I want to move in with my friends, but I'm tryin' to save for university, and I don't even know what I want to take once I get there. I just don't know. I need this gap year to figure myself out and I can't do it at home."

Gran sat up and brushed her fingers through her shoulder-length waves, the deep golden color reflected in the light from the lamp.

"Ye've such pretty hair," said Emily, remembering the first time she'd met Kathleen. Though no blood relation to the woman she called Gran, she was embraced and welcomed into the fold as though she were. Emily had always thought that if ever an orphan needed a home, Kathleen's home would be the place to be. Kathleen was the very essence of love itself, all encompassing.

"Don't change the subject," Gran said, giving her hair a final fluff before angling her body to face Emily. "I don't doubt ye need some time away. Have ye any money at all saved up? Could ye take a wee trip somewhere? Go backpacking or hiking? Lots of young people do that between school and university. Or go volunteer for some organization that works with the poor in a foreign country. Ye'd get to see somethin' of the world and help out, too."

Emily was quiet. Gran didn't understand. No one would. She knew who her real mam was, although the older she got, the images in her mind became less clear. She could remember things that had happened, but the people in them had no faces. All she had left of her mam were a few photographs in a little box Henry had given her. There was one photo in there that stood out among the rest, the one with her mam and a man, standing together near a river. The man was completely unfamiliar and she knew she'd never met him before. It was likely even Henry hadn't seen it there when he'd given the box to Emily. But Emily had seen it, and kept the little box close by, always.

And so the photograph had survived, somewhat wrinkled from all her handling of it, but a picture of a man with her mam, she looking so young and he looking so handsome beside her. It was a summer photo, the landscape behind them lush and green, like the path on the way to Ross Castle, with a river flowing past. She wondered where it was and if he was her father. Because as much as Henry and Siobhan had treated her as their own and given her all the love they possessed, Emily had always wondered about her real da.

Inishannon was a place to start. Ciara had once told her that she'd find answers there, when Ciara still had her psychic sense. She hadn't said much more than that, and now it was too late. Ciara didn't get visions anymore.

"I do have some money set aside," she began, "but I think I just need to stay in Ireland for a while, figure myself out. I'm feelin' a bit lost and I was wonderin' if it would be okay to stay with ye, just for a while. I'd be no trouble," she finished, hoping to allay Kathleen's fears that having a teenager, even if she was pushing eighteen, would be too much for her.

"Ah, ye're always welcome, ye know that. And there's Ciara's old room that ye can have. If she and Cian want to visit, there's lots of other rooms to choose from, but Ciara's was always the nicest, lookin' over the back garden as it does."

Emily jumped out of bed and ran to hug her grandmother, "Thanks, Gran, I promise I won't be any trouble. I promise!"

"Well then, we'll have to make certain ye aren't. Go to sleep now and we'll talk more in the mornin'."

Emily went back to her bed and pulled the blankets up around her chin while Gran turned out the light. It would be okay. She'd go to Inishannon and find her da, whoever the man in the photo was, and…

Suddenly, the thought of who he might be scared her. What if he was a criminal? What if he turned out to be a druggie like her mam? Is that where her mam got all her drugs? So many thoughts were bombarding her that she wanted to scream at them to leave her alone. Where had all those ideas of a knight in shining armor gone? Of the mansion on the hill? Of the friendly face in the photo welcoming her into his life, claiming her as his long-lost child?

A tear escaped her eye to roll down her cheek, leaving a wet streak that she swiped at. She hadn't realized she'd begun to cry.

Rolling over so Gran wouldn't know, she wiped her cheek with a corner of the sheet and closed her eyes, trying not to sniff as she snuggled farther down the bed, holding the blankets like a cocoon about her.

Kathleen lay awake long after she heard Emily's soft

snores, her breathing even and deep. Her mind was focused on what Emily was saying about the fella she'd been dating.

Dating? They'd been doing much more than that. They'd spent every waking minute together, and the only reason he hadn't attended this celebration with her was because she'd asked him not to. She wasn't ready for the next step, she realized, not sure of what the next step really was. And not sure if she wanted what it might mean.

Was she ready to share her family with him, ready to have him permanently in her life, as he seemed to want to be? Damian Lynch was a fine man, respected in the community and soon to be retired from his job in the hospital pharmacy. He'd been running the department for nearly thirty years and had told her that when he retired, which would be in a matter of weeks, he'd planned to help his son at the pharmacy at Inishannon. His son, Dylan, had bought it a couple of years back and Damian had said as how Dylan could use the help when he decided to go on holiday. It was something Damian thought would be a good way to retire, yet keep his hand in things.

Kathleen had thought it a great idea, had met young Dylan a few times and liked him. Young? No, he wasn't young, leastwise, not in his twenties. No, Dylan had to be at least in his mid thirties, of an age with her own son Henry, or maybe Brandon. But if Dylan had his own family somewhere, she didn't know, only knew he was single. She and Damian had never discussed Dylan's situation, just as she'd never gone into detail about her own family. They talked about them, but never got into the nitty-gritty. They'd been more interested in each other. All she needed to know of Damian was that he'd been married once and divorced, and his ex-wife was now somewhere in Ulster with a new husband and out of his life for good.

The other thing she knew was that Damian was a good man at heart. He'd never willingly hurt a soul, and that was enough for Kathleen.

But could she live with him? Or he with her? Whose house would they live at and could they share the space without wanting to be at each other's throats in a few short weeks? She was due to retire soon, too, although she hadn't mentioned anything to her family yet.

There was so much to think about, but no decision had to be made yet. It wasn't as if Damian had proposed. He hadn't mentioned a thing. And yet, sometimes, she got the feeling that he wanted to.

She yawned, noted the time on the clock across the room, and sighed. It was nigh on one in the morning, and she was still awake.

Emily mumbled in her sleep and Kathleen wriggled in the bed, getting into a more comfortable position. It would be good to have Em stay with her for a while. It would keep Damian at bay until she herself could figure out what it was she wanted.

That was about as settled as that argument went, she decided, and finally, after rolling over and punching the pillow to a more suitable lump, she gave herself over to a light sleep.

Chapter Four

Damian tucked his desk calendar away for the day. He was on countdown now, one month and three days to go. He would be so glad to go, so happy to turn the reins of the department over to someone else. His replacement was much younger than he had been when he started, but it had been a different era back then. Life was different, you had to prove yourself ten times over before they even looked at you. Yet he'd done it. To him, it had been his dream job. He loved it for all the challenges that came with it, the classification and cataloguing of it all. He would be sad to lose that part of his life, and yet he was tired. So tired of working and longing for a simpler, easier, yet still highly organized existence. Damian needed organization.

His ex-wife had hated that he was so systematic, but running a hospital pharmacy demanded that he know where everything was and that everything had been accounted for. And while she'd said she'd understood, she hadn't understood that he couldn't stop being that way once he was at home. Their home, she'd accused him more than once, looked much like his office at work, with everything boxed, labeled, and accounted for.

He was OCD, a man with an obsessive-compulsive disorder who absolutely needed everything to be just so, from his desk at work to the kitchen cupboards at home. He couldn't stand to have anything out of place and took exception to the way his wife rearranged the cupboards. It had precipitated an argument that had far-reaching effects. Divorce proceedings had followed.

Their only child, Dylan, had been away at school at the time. That made the divorce easier, Damian remembered. They'd sold the house, he'd moved into a flat near the hospital, and that had been that.

He didn't think it had bothered Dylan too much. He'd weathered his mother's desertion with a stoic resistance to tears and merely shrugged it off. He had been nearly twelve at the time and learning that young men did not cry.

Life seemed to settle down after that. Damian could keep house the way he wanted and Dylan eventually followed in his father's footsteps by going to university to study pharmaceuticals. It had been in his second year at the university in Dublin that Dylan began showing signs of stress. Damian found out later that the stress had nothing to do with university and everything to do with a girl he'd met and fallen in love with. Something went wrong with the relationship, Damian didn't know what, and next thing he'd heard was Dylan saying they were not seeing each other anymore. The girl had left him for someone else.

Dylan had buried himself in his studies after that, had graduated with honors, and was now the proud owner of his own pharmacy. Conveniently, that pharmacy was located in Inishannon, the same village where Kathleen lived.

He smiled to himself when he thought of Kathleen, a woman as short as she was round, yet with an energy that put much younger women to shame. His first wife had been a toothpick, all hard angles and bone. If he were a man to compare women, which he wasn't usually, he'd choose a woman like Kathleen. A woman whose curves were softened by the layers around her, not fat, but pleasantly plump, and all the more of her to love.

He did love her, but did she love him? Would she put up with his obsession that he still struggled to control? She'd been to his flat, had spent a few nights in his arms instead of going home to Inishannon to the big, empty house that she refused to sell. There was just her there now, her daughter having moved away and recently married.

There were other family members, he knew, scattered around Kerry and Galway mostly, but he knew little of them other than they were her grown children. Kathleen knew his son, Dylan, was the chemist in town. But Damian had never met her offspring, and in any case, he had only Dylan. His wife hadn't wanted children, but they'd had the one, and he'd be forever grateful for that. One was better than none, although he would have loved more.

Kathleen was lucky. She had grandchildren now, something he was looking forward to one day. Dylan had still not settled down to any one woman, had shown no indication of being serious about marriage, let alone serious about dating. He was beginning to wonder if perhaps Dylan was an arse bandit in disguise, but he didn't think so. His son had never shown an interest in men. No, he had an idea that his son was still hurting from the one that got away and no woman, no matter how pretty or how smart, seemed to be able to turn his head enough to banish the memory of that first love.

Love. Kathleen. The two were synonymous. He could feel an arousal building just thinking of her, of spreading her thighs, feeling the wetness, and sliding into her depths. Of lying atop her, like a life-sized cushion beneath him, all softness and welcoming warmth.

He shifted in his chair, thankful he was still behind his desk where the evidence of his thoughts was well hidden. Glancing around his office, he knew he should begin to pack up some of his binders and textbooks. The new person would need the space and have their own items to fill the shelves that were neatly overflowing. Even his piles of papers were organized, flagged, and waiting for a spare moment to be filed away. Damian disliked secretaries, preferring to do it all himself, properly, so he wouldn't have to do it all again. He hadn't met an assistant yet that could get it right.

So things piled up. But they were neat piles, he knew.

Feeling his arousal dwindle, he pushed his chair back, thinking it was time he left his office to check on the inventory one last time for this month. After that, he had plans to head to Dylan's pharmacy, see what improvements he could make there as his son had requested, and head over to Kathleen's to see if she was back from County Kerry yet. He could phone, but that would spoil his surprise visit.

Pulling his suit jacket from the coat tree by the door, he slipped it on, even though he knew it was probably too warm an afternoon to be wearing such a thing. Turning the light out and closing the door on his organized life, he put off the inventory for the morning, left the building, and headed for the parking lot.

He now had one month and only two days left to go.

* * *

"Here's the key to the door, Em. If ye'll open it, I can grab the bags from the boot."

Emily nodded, and taking the key to the front door, had it open, waiting for Gran to bring in their things from the car. They'd spent the morning in Killarney, packing up the items

Emily would need right away: her clothing and some jewelry, makeup, and shoes. Everything else could wait, they decided, now that the decision had been made.

"What's the hurry?" Henry had asked, looking hurt, and Kathleen couldn't blame him. He'd raised Emily from the time she was ten and had come to think of her as his own flesh and blood. And here she was, moving out without much of a warning, to stay in Inishannon.

"It's just for the summer," Emily had said, lugging out another bundle of goodies from her room upstairs. "And it isn't like I'll be very far away, less than two hours up the road."

And then they were gone, just Em and Gran, and arriving in Inishannon just in time to unload the car and put some dinner on.

Emily was thinking that a quiet night in her new abode with Gran would be a grand way to start her foray into her new life. She'd cook up a storm for Gran, give that woman a chance to put her feet up for once and be waited on a little. Emily loved to cook, inventing recipes, putting odd ingredients together and coming up with a masterpiece. And, according to Mam, was ever so good at it.

The doorbell rang, and Kathleen called to Emily to answer it while she put the bags away.

Opening the door to see a strange man on the doorstep was not what Em was expecting. However, being astute among other things, she wondered if perhaps this wasn't Gran's fella? She couldn't help the grin that grew, couldn't hide it, and asked, "Can I help ye?"

The man on the doorstop looked nonplussed and hemmed and hawed before anything intelligible came out of his mouth. Finally, he said, "I'm here to see Kathleen O'Farrell."

"And you would be…" Em let the words hang in the air,

the obvious question left for him to answer.

"I'm Damian. Damian Lynch. Is she at home?"

Coming down the stairs, Kathleen called out, "Damian, I wasn't expectin' ye. Come on in. Can ye stay to dinner?" Immediately, she was by his side, pulling his arm to bring him fully into the room and closing the door soundly behind him. "I see ye've met my granddaughter, Emily, come to stay for the summer," she added.

So this was the mystery man, Em thought, the one that had Gran tied in knots whenever anyone asked her about who she was seeing. Emily noted Gran's nervousness, her cheeks flushed with color that had nothing to do with having just gone up and down the stairs but, she suspected, had everything to do with the man before her.

They went into the sitting room and took seats before the lovely bow window with its mullioned panes across the top, the ones that looked like icicles, lined up and refracting the sunlight into myriad rainbows across the ceiling and far wall. Emily loved that window and thought that perhaps it was the best feature of the entire house.

"I didn't mean to interrupt anythin'," said Damian, having calmed down a little from his first meeting with Emily.

"Not at all," said Kathleen as a small chuckle escaped her lips.

Gran, chuckling? Emily hugged the observation to herself, thinking how much fun this summer was going to be. Gran had a boyfriend!

Kathleen continued, the blush still coloring her cheeks. "I meant it, the invitation to dinner, I mean. It's just some leftover ham and vegetables, and I'm just goin' to thrown some potatoes on the hob to cook. They're good with some butter, they are."

"Mmm, I love spuds with butter," said Damian, his eyes never leaving Kathleen's face.

"Love, will ye go start them? I'd hate for supper to be too late," she asked Emily, her eyes glancing at her quickly before turning back to Damian.

"Of course," answered Em, thinking it would be grand, she could just watch them from the kitchen while giving them some sense of privacy. Maybe they'd get it on, and she could watch like she did Da and Mam that one night.

She remembered how it went with them. Just last year it was and she'd heard a noise downstairs. Mam was lying on her back on the sofa, her legs spread wide, her opened robe revealing her naked body beneath. Da had quickly shucked his trousers and drawers and even though he still wore his shirt, she could see his lad, standing stiff and erect, and then he'd got on top and slid it inside Mam. Mam had sighed, said how good it was and then Da's arse, high in the air, the nads in his sac bouncing away behind him. It was too much to take in without giggling and she'd nearly given herself away, covering her mouth with her hand to stifle any sound.

And then they'd finished, and Da had collapsed onto Mam, his lad still inside her.

She'd snuck back upstairs after that, trying not to creak the one stair that always did, no matter what, and that time had been no different. But she'd been lucky and escaped detection. Yet it left her wondering. What would it be like? Mam seemed to enjoy it and Da obviously had. But Em didn't have a boyfriend that she liked enough to want to do that. She knew he'd have to be someone special because she wasn't about to try it just for the sake of the experience, although she knew some of her friends had done just that.

As she watched from the kitchen, she noted Damian

taking Gran's hand in his while they were talking, and since she couldn't really hear what they were saying, put the kettle on to boil for the tea that would follow supper.

* * *

Damian had been gobsmacked when Emily opened the door. If not for the fact that he'd been to the house many times, especially in the last few weeks, he would have thought he'd made a mistake. But then Kathleen had been upstairs and called out to him, and he knew he was at the right place. But who was the young lady with the flowing raven hair and deep blue-grey eyes that met him at the door? She looked nothing like his lady-love, and he was startled when Kathleen introduced Emily as her granddaughter. A quick thought came to him that perhaps she took after her mam, and would therefore not resemble her da's mother so much. Although the hair, he remembered from seeing photographs of her sons, that was where the hair came from. They were raven-haired to a man. Kathleen's daughter, Ciara, was the one who took after her mam, with her blonde hair that glinted a teeny bit red in the sunlight if that photograph on the table beside the sofa was anything to go by. Her eyes were different too, green like Kathleen's, not deep blue like her brothers. No, Emily didn't seem to take after Kathleen's side of the family at all.

Emily had left them alone, gone to start the spuds like her gran had asked, and she hadn't come out again. He suddenly wasn't sure what he wanted to say to Kathleen. And why was he there, if not to see if she was free to spend the night with him?

He supposed there wouldn't be any of that, now that Emily was there for the summer, and he braced himself for a lean few months. Then he thought up a way for them to be together, at least for a bit. "Come drivin' with me after supper."

"I don't know if I should go. It's Emily's first night here and I'd like to see her settled."

Not to be put off, he said, "Ah, well, she's a sweet girl and I can see ye'd like to do that. But I thought a quick drive, ye know, while she maybe settles into her room or whatever, and then we can be alone for a while." He hoped his suggestion would take root. The girl wasn't thirteen, after all. She looked to be about twenty.

"It's true, she could spend the time to organize Ciara's old room, I suppose. What did ye have in mind?"

He had to think fast. Where would he take her where they could be alone? It would be dark…and then he thought of the perfect spot. "How about we drive over to the old friary. I'm sure there'd be hardly anyone there after supper."

"What, the Timoleague Franciscan Friary, ye mean? I haven't been there in ages. It's a lovely spot, so peaceful. Yeah, I think that'd be grand," she said.

From the kitchen he could hear the tinkling of cutlery as Emily laid the table and could smell the aroma of the ham steaks and asparagus that wafted through the partially opened door. It was a clear sign that supper would soon be ready.

His mouth watered with more than just supper in mind.

Chapter Five

The sun hadn't quite gone down but was at that point in the sky where the shadows ran dark and deep, and the old graveyard looked spooky, although the atmosphere of peace and tranquility could not be denied. They walked hand in hand, weaving their way through the headstones, not caring that the light was too dim for them to read what was on them. It wasn't important, anyway. They weren't here for that.

Damian wondered if Kathleen was aware of the extent of his feelings for her, if she knew how much he wanted her, not just her body for sex, although that was ever so nice, but to have her in his life. Always. And why had he brought her here, if not to be alone with her? She must have known that if not for Emily's presence, he would have stayed the night.

"Ye're very quiet," said Damian, leading her from the graveyard to the inner walls of the sanctuary where it seemed as if they were in a church whose roof was the very heavens they stood beneath. Stars were appearing, twinkling through the atmosphere, and soon night would be complete. "Did ye not want to come out with me, then?"

A tug on his hand told him she'd stopped so he turned to look at her and hoped he didn't appear as crestfallen as he felt.

"It's not that, Damian, ye know I care for ye. It's just,

havin' Emily there…well, it's not somethin' I'm used to. Ciara was my daughter and had lived there all along until about a year ago, and since then, the house was my own with no one to mark my time. Now, all of a sudden, there's someone else to think of again, and I don't know how I feel about that. She's young, she's never known me to have anyone else in my life but my family. I don't know how she'd take it."

"Ye mean, havin' us share a bed and wake to find me in the kitchen makin' ye breakfast."

"Well, yeah, now that ye put it that way. I think I'm a bit embarrassed by it all, like."

He pulled her to him, wrapped his arms around her and planted a kiss on her forehead. "Ye're a special woman, Kathleen. I don't want ye to do anythin' that makes ye uncomfortable, and I get that it could cause ye a little discomfort. But she has to know ye're a grown woman and ye've a right to yer own life. And that sometimes, that life might include a man. A man in yer bed, no less. If we were married, she'd have to accept that."

"I know," she agreed, far too readily, he thought, "but I don't think I'm ready for that yet."

He rubbed her back lightly. She was wearing a simple shawl over her dress, a loose frock that was made for warm summer days and hotter summer nights, he mused. Looking around, he spotted a grassy area and pulled her toward it, saying, "Come sit with me here for a bit. We can stargaze, and it's protected from the wind. I'll put my jacket down so yer dress doesn't get dirty.

"From the grass?" she joked.

"Well, I'm assuming it's just grass but ye never know," he chuckled, thinking how glad he was that she seemed to welcome his suggestion.

The lay on their backs to see the stars straight above them. Theirs was the only car in the parking lot and no other noises filled the quiet save their own breathing. Damian felt his heart speed up as his hand traveled up her thigh and she willingly parted her legs for him. "Ye're not wearin' any hose," he said, surprised.

Shrugging, the movement barely detectable in the moonlight, she said, "It was too warm earlier, and I had sandals on. Can't wear pantyhose in those things without slipping out of them," she explained.

"Ah, well then, that's to my advantage, isn't it," he commented.

"Mmm," came her answer, followed by a long, drawn out sigh. "This is quite nice, even if it is on the ground."

"A nicer bed, nature never made," he said, and then, "do ye mind if I, ye know, do more than just get ye off with my hand?"

"So, ye mean to make love to me in a graveyard?"

Her voice held a hint of laughter and he couldn't help but join in. "It isn't quite in the graveyard. And if any in there can offer any hints, then I'll gladly listen."

He felt her hands on his pants, undoing the button and drawing the zip down. Moments later, her hand was on his lad, stroking it to its fully aroused state. It didn't take much.

She shucked her knickers, and he pushed his trousers past his hips to move between her thighs, and rubbing the tip of his lad against her flange until the wetness flowed and smoothed his way, he slid in, letting his breath out on a sigh. She felt so good beneath him.

"Are ye fine? The ground isn't too hard?"

"I'm grand. I don't care about the feckin' ground just now," she laughed, and then moaned as he began to withdraw, only to push inward again. "More, Damian, more, and don't stop."

"I don't want to come too soon. I want ye to come with me, to reach the stars at the same time as I do," he said between teeth clenched in pleasure. She felt so feckin' good. He was afraid he wouldn't last.

Her hand came between them, her fingers touching herself and he lifted a little to allow her access. It was an erotic feeling, her hand just there, stroking his lad as he slid in and out while she rubbed herself in exactly the right spot. They'd worked out at least this much in their relationship.

"How're ye doin'?" he asked again, not because of the ground but because he couldn't hold off much longer.

"Just about…ah, harder now, Damian, harder…"

He didn't need coaxing. A few good thrusts and he felt her inner muscles clench, heard her gasps of pleasure, her heavy breathing, and suddenly he was there with her, his body rigid with spasms as he spilled his seed deep inside. They'd worked out protection, too. She'd been on the pill for a while now, just in case.

The night deepened around them but neither wanted to move, to break the spell of the moment, but the sound of a car driving up, the glow of headlights, meant security personnel had arrived and were checking out the lone car in the parking lot.

"Quickly," Damian urged, in a husky whisper, trying in vain to hide the chuckle beneath his words.

"Where's me knickers?" asked Kathleen. "Oh lord, I can't find them." She was frantically feeling all over with her hands but obviously, from her panicked voice, hadn't discovered them yet.

"Here. I have them here in my pocket. No time to put

them on. Just smooth yer dress and pretend all is well."

They stood and Damian had his trousers done up and straightened just as light came around the corner. He had just leaned down to help Kathleen up from the jacket on which she'd been sitting when the voice from behind the torch spoke.

"Viewin' time is over," said the man, shining the light at their faces and then along their bodies to the ground where the jacket still lay. The light from his torch found their faces again.

"Sorry," Damian apologized. "We were sittin' down, stargazin'. Didn't realize it was so late."

"No harm done," said the man. "I'll lead ye back to the parkin' lot. There's plenty to trip up an unwary person. Don't forget yer jacket."

They followed him back to the car, Damian's jacket across his arm until they reached the car. He threw it into the back seat, and that's when he saw Kathleen's knickers hanging out of the pocket. Their eyes met and he would have sworn that she had turned beet red, although whatever she may have felt, she certainly was not alone. They sat down in the car and Damian started the engine, let it idle for a minute before their eyes met one more time. And then the laughter began.

He drove out of the parking lot, leaving the security guard behind to watch them drive away. Still laughing a kilometer down the road, he finally pulled to a stop outside her house, turned off the car, and handed Kathleen her knickers. "Would ye like to put them on?" he asked, unable to hide the grin he was sporting.

"I think I should, although I believe my dress will need a cleanin', anyway. I hope Emily has gone to bed. I don't want

53

to have to explain the moisture at the back."

"Moisture?" And then the lightbulb came on inside his head. "Ah, well. Yes, of course. I hadn't realized, but, yes." Then, because he really did feel as if it were his fault, he said, "I'm sorry."

Kathleen put her head back and laughed until the tears began to fall, and Damian laughed with her. "Did ye see his face past the torch?" she finally asked. "I would have given anythin' to see his expression when he saw me knickers hangin' out of yer pocket."

Damian felt himself turn every kind of red. "I did not," he admitted. "And I have to say I am glad I didn't. I don't think I could have come across so innocently if I had." At which point they both burst out laughing again.

They sat a moment longer while Kathleen struggled to get her knickers back on and though Damian had offered help, all he'd received had been a look of mock anger before she chuckled and thanked him.

"So then, is this how it's to be, do ye think, until Emily goes home?" he asked, wondering if he'd just opened up Pandora's box.

Kathleen shook her head. "I've no idea. I don't know that I'm ready to tell her I've a boyfriend and that she might find ye there some mornin', but I don't know what else to do."

Damian sighed and placed his hand over hers. "Ye know I care about ye. Have for a long time. Christ, it took me months to screw up the courage to ask ye out and even longer to take ye to bed. Ye'd think we were teenagers the way we're worryin' over kids findin' out. And now we're bein' discovered by security personnel in national monuments because we're too afraid to do it under the same roof as your grown granddaughter."

"She's almost grown. Not quite."

"She looks to be at least twenty," he said.

"No. Just seventeen, not quite eighteen. She's just finished school and wants to have a gap year but hasn't any idea of what she'd like to do at the end of it," she said testily.

"Hmm, I thought she was older. I'm sorry, I didn't mean to imply that this is yer fault."

"What? This? Our liaison tonight?" At his nod, she continued, "Ah well, that's not yer fault. 'Tisn't mine, neither. It just is. We either have to brave her opinions or continue to find other places to get together."

"What do ye think she'd say? I mean, this is your problem more than it is mine. Ye're the one that'll be lookin' at her every day. Not necessarily me." He could almost see the wheels turning in her head as she thought.

Finally, she said, "I'm still workin', still pullin' odd shifts so she'll be alone much of the time. I could stay over with ye sometime, could I not?"

It didn't take much to answer, "Of course. It's a grand solution. But I'm only workin' for another month or so, and then I'm retired."

Kathleen shrugged. "That shouldn't matter, should it?"

He shook his head. "I'm to be helpin' Dylan at his pharmacy in town."

"Ye mean the one next to flower shop here in Inishannon?"

"Yeah, that's the one."

"For the next month, at least, we'll have time at your place, then, and time enough to figure things out, don't ye think?"

Damian nodded and leaned toward her in a tête á tête move. "I'm pleased, ye know, that ye want to spend time with me in that way."

Kathleen blushed, a darker tinge to her skin that Damian could follow as it crept up her chest and neck and onto her face. As if she could read his mind, she leaned over the short distance and took his mouth with hers. His hand reached out and cupped a voluptuous breast, running his thumb across the front, bringing her nipple to a peak.

She sighed. "I have to admit, I want ye all over again," she whispered. "That's unusual for me. I've not felt like this for a good many years."

Damian's answer was to deepen the kiss and slide his hand up her dress to the curls now encased in her knickers. Ignoring the material, he pushed it aside and slipped his fingers in to rub her where he knew it would count. Her breathing quickened, and she stretched out as much as she could in the confines of the car until he abandoned her momentarily to hit the switch at the side of her seat to allow it to fall back.

Almost like a bed.

He then got out of the car and walked around to her side and had her stand. Pushing the entire seat as far back as it would go, he sat on it and beckoned, and she, being as adventurous as he, slipped her knickers off again and climbed in on top of him, the hem of her dress easily lifted to fall around them as she sat on him. It was a tight squeeze, and she giggled as he pulled the door closed. Although not closed as tight as it could be, it was closed enough.

Kathleen's hand soon had his lad freed, and he was once again inside her. Movement, restricted as it was, seemed to be enough as long as his thumb rubbed her clitoris. She braced herself with her arms outstretched, one on the window, the other on the driver's seat, and he lifted the voluminous folds of the dress that hung more like a shift to free one breast and play with her nipple. It was awkward, it was crazy. It was some of the best sex he could have imagined.

And Kathleen was about to come. Her breath came in gasps as she widened her stance as best she could. He could hear the wetness as he slapped against her flange, his lad buried deep inside, could smell her sex, or was it his? It didn't matter, it was heady, intoxicating, and the fact of easy discovery by someone, anyone, made it even more enticing.

She cried out her climax, something he hadn't heard her do before, as if it was so intense she couldn't keep it in. He joined her immediately, wondering how he'd lasted so long in the first place. It was more craic than he could remember having. Ever.

Kathleen looked down at the man beneath her dress and began to laugh. His head was literally buried in its folds where he'd managed to latch on to her nipple with his mouth, and it was comical to see him peering up at her through the broad neckline. Good thing it was elasticized across the bodice, she thought, or it would have torn for sure.

She felt him back out of her dress as she struggled to reposition her breasts inside her bra. It had been the most outrageous thing she'd ever done. She'd never before made love in a car, not even as a teenager!

"Jaysus, Damian, this has been deadly craic but I don't think I can do it again, I'm gettin' too old for this shite," she said, still laughing about it.

"I know what ye mean. Takes a bit out of ye, doesn't it?" He was joining her in laughter as she felt him begin to slip from her body.

"Wait, let me get my knickers," she said, trying not to laugh. With each chuckle that escaped, he slipped a bit more, and she was hoping to avoid the gush of moisture that was sure to follow.

"Ye can't slip them on in here, surely," he said, and from the sounds of it, was also trying to stem the laughter.

"No, but I can stand just inside the shelter of the car door and pull them on."

She opened the car door and stood, bent down to haul them up her legs when the porch light came on. Stranded, with knickers half up and half down, she straightened, wiggling her arse into them, only realizing as she settled them about her that they were on backward. "Ah, feckit, this is awkward," she exclaimed, and Damian laughed again, trying to tuck himself into his trousers.

Finally, suitably clothed, at least enough to enable him to walk around to the other side of the car, he grinned at her, illuminated by the light from the house. "Do ye think she turned it on?" he asked, nodding in the direction of the light casting a bright glow across the parked car.

"No, it's automatic. I don't know why we didn't trigger it earlier. Maybe we did, and just didn't notice. It's all good, though. I'll bid ye goodnight and call ye tomorrow."

"What? No kiss?" he asked, standing at the driver's side of the car.

She looked at him, studied his face for a moment, the crestfallen look, and then met the wink he cast in her direction. "Away wit' ye," she said, beginning to chuckle again, "we'll talk tomorrow."

With another wink, he waved goodbye and moments later was gone.

Kathleen stood, feeling uncomfortable with her knickers on backward and knowing she had moisture on her dress in places all too visible to someone looking for it. And that someone poked her head out the door, grinning from ear to ear.

"What are ye doin', playin' Peepin' Tom?" Kathleen scolded, readjusting her shawl to hide the wet spot she could feel.

"I heard a noise," said Emily, "I didn't mean to interrupt."

"But ye did. It's time you and I had a talk, if ye've a mind to stay the summer." She gave the now empty driveway a last look and went inside, past Emily, and up the stairs to her room. "Put the kettle on, I'll be right back."

Jaysus, she thought, feeling the material bunch up around her arse, it was hard to move with yer knickers on backward!

Chapter Six

Siobhan came home from work early, something she rarely did, but she'd been feeling so poorly what with everything turning her stomach, from the smell of the coffee on her coworker's desk to the odor emanating from the egg salad sandwich still resting on its wrapper. She couldn't take it anymore. Neither could she bring it up to her coworker, Freida, because Freida liked to talk. She'd want to know why coffee and egg salad sandwiches suddenly had Siobhan wanting to puke.

Freida would ask questions, and Siobhan wasn't ready to answer them. Not yet. She still hadn't told Henry and now he was beginning to act in an odd fashion, as if he knew. But if he knew, as she suspected he might, why didn't he just come out and ask? Why beat around the bush?

Well, she could say the same thing of herself, she knew. She should just tell him, get it out in the open, but she was so afraid of upsetting an already tense household.

Henry hadn't taken it well that Em had moved to Inishannon. It was a subject they no longer talked about. Emily and Kathleen had no notion just how hurt Henry had been when, without warning, the two had gone upstairs to pack up some of Em's belongings and march out the door straightaway. It was like a slap in the face for all the years of love they'd both put into her, because it wasn't just Henry that had been hurt by it.

Kathleen had seemed unaware of the emotional turmoil she and Em were leaving behind.

Perhaps this would be a good time to tell Henry of the coming event, she thought, pouring herself a cup of weak tea. Even tea had to be weak now, or she couldn't stomach it. Feckit, everything was changing!

Her figure hadn't altered much except for the space around her belly. She looked like she was getting pudgier. Not one for ever having had a slim, model's figure, Siobhan had long ago consigned herself to the fact that she was pleasantly plump and that's just the way she was built. No amount of exercise and diet was going to change her into a willowy shadow. She would always be built for comfort, as Henry liked to say. And now she would have more padding, at least for a while. At least until there would be no denying that she was pregnant, and how long would that be?

She took another sip of the tea, felt her stomach settle, and reached for some soda crackers, the kind with lots of salt on them. For some reason, she was craving salty foods.

Henry came in the door just then, interrupting her thoughts. He was all manly good looks, well built, broad of shoulder, and despite his nearly forty years, still had the body of a much younger man. It was a little silly, she thought, but she wanted him, just now, just like it was lately when she wanted food. It had to be now. If she could get him upstairs and maybe before he got into the shower, she could pull it off without him asking why she was home so early.

"Are ye in for a time or are ye rushin' back out again?" she asked, cutting off whatever he was about to say.

"No, I'm home. Don't have to go out again. Why?"

She almost chuckled at the confused expression he

displayed, his dark brows furrowed and his mouth slightly open. He straightened after pulling his work boots off and sighed loudly. "It's warm out there today."

She knew it was warm and had welcomed the cool of the kitchen, but despite the heat, had wanted hot tea. "'Tis," she agreed, pushing her chair out. He was waiting for an answer, she knew, so she stood and walked toward him, feeling like a feline in heat, all hot and bothered and wanting him with a fierceness that grew with every step. Reaching him, she began to undo the top button of his shirt and followed it with the next one, and the next.

Henry kicked the door shut behind him with his foot and Siobhan kept going until the shirt was undone and she was pushing it off his shoulders.

And then the smell of stale sweat hit her and she couldn't help the retching that had begun. Turning around, she ran to the downstairs loo, making it just in time to bring up the tea and crackers she'd just had.

Wetting the cloth, she ran it over her face, and looking up, met Henry's eyes in the mirror. There was no putting it off now.

"We need to talk," Henry said, and he didn't look pleased. He looked…serious, she thought.

"Yeah, Henry. We do. Give me another minute and I'll meet ye in the sittin' room." And then, "Henry?"

He poked his head inside the door, his expression now unreadable.

"Go have a shower before we talk. Please?"

She could see the confusion on his face but as he lifted his arm to sniff his arm pit, Siobhan covered her nose with the damp cloth and breathed deeply through it. Her eyes began to water.

"Yeah. Guess I am kind of ripe," he admitted.

"Now. Please?"

Nodding, Henry left her in the loo to clean herself up.

What the hell was going on, wondered Henry as he trudged up the stairs to the shower. She was coming on to him like she wanted him, and he was all for it. Then, suddenly, she was running in the other direction and throwing up in the toilet. Jaysus, don't let it be terrible, he prayed.

He stepped into the shower, quickly soaped himself up and rinsed off in a jiffy, all the while mentally preparing himself for the bad news he was certain was coming. She was going to tell him she had some terrible disease and was dying, and he didn't know if he could hold it together. Christ, of all the times he'd ever wished for a pint, this one topped them all.

Dressing quickly in a clean t-shirt and short pants, he was downstairs in record time, seeing Siobhan in the chair by the window, looking as if she'd been crying.

Jaysus, God, he thought, steeling himself, trying not to get emotional, trying hard to keep his own tears at bay. What would he do without her? How would he go on?

"Siobhan?" His voice came out husky, a rough whisper as he took her hand and knelt in front of her, kissing her forehead as he reached a level with her eyes. "Darlin? Ye must tell me, whatever it is. I'm here for ye. I won't ever leave ye. Never." The last came out on a choked, half sob and Siobhan's eyes widened.

"Henry, why are ye cryin?"

"I'm not," he lied, feeling the tear leave his eye.

"Don't lie to me. I can see ye're tears plain as day. What's wrong?"

He couldn't believe it. Here she sat, teary-eyed in the

63

window and she was asking him what was wrong? "Are ye daft, Siobhan? You, sitting here lookin' like a month of rainy weather and ye're askin' me what's wrong?"

He could tell she had to think about it as she opened her mouth, though nothing came out. Except a sigh. A very big, loud sigh.

"Ye'll find out eventually," she finally said.

Henry braced himself. This was it. This was when his life would change forever and it would be all downhill from here.

"The thing is, Henry, ye're goin' to be a father."

Not expecting her announcement, he stammered without having anything intelligible leave his lips.

"I'm pregnant."

He felt dizzy, felt the room spin and grabbed at the chair she was sitting on. Her hands clutched at his t-shirt and he felt the pull as if he was falling. And then the dizziness cleared and they were face to face and her lips met his.

Pregnant! After all this time, Siobhan was pregnant!

Standing, he pulled her into his arms, prepared to ravish her right there in front of the window before his mind rearranged itself. She wasn't dying. She had no deadly illness. He wasn't going to lose her.

What the fuck?

"Why the hell didn't ye tell me sooner?" he yelled. "I thought ye were dyin' and couldn't tell me. I saw yer belly get bigger and though it was a tumor in there. I was near out of my mind with worry and ye're feckin' pregnant?"

"I wanted to tell ye," she said, her face suddenly looking upset and the tears beginning to run down her cheeks, "but I didn't know how. Ye kept talkin' about the time we'd have together, just you and me without Em here, and I couldn't take that away from ye. I couldn't ruin that for ye because ye were so lookin' forward to it. And every time I thought of sayin' somethin', ye'd bring up how it was to be just us, and I just couldn't tell ye!"

They'd both been yelling and finally they stopped. Just stopped and stared, nose to nose.

Henry laughed. It started as a chuckle low in his belly, traveled up his throat, and erupted in a great guffaw that he couldn't hold back. Seconds later, Siobhan joined him and the two of them stood there, the fire of anger dying in their eyes as the joy of the news overtook them.

"Ye're goin' to have a baby. My baby," he said, and the tears started anew.

"I am," she answered, taking his hand and placing it on her belly. "I'm already startin' to show. I was so scared of what ye'd say."

He looked down at her breasts, those beautiful globes that were bursting her bra and thought how much he was going to enjoy them getting larger. But it still rankled that she hadn't told him.

"All this time I was so certain I was goin' to lose ye. I was so scared. I couldn't imagine my life without ye. And now we're to have a weyan of our own, and he'll have cousins to play with, just his age. It's a miracle."

But Siobhan just looked at him. "He? What makes ye think it's a 'he'? I'll have ye know, it feels like a girl to me," she remarked frostily.

"Girl, boy, I don't really care. I'm just gobsmacked, is all." He couldn't contain himself and pulled her close, and as he did so, she breathed in deeply and he was suddenly aware she was smelling him. "Better?" he asked, realizing now why she'd made him shower. The body odor from working all day in the hot sun had turned her stomach.

She began to laugh and nodded. "Yeah, much better. I had to come home because I couldn't stand the smell of food in the office. Not even Freida's coffee."

"But ye like coffee," he said.

"I did. But not right now. It's like the orange juice I had the other day after ye'd left. I drank some orange juice and then had some tea. Halfway through the tea, the orange juice came up but the tea stayed down."

"How do ye know the tea stayed down? How could ye tell?" The idea that anyone could detect the difference surprised him, and he wondered if her pregnancy was not going to introduce them both to an entirely new world of discovery.

"Don't be a neddy. The color, of course!"

"Makes sense, I guess." He was rubbing her back, felt like drooling into her cleavage but didn't, and kissed the tip of her nose instead. "I was wonderin, though," he hesitated, saw the twinkle in her eye and knew she was thinking the same thing. "Upstairs or here?"

"Upstairs. Ye know I'm not one for bein' an exhibitionist."

"Feckit, ye are, too!"

"No. Ye're thinkin' of someone else," she laughed, taking him by the hand and leading him toward the staircase. "Besides, I don't think I'm up to the kind of positions I'd need in order to do it on the couch."

Henry eyed the couch and remembered that night, not so long ago. They'd been hot for each other, and she'd come downstairs, untying her bathrobe as she went until she stood before him, exposing her nude body to his gaze. He'd immediately grown hard with wanting and the coupling had been as good as they'd ever had.

This time would be different, though. He'd make love to

her gently. He didn't want to hurt her. And that brought up another thought. "It'll be alright, won't it?" he asked.

"What? Ye mean, makin' love?"

"Yeah. Sex. It's okay? Won't hurt the weyan?"

She laughed as they stood at the edge of their bed and she helped him slip his t-shirt off before attacking the button of his short pants. "It'll be fine. Hasn't hurt any babe yet that I know of, and yer mam would tell us if it would."

"Does she know?" Her dress was soon off and he was working the clasp of her bra, freeing her breasts.

"Aaii," she said as the globes hung free. "They're a wee bit tender." And then, "No, she doesn't know. No one does, and thank God Ciara hasn't the sight anymore because I nearly fainted at the dinner when she looked straight at me and said I was knocked up, as if she knew. But then, she said later she couldn't tell, and I was ever so relieved."

"I'll be mindful of yer breasts, ye'll let me know if I get too rough with them, because I intend to enjoy them as much as I can before they're off limits."

"Oh, I'll let ye know, never fear."

His hands traveled down her sides, cupping her arse as he kissed his way down, past her breasts to the small bulge of her belly. "Hello, me son," he said before kissing the bulge, and received a light whack on the head. Looking up, he met Siobhan's eyes and couldn't help grinning. "I know, it could be a girl. Alright. Hello, my weyan," he said into her belly, and was rewarded with Siobhan's laughter.

His lips kissed her belly once again and traveled lower. Using his thumbs, he gently separated the folds of her sex and licked the tip of her womanhood, tasting the juices that had already begun to flow. Her hands cupped his head, running her fingers through his hair, holding him there. Slipping his tongue inside, he heard her intake of breath, felt the renewed pressure on his head, and wanted nothing more than to bring her off before laying her down and making her ready for him once again.

"I need to sit," she said, breathing hard, and Henry obliged her by allowing her to get comfortable on the bed, drawing the covers back before she lay down. It meant having to abandon what he was doing but it didn't deter him. He was back there the moment she was ready.

Her flange was open and glistening, the skin flushed and welcoming, and just the sight of it made Henry want to lose his load right then. But he held back, bent his head, breathing in the musk that was uniquely hers, and began to feast, tasting, tickling, drinking of her moisture until her hips began to move, to undulate as her body ramped up. As she cried out her climax, he kept his tongue in place, kept sucking lightly on her bud until she pushed at his head, a signal that she couldn't take any more. He sat up, quite pleased with himself, noting the flush of climax on her skin, the mottling of the blush that covered her breasts and halfway to her neck.

"Come into me, Henry. I want ye inside."

She didn't need to ask twice. Henry slipped inside her, felt her along the sides of his flute, wet, hot and welcoming. Languishing in the cocoon of her body, he took her mouth with his.

His hips began to move and she, always one so sensitive to his body's movements, joined him, wrapping her legs around him. And even though she'd just climaxed, he could tell she wasn't done yet, hadn't given up that there was another one there to achieve, and met him thrust for thrust.

Taking a ruched nipple in his mouth, he only once made the mistake of nibbling with his teeth. That had nearly stopped the entire process but he quickly switched nipples and reminded himself to suckle gently, that her breasts were now very tender.

She seemed to appreciate his gentleness and relaxed, growing wetter than he'd ever imagined possible. So wet that he nearly slid out of her as he prepared to thrust again.

Then slowly, despite the over-abundance of moisture, he felt her insides grip him, and knowing he could no longer hold back, let himself go, let the joy and thankfulness he'd felt at her news overtake him, and growled his climax as if he were a wild animal.

She was going to live! She was going to have his baby! Henry had never felt so overwhelmed in all his life as he collapsed atop her, his breath coming in great gasps.

"Feckit, Siobhan, ye'll kill me one day, I swear," he exclaimed, lying beside her, his lad slipping from her depths.

"Ah, Henry. If I wasn't already pregnant, I'd swear I would be now," she laughed.

He looked over at her, at the golden halo of her hair tumbled about her shoulders, at the misty look in her eyes, and knew he had never been as much in love with her as he was at that moment. "C'mere to me," he said, and pulled her close. "Later, we can talk about re-doin' Em's room into a nursery and whatever other plans we might need to make, but right now, I want to hold ye, maybe have a little kip. What do ye say?"

"Ah well, and I could sleep, that's for sure," she said, unsuccessfully stifling a yawn.

Henry hugged her close. "I'll make ye some supper soon, eh?"

"Yeah," she said, and closed her eyes.

Henry stared down at her and couldn't identify his

feelings anymore. They were too rich, too broad, too much. How the feck did he get so lucky, to love a woman to the depths he loved her, and then be rewarded with a child?

He pulled the covers over them and closed his eyes. He knew he wouldn't sleep but he wanted to lie there, to feel her in his arms and to thank God she wasn't going to die. For that alone, he was thankful. To have a baby on the way was more than he could have asked for.

And then his mind began to work, began to think of all the things they'd have to do to prepare for the weyan. Em's room was just the tip of the iceberg. They'd have to think of daycare, of Siobhan being off work, of a whole list of things. And then his mind thought of the property he'd seen and was prepared to sign the papers on, and saw that dream die in a puff of smoke, just like in a cartoon. Or would it?

As his mind went round and round, his thoughts became dreams and despite not thinking it possible just then, he drifted off to sleep.

Chapter Seven

Hank was looking out the window of his half brother's house, waiting for Brandon to join them for brunch. The women, Brandon's wife, Aine, and his own wife, Laura, were putting together the makings of a very fine meal. The weyans, Ryan and Meara, had already been fed and were down for a nap. It was blessedly quiet, and for that, Hank was extremely grateful.

"Any sign of him yet?" asked Aine. She'd sent Brandon out on an errand an hour ago and he still hadn't returned.

"Nah, but he'll be back soon. How long does it take to buy butter?" Hank asked, just then spotting Brandon's car coming back across the narrow bridge that led to Sam's cottage, and eventually, if a person continued on, to Ballycarbery Castle. The castle was a stone structure, all mystery and wonderment rolled into one. Except that they had insider information on how it ended up the way it did. Ciara had been there, in another life. It was still all too much to take in. To believe.

Minutes later, the door was heard to open and Brandon strode into the room, a small bag of something in his hand. "Got the butter," he said, proudly holding up the plastic bag.

"What took ye?" asked Aine, greeting him with a kiss and taking the butter from him at the same time.

"Ran into Sam so had to look at something he wanted to show me."

"Like it couldn't wait?" Aine cocked an eyebrow at him, leading Hank to wonder if the ability to do that wasn't something all women learned at their mam's knee.

"Ah, no. Well, it could've, I suppose, but he was so excited about it that I couldn't let him down. Brunch ready yet?" he asked on a rapid change of subject.

"Was ready thirty minutes after ye left, ye neddy," Aine scolded. "Never mind, though. Come and sit. We now have butter for the buns and that's all that matters."

An hour later, sated and sipping coffee, the sounds of a baby squalling from down the hall had Laura jumping up. Casting a quick glance at the long case clock at the far end of the open concept living space, she laughed. "Right on time," and disappeared, the sounds of the baby's cries louder, then quieting as she opened the door and lifted Meara from her cot. A moment more, and the sounds of Laura, humming a tune while she nursed the baby, filtered down the hall.

"Very domestic," said Brandon, a whimsical expression to his face, his lips twisted in a half smile.

"Your turn will come," said Hank, grinning because he knew that Brandon was looking forward to the day when he would enter the hallowed halls of fatherhood. Aine was more than halfway through her pregnancy and they'd already done the baby's room—a fortunate thing, thought Hank, because it meant a room for his own weyans, at least while they were visiting.

Every now and then, and because he'd named his daughter for her, he'd remember his sister, how she looked the last time he saw her. Her black, wavy hair had been blowing about her face, her eyes not quite gray, not quite blue, the same as Emily's. She'd been fat with child and Hank surmised that Emily had been born not long after. But he hadn't known he'd never see his sister again, or that he wouldn't know anything about her child until a couple of years ago. It was Siobhan who had lured him back with threats of a paternity suit, saying she'd been looking for him for years to let him know of his daughter.

But the timing was off, Hank knew, although there was that night before he left to marry his Canadian girlfriend that held the possibility.

Shaking off the memory, he reminded himself that Meara lived on in Emily and in her namesake. Excusing himself, he wandered down the hall to check in on Laura, to see if Ryan was stirring yet. The weyan often woke with a squeal of enthusiasm that would startle anyone out of a dead sleep. Peering round the door, he saw Laura in the rocker, Meara nursing happily, every now then slapping toothless gums as she lost suction, only to root furiously until she found it again.

Hank smiled at his daughter, at his wife looking so serene, and as Brandon had said, domestic. Laura's nipples had turned dusky as her time approached, and Hank thought it interesting that such a thing should happen. She hadn't acquired any of the other odd colorings that some women attained through pregnancy, but then, Laura was fair with a goodly amount of freckles that made up for any lack of childbearing tattoos.

Ryan was still sleeping, his soft snores like a little motor.

"Any movement from His Nibs?" asked Hank, indicating the small body on the pallet in the corner with a jutting of his chin.

Laura shook her head. "He stirred a little when Meara woke but went right back to sleep. I think he's still tired from the trip and everything."

Hank nodded. "It's a nice day. How about we take the

weyans out for a bit when he wakes?"

Laura grinned. "Sounds perfect. If he doesn't wake soon, I'll get him up or he won't sleep tonight."

Hank agreed. "Yeah, and it's a been a few nights. I haven't wanted to bother ye, but…" he let his words trail off and caught Laura's expression. If she hadn't been holding the baby or worried about waking Ryan, he knew she would have either hit him or chased him away. It would all be mock anger, he knew. Laura loved a good shag as much as anyone.

Just then, voices could be heard, and Sine's American accent carried into the hall. Liam's voice distinct, laughing at something that was said, and Hank quirked an eyebrow at his wife. "I think it's possible we're bein' invaded," he said, "and probably, unless we go alone, our walk is postponed."

Ryan began to stir and Hank knew he'd soon emerge from sleep, all tousle-haired and smelling of sweaty child. He'd be slightly disoriented but the boy's sunny disposition would soon take over, he knew.

As if on cue, Ryan opened his eyes, gave the room a worried glance before seeing his parents, and then pushing himself to a sitting position, scrambled off the small pallet they'd made as a bed for him and launched himself into Hank's waiting arms with his characteristic squeal.

"There's me lad," said Hank, hefting him up to his shoulders and ducking strategically out the bedroom door. "We'll meet ye in the other room when ye're done," Hank tossed the comment over his shoulder and went to greet his other half sibling. If anyone had told him three years ago that he would have a wife, two children, and five half siblings within that time frame, he would have called them all kinds of a fool. But it was true, and he couldn't be happier about it.

* * *

Michael held Niall's hand in a firm grip. "It'll be alright," he said.

Niall, usually disinclined to touch in public, allowed Michael to keep his hand in his grip. It was comforting, and Niall needed that reassurance just now. How could Michael maintain his composure at such a time?

"She'll be fine," Michael's smoothly accented words, whispered in the hustle of the hospital's maternity ward, were barely heard.

But Niall had heard. And worried still. "What if..?" He looked at Michael, at the crinkly hair cropped so close to his scalp, at the full lips and golden eyes, and hoped their child would look like that. He didn't care if it was a boy or a girl, he just wanted a child that looked like his lover. The woman was, like Michael, of Arabic extraction. It was because of her parents that she was in Ireland at all, and only coincidence that they had come across her. It had been their counselor's suggestion at the parenting clinic they'd visited on a lark. That day had changed their lives. "It isn't goin' well," huffed Niall.

"How can you say that? You have no idea what's going on in there, and furthermore, you've never seen a woman give birth and have no hope of ever doing so, if I have anything to say about it."

"Well, it's not like either of us will ever do it," said Niall, but he'd laughed a little, as Michael had intended.

A nurse slipped out of the room and Michael caught up to her. Niall watched, unable to clearly make out what was being said, but the woman smiled and Niall thought he could make out the words, "It's alright."

"Well?"

Michael shrugged. "Apparently, it's going well. We'll just have to sit down and wait."

"How much longer?"

Lifting his finely arched brows, Michael sighed and shrugged. "Don't know. I don't think anyone does, but she did say they were almost there."

"Almost there? What's that supposed to mean?" asked Niall.

Again, Michael shrugged.

Moments later, a man and woman entered the area and Niall had a feeling of panic wash over him. Tapping Michael's shoulder, he nodded in their direction. Their eyes met as they exchanged a look. A look that clearly communicated their fear. Without so much as an introduction, they just knew that these were Farrah's parents, and they were here to claim their grandchild.

He was a short, stocky, dark-haired man of Middle Eastern extraction, with eyes as black as night and a countenance to reflect it. Angry didn't cut it. He was furious, if his creased brows and lips stretched thin meant anything. She, on the other hand, was blonde, delicate, and looked very worried, her light gray eyes glassy as if she would break into tears at any time. Or maybe she'd already been crying.

And then the sound they'd all been waiting for, the cry of a newborn, could be heard through the closed portal beyond, and Niall and Michael forgot all about the couple who were likely the woman's parents and moved closer to the door. A short time later, the midwife came out and spotted the two men.

"Come inside and I'll let ye hold yer wee daughter," she invited. "She's a bonny, wee lass," came the thick Scottish burr. "I'll let ye hold her for a moment, but we'll need to get her measurements and stats before releasing her to ye. She'll be here for a day or two, just to make certain all is well."

"And the mam," asked Niall, "how is she?" They had moved into a small anteroom attached to the room where Farrah gave birth.

"She's fine," answered the midwife. "She hasn't seen the bairn, hasn't wanted to, and it's for the best. She'll recover much faster this way."

Nodding, Michael stood with his chest to Niall's back, leaned over his shoulder as the midwife placed the small bundle into his lover's arms. Stroking the soft, downy head with one hand, he kissed Niall's cheek and put his other arm around him and hugged. "She's ours," he said, and Niall could hear the emotion in Michael's voice, right next to his ear.

"Yeah, she is," he agreed, feeling the same sense of joy, excitement, and a million other things he couldn't put a name to, all clogging his throat, making it difficult to talk.

"What shall we name her? Of everything we discussed, we hadn't really thought of names."

Niall suddenly realized that Michael was right. They hadn't thought of names at all. "Might take some thought," he suggested, "maybe we'll have to have a conference with the family."

"We could name her for our mothers," Michael proposed.

"I think she should have one all her own," Niall replied, feeling very certain he didn't want her called Kathleen, or Nasra. "She doesn't look like either one of those names."

Michael laughed, a soft sound that the baby seemed to respond to.

"Here, you take her for a minute," said Niall, handing her over to Michael's arms, watching as his mate carefully jostled her to finally cradle against his chest.

"Gosh," was all Michael could say. "She's so light. So pure and innocent. I can't believe she's ours."

"Dawn," said Niall suddenly. "We should call her Dawn."

Michael met Niall's eyes and Niall saw the shimmering of emotion that matched his own. "Yeah. Dawn. We can work on a middle name later," he managed to choke out.

"Dawn O'Farrell-Johnson," Michael grinned. "Quite a handle but I'm sure she'll get used to it. But shouldn't she have an Irish name, too? After all, we do live here and you're Irish."

"Yeah, but ye're English."

"Dawn is English enough. I'll think on an Irish name and let you know."

Niall thought a moment and nodded. "It's only right. I gave her one name, ye'll give her the other. Deal."

A ruckus outside the room could be heard, voices raised and a bustle of footsteps all gathering outside the door. The two exchanged glances, a silent acknowledgement of pending trouble.

The midwife reappeared and took the baby from Michael's arms, saying, "We have a situation outside. I'll take her to the nursery now, but if I could please ask ye to bide a time here until they get things settled down oot there, it would be for the best."

Nodding, they watched her slide out the door, got a quick glimpse of the couple they'd noted before, the man's fist in the air as he gesticulated his anger. It was his voice they heard, raised in anger.

"I wonder if it'll be okay if we go see Farrah to see how she's doing. I don't want her to think we've abandoned her just because she's finally given birth," murmured Michael, so close to Niall's ear as they craned their necks closer to the door.

Niall slipped to the other door that connected Farrah's

hospital room to the one they were in and opened it. No one seemed about, and Farrah lay alone in the bed. Every now and then she looked toward the outer door and bit her bottom lip. She was worried. Or scared.

"Farrah?" Niall called softly, and Farrah looked his way and smiled.

"Oh, I'm so glad to see you," she heaved on a sigh, looking suddenly relieved.

Calling over his shoulder, he beckoned Michael with him and the two went to sit by Farrah's bed.

"I'm sorry we haven't even any flowers for you, for all the work you did bringing our baby into this world. You did a fine job," said Michael, taking Farrah's hand in his and clasping it warmly. Niall watched and wondered, as he sometimes did, if Michael was looking for another woman, or if he was still content as they were? You never knew with Michael, although he'd promised fidelity, promised his womanizing days were over, when they wed last year.

"Take the seat beside the bed, Michael, I'll stand," said Niall, moving to the other side and leaning over to kiss the top of Farrah's head. They had become friends over the past few months and he truly liked the woman, whose genuine sweetness always shone through.

"You boys are going to ruin me for life. I'll have to find a gay man who will have me because none of my manly boyfriends have ever stepped up to the plate, hence the condition I'm in. Or was in," she amended, rubbing her now-flat belly.

"How are you feeling?" asked Michael, retaining hold of her hand and caressing it in an absentminded way.

The noise in the hall was not diminishing and Niall wondered how long they'd have to wait for the parents to leave. It seemed obvious that Farrah didn't want to see them if she truly was aware it was them.

"Good," she replied, nodding. "I'm good. It went well, no tears, no stitches, everything went swimmingly." Biting her bottom lip again, a sign that Niall now recognized as nervousness, or maybe anxiety, she asked, "Have you seen her?"

"Oh, so ye know it's a girl?" Niall wondered if she regretted not seeing her baby before it was whisked away, but didn't ask, and at her nod, he said, "She's grand. We've named her Dawn, just haven't thought of an Irish name for her yet."

"Dawn. Very pretty." She smiled tremulously, and looked suspiciously as if she were about to cry.

At once the door to her room burst open, halting any sign of tears or anything else, and in marched the short man with fire in his eyes.

"Whore!" he screamed at Farrah, and Michael spun around in the chair.

"Your dad, Farrah?" he asked, ominously quiet, and all Niall could think of was that this was not going to go well. From down the hall he heard the rumble of heavy feet, likely hospital security, hopefully the garda.

Michael was stoic as the man took the few strides to stand before him, glaring down at him as if Michael was midget. A midget that stood six feet and an inch but was at a disadvantage, still sitting in the chair.

Farrah's father was shorter by a good six inches, but he was standing over Michael's half-seated form, his black eyes meeting Michael's golden orbs, neither one turning away.

"You took advantage of my daughter, you…" he spat at Michael. But before Michael could say a word, the man's meaty paw grabbed Michael's shirt front with an iron grip, a grip made from a fist the size of a sledgehammer for all the man's smaller stature. The other fist came from nowhere, flying downward in an overhead arc, smashing into Michael's nose. A solid thump, the sound of breaking cartilage, and Michael's howl of pain were augmented by blood gushing everywhere.

Farrah's screams rent the air, Niall felt the rage erupt in his chest and launched himself at the man before he could land another punch. And then hospital security was there, followed quickly by two burly cops, and all mayhem broke loose.

Niall let the garda do their thing and grabbed Michael to drag him out of the way. From the corner of his eye, he could see the stocky form of Farrah's father grappling with the four, knowing he would eventually go down, wondering how long it would take.

Then suddenly it was over. The cuffs were on and he was being dragged away and all that was left was the blood on the floor from Michael's broken nose and the heart-wrenching sobs of Farrah in the bed. Outside the door, the tiny, blonde-haired woman stood, the same expression on her face as she'd had before, and Niall, glancing up to see her, recognized the biting of the bottom lip and knew for sure she was Farrah's mother.

Not knowing what devil prompted him to say it, he spoke to the woman. "If ye'll be civil and kind, I'm sure yer daughter could use some comfortin'. If not, I'll ask ye to leave, quiet like, hmm?"

As if she didn't know what to do, her eyes following the last of her husband's tirades as they dragged him down the hall. They all heard his ranting, his not-so-veiled threats, and she swallowed visibly as if her fear still lingered, even though the menace had been removed. Then, stepping across the threshold, as if in that alone she was defiant of her husband, she went to her daughter's bed.

"Farrah?"

"Mum?" Farrah looked up from the bed, gulping her last sob.

"Oh, my darling!" And then the mum was there, hugging her daughter, the two crying.

Niall was still holding the towel he'd dragged from the private shower inside the room to Michael's nose, still bleeding. The towel was still soaking up blood, growing redder despite the pressure Niall was using to staunch the flow.

Seconds later, a nurse entered the room, obviously to ensure Farrah's well-being, as she first went to her before noticing the two men on the floor on the other side of the bed.

"Could I get some help here?" pleaded Niall. Michael wasn't breathing so well.

With one look, the nurse left the room, and Niall hoped it wasn't because she was hoping to find something better to do. He hoped she'd gone for help. Help was confirmed with the appearance of a wheelchair.

"Get him on this, we'll take him to the ED. Looks like his nose is broken. I'll get the doctor to look at him."

Niall glanced at Farrah as he helped the nurse get Michael into the chair. He was worried as hell that once he left, Farrah's mam would change into some hellish creature that would finish her off, and yet, if he didn't follow Michael to the ED, he was afraid that he'd lose him in the chaos.

Farrah took care of his quandary. "It's alright. I'll be fine here with my mum. You go ahead."

He took quick note of her eyes, drying from the tears she'd shed and the half smile on her mother's lips and the nod that went with it.

"I'll see she's alright," said the woman, and Niall had no choice but to believe her.

Chapter Eight

Later, Niall wasn't sure where he should be, beside Michael's bed as he slept off the rest of the anaesthetic from the emergency surgery he'd needed to reset his nose, or go to see his newborn daughter, maybe feed her and cuddle her before laying her down again in her small cot. He'd already made the journey through the halls several times back and forth between Michael and Dawn, and once to see Farrah, whose mother was still with her. Something was not right there, and it worried him because he couldn't figure it out.

As he plunked his coins into the coffee donations can in the patients' lounge, he poured himself another cup of the oil-like brew. It was overly strong, made him grit his teeth to swallow it, but seemed to be something he needed just then. As he did so, he realized that he hadn't called anyone yet to tell them the news, that their baby was born and that she was wonderful, and all those things that a new father would say to their family about such things.

Pulling his phone from his back pocket, he thumbed the number onto the keypad, checking the time as he did so. Just past eight. Not too late.

A moment later his mam's voice answered, "Kathleen speakin'."

He must have caught her at work, he realized, but

marshalled on. "Mam, it's Niall. Got a minute?"

"Oh, o'course, Niall. What is it?"

He felt the tears come, choke his throat, and he sniffed loudly, not meaning to, and then felt girlishly silly.

"Niall?" Kathleen's voice sounded worried now.

Well, with everything that had gone on, she might still feel that way after he told her.

"Some good news," he began, "but also some not so good."

"Niall, ye'll have to be quick, love, I'm at work," she said quietly, and he knew that she was not in a place where she could talk easily.

"Ah, sorry, em…it's, well, we're fathers now, Michael and me. Farrah had a baby girl this afternoon. We named her Dawn. Just don't have a second name for her yet."

Kathleen's squeal of delight could be heard even when the phone was pulled from his ear, but he couldn't leave the conversation there.

"That's not all, Mam. It's not all good and before ye worry, the baby's fine. It's not that. It's…well, Farrah's parents somehow found out she was here, and her da came bursting into the room and planted one right on Michael's nose. They had to fix it surgically."

There was silence on the other end of the line. "My God, Niall, is he goin' to be alright?"

"Yeah, Mam, he is. He's sleepin' now, his eyes already lookin' black; blacker than Brandon's when those plonkers hit him with the telephone."

"And yer wee babe?"

Niall sighed. "She's fine. I fed her tonight. And Mam, it was ever so nice to hold her and to cuddle her and to know she's ours. I've never been so…"

"In love," she finished for him. "Ye're in love with yer new daughter and that's how it should be," she said, and he could feel her smile through the phone.

"I'll send ye a photo tomorrow. With all the shite that went on today, I didn't get a chance to get one," he apologized. "But Mam?"

"Yes, love?"

"She looks a little like Michael."

"Ah, that's good then. I can tell ye're happy about that. It's what ye wanted."

Nodding, even though his mam couldn't see, he finally choked out a "Yeah," before wishing her a good night and cutting the connection. Mams were amazing people, making you feel better even when the odds were against it.

Michael was still sleeping, and likely would all night now, so Niall left him and wandered past the nursery, hoping to get another glimpse of his wee girl. But she, too, was sleeping and so he didn't disturb her, either, didn't go in because he knew there were babies in there who were very sick. Normally new mothers kept their babies with them but this was a special case. Babies like Dawn were sent to the nursery, which was attached to the neonatal unit. It was quite possible, if all went as planned, that Dawn could go home with him tomorrow. In fact, if everything went his way, he could take Michael home, too. They'd have time to be a family for a few days before Michael would go back to work. Niall had first dibs on paternity leave, Michael would get his later; but Niall thought he'd need a couple of days to get over his injury. At least, that's what they'd tell the company.

Feeling much better about things, he thought he'd look in on Farrah, even though visiting hours were now over for the main hospital. But this was a maternity ward, and things were different.

As he rounded the corridor to her room, he met her mother coming out the door, pulling it closed behind her. Without any hesitation, she looked up at him and said, "I'm glad you're still here. We need to talk. Let's go get a coffee."

Without waiting for an answer, and despite the fact that Niall still held the paper cup of coffee in his hand, she marched down the hall to the same patients' lounge he'd just left. With a look over his shoulder at Farrah's closed door, he sighed with impatience and followed her mother. She was waiting for him, although he was only steps behind her, and being late as it was, the lounge was empty but for them.

They stood facing each other, the slight, diminutive woman he'd seen earlier no longer in attendance. In her place was a raging gargoyle, every bit as menacing as those that graced the cornerstones of some buildings around town.

"How dare you," she hissed, quietly, if it was possible to hiss quietly. He supposed it was because she did it admirably well.

"How dare I what? Help your daughter? Pay for her medical bills? Ensure she was well looked after throughout her pregnancy? Just what is it ye're how-darin' me about?"

That seemed to set her back on her heels. Niall didn't get a lot of the nuances of relationships, he just wasn't made that way, but he did know how to stand up for himself. He had learned that last summer on Liam's film set when he and his brother had traded places.

He'd love to trade places with someone right now. Anyone would do.

"You, or was it your friend, ravaged my daughter and got her pregnant. And then you had the audacity to make her give it up. Her own baby, her own flesh and blood. My grandchild!"

Niall took a deep breath and put his coffee on the small table beside one of the chairs. This wasn't going to be easy. Putting his hands up, palm out, he blew out a breath. "Calm down and back up, if ye wouldn't mind. Ye haven't got all the facts straight."

"What don't I have straight? She's just given birth to your daughter. She said so."

"Hmm," he nodded, "my daughter. Yes. My daughter because I'm adoptin' her. I never had sex with Farrah, and neither did Michael." He suddenly wasn't at all sure how much he should tell her, yet all the paperwork was legal. Their lawyer had assured them of that when they drew up the contract.

"Well one of you must have in order for her to become pregnant and then claim the child as yours."

This, thought Niall, was beginning to make sense. People believed what they wanted to, after all.

"Yes, we claim the child as ours, and no, neither of us had sex with her." Seeing her before him, trying to stand tall, to be the gargoyle he'd thought her and suddenly failing, softened his heart just a little. Perhaps it was the quiver of her lower lip, thin with the lines of age creeping in, or maybe it was her overall look, the look of someone who knew they'd lost the battle.

He thought for a moment while she stood silent, mulling over his words. If he were Michael, he'd tell her that he and his partner were gay and they'd both make the very best of parents for that wee little girl. Their little girl. But he was Niall and was never a hundred percent sure of himself, always with the shadow of a doubt, even though the truth was staring him in the face.

"Why would you want a child that isn't yours?" she asked suddenly.

"But she is," he answered without even thinking. He and Michael had thought of the baby as theirs months ago, the moment Farrah signed the papers.

"Nonsense. A baby belongs with its mother."

"Yeah, well, she'll have two fathers instead."

The implication had finally dawned on the woman's face. "No granddaughter of mine will be raised by two gay men. Never! I'll see you in court first," she hissed.

So, thought Niall, we're back to the hissing gargoyle. "That's unfortunate that ye think that way because our lawyer, the one that drew up the contract that your daughter willingly signed, says she's ours, and we've nothin' to fear. So I'd suggest ye just get used to the fact that Michael and I are her parents and nothin' can change that."

"I have rights, too," she argued, the only thing missing was the stamping of her foot, and Niall had no doubt she'd do just that, given the chance.

"Ye do. Under our rights as her parents. If ye want to see her, we have no objection. We told that to Farrah as well, but she didn't want any contact. Her plan was to have the baby and go back home as if nothin' happened."

"That's ridiculous. No mother can do that. A woman can't just pretend nothing happened when she's just given birth."

Sensing he was getting nowhere fast, Niall changed tactics. "Just what did Farrah and you talk about? She's been fine with everythin' all along. She even asked to have certain clauses removed from the contract that we were good with, like visitation and such. She made it very clear she didn't want that. So, I'm not certain what yer aim is, but that weyan goes home with me and my partner. Ye'll recall my partner, the one yer husband assaulted without cause? I think that's likely good for a court case in itself."

89

A loud gasp of indrawn breath and widened eyes showed Niall had hit the mark. She'd forgotten that little incident.

"Would ye like to see Michael? He's sleepin' now, but ye can see the damage that was done, see how black his eyes are and know ye've caused him more than one kind of pain. They had to do emergency surgery to fix his nose so he could breathe. I hope they got it right, because he was very fine to look at and I'd hate to think any of that has changed." Niall could stare anyone down with his unemotional personality, and this was no different. His words, delivered in his matter-of-fact, deadpan way, had the desired effect. She backed down.

And sat down.

Niall took the opportunity to do the same.

"I'm sorry for what my husband did, but he was so angry. His only daughter, ruined."

"I hardly think ruined. Maybe if this was a hundred years ago ye might have that thought, but not in this day and age. But it says somethin' about her upbringin' that she had to run away rather than tell ye she was pregnant. And go to all the lengths to cover it up, as well. It has all the earmarks of a male-dominated household where the women have no say. Believe me, after living with Michael and hearing the stories he's told me, I know what I'm talkin' about."

"It's not like that," she broke in.

"Not like what? Farrah too afraid to tell ye? Too afraid ye'd throw her out? Too afraid ye'd send her to relatives in her da's home country where she'd quietly disappear? And, might I remind ye, she's twenty-three. Old enough to know her own mind and not need yer permission for anythin'."

Farrah's mother sat silently, and once again, a feeling of softness, of pity, wove its way through Niall's gut. He knew he'd hit home with his remarks because of what Michael had told him from the stories he'd had from his own father. God knows what any of them would to do the poor plonker who got Farrah pregnant in the first place, he thought.

Standing to refill his coffee, even though he'd had enough, he pulled out a second cup and filled it for Farrah's mother. He pointed to the powdered whitener and the sugar, to which she shook her head, and then handing her the cup, said, "Ye know, even though we kind of met a short while ago in yer daughter's room, I never learned yer name. Mine's Niall. Niall O'Farrell-Johnson, and my partner's name is Michael. Same last name." He waited for the news to take effect.

"Same last...? Oh. I see." It was evident that she'd suddenly taken note of the platinum ring on his left hand, the one with the small diamonds across the top, cradling the slightly larger emerald-cut stone in the middle. It was a masculine ring, with feminine attributes.

"And yer name is...?" he prompted.

"Sylvia," she answered, grimacing at the bitter coffee she swallowed. "My husband's name is Anwar. He's Egyptian Arabic, born and raised in Alexandria, moved to Cambridge to attend school, and that's where I met him. We just hit it off. He never showed any tendencies to possessiveness or jealousy until a couple of years ago."

Well, he'd got more out of that simple question than he'd thought possible, he mused, wondering where to go from here. He didn't do touchy-feely. That was Michael's thing. But he did know how to commiserate with someone. He wasn't that immune to another's feelings.

"Sylvia, did ye never think for once that Farrah hadn't wanted this child but didn't know how to tell ye?"

"What do you mean, didn't want this child? She had

a boyfriend we didn't know about, they had sex, and she became pregnant. Wanting had nothing to do with it."

"Well, ye may be right there, and the circumstances of how she got that way may or may not play a part, but the fact is, she was pregnant, wasn't ready for a child, and chose to give it up to people who wanted it. That's why she came to Ireland. That's why she did her research and knew there were folk here who would be only too happy to have a child. Any child. Michael and I, we weren't lookin' for perfect, although that's what Dawn is. But we'd love her anyway, sick or well, even if she had twenty toes instead of ten. Because that's what love is and that's what a parent does. There are no conditions to love. It is, or it isn't. And ye can't throw a child away just because it doesn't meet yer expectations. And I fear that's what ye're doin' with Farrah. She's disappointed ye, made ye look at yer own relationship maybe, and left ye wonderin'. Ye've a beautiful daughter in Farrah, Sylvia. And Michael and I have a beautiful daughter in Dawn. Can't ye just leave be?"

"No, I can't! And neither can Anwar. That child is our grandchild and nothing will ever change that. She is ours and Farrah had no right to…"

He didn't let her finish. It was time to fight the gargoyle. "She had every right!" he exclaimed, feeling his face flush with anger. Michael used to tell him that, that his face would get red when he became extremely angry, and he'd seen the same happen when Liam's emotions got the better of him. And if this wasn't a case for extreme anger, nothing was. "Farrah is a woman in her own right. Ye've raised her, she's tried to do her best by ye, but the fact is she's a grown woman and ye've no claim on her. Ye're rippin' her apart emotionally, and it needs to stop."

"She needs a psychiatrist," Sylvia spat out.

"She has counseling from one of the best, recommended by someone who knows a lot about good counselors, and she's still seein' him." Both Brandon and Aine had recommended Brandon's counselor, Sean Graham, and Farrah had agreed, so they'd rented a flat for her in Kinsale where she could be by the sea, enjoy the small town, and be close to her counselor. Niall continued. "We have her health covered, Michael and I. We wanted her to know that we cared about her, too, not just about the baby. It wasn't ever just about the baby. We saw someone in her who needed a little extra care, and since we loved everythin' else about her, thought that maybe we could be the ones she could turn to, in exchange for havin' a baby for us, one that we'd never be able to have on our own."

Sylvia set down her now empty cup. As bad as the coffee was from sitting there half the day, she'd drunk it in record time, he noted. Niall thought she'd likely be able to down a pint just as quickly. Yet there was a stubborn set to Sylvia's jaw that didn't bode well. She'd made up her mind that she'd have her granddaughter, come hell or high water if Niall wasn't mistaken.

"I'm sorry it's come to this," said Niall, not really meaning the phrase as an apology. "Ye'll just have to get used to the fact that Michael and I are Dawn's parents. Period. End of subject." He stood to go and Sylvia followed him with her eyes. He knew, because he stopped at the door and met her stare for stare. "If ye want to see the weyan at some point, we can discuss that. But make no mistake, it will be at our say so, not yers."

He left Sylvia to digest his words, and then retraced his steps back to Farrah's room. The halls were quiet, even though it was just half eight, and he knocked softly, poking his head in when he didn't hear an answer.

She was sleeping, and not wanting to disturb her, he closed the door again. There was nothing left for him but to go home, although he couldn't resist one last look at his wee girl.

Back inside the nursery, he met one of the specialty nurses in charge. "Is it time for her feeding?"

"It is," answered the nurse with an indulgent smile. "She'll need her nappy changed as well. Have ye ever done that?"

Niall shook his head, but how hard could it be?

The nurse crooked a finger at him and he followed her to where the baby lay in her cot, just beginning to wake.

"She's already passed the meconium, so that's good."

"The what?"

"Meconium. It's something all healthy newborns pass, their first feces. Very gooey stuff, ye're lucky she's already done it."

He couldn't help but like this nurse, someone who looked like she was right out of school but seemed to know her business. He watched carefully as she unwrapped his baby, removed the wet nappy, and took a cotton-tipped swab to clean around the umbilical cord, handing a second swab over to Niall so he could do it, too. He liked that she made him, that she wasn't all show-and-don't-touch. When he was done, she helped him wipe her down and put on a new nappy, and then showed him how to swaddle her in the small, light blanket while he fed her.

Niall took the bottle she held out for him and placed it in Dawn's mouth. Immediately, the baby began to suckle, her deep blue eyes staring at him through lashes that were almost invisible. The nurse had told him earlier that they would grow more and that her blue eyes would change color by the time she was three months. He didn't care. He loved her.

As he sat in the rocking chair feeding his baby, he didn't see Sylvia's angry face, staring at him from the hall through the glass of the nursery windows.

Chapter Nine

In Brandon's kitchen, where everyone seemed to gather, Liam and Sine, along with Brandon, Aine, and Hank, were standing and chatting when Laura finally walked into the room carrying Meara. Ryan was munching on raisins and it looked to Laura as if everyone was on the verge of going out.

It was soon confirmed. "We thought it a lovely day to take a blanket and sit out by the castle. We've some drinks and snacks in the car and wee Ryan can let off some steam," said Liam.

"Oh, that sounds lovely," said Laura, relieved that they would be going out after all. "Ryan could use some space to run and I could sure enjoy sitting in some sunshine with nothing better to do than soak it up."

"It's a rare day out there to be sure," said Liam.

"I'll help you get some things together for the wee ones," offered Sine, causing Aine to remark on her accent.

"Ye're beginnin' to sound Irish, ye are, only ye've to learn it's weyans. Ye have run the two words together." But her admonishment was all in jest. They'd all teased Sine about her accent—part Chicago, part Irish—ever since she and Liam married.

"Yeah, yeah, yeah," Sine intoned, laughing, and as she stood and stretched, a hand on her back, her very pregnant belly thrust outward, she groaned. "Oh, too many nights in a bed not my own."

"Are ye sure ye want a picnic then?" asked Aine, quirking a brow at her sister-in-law. "Ye're due at any time now."

"Nah, I'm fine. I'd rather go on a picnic."

Laura wondered, too, if it wasn't better for Liam to take her back to Galway. But other than a sore back, normal at her stage of pregnancy, Sine still wanted to go picnicking instead.

"Right then, off to Ballycarbery as soon as everyone is ready," said Liam, heading out the door to the car.

Half an hour later, after gathering up kids, car seats, and assorted paraphernalia, they had laid out a blanket in the sunshine at the rear of the castle where the shade was beginning to grow. It was nearing the hottest part of the day and they'd soon welcome the cooling shadow of the uppermost tower and a light breeze from the sea.

Laura rummaged in the diaper bag, looking for the baby wipes she was certain she'd put in it. "Oh, frig, I guess I forgot them," she muttered as she continued rummaging.

Looking back the way they'd come through the bawn of the castle, Sine said, "Wait, I think I see something." She rose to get it but Liam stayed her with a hand to hers.

"Wait here, I'll get it."

"No, it's okay. I feel like I need to move." She waddled over to where a white plastic object was sticking up in the grass, leaned over, and held it up. "Got it," she said, waving it in the air, only to suddenly grab her abdomen, crying out, "Liam!"

A gush of liquid rushed down her legs and the immediate cramping could not be denied as Sine doubled over in pain. Liam was suddenly at her side, about to scoop her up but she pushed him away and crumbled to the grass. "No, don't!" she cried.

Aine ran over and Laura noted the professional in her emerge. This was Aine the nurse at work, and as she began barking orders, people began to scramble, doing exactly as she asked.

Within minutes, they had the picnic blanket laid beneath Sine where she'd collapsed. She was refusing to move and had begun making the unmistakable sounds of a woman not just in labor, but of pushing, thought Laura. Handing the baby off to Hank, she shooed him away with orders to keep tabs on the kids and keep any onlookers at bay. There were a few tourists enjoying the castle in sunshine.

"Liam, sit her up," commanded Aine, and Liam did as instructed, going behind his wife, sliding onto the ground behind her, and propping her up on his chest, his long legs on either side of her.

"Christ, she's havin' it right now," and then, "don't push until I tell ye to," Aine said to Sine, and Sine, panting, trying to hold back on the urge, nodded.

"Breathe with her, Liam, like this." Aine looked directly at Liam, who wasn't getting it.

"Sine, look at me," said Laura, squatting down beside her and picking up a sweat-soaked hand, holding it, letting Sine squeeze if she needed to. "With me, come on now," and then began the breathing exercises that would get Sine through.

The others stood guard providing a screen of privacy, all except for Hank, who was busy keeping Ryan from running amok and Meara, who was happily cradled in her car seat, cooing at the toy Hank was holding for her.

"I need a towel or a blanket, something to wrap the babe in," called Aine, and with a nod, Brandon raced back to the car for the emergency kit they'd all seen in the car's boot when loading up earlier. Minutes later, panting, he unwrapped the blanket, soft and clean, and none too soon.

"Now push, push as hard as ye can, I've almost got the head out." Aine was all business, hardly acknowledging the new blanket.

Sine groaned, a raw, raspy sound emerging.

"Try not to make that noise in your throat. Just push. Okay, the head is clear, now, wait for the next contraction and then push with all ye've got!"

The next contraction came with her next breath, and with a final grunt and another gush of liquid, the baby burst forth from Sine's body, and Laura took a moment to see the form of the new baby turn from a sickly gray to burgeoning pink. Seconds later, a newborn's cry split the air and the group of onlookers that had gathered a respectful distance away sent up a cheer.

Sine laughed, her head sweat-soaked and dripping, face flushed with the effort of pushing, and Liam, kissing the top of her head, holding her against him still.

All this Laura saw through a haze of memory of her own birthing experience a scant three months before. And as Aine tied the cord with the strip of gauze wrapping from the emergency kit, she had Liam undo the back of Sine's dress so they could lay the baby skin to skin on her chest. That done, she laid the clean blanket over them both.

"Did anyone think to call an ambulance?" asked Aine as she placed heavy wadding between Sine's legs. "She's goin' to need some stitches, the baby came so fast."

"On their way," said Brandon, "shouldn't be too long now. By the way, what is it?"

"A boy," said Sine through her tears of happiness. "We have a boy!"

Laura was certain that if there was a pub band anywhere

nearby, they'd certainly break into song, and when the ambulance arrived a short time later, everyone had relaxed into a jubilant mood. "How far is the hospital?" she asked no one in particular.

"Just up Valentia Road. Quite close," answered Brandon.

Even if the hospital had been across the road, it wouldn't have done much good. The baby had come so quickly, thought Laura.

"Well, that was certainly a bit of excitement on a sunny day," remarked Hank as they gathered up the remnants of their picnic. Liam had gone in the ambulance with Sine, and everyone else was pitching in to make sure nothing was forgotten in the long grass behind the castle.

"Well done, Aine," Laura congratulated her sister-in-law. "We are all so fortunate that you were here."

"Me? What about you? Stepping in like that and controllin' her breathin'. She was startin' to hyperventilate until ye stepped up to the plate. Well done, yerself!"

They both grabbed the last of the bits and pieces from the ground and followed their men back to the car.

"I'll get Brandon to drop me at the hospital. I need to write up a report. Plus, I need to see that Liam is okay. He looked a little shell-shocked."

"I'll say. I don't think he ever thought for one minute that he'd be assisting at the birth of his son out here," replied Laura, glancing around at the magnificence of the castle. She remembered her first sight of it, as the morning sun first kissed the castle walls, piercing the window openings to alight on the grass, wet from a night of rain. Hank had proposed just there, she remembered, as they passed through the bawn and the outer wall toward the parking lot.

The parking lot had a few more cars than when they first

arrived and some were gathered near their own with people asking questions. Laura heard "a baby," and "wasn't that Liam O'Farrell," among others. To the first question, she heard Brandon reply, "yes, a boy," and to the other, she had to giggle to herself.

"No," she heard him say, shaking his head. "No, he only looks a lot like him. Gets that all the time he does, especially when his name is Liam as well."

Laura could have sworn there was a "but" in there from the expressions on the faces of the onlookers. There was no mistaking Sine's coppery locks, and with Liam's well-known face, putting the two together was a given. Still, the ruse kept people at bay long enough, and the family hid the smirks they were wearing, happy at keeping secret both Liam's and Sine's fame, at least this once.

Loading up the vehicles they'd arrived in, they placed the two children in their car seats and drove away. Laura would bet dollars to donuts, as her father would say, the tabloids would be full of the news in a matter of days, if not hours. Not much got past them and she didn't believe for one minute that every onlooker there would not see past Brandon's lie.

Upon arrival at Brandon's home, they noted Cian and Ciara, just getting out of their car.

"We tried callin'," said Ciara as they greeted everyone, "but no one answered. Where've ye been?" She was looking around as if doing a head count, and then, "Oh, my God…it's Sine…she's had the baby!"

Laura laughed, because she'd been the recipient of Ciara's intuition before. And even though Ciara had said she didn't get visions anymore, Laura wasn't so certain that was so. "You sure caught on to that one quick. So, without anyone telling her," she turned in admonishment to the others, then back to Ciara, "guess what she had."

Ciara's face softened and without hesitation, she said, "A wee lad. What'll they call him, do ye think?"

"No idea," said Brandon, "but I think Laura may be right about your talent. It may be resurfacing."

"A lucky guess," she said. "Let's go inside and ring Mam and Henry."

"Isn't she workin' tonight?" asked Brandon, and Ciara's face scrunched in thought.

"Ye could be right, and I know how busy her floor can get so maybe we could wait until mornin' and let Liam call. In the meantime, should we call Henry, do ye think? He and Siobhan may want to join us for dinner."

"Now that's a grand idea. We could drive up to Killarney and tell them in person," Brandon suggested.

"Sounds grand, but we've the weyans," said Hank.

"Oh, right. Forgot about them in all the excitement," said Brandon. "And Aine's not back yet, either. Why don't we just go down to the pub? Its fare is as good as any, and they've a good band playin'."

"Ye're all out to lunch, ye are. Hank and Laura won't be wantin' to haul kids out to the pub," scolded Ciara, and then turning to Laura as if looking for confirmation, asked, "would ye?"

"It's okay," answered Laura with an indulgent smile. "The kids are tired and I'm a bit tired, too. We can stay here and wait for Liam to resurface, and Aine, too. You guys go ahead."

Echoing Laura's thoughts, Hank said, "Yeah, it's grand. Laura and I will stay here and have a quiet evenin' to ourselves, and maybe a bit of somethin' else."

Laura felt herself blush, even though she was hoping Hank would elect to stay behind for just that reason.

"If ye're sure," asked Brandon, and at Laura's nod, everyone filed out the door.

"We'll tell Liam and Aine where ye are when they get home. They may want to join ye," Hank threw over his shoulder as he met Laura's eyes.

"So," he whispered when finally the front door closed on the revelers. "How long before the weyans are asleep?"

Laura's answer was brief but realistic. "Way too long."

Two hours later, both weyans were asleep and Hank turned to his wife, a suggestion of adult time in his heated gaze. "Let's not waste precious time," he whispered as they took a last look at the two babes, Meara asleep in the cot, fist in her mouth, and Ryan cuddled up on his pallet, cheeks flushed in sleep, softly snoring.

Hank led her to their room, the next down the hall, and drew her inside and into his arms. Without preamble, he slipped his hands beneath her t-shirt and caressed her skin, hands splayed across her back, keeping her close. His lips touched hers and she opened for him, tongues dancing, enticing, pulling each other in.

Hank's hands inside her clothing had Laura moaning her delight as one moved to cup the mounds of her breasts, the other to slide inside her jeans, popping the snap as he did so. He felt her shimmy her arse as he pushed them down, and then her jeans and knickers were off, her bra following, and it was his turn to undress.

She helped him undo his own jeans, and as she pushed them down, he hauled off his t-shirt and flung it aside, his jeans and shorts following the same arc. He led her to the bed, and no sooner was she on her back than he was beside her, stroking her, planting kisses across her breasts before laving an erect nipple with his tongue. A bud of milk appeared, and

103

he sighed. "Mmm, dessert," he crooned, and Laura chuckled.

"Keep that up and you'll start a flow." And then, "Jesus Christ, I told you," she swore as the milk came out in a rush, and Hank could no more staunch the flow than he could suckle it fast enough to stem it.

Reaching for one of the t-shirts on the floor, he grabbed it and placed it across her breasts where the material soaked up the excess until the moment passed.

"Is it safe now, do ye think?" he asked.

Laura met his gaze with a raised brow and shrugged. "Not sure, but I think the pressure's off. Shit, I didn't see that one coming," she giggled, then lifted part of the t-shirt to wipe the milk from Hank's forehead and dabbed at the spot in his hair.

"Ye got me a good one," he joked, joining her in laughter. Lifting the shirt and peeking beneath it, he dabbed at her breasts, noted only a light beading of more milk, and tossed the garment on the floor. "We can shower later," he suggested as he bent once more to his task. "I'm not done here yet, though."

He followed the planes of her abdomen down the softened belly she had tried so hard to firm up after Meara's birth. Hank didn't care. He'd cited it as scars well earned and a baby belly being something to be proud of. He knew Laura didn't agree with him, that she mourned the loss of her pre-baby figure, but her shape wasn't important to him. He loved her, stretch marks and rounded belly be damned.

Spreading her legs, he settled in to suckle on her mound since her breasts seemed a bit too trigger-happy tonight. Sliding his tongue inside, he tasted her juices beginning to flow, heard her moans of pleasure, and focused on her bud, the part that had her writhing beneath him in no time at all. Her scent was intoxicating and he felt himself grow hard with wanting her.

Lifting his head from her box, he slipped a finger inside, although he knew it wasn't a substitute for his flute. He'd soon be there, he just needed to know she was ready. Her eyes were closed tight, her bottom lip sucked into her mouth as she enjoyed what he was doing.

Crawling higher on her body, placing his lad at her entrance, he was just about to press it home when the unmistakeable sounds of voices could be heard, the noise that said others were now home.

"Just be quick," came the panicky voice from beneath him.

But Hank had lost it. His concentration broken for just that one moment had been like a bucket of cold water, and Laura, so close and on the verge, suddenly swore.

"Crap! I was so close. So close," she stressed.

It was frustrating, to say the least, thought Hank. "I'm sorry, love, that was my fault. I just should have continued."

Heaving a sigh of acceptance, Laura rolled from beneath him. "Never mind. Let's get dressed and go tell them where the others are."

Nodding, Hank drew on his shirt, pulled on his jeans without worrying about his shorts, and went out to meet Aine and Liam, leaving Laura to make herself presentable.

"Well then, how's the new mam and babe?" asked Hank, walking into the kitchen to see Aine filling the kettle. Liam looked like he'd been through the ringer, thought Hank, taking in his half brother's unusually ruffled appearance.

"They're both doin' well," he said, "but as it was a field birth, they're keepin' them both for a while. Especially Sine. She ripped arsehole to breakfast," he said, shaking his head.

"Ouch," said Laura, coming up behind them. "That's going to make her recovery a little bit tougher."

"It will," acknowledge Aine with a rueful slant to her mouth, "but what can ye do when the babe's comin' and naught can stop it. If there'd been time, I could have stretched her a wee bit, but he just barreled through there like a cannonball."

"It was definitely fast," observed Laura. "Maybe that's why she had an aching back for the last day or so. She was really in labor, and no one knew."

Aine was in complete agreement. "If I'd thought about it, about her bein' so close to her time, I'd have suggested that she and Liam beat it home to Galway days ago, right after Emily's graduation dinner. But they seemed so blasé about it that I thought everythin' was well in hand. I'm surprised Kathleen didn't order them home right away, though."

"Ah, Mam had her own things to think about, from what I've heard. I talked to Henry tonight," Liam said, defending his mam.

"Oh, and was he happy for ye?" asked Hank, knowing even as he said it that it was a silly question.

"Yeah. And then he dropped a bombshell on me."

The trio waited, and when Liam turned after pulling the kettle from the hob, he was met with expectant stares.

"Siobhan's pregnant."

If the three were curious before, they were now completely stunned.

"It's true," he managed, pulling out the teapot and throwing in a handful of loose tea before filling it with boiled water. "He'd thought maybe Siobhan was dyin', had been too scared to ask her what was amiss, and then she told him. Seems she was scared he'd be angry. Ye'll recall we were all talkin' at the dinner about how they'd have an empty nest and all that time together for the first time in their married years."

"And that's it? She was pregnant and afraid he'd be angry?" asked Aine.

Liam nodded.

"Crazy." She shook her head, laughing. "But I'm ever so glad for them. I know they thought they'd never have their own, that Emily would be their only child. I'm so happy they'll now experience raising a child from the cradle up."

Liam's eyes squinted as he handed down teacups to Hank, who'd stepped over to the counter to help. "What's wrong with yer hair?"

Hank's hands went up to his head, touched the milk-dried clumps of hair sticking up and felt his face flush. Behind him, Laura burst out laughing.

Sudden dawning showed on Aine's face, but Liam was still confused.

"I don't follow ye." He was squinting at the strands of Hank's mop of hair, stuck together as if it were caked with gel.

Hank took in Laura's blush, the sideways moue of her mouth, and burst into laughter, leaving Liam in the dark.

"Let me go take a quick shower," said Hank, excusing himself before beating a hasty retreat down the hall.

"Oh, no you don't, not before me," cried Laura, running after him.

Liam looked to Aine. "Did I say somethin' funny?"

Aine, herself, was having a difficult time gaining control. "Ah Liam, ye can be thick as a brick sometimes, I swear."

"What?" he questioned, arms akimbo.

"I think, if I'm not mistaken," she began, "they were tryin' to make love when Laura's milk began to flow. And once that starts, there's naught to be done except let it go."

Liam's face was scrunched in thought. "So, that stuff in Hank's hair is…"

"Milk," Aine finished for him.

"Ah, coitus interruptus, but not the usual way," he joked.

Nodding, she turned to the teapot. "Let's have some tea. I think I can put together a meal for us. Ye must be famished, likely yer backbone and stomach are meetin' by now."

"Come to think of it, I am a wee bit nibbly."

Minutes later, Aine had bread, cheese, some cold meat, and a salad put together, perfect for a warm summer evening.

Neither of them thought to ask where the others were.

Chapter Ten

Emily had landed herself a job at the flower shop next to the pharmacy on the main road going through Inishannon. She'd been delighted to begin the process of learning all about the plants she was handling, how to write up orders, and one of the more enjoyable aspects of the job, how to make up a bouquet.

"What's this stuff called," she asked Dharia, the store owner-operator, as she held up a stem of almost circular leaves of a blue-green color. "It has a strange smell."

"That's eucalyptus, that is. We use it in a lot of arrangements. Nice, isn't it," Dharia remarked.

Emily agreed and went about laying out the flowers on the paper as Dharia had taught her, to end up with a properly set up bouquet. As she did so, she noted the red spot on her hand, how itchy it was becoming and then, almost before her eyes, how more spots began to appear. Her hands felt as if they were swelling, and she gaped in fear as she lifted them before her face, noting not just swelling and red dots but that her hands looked sunburned. "Dharia, look," she cried. "Look!"

"Oh dear," said Dharia, reacting by pushing her toward the sink. "Quick, wash yer hands with some soap and water. Ye've come into contact with somethin' ye're sensitive to."

Emily did as she was told and soon the symptoms

subsided, the swelling less but still noticeable.

"Let's see," said Dharia, taking Emily's hands and checking them over, then added, "go to the pharmacy next door and show Mr. Lynch. He's the pharmacist there. He'll know if there's somethin' ye can put on it."

Thanking her, Emily did just that and soon found herself showing Mr. Lynch her red and puffy hands.

"A contact allergy?" he asked, and at Emily's nod, said, "Here, try some of this. It's a mild cortisone cream. Now, use it sparingly—a little goes a long way, as the sayin' goes."

Emily thanked him and then realized she didn't have her money with her. It was still at the shop.

"Never mind. Ye can pay me on yer next break. I know where to find ye," he joked, and Emily, thankful that he was so understanding, promised to do just that.

As Emily got back to work, Dharia held out a pair of medical-style rubber gloves and was adamant that Emily refrain from touching the eucalyptus without wearing them.

"How do ye know it was that?" asked Emily, curious.

"It can sometimes have that effect on people. Have sensitive skin, do ye?"

"Not that I'd noticed, but maybe," conceded Emily. "I have a mild sensitivity to cheap perfume," she shrugged with a roll of her eyes. "I'm okay with the good stuff but if someone comes close to me wearing the other, I'll get a nasty headache."

Laughing, Dharia put in, "Well, whatever man takes yer eye best beware ye're not a cheap date."

As they worked, Emily asked, "How well do ye know Mr. Lynch?"

"Who? The chemist?" At Emily's nod, she said, "Not well. Just that he's the chemist, a nice fella, genuine like. Why?"

"No reason. Just, me gran knows another chemist with the last name of Lynch, says he works at the hospital, but he's retiring soon."

"Ah well then, that would be the elder Mr. Lynch, this 'un's da."

"Oh. Now that I think on it, I believe Gran said somethin' about that."

Emily thought back to that first night, just a week ago, when she'd moved in with Gran. She'd organized her things in the room her Auntie Ciara used to occupy, and as Gran said, it had a lovely view of the garden out back. But after a while, when all her things had been put away and she'd grown bored, she'd kept an ear out, hoping Gran would soon return.

Eventually she'd heard the car in the drive, and peering through the window, had seen Damian go from his side of the car to Gran's, and then seen Gran's knickers come off. Not able to help herself, Emily watched in fascination as the two got it on inside the front seat, Gran on top, Damian beneath her with the back of the seat laid down as far as it could go.

It was difficult to make anything out, but she'd give a hundred euros they were shagging, just as she'd caught her mam and da that night, not so long ago, shagging on the couch in the living room. As the figures in the car moved, so did the car, ever so slightly, and Emily found herself instinctively rocking her pelvis back and forth, feeling herself becoming aroused. She hadn't yet actually had sex herself, but she was certainly no ignorant school girl.

After a while, the two in the car finished, and as it was dark, Emily thought maybe Gran would like a light so she didn't stumble on the way in. Flicking the porch light on, she went into the kitchen to put the kettle on. She and Gran could have some tea while they talked about whatever it was that came up.

She hadn't intended the night to turn out as it had.

Gran hadn't been just angry. She was pissed. Pissed that Emily had seen her doing something a schoolgirl might, as if she was hoping not to be caught, but being caught anyway. They'd had it out, and Emily felt like an intruder. All she'd wanted was to spend time with Gran. She remembered all the times they'd visited as a family, whether at Gran's or her great-grandparents' home in Garrettstown. It had been fun, and she'd just wanted that camaraderie again, to enjoy it one last time before heading off to university next year. Especially when she hadn't ever thought just exactly what it was she wanted to go to university for. She was hoping this year would tell her.

Instead, she and Gran had nearly come to blows. The memory of Gran going upstairs with the material of her knickers bunching up against her arse showing through the backside of the dress nearly had her guffawing, and to stifle it, she went into the kitchen to pull out the teapot. The humor in the situation was dampened by her gran's anger.

The law had been laid down that night. Damian was going to be a guest in the house, she'd been told. Not necessarily often, but a guest nonetheless, and he'd be the kind of guest that would be sharing her gran's bed, and if Emily didn't like it, she could take herself off back to Killarney.

Emily had listened, red-faced with shame. She'd done a childish thing by watching them, although she knew that if she'd given it another thought she could have got away with it. If only she hadn't thought Gran might need a light to see by.

It was better now, though, thought Emily as she dusted

the gifts on the shelves near the door. Once Gran had said her piece and the ground rules were laid out, they'd finished their tea and gone to bed.

Gran hadn't retired yet so Emily could be expected to be home alone sometimes, and maybe for two or three days while Gran worked late shifts and slept at Damian's.

That gave Emily ideas. If she met a fine fella, she could have him over on those nights...

The store phone rang, jolting Emily out of her internal scheming, and as it was her job to work the front counter, she went to answer it leaving her thoughts behind.

* * *

Dylan Lynch watched the young woman walk out of his door. There were no other customers just then, the day was quiet, and so he let his mind wander. There was something familiar about the girl, though he couldn't put his finger on it. He'd ignored his first instinct, which was to find out more about her, such as her name, and went about the business of running his pharmacy. Although...he paused. She was a looker, and he hadn't been interested in anyone since...

The bell over the door jingled as it opened. Normally, he would keep the door open on a day like today with the sun beating down outside, but he was alone, the other employee he had was on a day off. Without the jingle of the bell, he'd never know if someone was there or not unless they spoke, and he made a mental note to one day replace the small bell with a proper light that triggered a chime whenever someone walked through it. He hated those, though. Hated the sound of them. He much preferred the old-fashioned bell.

Looking up, he saw his father striding toward him.

"Hello, me lad," Damian grinned as he greeted his son. "How's business today?"

"Da, good to see ye," he answered, grinning back, holding out his hand in greeting. "To what do I owe the honor?"

Shaking his head, Damian said, "Oh, nothin' at all, just in the neighborhood and thought I'd drop in."

"Ye're not on shift today then?"

"No," answered his da, "I'm letting the new fella have some time alone. Worked this mornin', thought I'd take the rest of the day, it's so nice out there." He pointed with his thumb out the window where the day was, as Dylan knew, very warm. "It's a might warm in here. Why don't ye have the door open and let the air circulate?"

"Ah," answered Dylan, "we had an incident a short time ago, some gligeens from up the way decided to take advantage of the open door and no clerk at the front. Nearly got out the door with a hundred euros' worth of goods but for the cop who walked in just then, looking for somethin' for a cough. I looked up just in time to yell at the thieves and the officer merely filled the door with his body. Those eejits didn't have a chance," he finished with a broad grin.

"Well, if I'm to help ye here at all, I can install one of those electronic signals so ye can have the door open and still know when someone comes in."

"No. Hate those things. I'd rather install air conditionin'."

"Well, we can do that, too," Damian offered.

A moment later, the bell jingled again and the young lady that had come for cortisone cream was back, her hands tugging on the long strap of her purse slung over her shoulder.

"Ah, come to pay, did ye?" Dylan asked, winking at his da as he moved behind the counter.

Looking up as if she just noticed him, Emily said, "Oh, hello, Damian. I'd forgotten that Gran said yer son owned this pharmacy."

"Hello, Emily. Yes, this is my son, Dylan. Dylan, this is Kathleen's granddaughter, Emily."

"Hello then, Emily. Now I've a name to put to yer face, I won't forget. I've known yer Gran for a while now." He had seen Kathleen O'Farrell come into his shop now and then when she needed something, although it wasn't often. He hadn't really known her until his da confessed to seeing a woman on a regular basis. Dylan, as curious as any might have been, had finally wheedled his da into telling him who the lucky lady was.

Dylan had little to do with his own mam, happy to have his da for companionship on his own odd days off when his clerk could handle the load. Besides, his mam was long gone with the fella she'd married and wanted nothing to do with her son.

Dylan was happy being single, although he sometimes thought wistfully of the one he let slip away. But he'd been young, in university, and hadn't the time for a serious relationship. And then the years had gone by and no one had taken his fancy.

Emily paid for her purchase and went back to the flower shop, and Dylan turned to his father. "She doesn't look much like her gran, does she," he said as a matter-of-fact statement.

"No. I expect she takes after someone else in the family. Kathleen's sons are all raven-haired so I imagine Emily takes after her da. She's the only daughter of Kathleen's eldest."

Nodding, Dylan checked the clock. "It's near to closing, and it's been a rare quiet day. How 'bout a pint?"

Damian smiled, and Dylan knew he had him. "How could I not?"

* * *

Kathleen finished her shift and instead of heading home,

115

or even to Damian's flat, drove into Cork City's downtown center to do some shopping. She had a baby gift to buy for Niall and Michael, and, she suspected, a whole lot of other things the lads might not have thought of. One hour became two, and before she knew it, she had a boot full of items—enough to keep a family going for a full year, she surmised, but happy with her purchases, nonetheless. She'd drive up to Dublin on her next day off and visit with the lads, as she liked to call them.

Stopping in at Damian's, she noted the absence of his car and instead of staying the night as she usually would have done, decided to go home instead. Within the hour, she was unloading her car outside her door when Damian's car pulled up. About to call out a greeting, she stopped midsentence when Emily emerged as well as Dylan, Damian's son.

As she struggled with the package in her arms, she shook her head. "Now if that isn't a trio of trouble, I don't know what is," she exclaimed. "Each of ye grab somethin' and help me haul it inside, and then ye can tell me where ye've been."

"What did ye buy?" asked Emily, peeking inside one of the packages and pulling out a stuffed, pink bunny. "Oooh," she squealed in delight, "Liam and Sine had their baby?"

She looked overjoyed but it didn't matter who had it, a baby was a baby. "No, not Liam and Sine. The lads' baby was born yesterday, and they've got her home now, just today. Seems it didn't quite all go as planned but they've got a wee girl now, named her Dawn. So I popped into town after work and picked up a few things." As they brought the packages up the stairs, having got everything out of the boot, Kathleen asked, "So, where've ye been?"

"Down the pub," said Damian. "Dylan and I took Emily to dinner and had a pint."

"Not Emily, I hope," said Kathleen with a leering glance at her granddaughter. She knew firsthand of Emily's liking for the black.

"No, not at all. She's too young at any rate. We watched, Dylan and I did, that she had only a cola."

"That's good then, that is," she answered, releasing a breath she was only just aware she'd been holding. "Come inside and I'll make some tea."

"We brought ye some dinner," said Damian, holding up a paper bag like an offering to the gods.

Putting her parcels down inside the door, Kathleen took the offering and peeked inside. "What did ye bring me?"

"They had some cottage pie," said Emily. "It's not as good as yers, nothin' ever is, but it was tasty and we thought as how ye might want somethin'. We just meant to be home a wee bit sooner than we are," she apologized.

"Don't fash yerself. Ye had no notion of when I'd be home, after all. And I nearly stayed in Cork at yer place, Damian, only yer car wasn't there and I just had a thought that I should come home."

"I'll take it ye've not eaten then," he said, laying his share of the loot from the car on the coffee table by the sofa. He'd grabbed a bag with handles and had been able to wrestle both the gift and the food into the house without dropping either one.

"No, so I'm ever so grateful ye've brought me somethin', otherwise I'd be lookin' to see if there was somethin' left over in the fridge."

"There was," said Emily, "only I had it for lunch. Can I look inside the rest of the bags to see what ye've bought?"

"Of course," answered Kathleen as she went into the kitchen to get utensils to eat with.

As Emily pulled each item from its wrapping, she became more and more excited. It was like watching her at Christmas, thought Kathleen, and was pleased with herself for finding what seemed to be the perfect gifts.

"I'll have to send them some flowers from the shop," said Emily, leaving Kathleen to wonder how many people Emily knew would suddenly receive a gift of flowers as she became more adept at telephone orders through the store.

Dylan watched Emily as she sorted through the things her grandmother had bought. He thought her cute, loved her enthusiasm and how sweet she was, with an air that seemed to speak of her naiveté. She was young, certainly not as old as she first appeared to him. And although he knew she was young, especially as his da wouldn't allow her anything but cola, he was attracted to her vivacity, and, if he was honest with himself, her youth. There was something simply seductive about her that he couldn't quite put his finger on.

Her laugh was enchanting, her smile like a jewel to a crown. Her eyes held a little bit of mischief that he was certain was there in droves and would show if he ever got to know her better.

Then suddenly Kathleen yawned and he looked at his watch. It was after ten. "Jaysus, I hadn't realized the time. I guess I need to be off. Da?"

The question hung in the air. "Oh, right. Eh…ye can take me car with ye, just if ye wouldn't mind comin' to get me on yer way to the pharmacy in the mornin'?" Damian winked at his son and Dylan darted a glance at Kathleen, who seemed to be blushing just a little.

"Oh, of course. I'll see ye tomorrow, then."

Nodding his goodnight, Dylan stepped toward the door and Emily, as if she were the hostess instead of her gran, stood and said, "I'll walk ye out."

That, thought Dylan, was precisely what he wanted, and as soon as they were outside on the stoop and heading down the stairs, he said, "Would ye like a ride in to work tomorrow? It's not like it's out of my way, and I'll be needin' to get Da, as well."

Emily laughed, and again he was taken in by the sound and how it animated her face, like a Christmas tree that was pretty by itself but so much more when the lights came on.

"That'll be grand. I could walk it, have done this past week, but a ride is so much nicer, thank ye."

And then, because Dylan was often impulsive, he leaned over and kissed Emily's cheek, watched as she put her hand there and giggled. Yes, she was very young.

Saying goodnight, he left her standing in the drive as he made his way down the road. And for the first time since he let that one get away, Dylan felt the stirring of emotion, of becoming interested in going out on a date.

Chapter Eleven

Dawn had turned out to be a very good sleeper, at least she was that first night home, thought Niall as he rose to brew a pot of coffee. Michael, still in bed, had been restless, complaining of the packing inside his nose and how it felt as if it were slipping.

"Why don't ye just pull it out?" Niall had asked, and was shot a look that had daggers imbedded in it. "I'm serious. It's only in there to stop the bleedin', and by now, I'm sure the bleedin's done with."

Again, Michael's expression bore the look of someone who highly doubted the sanity of the man next to him. Still, the feeling of the wadding, slipping, or moving, or whatever it was doing, must have been uncomfortable enough because he'd finally got up the gumption to pull at it. Golden eyes squinting against some kind of pain, real or imagined, he'd gingerly tugged at it until the wad slipped free. It was bloodied and disgusting looking but Niall's tolerance of blood and guts had been honed in the best family possible. All of his siblings, himself as well, had put their mother's talents as a nurse to good use. The sight of blood was nothing to him, not even the gooey and stinky variety.

"Here." He fetched the trash bin and held it out for Michael to drop the offending wad into. "There. Done. Feel any better?"

Michael gave a tentative sniff. "Yes, it does, actually. It feels much better. I don't think I'm ready to lay flat on my back as usual, though. Not yet, anyway." Michael shook his head lightly at the offer of a third pillow. "Two's enough, thanks."

The baby's whimpering cries drifted down the hall from the second bedroom just then, and since Niall was already up, he went to get her bottle and put it in hot water to heat. He'd been warned against putting it in the microwave oven, although he wasn't sure why. Minutes later, he had the baby changed and ready for her bottle, only to turn in time to see Michael standing at her door, warmed bottle in hand.

"Would you mind?" he'd asked, a hopeful look in his eye, and Niall couldn't have denied him that time. It would be Michael's first effort at feeding their daughter, and so with a few quick instructions, for neither of them had ever changed or fed a baby before having Dawn, Niall passed along to Michael the tips he'd received from the nurses. A quick look over his shoulder as he went to get dressed told him all he needed to know. They'd be fine.

Later, as if his thoughts of Michael and the baby called them, he looked up from pouring his coffee to see Michael walk in with the weyan on his shoulder, held there by one broad hand upon her tiny bottom. His face bore the ravages of his broken nose: eyes blackened halfway down his cheeks and across the bridge of his nose, which, Niall was pleased to see, was still as handsome as ever. And with the dark shadow of his beard and tousled hair, Michael was his dream come true. Without hesitation, he walked over to him and kissed him full on the mouth, rubbing his back as he hugged him good morning.

"Want a coffee?" he asked, and Michael nodded, not

quite awake yet, for all he'd been feeding their child.

"I've a question for you," said Michael, sipping gingerly at the hot brew, and at Niall's nod, continued. "The other night after my surgery when I was still rather dozy from the meds, did you come and sit with me?"

"Yeah, I did. Ye were mumblin' things and we had some sort of conversation, like, though I'm not at all clear what it was about. Nonsense, mostly."

"Did you have a woman with you?"

Niall scrunched up his face. "Woman? No, just me. Why?"

Shaking his head, Michael had that look about him that said he was thinking, or rather, trying to clear the cobwebs from his brain so that he could. "No bother, just that I could have sworn there was a woman there."

Curious, and having a feeling about where this was headed, Niall asked, "Can ye describe this woman?"

Michael shook his head. "Not really. Not much, at any rate. I had an impression of an older woman, blonde hair done up on top of her head or something. Either that or it was short. But I think not."

"Did this person say anything?"

Nodding his head, Michael again took on the look of someone trying to retrieve a memory that was a bit elusive. "Something about Dawn. Something about the baby being hers. Made no sense whatsoever. May have been a nightmare because we'd been waiting so long for our little angel."

Heaving a sigh, Niall sat down at the table, gesturing for Michael to sit, too.

"Do you know something about it?" asked Michael.

"Yeah. I do. Sounds like it was Farrah's mother. She's been quite adamant about wanting to keep her granddaughter."

"Oh, so now they're being supportive?" Michael said, dripping sarcasm.

"Hardly that. I just think there's trouble ahead is all. She cornered me as I was goin' in to see Farrah. I wanted to see if there was anythin' I could do for her before I left. I'd already gone to see ye, and since ye were sleepin' sound, like, I thought I'd check in on her. As I'm about to open her door, her mam exits, takes one look at me, and says we need to talk. She was quite insistent that it was her right to see Dawn, and I agreed, only I told her it would be up to us as to when and how. That was the part she didn't like."

"Did she threaten?"

"No. Didn't have to. But it was there until I reminded her about her husband hittin' ye. I left her to mull that over. She maybe went to see ye after I left, I don't know. I went back to Farrah's room but she was sleepin' as well, so I went to the nursery, changed and fed Dawn for the nurses, and then came home. I never saw Sylvia again. I think perhaps we're at a stalemate for now. But I can't help the feelin' that there's trouble yet to come."

"Nathan said he'd covered everything in the agreement," said Michael of their lawyer, unconsciously patting Dawn's nappy-covered bum as she fussed and stuffed her tiny fist in her mouth.

"He did. But I don't think that's where the trouble will come from because Farrah was given every opportunity to back out and didn't. Furthermore, all her expenses have been covered, and will continue to be for the next three months, giving her plenty of time to recover. Add to that the fact we hooked her up with Sean, so put mental health taken care of on the list, too. No, I don't think the threat will be Farrah herself but perhaps the pressure her parents will put on her.

123

I think she's been raised in a very traditional way, and even though she's twenty-three, as far as her parents are concerned she must still toe the line because she's neither married nor has a man, like a brother, for instance, to look after her."

"That's fucking archaic," sneered Michael.

"Watch yer language. We've a weyan now."

Michael smiled as he hugged the baby to the warmth of his neck. "I will when she's older. For now, I think we're safe."

Huffing his disagreement, Niall said, "Back to Farrah. How're we to handle this?"

Shrugging and sipping his coffee, Michael only shook his head. "I don't know. Maybe we need to wait and see what pops out of the woodwork? Did you see her yesterday before you came to get Dawn and me?"

"No. Wanted to, but didn't. I think her folks were there and I didn't believe it was the right time for me to make an appearance."

"Did her mum post bail?"

Again, Niall couldn't say for certain. "Haven't heard. I imagine ye'll be contacted to see if ye want to press charges. Do ye think ye will?"

"Part of me says yes, of course. But the other parts tells me to wait. I think I can do that, for a while anyway. It might provide us with a bit of leverage."

"Leverage? How so?"

"Well, think about it. If you've assaulted someone without cause, and caused them bodily harm in the process, don't you think you'd be on tenterhooks, wondering if you were going to get your arse hauled off to the hoosegow?"

Quirking an eyebrow, Niall had to concede the point. "Ye may be right. Can't say as I'd want to be in that bugger's shoes."

"Now who's using language?" Michael taunted, and received a snicker in turn.

"Fair enough. I'm famished. Shall I make us some nosh?"

"Yeah, what did you have in mind?"

Pulling out bacon and a few eggs, Niall began throwing together some breakfast while Michael went to put the baby back to bed. Moments later, Niall felt Michael's arms about his waist and the warmth from Michael's lips kissing the back of his neck.

Niall turned in his arms. "Feelin' better?"

"Maybe," answered Michael. "I think we're about to discover what it's like to be parents." At Niall's questioning look, he said, "You know…breakfast with food, or breakfast with sex."

"And the answer is…"

"If you promise not to touch my nose, I'll let you lead me to the bedroom."

They left the food where it was.

* * *

It was midafternoon before Niall made it back to the hospital to pick up Farrah and take her back to the small flat they were renting for her when she relocated to Dublin to have the baby. Her flat in Kinsale was still there, if she should choose to take up the offer of further appointments with Sean Graham, the counselor they had enlisted. Niall was hoping she would. Sean was an excellent professional with a good track record, and if his thoughts about Farrah were correct, she would need Sean's expert help.

As he neared Farrah's room, he heard voices through the partially opened door. So, her parents had made it back to see her. Standing just outside the door, he could hear the words, clearly spoken, and Farrah's objections, even more forceful.

"I am not going back with you," she said, and Niall could envision her, tight-lipped and eyes flashing as she glared at her parents. She had gumption, the woman did.

Her father's voice, stern and unforgiving, came through loud and clear. "You will pack your bags and come with us now. You can take us to where they live and we will pick up the child."

The child, thought Niall. Not your baby, not your daughter, but the child. No way in hell.

He stepped inside the door as if he'd just arrived, pretended to be all sunshine and roses, and smiled at Farrah to put her at ease. She immediately responded with what looked like relief, as if the garda were at the door and she was now safe. "Farrah, ye're lookin' well today. Are ye ready to let me take ye home?"

The imposing figure of her father stood in his way. Unfortunately for Anwar, he was nearly a foot shorter than Niall and Niall had been taught to use his fists by the best of them, namely his big brother Henry.

Niall took a deliberate step closer to Anwar, and Anwar backed away.

"My daughter will be coming home with us," Anwar stated, squaring his shoulders and posturing in what Niall thought a good impression of a badger.

"Will she now?" asked Niall, and then meeting Farrah's eyes, said, "I wonder if that's what Farrah wants."

"What she wants is of no consequence. We will go home and put this matter behind us and she will learn her place," Anwar declared.

Raking his gaze from the top of Anwar's head to his toes, Niall met the other man's eyes directly. "Her place? And tell me, what place would that be? Walkin' behind a man ye pick

126

as her husband who might be sixty years old if a day? A man who might backhand her or beat her if she decides to share her own opinion with him? I think Farrah can make up her own mind, and I think it's time ye realized that."

"She cannot go home with you." He was like a short, brick wall, unwilling to be moved. "You are a man, and you are not related to her."

So, they were down to that. "Well, I'm a married man, and Farrah has nothing to worry about on that score. We've been lookin' after her these past few months and we don't intend to stop just because she's given us a daughter. We aim to see she's well enough to go back to whatever life she chooses. And if ye don't mind yer manners, it may not include ye. This is Ireland. Not whatever country ye came from before ye hit England. Last I heard, Farrah was English, and that's a free country."

Ignoring Niall, Anwar turned to Farrah. "You will come now."

Rolling her eyes, Farrah repeated what she'd said earlier. "I will not. Now, get out of here, all of you, so I can change and pack my things. Niall, I'll be just a moment."

He met her eyes, nodded, and stood aside so that her parents could leave first. He was not going to allow them any more contact with her than they'd already had. He needed to speak to her. "Farrah, may we speak? Privately?" He glared at her parents as he said the last word and could see her father puff up his chest as if he would object.

"I'm not goin' to ravish her, for God's sake," he swore. "I'm just goin' to talk."

They left the room, Sylvia hiding the gargoyle personality he'd seen the other night and casting him a glance that was almost pleading.

When the door closed, he pulled the curtain across the bed, hiding Farrah from his view. "There, ye can dress and we can talk and then I can take ye to yer flat, if that's what ye want, but ye need to tell me, Farrah, if ye're alright."

He could hear the rustling of the bedsheets, heard her open the locker and remove her clothing. "I'm fine. Really. I just want to get out of here and go back to my old life."

"What? Go back to them? To the prison they made of your life?"

"It wasn't that bad. And Daddy isn't quite the prehistoric father you make him out to be. He has some old-fashioned ideas, but he really means well."

"Well enough to break Michael's nose without a by-yer-leave."

A moment's hesitation and then as she resumed dressing, said, "I'm really sorry about that. He felt terrible about it later when he found out that we were all just friends."

"Humph. He can go on feelin' terrible, especially if Michael decides to press charges."

"He wouldn't do that, would he? It was all a misunderstanding."

Misunderstanding was an understatement, thought Niall, a very big understatement. As far as he was concerned, Anwar deserved to be convicted and pay the fine or do the time, whatever his punishment was to be. But this wasn't about what Niall wanted. He needed to know what Farrah wanted.

"Farrah, are ye sorry ye gave up yer wee girl?" There. It was out. Let Farrah say what she would.

"No." But there was no conviction in her tone.

He gave her some time to say more, to gather her strength to refute the seeds her parents had planted.

"No," she repeated, and then pushed the drapes back so

they were eye to eye once again. Picking up her small suitcase from the locker, she laid it on the bed and flipped it open. "We made an agreement, and I intend to stand by it."

"That's good, and I'm glad for it, but yer folks were hard on ye. They were really layin' the guilt trip on ye and I need to know if Michael and I have anythin' to worry about, later on?"

"Like what?" She paused as she picked up her toothbrush and toothpaste from the sink.

It was Niall's turn to pause. "Like a couple of months, or a couple of years down the road, we get an order to appear in court over a custody battle."

Resuming her packing, Farrah gasped. "I wouldn't do that to you. You've been amazing, so brilliant and helpful. I don't know what I would have done without you. And you've paid all my bills. I'd never go back on our agreement."

"Yer parents are puttin' pressure on ye. That can be a nasty thing to overcome and I just need to be clear that ye'll not go back on yer word."

"Niall," she came around the bed then and stood before him, and taking his hands in hers, said, "You and Michael have been the best friends ever. I hope you will continue to be those friends. Giving up my baby is hard, I won't deny that, but I know it's best for her. And with Sean's help, I will get over it. Besides, I kind of like Kinsale. Maybe I can get a job there and restart my life."

They were so close, the top of her head coming just below Niall's chin. If ever he could have been tempted by a woman, Farrah would be it, he thought, and then realized that if he was thinking along those lines, then surely, Michael could be tempted, and if Farrah were around, might be.

"Ireland isn't England," he stated, slipping his hands

from Farrah's cool grasp. "I think ye need to go back there to begin yer life. Not to yer parents' home, but to one of yer own. If ye want to go now, we can help ye with that. But Kinsale is just a bit too close, at least for now."

"Oh, I won't come looking for you, bugging you to see the baby or stalking you if that's what you think." She looked honestly horrified that he would think that of her.

"It's not that so much as…never mind." He hesitated before going on. "I just don't think it's a good idea."

A banging on the door was followed by her father's voice. "Farrah. Hurry up."

As she rolled her eyes yet again, Niall couldn't help but hide the smirk he wanted to let loose. Her father was nothing if not persistent.

"Ye don't have to go with them. I'll take ye to yer flat."

She heaved a great sigh and put the last of her things in her suitcase. "I'm sorry, Niall. I need to spend a bit of time with them, to let them know I've done the right thing and that I'm not going to go home with them, at least, not yet. Maybe when this is all over, when we've all got on with our lives, I can go back to England. But for now, I'm going to spend until the end of the month at the flat here and then go back to the one in Kinsale and recoup there for the following three, just like our agreement. After that, you will have fulfilled your end of the bargain, just as I have fulfilled mine, and we can part company. And you can rest assured I will not try to contact you."

Suddenly, Niall wondered if he wanted to lose her, to let her go back to her old life, but he knew it had to be this way. Nodding, he said, "Right. Well, give us a call and one of us will take ye to Kinsale when ye're ready. After that, we'll say our goodbyes and that'll be that."

"No. This is goodbye, Niall." She leaned over and kissed his cheek and he smelled her perfume, the unique scent that seemed to be hers, and was ashamed to feel himself become aroused.

She left him standing there, feeling confused and sad as she opened the door, and with suitcase in hand, walked the length of the corridor with her parents to the elevator and out of his life. He sat down hard on the chair in her room and gripped the edge of the square chrome arms with his fists. Leaning back, angry with himself without really knowing why, he closed his eyes, only then realizing how tired he was. If not for the short back on the chair, he could have cheerfully fallen asleep. Instead, he opened his eyes again, felt the emotion in his throat as he swallowed, and rose to stand before the window.

They would never see her again, and that would be for the best. They had a small album of photographs they would show Dawn one day, photographs of her mother, of the friendship the three shared while Farrah grew bigger in each one.

He sincerely hoped he wouldn't be hearing from Farrah's parents again. Anwar's stance when he'd first walked in had taken him by surprise and instinctively he knew that had the man been taller, he might have ended up as had Michael. But then, Michael had been sitting, and the punch had taken him unaware.

As Niall's eyes roamed the line of parked cars outside, his gaze caught the movement of three figures emerging from the building. It was Farrah and her parents. He watched as her father reached for the suitcase and Farrah held it away. She was backing up, and to Niall, several stories up, it seemed she had no intention of going with them after all.

She was backing away. They were arguing, although he couldn't have said what was coming out of their mouths, only that Farrah was being forceful, making her desires known, loud and clear. And those desires were not in tune with her parents.

Her mother grabbed Farrah's arm…in supplication? Farrah shook it off. Her father tried to do the same but Farrah had stepped back.

And then she was walking quickly away, and with a quick glance over her shoulder, began to run. Her parents, thankfully, stayed where they were, her mother grabbing Anwar's arm when he would have given chase.

No. It wasn't over. He made a mental note to call Farrah later, or maybe just show up at her flat to make sure all was well. Maybe he'd send Michael and save himself the pain.

And maybe hell would freeze over. If that was what a few minutes alone in her presence did to him, what the feck would it do to Michael? Michael, who could love both men and women, who had been so faithful since their marriage but had betrayed Niall prior to that event. He loved Michael with all his heart and he didn't doubt Michael's love for him, either. This morning had been proof of that.

They'd been intimate in a rushed kind of way, as if they were both worried that Dawn would wake at any moment and they'd have to break apart, right in the middle of it all. But that hadn't happened, and so they'd made love with all the intensity of a night of passion, but with the necessity of speed.

He'd let Michael penetrate, let him take it as slow or as fast as he wanted, and couldn't help but join him soon after. Just the feel of his lover inside him, of Michael's hand on him afterward while Michael's lad relaxed and slipped out, had been enough to bring him off.

Between thoughts of making love with Michael and Farrah's scent still in his nostrils, he was feeling aroused again.

Farrah's parents were gone when he came out of his reverie. Farrah was gone, hopefully to her flat, and hopefully alone.

Inhaling deeply, he turned and left the room, traced Farrah's steps to the same elevator, and let himself out of the building for the long drive home.

Home. They would be moving soon. The flat was too small for a family. They'd wanted a garden for Dawn to play in, a neighborhood that was family friendly, and they'd found it in a village just outside of Dublin.

For now, though, they were still at the flat, and as he wove through the impossible traffic of Dublin, he knew he was glad they were moving. It was to be a new beginning for everyone.

Chapter Twelve

Henry had made the trek to Galway for one specific purpose, and that was to pick up the car seat and other baby paraphernalia Liam and Aine had ready at their house on the coast and were now in need of. Emily, having gone to Killarney to retrieve more of her own things, had asked to tag along and Hank thought it a good idea. He hadn't yet told her about the baby he and Siobhan were having, and he wasn't sure how she was going to take it. She'd been the only one in their lives for so long.

His siblings now knew of the coming event. Henry had told them when they called to give him the news about Liam and Sine's new arrival. It seemed to be happening all at once, like a baby boom all of their own, he mused. First Niall and Michael had adopted their child, having waited six long months for Farrah to give birth. And then suddenly of an afternoon and on the same day, Sine gave birth at Ballycarbery Castle. Thank God for Aine's presence, otherwise it could have been disastrous. She was still in hospital because while the birth was fast, it had ripped her from stem to stern and now she wasn't doing so well. He had no doubt that in time she'd be well, but for now? He only hoped Aine wasn't blaming herself for the infection that had set in. At least the weyan was thriving.

His musings came to a halt when they arrived at Liam's

house after a two-and-a-half-hour drive from Killarney. Emily, having arrived in Killarney the night before, had made the house feel right again, as if, in her absence, the balance inside their home had been upset. It had felt empty.

"I never thought to ask, how was it, sleepin' in yer old room again?"

"Grand, it's home, after all. And it's nice to know it's there, even though I need to move forward," she answered, a wistful smile creeping across her face.

"Do ye like livin' with Gran?"

"Yeah, it's good, like. Though I didn't know she and her boyfriend were that close," she laughed, emphasizing her last two words. "They're quite randy, like."

Henry nearly drove off the road. "What? What are ye sayin'? Ye shouldn't be talkin' of yer gran that way."

Looking hurt, Emily apologized. "I didn't mean anythin' by it. Just that I think I'm in the way, and maybe I should be lookin' elsewhere to live."

"She gave ye the talk, did she?"

Nodding, Emily admitted to feeling chastised. "It was ever so embarrassin'. I imagine it was for her, too. And then I woke up one mornin' and Damian was there at the table, havin' coffee and breakfast. Gran gave me a look and so I pretended naught was amiss and took myself off for the day. It was all a wee bit awkward."

"Well, yer grandda's been gone many years. If she's found somethin' to like in Damian, maybe ye should just grow up and leave off? It's her house. She can do what she likes."

"Ye see, that's what I mean. It's her house and I'm an interloper. I know I'm welcome, she'd never turn me away, but I can't help feelin' I'm crampin' her style, like."

"Ye're hardly an interloper, Em, and the whole idea of ye movin' to be with yer Gran was to help ye spread yer wings. Ye're a bit young to have to fend for yerself and it seemed this was an easy way to do it. I'll mind ye, it was yers and yer gran's idea."

"I know, but maybe it was a mistake."

"So, what are ye sayin'? Ye want to come home?"

When Emily bit her lip, Henry knew she'd been thinking about it.

"Would it be so bad? Do ye think I could?"

"Ah, darlin', it's only been a few weeks. Why don't ye give it some time. Spend the summer as planned and see how it goes? Ye've a job ye seem to enjoy and ye wouldn't want to suddenly quit on them. It's not right."

"Then I could look for a flat of my own in Inishannon."

"That's expensive, that is."

"Uncle Hank left home at my age. My mam even younger."

Henry couldn't refute that. "Yer Uncle Hank had good reason. His mam had died, he had no choice but to be on his own. And look what happened to yer mam, unfortunate though it was. Besides, it's different for a young man…"

"Why?" she broke in before he could say the rest. "Why is it like that? Just because I was born a girl shouldn't mean I can't take care of myself."

He was about two heartbeats away from shaking some sense into her. She'd always had a bit of a wild, independent streak, likely from the upbringing she'd had before she came to live with him. Meara had carted her around the country, sometimes leaving her alone while she went in search of her next fix. It scared him silly when he thought of what Emily had seen and endured at an early age.

"Em, I want ye to stay with yer gran, just for now. And while Siobhan and I would take ye back at any time, there's somethin' ye should know." They had arrived at their destination and were now parked in front of Liam's refuge from the world, the great stone manse hidden behind a bower of yew trees, the long, serpentine drive through the acre between road and house like a drive through a park.

They stepped out of the vehicle and Henry unlocked the gothic arched door with its massive, black hinges across the time-blackened wood, and followed Emily inside. He shut it behind them as she walked over to view the coastline from the floor to ceiling windows in the sitting room.

"What should I know? If it's the facts of life, ye're too late," she giggled.

Henry's head shot up. "What?" All kinds of images flashed through his mind, images he wasn't ready for.

A sudden dawning showed on Emily's face as she must have realized her mistake. "Oh, no, not that. No, I just mean that I know about the birds and the bees, is all."

Letting go a huge sigh of relief, Henry realized his stomach was rumbling. Opening the fridge, he checked the contents and then, closing it, opened the cupboards instead. He found some interesting canned soups and pulled one out, then began rummaging around looking for a can opener. In no time at all he had the soup in a pot, warming on the hob.

"Come and sit while I get some lunch together."

She found a seat at the high counter and as Henry put some buns on the table, Emily noticed the bottles of beer next to the fridge. "Oh, can I have one of those?"

Henry looked to where she was pointing and frowned. He'd known Meara had given her alcohol sometimes, and while it was never a whole bottle and maybe only a sip or two from her own, he disagreed with it. As a man who straddled the line with alcoholism himself, he'd vowed never to touch another drop once Siobhan had read him the riot act. Looking back at Emily, her face a display of innocence, he said, "I think not."

"Ye're no fun," she complained.

"Ye're not yet eighteen."

"A couple more weeks, that's all."

"Humph," Henry answered, and pulled a bottle of juice from the fridge and poured them both some of that instead.

He served up the soup into two bowls, then sat down next to her and watched as she tucked into her meal. They were halfway through when she asked, "So, what is it ye wanted to tell me?"

It would be alright, he knew. She'd probably be excited. So why did it seem so difficult for him to tell her? Clearing his throat and breaking open yet another bun, he said, "Siobhan's pregnant. Ye're goin' to have a wee sister or brother in about six months."

Emily dropped her spoon, gasping and nearly choking on her soup. "Eee, that's grand!" she exclaimed, jumping down from her chair and hugging Henry, a difficult task since he was still seated.

"Oh, come on, Da, that's got to be worth a wee dram of somethin' to celebrate with."

"Over my dead body. At least not until ye're eighteen. No. Finish yer soup and help me get the baby stuff together, and for God's sake, don't let me forget the car seat."

She was fairly buzzing in her chair as she downed the rest of the soup and helped him clean up the mess. A short time later, they had put everything itemized on Liam's list in the van, including the suitcase Sine had packed for the hospital, which, according to Liam, also contained the clothing to bring the baby home in.

Off they went, Henry ruminating on the drive ahead while Emily played on her phone. It was enjoyable, this simple act of being together with his daughter, to enjoy the time they shared and take it for what it was. She wouldn't be his for much longer. She was on the verge of adulthood and one day, he knew, a young man would come to claim her. It had him shaking his head at life. In the space of a year, his daughter was grown and out the door and a new baby would be born to start the process of raising a child all over again.

Henry wondered if he'd be up to it, and then had to laugh at himself. It wouldn't matter. It would happen anyway.

* * *

Hank and Laura, having left their two children in Ciara's and Cian's care for the next two hours, had just come from visiting Sine. She was still feverish, but seemed to be improving they were told, and through it all, she'd managed to keep breast feeding. The baby, still nameless, was staying in her room until she was well enough to go home.

As they left the hospital, Hank broached the subject he'd wanted to talk to Laura about since returning to Ireland. They took the car and drove northeast along N70 to Rossbeigh and parked, looking out at the water and the small, broken down fortress on the spit of land beyond. There were few people on the beach, mostly enjoying the view and the sun, their presence so sparse as to make it seem as if he and Laura were alone. The sand, a grain as soft as talc and as light in color as any in Ireland, slid into their shoes despite their efforts against it.

Hank took Laura's hand on impulse, pulling her close for a slow kiss.

"What was that for?" She was smiling up at him, and he felt suddenly guilty because although the kiss had been genuine, he had ulterior motives for it.

"Because I love ye." That sentiment, too, was genuine. And while the thoughts in his head were no less legitimate, he knew she'd misconstrue the sentiment of the kiss once he broached the subject that was burning in his brain.

They walked a short way until the sea came between them and the small fortress. "Want to try?" he asked. "It isn't deep."

She looked down at the water separating the fortress from the rest of the beach and a grin spread across her lightly freckled countenance. "Let's do it."

They shucked their sandals and picked them up, then stepped into the cold water of the bay. Laura gave a squeal as the icy water hit her toes, and then they were both running across the gap, laughing as they went and splashing more water than they thought possible. They hopped onto the land on the other side, lightly soaked from the waist down.

"I'd suggest we strip off and dry in the sun but I'm not into displayin' everything for the beachgoers, and there's no privacy inside the fort." Hank cast her a cheeky grin.

"No, it doesn't look like it has many walls high enough for that," she observed and grinned back.

Slipping their shoes back on and taking her hand once again, Hank led her the few meters to the fortress and peered inside. Rubble, coarse grass, and sand covered the ground, looking as wild as any along the coast of Kerry.

"It's kind of neat, I think," she said, looking up at the four walls that had once stood to an impressive height.

Hank nodded, took a breath, and pulled her down beside him on one section that was high enough to sit on, low enough that they didn't have to crawl up to it. "Can I talk to ye about something?"

Shrugging, she answered, "Sure. You know you can. We've always been able to talk."

"Yeah, and when words failed…"

"That's why we have two kids," she finished, and they both chuckled at the truth of the statement. They'd always talked and made love. Even when things felt wrong, they'd always been able to do one or the other, and through words and actions had resolved many issues.

Hank sucked on his lip, suddenly unsure of what he was about to ask of her. "I was wonderin' if ye might want to extend our stay in Ireland just a wee bit longer?"

That seemed to catch her off guard. "Longer?" At his nod, she continued, "I guess it depends on how much longer. Are we talking weeks? Months?"

"Years."

"What?"

Gobsmacked, that's what she was.

"Years. I was wonderin' if ye'd mind movin' here for a time. We could rent our combined properties out at home, which would give us an income, and stay here for a while; let Ryan and Meara get to know their Irish cousins."

"They can get to know their cousins through visits. We can come here every few years and they can come to Canada every few years. It isn't like Ireland is the only country involved in this family. We're Canadian, too," She argued.

"I know. I just…"

"Look, I understand that being here, being with people you've come to know and love as an extended part of the family that is truly yours, is a real draw. I get that. I just don't think we need to relocate for the rest of our lives. I have a good job back in Canada, and in six months, I'm due to go back to that job. And I will."

He filled in the unspoken words inside his head, with or without you. "Would ye think about it? Maybe stay for… say…maybe the next six months; give it a try?"

She stood and walked to the farthest edge of the fortress interior as if put as much distance between them as she could. "I don't know," she stated flatly, crossing her arms in front of her. "I like Ireland, it isn't that."

"Then what?" He'd moved to stand beside her, wanting to take her into his arms, to let her know it would be alright.

"It's a big move. It's really sudden. We have stuff at home. Stuff in the fridge, the kids' playthings, the rest of their clothing. Our clothing. I can't live for the next six months with the stuff we brought with us."

"We can buy more."

"We aren't rich! I don't know if we can manage all this, what with a mortgage covering the new house and the rebuild on your cottage, and me being on maternity leave with a reduced paycheck. I just don't know."

"I've a nest egg. Ye know I do."

"A nest egg for emergencies. Hank, this isn't an emergency, it's madness."

"Ah, but wouldn't ye like to go mad, just for a time?"

"No. End of subject. No."

He chewed his bottom lip in thought. "Does that mean no, as in I can't use my nest egg, or does it mean no, as in ye'll not even consider a six-month extension?"

Shaking her head, she moved off, clearly not wanting to be too close to him just then. "I don't know. It's too sudden. I need time to think."

He felt a little better at that. She'd always been the

hesitant one. Before they were married, he'd had to leave her in order for her see how much she missed him, how close they'd become. She'd had to learn that he was as much a part of her as she had become to him.

And she'd finally followed him to Ireland once she realized how much he meant to her.

"Alright. We've another week here. We may as well enjoy it. But I'd like to discuss it again before the week is out. Deal?"

Laura gave a reluctant nod.

They retraced their steps in a much less enthusiastic mood than when they'd crossed the gap less than an hour earlier. The tide had been on its way out then, and now it was at slack water, neither ebbing nor flooding. They crossed the gap with ease, hardly dampening their clothing at all.

Laura was in a mood, Hank knew, and he'd put her there. Too late for regrets, he opened the car door for her and then got in the other side to drive back to Cahersiveen. Their two hours of freedom were up.

* * *

Laura's head was spinning. Of all the idiotic ideas Hank had come up with in the past, this was the biggest. To move to Ireland? She hadn't lied when she said she liked Ireland, loved it, in fact. The green, rolling hills; the rocky, furze-covered landscape of the mountains; the lushness of the valleys; the purity of the streams. Everything was beautiful, and if the whitewashed cottages dotting the landscape weren't enough to draw you in, then the wildness of the many ruins, stone forts and fortresses, would add to the magic of it all.

There was little about Ireland she didn't like. Maybe the fact that you could drive around the Ring of Kerry in an afternoon, including a stop for lunch. Nothing was very far away, at least not in terms of her life in British Columbia, where a three-hour drive still wouldn't get you to the coast from her home in the interior. Still, it wasn't enough of a drawback, in her books, to dislike a place. No, it was the way Hank had said it, the pleading in his voice, the expression in his deep blue eyes. Eyes she could never say no to. He wanted this. Or at least he thought he did. Maybe, when he'd stayed here for six months, he'd realize what they had in their little mountain homestead? They had acres to themselves and the kids, miles in which to ride snowmobiles, ski, and hike without running into another living soul because between the two properties, her cabin and Hank's original site down the road, they had acres to spare.

All that aside, she knew she would miss her friends, Kerry Gallagher, whom she worked for as a legal researcher, and her friend Sarah Chan, who'd lived across the hall in the condo where she'd resided when Hank came into her life. She and Hank now had a three-bedroom home in town, a home with a nice backyard and a swimming pool to cool off in during those hot summer days when they weren't up the mountain. But it was her friends she'd miss the most. And her life.

What kind of life would she have here, with only Hank's relatives as friends? She liked them all well enough and had been accepted as one of the family without any questions asked. The Irish, she'd learned, were an inclusive, happy bunch, whose lives were better when shared, and whose proclivity for joy seemed to be a part of the overall package.

Still, she hesitated. Would Hank remember her, once he regained his life here? He hadn't been all that happy in the past and had gladly given up Ireland for what he'd found in Canada. And until they'd begun returning for visits after that first fateful trip, he'd never mentioned wanting to return for good. And yet, that's what this felt like. It felt like he wanted to stay. Forever. And forever wasn't what Laura had in mind.

She thought of the kids, of them growing up without a Canadian identity, of not knowing about maple trees and the coureur des bois, of the kind of Hallowe'en where costumes had to cover snowsuits. She'd grown up back east where fall colored the Gatineau Hills in a patchwork quilt, and where, in spring, the maple trees ran thick with sap to be quickly boiled up in long vats that turned the clear liquid into precious maple syrup. It was called, the sugaring off, and her Canadian roots were as deep as the maple trees that lined the hills in Quebec. Though she no longer lived in the east, she loved her western home just as much.

Her move west had been to escape domineering parents. They hadn't trusted that she was smart enough to be on her own and so she proved to them just the opposite. She was not only smart enough, she'd wangled herself into a good position at the best law firm in town.

So the town wasn't Vancouver. So it didn't have the glitz and glamor that her parents enjoyed on trips to Montreal or Quebec City. It didn't have huge crowds, either.

That was one of the positive things about Ireland. Killarney, where Hank was from, might be crowded during tourist season where the traffic crawled to a halt through the main thoroughfare in town, but it suited her just fine because, during the off season, it appeared relatively quiet.

Of course, Hank's family was a big draw to him, whereas Laura had only had her parents; no cousins that she knew of and no living aunts or uncles. She'd had an aunt, but that woman, a person Laura had loved more than her own mother, had died at an early age. Laura understood grief—she and her aunt had been so close—which was why she also understood Hank. He'd come back to Ireland to look for answers, to fix his past so he'd be free to wed her. She hadn't known it at the time and only learned of his purpose during that first visit.

She recalled when he took her to the graveyard at Killegy, where the thirty-foot stone Celtic cross faced Killarney town, and told her the story of his family and those buried in the ancient graveyard.

That day at Killegy had been magical.

He'd taken her hand, determined to show her something he'd only recently found himself, the graves of his great-grandparents.

"She had only two children, the first being a girl who grew up to be my grandmother, the second a boy who died in childbirth. He was buried here. She died hours later, unshriven and therefore not able to be buried in a proper Catholic graveyard. She wouldn't have wanted it anyway, so I've been told.

"My great-grandfather did his best to raise the young girl but soon gave the care of her over to his sister's family. The story goes that once he was certain she was in a good place, he took himself off and was never seen again. They think he took a boat out to sea to drown himself in sorrow. It's all legend, family legend, but it explains why she is buried here, and he is only mentioned on her headstone. I'll show you when we get in there," he said, speaking of the headstone. "My half brother Henry had a proper stone erected a couple of years ago. They are his heritage too. What the phrases mean, the difference between 'of Killarney' and 'died at Killarney', is that if a person is from Killarney, it says so. But my great-grandfather was not from Killarney and not buried here, therefore it only says 'died at' instead of the name and the words 'of' or 'from'."

"But you said they don't know where he died," she'd objected.

Hank agreed. "There may be more to the story. I hadn't been born yet." His blue eyes had crinkled in laughter.

They were walking up the grassy lane, over the stile, taking care to keep clear of the stinging nettles close by.

"The leaves are harmless, but those little spikes can leave nasty blisters and festering sores if you come into contact with them. Horrible, nasty things," he explained, holding her hand as she scrambled through the deep V of the iron fence and landed neatly on the other side.

She grasped the rust-mottled rungs carefully, warily eyeing the nettles close by, glad to be through the stile unscathed.

Safe on the other side, they walked up the cart path toward the hill where, on their left, stood the great Celtic cross, dark gray in the lighter gray of the pearled sky. Clouds seemed not to be moving at all though the breeze blew briskly across their faces and whipped her titian hair about and she remembered wishing she'd tied it back.

Minutes later they came to another gate, another stile, this one with no nettles, and she sprang through it, eager to see what was on the other side. Beneath the huge yew trees, the leaves provided shade and a kind of peace. The graveyard didn't seem creepy at all.

He led her through bluebells, hundreds of the foot-high plants spreading a blue carpet before them through a graveyard punctuated by headstones, tombstones, and the fenced-off stairs to a mausoleum below one of the larger tombstones. Beyond was the cross at the edge of the hill. Like a great, gray sentry standing guard over those in eternal repose, it faced inland, many miles from the sea and the man who'd drowned in those water's icy depths.

"If you ask anyone in town about this graveyard, if you ask them where Killegy graveyard is, most won't know. Especially people our age. Unless they've family here, they won't have heard of it," he explained.

"Is that because most of them are Catholic?" she'd asked, genuinely curious.

Shrugging, because he didn't know the answer to that one, he led her from the cross and showed her other graves, told her about the people who had lived and died in the land of his birth, some of whom he had known as a young boy.

They circled round the graveyard, trying to avoid crushing the multitudes of flowers without luck. It was impossible to step through the mass of blue without flattening the stems in their wake. He reached down and, cupping his hand around a stem, pulled upward, relieving it of the delicate petals, releasing their fragrance in the palm of his hand.

"Here," he'd invited, "smell these."

She'd closed her eyes in delight, inhaling the delicate scent that had brought a smile to her mouth, lips curved in obvious enjoyment. "Oh, that's so lovely," she'd said. "I've never smelled bluebells before. Come to think of it, I don't think I've really ever seen bluebells before."

They took a step and were suddenly beside an ivy-covered structure, the missing door inviting them to the dirt-covered floor within. It was obvious that no panes of glass had ever graced this structure, and on the opposite wall was an engraved stone that Hank read out for her.

"This church of Killegy was built as a family mortuary chapel by Maurice Hussey of Cahirnane late colonel in the army of King James II.

148

At his death in 1714 his body was borne here by his four sons and buried at midnight by torchlight."

They stood in silence a moment before he asked her if she felt creepy in the cold depths of the stone structure. It was small if it was supposed to be a house, although if the house were meant for the soul of the individual, then it was big enough. Roughly twelve feet long and eight feet wide, with a window at either end and a short doorway in the side where you had to duck to get through, it was compact if nothing else. The dirt floor was solid beneath their feet, leaving dusty footprints where they stood.

"Not really. I think it's rather peaceful here."

"Oh, well. I thought I'd wait to tell you this part. Henry has a friend whose dog will absolutely not cross that threshold. It refuses to budge or set one foot inside and whines like the bean sidhes are after it if you try to coax it inside."

"Really? That's amazing. I feel nothing."

"Well, it isn't a place you want to be after dark, I can tell ye that," he grinned, and she didn't doubt that at all. "Here," taking her hand, he brought her out of the tiny structure and wove her through the grass where large stones stuck up at odd intervals. "See these three tucked close together? They are my great-great-aunties, stillborn and, like my great-grandmother and her child, unable to be buried in consecrated ground. But these have no headstones because they were too poor to have any made. So they marked their graves with simple stones, just to show where they are."

Laura had gazed about, suddenly aware that many rather large stones protruded through the ground, higher than the grass. "All these stones signify people buried here, too poor to have headstones made?"

She was filled with part wonder, part sorrow, even though

she didn't know who these people were.

And then he continued telling her what he wanted her to know, the reason he'd brought her here. "This is where I'm from. These people are my family. And while you might think it something interesting, to me it's completely amazing. This family, in this graveyard, including those people over there who I had known as a young boy, are all very real to me now. I had no knowledge of family before this visit, beyond my mother and my sister. Sadly, I didn't have money for a proper grave for my mother, so she's buried in the paupers' field on the other side of town. Just a simple white cross marks her spot."

"How sad!" exclaimed Laura.

"It is, in some ways. But my new siblings, they showed me this place, told me the stories of my great-grandparents, my aunties. It's sad about them, too, but life goes on. I'm here, with a whole new aspect to myself and my life. How can I be sad about that when I suddenly feel like I'm not alone anymore?"

* * *

That day still resonated within Laura, reminding her that when he'd left Ireland, he'd thought he'd had no one, no family anymore. He'd arrived in Canada, a lone soul but for his new wife. Eventually, that marriage had failed and he'd headed west for another new beginning, and now he had her, and she couldn't regret that new beginning for herself, either. He was something she'd been looking for all her life, especially after learning that her first husband had been more than unfaithful. Laura knew that Hank was the kind of man she'd hoped for in her first marriage, yet here she was in a second marriage, with two children, and a husband who now wanted to leave what they had—all the good things that added up to their lives in the mountains of British Columbia—to move back to Ireland. For what? For a prolonged visit? Or forever?

Her mind was working hard at trying to unravel her feelings. Could she stay another six months? What would it hurt?

Brandon's house on the hillside over Cahersiveen came into view and she still hadn't come to any decision. If they stayed, they'd have to find a place to live, and it would have to be furnished, and they'd have to buy clothing, and toys, and...

The list seemed endless. Overwhelming. And it was all Laura could do to put a smile on her face when they pulled into the driveway and saw Brandon and Aine playing with the two little ones in the front yard. Or rather, Brandon was playing with Ryan and Aine was holding the baby, who looked like to be asleep in her auntie's arms.

It melted her heart and filled her with a confusion of feelings she didn't know how to handle.

Chapter Thirteen

Emily put the order for a bouquet of flowers through to the shop in Cahersiveen and to one in Dublin and hung up the phone. She was so happy to be an auntie! A girl for her uncles, Niall and Michael, and a boy for Uncle Liam and Auntie Sine.

Few knew she was related to Liam O'Farrell, the actor, let alone that his wife was also a famous actress who still used her maiden name, Maguire, on screen. To the family, they were normal people who went by Mr. and Mrs. O'Farrell. And now they had a baby to add to the group, a baby named Aedan Daithi O'Farrell, the second boy born in this new generation and not a Henry nor a Ryan after their grandfather. Uncle Hank had taken care of that, she grinned to herself.

Uncle Niall and Uncle Michael had claims to the first girl. Dawn was such a pretty name and recently, Michael had proclaimed her middle name to be Grainne. A fine, strong name; a name given to an Irish heroine and fitting for their wee girl, she was certain. Emily hadn't seen her yet, but the lads, as the family had termed them, had promised that perhaps when Uncle Michael's eyes were less bruised from his broken nose, they'd venture forth.

Of course, that hadn't stopped Gran from going to see them and snapping a million photos, too many to send all at once through email. But she'd shared many and so now

Emily knew what Dawn looked like. She looked like Uncle Michael without the black eyes, another thought that had her grinning.

The bell jangled on the door as it opened and Dylan walked through, sighing an audible relief at the blast of cool air. His pharmacy was still without air conditioning and the heat wave was ongoing. He closed the gap between the front door and the desk, looking to her like a Celtic god, fair-haired and blue-eyed and with a look that brought out her romantic streak. She thought him so handsome, although she knew he was too old for her. He had to be at least twenty years her senior, but she fancied him nonetheless, and what would it hurt, she wondered, if they dated for a while? After all, he was a mature man that could show her much of life that, at the moment, seemed to be a mystery to her. So what if they never married? While she would be looking for a full-time relationship eventually, she was curious about many things in the meantime and she briefly imagined them dating.

He planted his hands on the counter in front of her, and looking her in the eye, said, "If ye've time, I was wonderin' if ye'd like to go for lunch? As reluctant as I am to leave the cool air in here, I've no one to eat with and they've cottage pie at the pub. Are ye game?"

Leaning over so they were close enough to kiss, she grinned at him, "That sounds like a grand idea. Let me check with Dharia."

She came back a moment later, her purse dangling from its long strap off her shoulder. "Let's go," she said, and walked through the door he was holding open for her.

The pub was dark and gave the impression of coolness, though it was hardly that. The open door invited people in, the wooden benches comfortable and cool although the temperature inside was only slightly less than outside. They sat at a table in a corner near the window that opened out onto the street. A rear door was ajar somewhere, and a light breeze could be felt now and then, flowing through the establishment.

In no time at all, the cottage pie was before them, and while Dylan ordered a black, Emily had to settle for a cola.

"Here, want a sip?" asked Dylan, a twinkle in his eye.

Emily looked at the Guinness in his glass and gave a wistful sigh. "No, thanks. I'd better not. I promised Uncle Henry."

"Ah, just one sip. No harm in it."

Again, she shook her head and dug into the pie, breaking through the crust of mashed potatoes to the meat and vegetables beneath.

"Ye aren't livin' at home anymore. Ye're on yer own, more or less. Ye can do what ye like," he said, taking a long, cooling draught before setting it down and licking the foam from his lip. "Ye're missin' somethin', ye are."

She looked up and giggled. He still had a speck of foam at the corner of his lip and she couldn't resist taking a finger and wiping it away for him. Then, just to prove her independence, she put her finger in her mouth and sucked it clean. "All gone," she said, laughing.

Dylan's eyes widened and then he, too, dove into his pie.

From across the pub, the young bartender, Fionn, watched the two in the corner. The girl was pretty, with her long, flowing mane of wavy black hair. Her eyes, from what he could tell, were a shade of blue, or maybe gray. He'd seen her at the flower shop when he'd bought his mam a small gift for her birthday. The shop had some gift items besides selling flowers, and there were always unique tidbits to find.

He'd found the girl to be a tidbit he wanted to get to

know, and he wondered about the man who was with her. He recognized him from the pharmacy, but other than that, knew little about him. To Fionn's way of thinking, he was far too old to have an interest in her.

He wiped down the counter and went to pull an ale for a new patron. It was as thirst-quenching a drink on a hot day as any he knew.

Looking up after pulling the draught, he saw the two stand to leave and the pharmacist approaching to pay the bill.

"I can get my own, Dylan," the girl protested when the man pulled out money for both meals.

"It's no bother. I've never asked a lady to lunch and then let her pay for it. It's not right," he said, handing over the money.

Fionn took the bills and handed back his change. The man gave him a nod of acknowledgement, but Fionn had eyes only for the girl. She looked at him, smiled, and he winked in return. She took her time looking away, as if to assess him more fully. It was as much as he could hope for, and before his shift began tomorrow, he promised himself, he would stop in at the flower shop and ask her out. There wasn't a lot of entertainment to be had in Inishannon, but being so close to Cork City, it didn't need to have much.

And Fionn had a car.

Outside the pub, Dylan and Emily stepped around the vehicles parked along the street and crossed over to the shady side. "Have ye met the lad back there?" asked Dylan, waving a thumb over his shoulder, pointing at the pub as they walked the short distance back to their respective stores.

"No," answered Emily, "he seems a nice fella, though."

"He's alright," said Dylan, not wanting to enlarge upon the boy's attributes more than that. After all, though he knew

Emily to be young, and as she seemed to be between male company, he deemed her fair game, as the saying went. He'd only asked because he'd seen their eyes meet, saw the interest in the lad's gaze as he paid for the meal. Moreover, Dylan wanted to be number one on her radar, the gap in their ages notwithstanding.

To further that end, Dylan wondered briefly if she or her gran had any plans for the weekend. They could go somewhere on Sunday after church if she hadn't anything else to do.

Then suddenly she turned to him, saying, "Thanks for lunch, but I've got to get back to work now. See ye later, maybe," she called, and scurrying through the door with a quick wave, left him standing alone on the street.

It was his own fault, he realized later when he thought about it. He'd been woolgathering, not paying attention to her at all on their way back to work. And she, young thing that she was, likely thought he wasn't interested in her.

Promising himself to do better next time, he wandered back into his pharmacy to sweat the rest of the day away.

* * *

Sunday dawned warm but cloudy, a portent of rain to come. And that was okay by him, thought Fionn as he hauled himself out of bed. He'd caught Emily just before she left the store yesterday, and she'd given him her gran's address, saying she'd love to go for a drive. They'd made a date for ten, hoping to make the most of the day before them.

Hastily tidying his compact car, throwing out the remnants of the previous weekend's party, he left his small cottage and picked Emily up at the appropriate time. By the way she sneaked out the door, he was wondering if her gran had wanted her to attend church.

Greeting her with an ear-splitting grin as she got in the car, they sped off toward the beach near Old Head Kinsale. There were two or three beaches that lined the road between Garrettstown and Old Head to choose from, and they would have the option of going into Kinsale itself for a nice dinner. At twenty-two, Fionn felt himself worldly and generous. Especially when he had someone as pretty as Emily by his side. Cute, vivacious, and playful, she seemed to be the perfect girl for him.

For now, at least. He wasn't sure what he wanted for the future, but at a time when his mates were having different women every weekend, being stuck in small place like Inishannon held few options, unlike, for instance, working in a pub in Cork. He would have loved to have done that but hadn't been lucky enough to find a place with any openings for the summer.

He hadn't regretted his decision to stay in Inishannon. It was small, the pay was decent, and he was able to afford his own place, even if it wasn't especially fancy. It was home. The owners of the big house on the front of the property allowed him the use of a small sunroom at the rear next to his cottage, where he could paint when the muse prompted. He was a student of art and spent most of his time, when not tending bar, working in either oils or acrylics, trying to decide which he liked better.

Emily looked across at Fionn and bit her lip in wonder. How did she get so lucky? Dylan was a fine fella and he seemed interested, but he hadn't asked her out at all with the exception of that one day at lunch. But here was Fionn, all handsome good looks and full of charm, and a smile that brought a twinkle to his eyes. His hair, a light brown, was flecked with golden streaks that brought out the color of his eyes, eyes that could be green or hazel depending on the light.

He had a profile that could grace the cover of a magazine, she thought, eyeing the long, straight line of his nose and the chin that was almost strong, but certainly not weak. His lips made her want to kiss them. They were full, unlike Dylan's, whose lower lip was full but the upper lip was so much smaller.

And why had her mind wandered that way? Was it because this was the first time she'd been on a date with someone who was older and not from school? Killarney had no shortage of young men that could have caught her eye but the sad truth was that none of them interested her, except for maybe Kevin at the phone store. But rumor had it he was taken.

In no time at all, they passed her great-grandparents' house and drove farther along where the road curved past a B&B and down to the Garrettstown Beach. They stopped there, where the food stand was perched on the opposite side of the road and the hot tub tent was available for anyone who wanted to rent it for a time. The clouds that had covered Inishannon had given way to brilliant sunshine at the shore, and neither Fionn nor Emily wasted any time removing their outer wear to display the swimwear beneath.

He was even handsomer in a swimsuit, thought Emily, eyeing his lean torso, the well muscled arms and calves, and the taut belly with a well-defined six-pack showing above the waistband of his swim trunks. His chest was lightly haired, and it was all she could do to refrain from running her fingers through it. Maybe she'd get a chance later, she thought with a grin.

At a whim, she'd worn a bikini, a garment not suited to the wild surf of the sea but perfect if looking to attract someone's attention. And if she read Fionn's eyes aright, he was paying very close attention.

Stepping toward her, he took her hand. And eyeing the low rollers coming in, both ran toward the water, screeching as the cold waves hit them before falling headlong into the surf. Emily was a strong swimmer and so was Fionn, and as the sun rose higher in the sky, the two alternated between playing in the waves and warming up on their towels on the beach.

Early in the afternoon when they'd emerged soaked and shivering from the surf, Fionn asked, "How about the hot tub? I'm feelin' chilled. Are you?"

Emily agreed, and minutes later, they'd paid their euros for twenty minutes of soaking. As she put her feet in the steaming water, she felt the warmth crawl up her body and couldn't help the sigh of pleasure that escaped her lips.

Fionn sat on the bench beside her, placed his arm over her shoulders and pulled her in for a kiss. They were alone in the tent and he wasted no time in getting to know her better. Her eyes told him everything he wanted to know. She was eager, and he was chubbed with wanting, although not here. Not yet. Instead, he leaned over and, slanting his lips across hers, felt the answering pressure of her own. Emboldened by her response, he opened his mouth, encouraged when she did the same, and reluctantly released her when they'd both run out of breath.

Her expression said it all. She wanted more.

He slid his hand beneath her bikini top, thumbed her nipple erect and was completely taken by surprise at her reaction. She'd reached down to cup his manhood, was running her hand along its rigid length and if he wasn't careful, she'd have him tossing his load right then and there.

So, even though they'd just got in, he couldn't resist asking, "Once we've warmed up, would ye like to see my place? It isn't grand, nothing big, but it's mine if ye've a mind to."

Her nod was all he needed and later, when her bikini top had been readjusted and they were sufficiently warm, the two were walking with long strides toward his car at the end of the line.

"It's just a wee cottage, mind," he said as they drove, "nothin' fancy, as I've said. There's a big house at the front of the property and I rent the cottage at the back. It suits my needs and is quite private. You'll see. I think ye'll like it."

Forty-five minutes later, they pulled up before the small cottage. It was self-contained with a small hob in the kitchen, which was also the living room and bedroom, and had its own toilet and shower. It wasn't big but it was private, as he'd described, and right now, it was privacy he was looking for.

Opening the door, it was impossible not to see everything at once, the row of cupboards, the fridge, hob, and sink, all in a line against one wall with a small table beneath the window next to the door. Across the room on the opposite wall was the television and a small sitting area. Beyond that, at the back of the house and next to the loo, was the bed. He breathed a sigh of relief because he was fairly certain he'd made it up this morning but wouldn't swear on a stack of bibles if he had or hadn't. He'd been too eager to see Emily, as if a part of him was worried she might have changed her mind.

He needn't have worried because when she stepped inside, her smile told him all he needed to know. "It's really cute," she said, openly admiring the compact space if her expression was anything to go by.

"Do ye like it, then?" he asked, suddenly nervous. His stomach, not having eaten since downing the leftover pizza from last night at breakfast, chose that moment to come to life, making its empty state well known.

Emily giggled. "I'm a bit hungry, too. We didn't grab anything from the chipper before we left."

Closing the door behind them, Fionn went to the cupboards and checked to see what he could possibly throw together for a meal for the two of them. He was handy at cooking, had a flair for making meals out of almost nothing, but was sorely disappointed when the cupboard revealed itself as close to empty.

Not one to give up so easily, he opened the fridge and pulled out some eggs. "Ye like omelets?" he asked, his head still in the fridge, rooting around in the crisper for any fresh vegetables.

"Yeah, I do. Can I help?"

"Grand," he exclaimed, and handed out a tomato and sweet pepper. A small onion soon followed and as a last whim, grabbed the block of cheese. "Here," he said, pulling out a cutting board and a chef's knife, "I'll get ye to chop up the whole of the tomato, maybe half of the pepper, and a few slices of the onion. I'll grate some cheese and we'll have lunch in no time."

The domesticity of the scene was not lost on him. Emily and he cooked in the kitchen as if they'd been doing it all their lives. He'd never had a girlfriend so eager to jump in and help. Most of them wanted to be waited on like princesses, but Emily wasn't like that. Clearly, she liked to take part. He hoped she'd take part in his version of dessert, too.

Soon after, Fionn had food on the table, clean utensils— he had to wash up an extra fork—and had pulled two blacks from the fridge, offering one to Emily. She hesitated only a minute before a broad grin emerged, showing her white, even teeth and bringing out a sparkle in her eyes.

161

As they ate their meal, all Fionn could concentrate on was removing her sundress and the bikini she still wore beneath it. His heart hadn't stopped thumping since the hot tub, although it had slowed its rapid pace to double time, speeding up again when he thought of the afternoon still to come.

They talked little during the meal, but were soon finished, Emily signifying her sated state by leaning back in her chair and stretching. "That was delicious," she sighed, casting him a cheeky grin.

Taking that as his cue, Fionn stood and held out his hand for her, saying, "Leave the dishes, I'll do them later."

Emily chuckled and ignored his hand, grabbing both her own plate and his and putting them in the sink, running water over them to soak. "If ye leave the cheese on them, it'll turn to stone and ye'll never get it off without a struggle."

"True enough," he agreed, and was swept up by her cleaning spree, even though it had been the last thing on his mind. And as he turned after putting the empty bottles away, he found himself standing in front of her and nothing, he thought now, would stand in his way of having her. Taking her hand in his, he led her over to the bed and pulled her close. "I've been thinkin' about ye ever since we left the hot tub. I won't deny wantin' ye."

Emily stepped closer and boldly slid her hands up his back beneath the cotton t-shirt he'd pulled on at the beach. He was still wearing his swimming trunks, though like her suit, it had long since dried.

His hands crept beneath the dress she wore as he helped her to remove it over her head. His t-shirt came off and then her bikini top, exposing full breasts with rosy nipples peaked and hard. Fionn's breath caught in his throat and he had a sneaky suspicion his hands were shaking but he ignored the

162

feeling and slid trembling fingers into her bikini bottoms, pushing them off, holding her while she stepped out of them. His own shorts came next and then he was pulling her into his embrace, skin to skin, belly to belly, groin to groin.

He tucked his lad between her legs, rubbing the length of it along the folds of her flange, igniting her senses and feeling her passion build. Beneath her ribcage, her heart was thumping, just as rapid as his own.

His hands slipped down her sides, cupping her bottom, pulling her close. His lips took hers, her mouth opened, and their tongues danced. Little moans of pleasure escaped her throat through her mouth, and he felt the rumble of it in his own mouth, tasted the remnants of Guinness and lunch, and knew she was as eager as he.

Her hands were working some magic of their own. Her fingers had thrust through his hair with a fierce determination, as if cupping the back of his head could bring him closer than he was. Her other hand had roamed to his arse to massage his cheek before tentatively sliding a delicate finger between the crack across his hole.

It had made his heart beat so fast it was all he could do to breathe.

"Just a minute," he said, his breath coming out ragged and rough, "I have rubbers here." He opened the small drawer in the nightstand and took out a foil pack. "Want to help?"

Emily's grin was anything but tentative, and taking the small packet from him, she opened it and carefully removed the coiled rubber inside. He wasn't sure if she'd ever done this before but it seemed she had because she knew exactly what to do, to place it at the tip and roll it down his length.

Their lips met again and his fingers found her nipples, hard and tender. He found that out when, in his excitement, he'd rubbed too hard and she'd let out a squeal that had him temper his exertions. Instead, he held her breast in one hand while his tongue laved it well and heard her intake of breath as she grabbed for him.

Unable to stem the momentum, he pushed her lightly to lie down on his bed and wasted no time crawling after her to lie atop her and resume their foreplay. He continued to tease her nipples with his tongue as she slid her hands down his torso to grasp the globes of his arse, pulling him to her. But as keen as he was to enter her right then and there, he needed to ensure she was ready for him, for this.

Fionn kissed his way down her belly and found her mound of pleasure. She was definitely wet as he suckled her clit and thrust his tongue inside her canal. She tasted of the scent that tingled his nostrils and heightened his senses, a particular scent that was hers alone and although this was not his first foray into lovemaking, Fionn felt as if he'd never achieved this same intensity before.

Emily's body writhed beneath him as if she was searching, reaching for something just beyond her grasp. Her breath came faster, gasps escaped her lips, little pants that were becoming more voluble with every intake of breath. Her hands pulled at his torso, pleading, needing, until finally she cried out her pleasure, and Fionn knew the moment had come. Without preamble, he scrambled up her body, grabbed his lad so hard with wanting, and slid inside to thrust his way home. Only the widening of Emily's beautiful eyes and the louder cry that pierced the confines of the room told him something was not quite right. But by then he was pumping and Emily was back to writhing, and as Fionn released his seed into the condom, one thing was clear.

Emily was crying.

Chapter Fourteen

What in feckin' hell? Fionn felt like a heel. Worse. He'd acted like an animal, interested only in rutting and getting it off. It had never occurred to him that Emily was a virgin; she'd been as eager as he.

Yet why else would she be crying?

"Did I hurt ye?" he finally asked, still breathing hard from his exertions.

"Only a little," she sniffed, "but it's fine now. I'm fine. I don't even know why I'm cryin'," she laughed, wiping the tears from her face with her fingers.

Fionn reached over and plucked some tissues out of the box on the side table. "Here, use this," he said, and then took one for himself as he withdrew from her body. Nothing like tears to throw cold water on a man's libido, he thought.

As he watched her wipe her face, he pointed to the loo. "Toilet's in there, if ye need it."

She nodded and disappeared inside, closing the door solidly behind her.

"Grand," he whispered to himself, "just feckin' grand. I've made a mess of it and she'll never want to see me again." He wiped himself clean and drew on his shorts again, thinking that she'd likely want to go home now. It was just mid afternoon and there were any number of things they could still do, and if it was any other girlfriend, he'd try to get her interested again. But this was Emily, and he was now beginning to wonder if he'd ruined everything.

She came out of the loo, looking embarrassed at her nudity, and scrambled to get her bikini back on.

"Here, let me help ye with the clasp," he offered.

She brushed his hands away, a frown of irritation creasing her brow. "No, it's okay. I've got it."

Clearly, his help was not needed and she didn't seem like she wanted him to touch her.

He watched her pull her sundress over her swimsuit and run a finger through her hair to comb out her tresses. He'd loved seeing the black strands splayed out across the pillow beneath them.

"Emily, were ye a virgin?" he asked, as gently as he could. He didn't want her to think it was a mark against her.

She nodded, and he went to her, put his arms around her. "God. I wish I'd known. I wish ye'd told me. I would've been gentler, but ye seemed to know what ye were doin'."

Emily laughed a little at that, allowing him to hold her before she seemed to relent and melt against him.

"I thought ye'd be angry, or not want to do it." Her words were muffled against his chest and he tilted her head up to meet his gaze.

"Why would I not want to? I've wanted ye since I met ye."

Shrugging, she mumbled into his shirt, "I just thought ye'd think me too young."

That stopped him cold and he took a step back, putting space between them. "How old are ye, then? Surely ye're, what, nineteen?"

"No. Seventeen."

He felt his face drain of color. "Jaysus! Ye could have

told me. I'd have held off," he swore.

"See? That's why I didn't. I didn't want ye to stop."

"Why? I'm not into ravishin' little girls," he protested.

She spun on him then, all hundred and sixty centimeters and maybe eight stone if she was a pound. "I'm not a little girl. I'll be eighteen in a matter of weeks."

"Well ye're not eighteen now and I'll not be charged for rape!"

"Rape? I wanted ye to do it. I didn't want to be a virgin anymore. I was likely the only girl left in school who'd never had sex by graduation. I was tired of feelin' left out."

Her voice was rising but so was his and he matched her anger, tone for tone. "So ye thought ye'd find someone to fuck ye? Is that it? Would anyone do? Why not the chemist? He's got eyes for ye, anyone can see that."

That stopped her in her tirade and her eyes widened in surprise. "Dylan? But he's old enough...never mind. Just never mind. I'll leave now."

"I'll take ye home."

"No, it's alright. I can walk. I need time to think."

"Emily..."

"What?"

He didn't know what to say, didn't know how to make it better. His anger was spent. His voice was quiet. "I'm sorry."

"Yeah. Right."

She left him standing in the middle of his small cottage and feeling worse than ever. It had been a mistake to bring her here, he thought, to bring her to a place where it was all too easy to take her to bed. He should have followed his instinct and just had a little fun in the car, a little finger fucking, bring her off and take her home. It would have maybe eased the way.

But she hadn't told him she was underage, and he shivered at the thought. She was so womanly, so worldly seeming, yet tempered with a youthfulness that excited him. She was woman and child all rolled into one and wrapped up in a body that called to him, even now.

He doubted she'd ever want to see him again.

* * *

Emily walked down the road, the strap of her tiny purse slung over her shoulder and her towel rolled up beneath her arm. The clouds were rolling in again but she didn't care. Gran's house wasn't far.

She passed the great stone edifice of St. Mary's Catholic Church, giving it a cursory glance but refrained from going in or even wandering through the graveyard at the side of the building as she sometimes liked to do. But today, after doing what she'd done, was not a time, she felt, to visit a house of God. Church going had never been high on her list of priorities, even though now, when she was feeling as if she'd just committed the worst sin of all, being able to talk to someone—especially someone who would be a stranger in a place of authority—to absolve her of her sins and therefore her guilt, would be a boon. It would be like visiting a doctor you'd never met before, and him or her having the right to check you over. A priest could hear her confession, tell her how many Ave's and Hail Mary's to recite, and absolve her of her sins.

A fat raindrop hit her forehead, surprising her out of her musings, and she looked up to see the largest, blackest cloud moving across the sky overhead. Another drop hit and she knew without a doubt she'd be soaked through in minutes.

She didn't care. She merely put the towel over her head and shoulders, using it as a shawl, and continued walking.

Her determined, powerful strides would get her home soon enough.

A car pulled up beside her and slowed, keeping pace as she walked. A part of her hoped it was Fionn, but a sideways glance told her it wasn't. As the window rolled down, Dylan's features appeared and he called out to her, "Hop in. I'm heading to yer gran's anyway. Come on, I'll give ye a lift."

The rain was pouring steadily now, the few drops quickly turning into a deluge. And although not especially cold, she was beginning to shiver from being soaked and exposed to the wind that had come up. It didn't take much to assess her predicament; freeze on the way home or take a ride. Without further thought, she yanked opened the door and slid inside, apologizing as she did for getting the inside of his car wet.

"No bother," he said, laughing at her. "Ye look like a half-drowned moggie," he exclaimed, as she used the sodden towel to squeeze the excess water from her hair. "I don't think that'll do much good," he nodded at the towel, "but we're aren't far from yer gran's place."

"Is yer da there, then?" she asked, and Dylan nodded.

"Yer gran invited us for dinner, and since I wasn't doin' anything else, I decided to go over a wee bit earlier. Ye've been out for the day now, have ye?"

She nodded. "Went to the beach with Fionn. It was nice at Old Head, the sun was shinin'."

Dylan's face wore a frown as he took in her very wet clothing and hair. "He didn't give ye a ride home? What kind of fella does that on a day like this?"

Emily giggled. "It wasn't like this when I started out. He lives just past St. Mary's, maybe a kilometer along the road. It wasn't so far if the weather had stayed good, but the clouds came over and, well, here I am."

He took in her wet appearance and harrumphed. "Still. He should have given ye a ride. I've a mind to talk to him, next time I see him."

"No, don't!" she exclaimed quickly. "I mean, it wasn't his fault, like. I wanted to walk home. He offered to drive, but really, I wanted to walk."

One look at Dylan and Emily knew he didn't believe her, but it was the truth, after all. Partly. She hadn't wanted Fionn to drive her because she had cried, and then he'd yelled at her because she hadn't been eighteen, as if she'd charge him with anything. She'd wanted it. Had jumped in with both feet.

So why did she feel so terrible?

She had little time to further contemplate her feelings because they had pulled into the driveway at Gran's, dodging raindrops as fat as balloons to get inside. And while Dylan stopped just past the door, she continued on up the stairs and into her room to step into a warm shower and put on dry clothing.

* * *

She arrived downstairs a good half hour later, her hair still damp but without the bedraggled look she'd sported on her way in. Dylan thought she was the most beautiful thing he'd seen in a very long time. Ever since…

No, he wouldn't go there. That was a long time ago. Still, there was something hauntingly familiar here, but memories were fickle. The mind changed things to what you wanted to see.

Kathleen was busy in the kitchen and his da was helping out, which left Dylan in the living room, a cup of tea by his side. "Would ye care for one?" he asked, nodding his head toward the cup.

"Yeah, that'd be grand, thanks." She sat down while he

poured out for her. It was strong but hadn't been sitting long enough to get cold.

"Milk? Sugar?" He indicated the items on the tray and then picked up the plate of biscuits to offer her one.

"Ye're quite domesticated, ye are," she giggled, picking up a sugar biscuit and taking a small bite out of it.

"Yeah, that's me. Just like an old hausfrau," he joked.

"Hausfrau? That's German, isn't it?"

"Yeah, means housewife. I had a friend at university from Germany. He used a lot of German idioms, and that was one. I was always the one to clean up, so I became the hausfrau."

"That's hilarious," she observed, sipping her tea.

Despite her young years, she reminded him of some long ago young woman, maybe in a frilly dress, sipping tea out of a delicate cup while wearing lace gloves. Kind of like the gloves little girls wore at their first communion, and he said as much, laughing as he did.

"I never had a communion, not 'til much later," she told him. And before he could ask why, she continued speaking. "Mam was into drugs so we moved around a lot. People didn't want us hangin' about, called us tinkers or travelers. Our black hair didn't help any. They really thought we were no better than gypsies."

"So ye never had any formal upbringin'?"

"No, not until Uncle Henry found us. Or, rather, Mam found him."

"I don't understand. I thought Henry was yer da." Damian had told Dylan about Emily, as much as he knew, anyway, and all he'd said was that Emily was Henry's daughter, come to live with her gran.

"He isn't. I don't know who my real father is," she explained.

"Then ye aren't related to yer gran or Henry, not really?" he asked. It was difficult to ferret out information when she was handing out in bits.

"No and yes." She laughed waving her hand in front of her face as if to wipe the slate clean. "Let me start at the beginning."

Dylan was all for that!

"Like I said, Mam was into drugs. She was goin' out with some fella up Dublin way but accordin' to her, he didn't want a relationship. Guess he was only into it for sex. Anyway, she got pregnant and left him. Maybe he didn't want the complication, maybe he didn't know. My birth certificate just says 'unknown' beside the space for the father's name. I was born in Dublin though we didn't stay there, we moved a lot. I seem to recall always havin' a different house, different rooms, different da. She called them my da, and then later it was replaced with uncle. I had a little schoolin'. She tried to stay in one place throughout the school year so's I could learn a thing or two, but then she'd be off again because money would run out, she'd lose her job, or somethin' else would happen.

"Eventually she decided we should look for my real uncle, her brother. His name was Hank. She never did find him. We went back to Killarney where she'd grown up but didn't find him there so she began lookin' elsewhere, wonderin' where he could be, and eventually ended up here. She was walkin' down a street one day and found Henry, thought he was Hank, and started talkin' to him, like. Suddenly, she realized it wasn't Hank, and…"

Dylan held up a hand. "Hank?" He was getting a squeamish feeling in his gut. He could feel Emily's eyes on him, wondering if he was alright. In truth, he didn't know.

"Yeah. Hank is my real mam's brother, and Henry is a half brother. So, I'm related to Henry through his da. Gran is no relation other than an adopted gran, but I love her all the same," she explained.

"What was yer mother's name?" The question came out in a voice tight with emotion. He felt his hands begin to shake, the implication of her words as they settled in his head. His stomach was doing its best to keep the tea contained.

"Mam's name? Meara. Meara Mulligan."

Dylan stood as if shot out of a cannon. "And ye say this fella she was seein' was in Dublin, and didn't want her?"

"That's right. Leastwise, that's what she told me."

"Emily, how old are ye?"

"Seventeen. I'll be eighteen in a couple of weeks. Why?"

"God." He stood and turned away from her to look out the window, crossed his arms in front of himself to stop his hands from shaking. His whole body felt like a vibrator. He was going to be sick.

"What? Dylan, what is it?"

He couldn't answer immediately. His heart was thumping madly in his chest. It was hard to breathe. Finally, he swallowed against the emotion in his throat, saying, "I was in university, midway. I'd met yer mam, fell head over heels for her. But she had a substance abuse problem. I didn't notice at first. She was careful to hide it, would binge drink sometimes. Days would go by when barely a drop would pass her lips, but then, when we were out in a crowd and everyone else was drinkin' too, she'd really go to town.

"But it was the other stuff she couldn't shake. She'd sneak off and get high, come back when she'd come down, but I could always tell. There was always the sleepiness about her then, the glassy look to her eyes. And I couldn't handle it.

I just couldn't handle it.

"Then, one day, she said she was goin' to the doctor. She'd been gainin' weight, unusual for her. She could eat me under the table and never gain an ounce, whereas me…well, ye see what I'm like now, I've a bit of a paunch, although I've tried my best to work it off."

"Dylan, what are ye sayin'?"

He still hadn't turned. Couldn't yet look her in the eye. "I often wondered why she never returned, ye know? She said she was goin' to the doctor's and then never came back. I thought maybe she had gone on another drug spree. We'd argued a lot that week. Hell, we argued more than just that week, but even as she left, I remember sayin' that I couldn't put up with her drug use anymore, and if she wasn't willin' to get clean, I didn't want her around. And maybe that's why she left."

"Ye knew my Mam?"

Nodding, he felt a tear slip down his cheek and hastily wiped it away. From the kitchen, he heard movement, then silence. Kathleen and his da were standing in the doorway. He could feel their presence without having to look. How strange things were that it had come full circle. He was standing in the room with his daughter, a girl he'd had romantic thoughts of as recently as the car ride over. Hell, he'd taken one look at her with her dress plastered to her body, the outline of the bikini beneath, and had chubbed up. He was glad for the driving to take his mind off things, and by the time they'd arrived at her gran's, his erection had dwindled although the randy thoughts hadn't.

Until now. Oh, God. He was ever so thankful he'd never asked her out, had never followed through with the thought of having her in his bed. He'd known she was young although he had thought her closer to twenty, but still, he'd suspected he was too old for her in many ways.

He should be jubilant to find a daughter he hadn't known existed. But here he was, ready to flee instead.

"Dylan, is aught amiss?" asked Damian.

Dylan looked to his father, to Kathleen standing there beside his da, and to Emily, mouth open. He could tell them nothing and leave. Or he could finish Emily's story, fill in the gaps and admit to being her father.

At least, he thought he was her father.

"I loved her," his ragged voice choked out. "I loved her with everything that I am, and she left. No word of goodbye, no 'see ye later.' She just left, and I never knew what happened to her, and after a while, I gave up. I didn't know where to look, had my studies to follow through with. And eventually, tried to move on with my life. Without her."

"Dylan…ye're my da?"

Dylan turned to face Emily, saw the tears in her eyes, and shook his head. "I don't know. I just don't know." Emotion was never an easy thing for Dylan. He'd lost his own mam to another fella when he was just a weyan, and then he'd lost Meara to drugs. He lost women. That was what he did, and eventually, he'd consigned himself to the fact that he wasn't good enough for anyone because they'd only leave him in the end.

"I need to go. Sorry…I need to…"

"Dylan." His father's hand was on his shoulder but Dylan shook it off.

"No. I have to go," he choked out and left.

* * *

Emily stood frozen in place, watching Dylan leave. Too much had happened in one day for her to think rationally, and she turned and fled up the stairs as fast as she could.

Hard on her heels, Kathleen followed her into the bedroom that Ciara had occupied, the one overlooking the back garden with its lovely view of grass and flowers.

"Em, oh my darlin' wee girl," Kathleen cooed, laying her hands on Emily's stiff back as she gazed unseeing out the window. "C'mere to me now," she said gently, pulling Emily into her embrace.

Emily let her, allowed herself to be cuddled as she had when her mam had died and Henry had taken over her care. Kathleen, Gran, had always been there, had stepped up and adopted her so she wouldn't get lost in the system, and then allowed Henry to raise her. Henry and Siobhan.

"He doesn't want me," she cried into Gran's shoulder. "He left. He doesn't want me. Didn't want Mam then, doesn't want me now." She pulled out of Gran's arms and took a tissue from the box by the bed. She blew her nose and deposited the tissue in the bin. Then, sniffing back the next onslaught of tears, straightened up, saying, "I need to show ye somethin'." She went over to the wardrobe where the doors were closed against her multitude of belongings, and opening it up, took down the small box of mementos she'd had from her mam and pulled out the few photos inside.

"Here," she said, "come and look." The top one was of Meara, looking much as Emily did now, she knew, but it was the next one, as difficult to make out features clearly as it was, that caught even Gran's attention. "It's Dylan, isn't it."

Kathleen took the photo from Emily's fingers, held it so the light from the window brought out the semi-faded colors, and then handed it back to her. "I think so. But ye won't know for certain if it is him unless ye ask him."

Shaking her head, Emily sniffed. "I don't need to ask

him. I've eyes, just as ye do. I'd forgotten for a time that I had this photo. But there was somethin' about Dylan I just couldn't put my finger on, somethin' that was familiar, as if I'd seen him before. And now I know. It was here all along, in this box."

"Does Henry know about this photo?"

Emily looked at Gran then, at the worry in her eyes, at the compassion in her face. She was getting older, there were streaks of white in the pale blonde strands around her face, streaks that Emily had thought of as lighter blonde. It was as if she was seeing her gran for the first time.

Gran's eyes wrinkled in a smile and pulled her in for a hug.

"He was the one who gave me this box, said it was my mam's things and I should have them," Emily sniffed through her words. "Maybe he never even looked inside."

"Maybe not. But it doesn't matter now."

"If Dylan really is my da, then that would make Damian my grandda, right?"

She could feel Gran's head nodding in assent. "That would be right," she agreed.

Emily pulled away slightly and met her gaze, smiling through the tears drying on her face. "Then ye need to marry Damian so's I'll have my gran and grandda together."

Chapter Fifteen

The following week passed quietly and yet all too slowly for Emily's liking. She hadn't been to the pub and so hadn't seen Fionn, and for that she was glad. She wasn't sure what she would say to him, or what he might think of her. She felt herself blush when she recalled the afternoon in his arms, the way she'd thrown herself at him, begging him to take her.

And he had. It was afterward, when he realized she'd been a virgin and not yet eighteen, that things got rough. It didn't make sense that he was afraid she'd charge him with rape. It hadn't been rape…not even close. She even fancied herself a little in love with him, which was why she'd been so keen to lie with him and have him make love to her. She'd never felt like that with anyone before, and for him to turn it around, as if he did that sort of thing every day with different women…well, maybe he did. In any event, he'd made it clear he didn't want her and was very quick to say he'd get her home.

Only she couldn't stand to see the look on his face, as if she was now something tainted and used. So she'd saved him the trouble and walked home instead. She thought, from his expression, that he'd been relieved.

And then to finish off that day was the news that Dylan was her real father, a flesh and blood man, someone who'd known her mam and had loved her. Someone who didn't want a daughter, though. It was the second time in a day that a man hadn't wanted her, and neither one seemed to want to change that in any way. Dylan had stayed in his pharmacy, hadn't set foot inside the flower shop, not even to take advantage of the cool air.

She wanted nothing more than to go back to Killarney, back to the people she'd come to know as Mam and Da, and forget that she'd ever moved out. She'd find a job in Killarney. And maybe she'd go to college or university in the autumn instead of working through her gap year. There were things she could do. She could even spend a year in Canada with Uncle Hank and Auntie Laura and their two weyans, but then she realized she'd likely get roped into being a nanny for the two and quickly squashed that thought.

The bell over the door jingled, but Emily ignored it. She wasn't in the mood to be cheerful or even helpful. If someone wanted something, they'd have to get it themselves, she fumed.

A shadow was cast across the blotter on the counter in front of her where she was writing up orders. Dharia was in the back, putting together arrangements, and Emily was alone at the front. There was no help for it, she would have to deal with this person.

She looked up to meet Fionn's eyes. "Hi. Somethin' I can get for ye?" she asked, as if he had been a stranger off the street, only not nearly so polite as she should have been.

Fionn shuffled his feet and cleared his throat. He looked uncomfortable and even wary. "I, em, I was wonderin' if ye'd help me out with somethin'," he stammered.

She met his gaze with a deadpan expression and as uninterested a look as she could. "Sure. What do ye need?"

Fionn scratched his head. "That's the trouble. I'm not sure."

Emily sighed in exasperation. She just wanted him gone, so closing the order book with a thump, said, "Give us a hint. Flowers? Gift item? I need somethin' to go on."

"Flowers, I guess."

"Good. That's a good place to start." She wondered who they could be for and then dismissed the thought as none of her business. Coming out from behind the counter, she took him over to the row of coolers where arrangements were displayed and where cut flowers lined shelves inside the coolers, and outside, standing in bins of water on the floor. "See anything ye like?" She stood with her arms crossed, more from trying to keep warm from the blast of cold air coming from the vents overhead than any displeasure she found in his presence.

Fionn hemmed and hawed. "What do you like?" he asked, stressing the "you."

"Me? Not sure. I like them all. Dharia does a fantastic job of arrangements, but cut flowers are nice, too. Who's it for?" And then, realizing what she'd just asked him and how awkward it was, followed her statement up with, "Ye don't have to tell me, it's just…it makes it easier if I know if it's for yer mam, or someone else, like."

"Ah, well, it's not for my mam but it is for a girl. Someone I don't know very well."

Grand, she thought. Just feckin' grand, as Da would say. He's already got another girl lined up and it hasn't even been a full week since…

"Right," she said. "That doesn't make it much easier but think of her coloring…is she blonde or dark…maybe get flowers that would contrast with her hair. Ye know, some people have lovely pink cheeks and flowers can bring that out."

"Ah, no pink cheeks. What about red flowers, do ye have any of those?"

"Lots," she said, moving toward the end of the cooler where they'd just had a shipment of roses and carnations, all in various shades of red and all in excellent condition, even for the heat outside. "If ye don't fancy cut flowers or arrangements, but ye'd still like to stay with red, ye can get azaleas, or red and purple fuchsias, even though fuchsias grow wild here and are an abomination to some peoples' way of thinkin'.

He laughed at that, and despite her angst at seeing him, she felt herself happy to be in his presence.

He sighed heavily, shaking his head. "I just don't know." He pointed at a plant, its small, slightly round petals streaked inside with little dots of color. "That's kind of interestin', like. What is it?"

Emily grinned. "That's alstroemeria; it's my personal favourite."

"Oh, okay. Does it come in just that one color?"

"No, we have lots of different ones. There are mauve, white, and some peach-colored ones."

"What would they look like all together?"

Shrugging, Emily opened the cooler and took a few of each out of their respective jugs of water and put them together in her hand. "What do ye think? Do ye like that?"

Dylan hummed. "Yeah, I guess. Do you?"

Laughing, Emily said, "Ye neddy, it's not whether I like it or not, is it? But because ye asked, yeah, I do. I like bunches of color all splashed together, just like they come in nature."

"Well then, if you like it, that's good then."

She pulled a few more strands to fill out the gaps, and at his nod, added a bit of greenery. "It'll just take me a moment to wrap these up. Are ye takin' them to the pub? If ye do, ye'll need to put them in water."

"Ah, no. I'm not."

"Right. Just give me a moment and I'll get these ready for ye. There's cards here if ye'd like to throw one in."

He eyed the cards and flipped through them, choosing one. "I'll just go here and write on it," he said, indicating a small wrought iron café table with a plant and some gift items on it.

"Yeah, fine," she said, figuring the cost and pulling out the paper to wrap around it.

He brought her the card in a small envelope and paid for the flowers, and as she watched him head for the door, part of her was glad he was going, part of her wishing he would stay. For all she was angry he hadn't wanted to be with her after all, she realized she still had feelings for him, and she hurt.

Then, suddenly, at the door, Fionn turned and walked back in.

"Forget somethin'?" she asked.

He looked nervous, as if he didn't know why he was there. "No, I didn't. It's just…well, these are for you." He thrust out his hand with the carefully wrapped bouquet with its riotous color, a bouquet Emily had put together and was envious of doing so, thinking it would go to someone else.

"What? Fionn, are ye daft?"

Laughing, he nodded. "Maybe. I wanted to apologize, to tell ye how sorry I am for last weekend, the way we, ye know, the way things were left. I hadn't meant it to be like that, and I'm sorry."

Emily didn't know what to think. "A simple apology

would have worked," she scolded. "Ye didn't have to go through all this."

"Oh, so ye don't want them, then?" He reached over to take them from her but she held them away.

"No. I mean, yes. Yes, I want them but ye didn't need to do this," she said, gesturing at the bouquet.

Leaning on the counter, Fionn said, "I wasn't sure what kind of a reception I'd get. Ye haven't been to the pub all week and I've not seen ye out anywhere, so I was thinkin' maybe ye hated me."

She took in his expression, the playful crook to his smile, the biting of his cheek and the wink of his eye, and began to laugh. "Well, as we're bein' truthful here…and we are bein' truthful, are we not?" At his nod, she continued, "As we're bein' truthful, I've missed ye, and I didn't know how to ask if ye still wanted to see me. I thought maybe ye didn't, since ye hadn't been by."

"Ye could have come to me," he whispered, his lips suddenly near enough to press her own against them, a playful peck, tentatively, and then harder. The bouquet was left on the counter as she leaned into his kiss, his tongue meeting hers, her world spinning, mad with joy.

She wanted to crawl inside him, become part of him, suddenly hating the counter that stood between them. Fionn's arms snaked around her back as did hers around his shoulders and up through the mass of glossy brown hair she loved to tousle with her fingers. He tasted of the draught he must have had at lunch, smelled like the pub he worked in, beer over-ridden with his own manly scent, and Emily was certain she loved him.

The bell over the door jingled its merry sound and they broke apart with a guilty lurch, grinning at each other like silly kids.

Dylan stood at the door, and it was all Emily could do to keep from running away. He was the last person she wanted to see, especially just now.

Fionn cast a casual glance over his shoulder, and seeing Dylan standing there, said quietly, for her ears alone, "I'll stay if ye want." He quirked an eyebrow at her, waiting for her response.

"It's okay. I'll stop in at the pub when I'm off…" she left the sentence hanging, half statement, half question.

Nodding his agreement, Fionn left.

Emily observed the man she now knew was her father, and caught herself seeking the similarities between them. Perhaps it was his stocky build, because from what she remembered of her mam, she'd been a toothpick on stilts. Even Uncle Hank was built that way, tall and very lean. And while Emily acknowledged that she didn't have a lot of height, she was neither stocky nor lean, but seemed to fall into a category that could best be described as average. If there was anything else to bind the two together, she'd yet to learn of it.

Dylan approached the counter, taking a quick look behind him as if to ensure himself that Fionn really had left. "Have ye got a minute?" he asked gruffly.

Unfortunately, she did. The shop was empty just now, Dharia was still in the back, and she couldn't think of any excuse that wouldn't be outright rude. Instead, she nodded and reopened the order book she'd been working on.

"I'd like yer full attention, if ye don't mind," he ground out, and as she looked up from her work, she noticed the furrowing of his heavy brows, the crease between them, and the rim of his lips tight across his face.

Chagrined because she knew she'd been rude, Emily closed the book again and straightened her posture as if that would give her all the courage she needed. "Right, I'm listenin'."

"Did yer gran talk to ye at all, tell ye what I wanted?"

"Ye mean about the DNA test?" He nodded, and she picked up her purse from beneath the counter. "I don't think we need it."

His expression had changed from almost angry to curious as she slipped the photo from a side pocket where it had been kept safe from being bent more than it already was. Showing it to him, she said, "This was in a box Henry gave me after Mam died. He said it was hers and I should have it. Had a couple of photos in it. This was one. I'd always wondered who the fella was, and until that day in Gran's front room, it was always a mystery. But not now."

He picked up the photo and looked carefully at it. "The River Liffey. We'd had a lovely afternoon and were takin' a walk. This was soon before she left. She'd said she wanted to tell me somethin' but never seemed to get around to sayin' it. Instead, we found ourselves walkin', and I had a small camera with me. We'd often do that, for somethin' to do," he said by way of explanation. "We'd go somewhere, take a few photos, and then I'd get them developed and we'd have a laugh over them. I gave this one to her the next day. She was gone the day after that."

She watched him as he spoke, took in the emotion in his voice. Whatever he felt, it seemed bloody difficult for him to express it. "Ye never signed it," she said.

"Sign it? Why would I sign it? It was just a photo, like all the others. I hadn't expected her to bolt. In fact, just the opposite. We'd talked of marriage." He stopped then, cocked his head, still studying the photo. "Ah, but I'd told her I wanted to start off clean, that I wanted her to be clean when we married, no drugs. I suppose, in a way, I was tellin' her it was either me or the drugs, but she couldn't have both. Guess we know how that turned out." Dylan handed her back the photo and she slipped it back inside the purse.

"I have more photos if ye'd like to see them sometime," he offered, sniffing and clearing his throat. "I never had the heart to toss them. Been cartin' them around since she left."

He was shuffling his feet, and his hands were stuffed back in his pockets.

"Is there somethin' ye wanted to say?" She suddenly wanted him gone because if he stayed there much longer, she'd burst into tears and she could see people gathering at the window, pointing at the display, and knew they'd soon have customers.

"Ah, just that I'm sorry for the way I reacted the other day. I had to get away, to…"

"Think," she finished for him. "Yeah, I know. I figured as much."

The outer door opened and Emily smiled and called hello. "I'll be with ye's in just a minute," she finished.

"Right. I'm off then. I'll call at yer gran's. We need to talk more."

"Yeah. Sure, I guess."

"No, I mean it. If I'm to be yer da, then there's things ye ought to know."

Emily bit her lip, deciding what to say. "We'll see," was all she could come up with.

Dylan turned to go but stopped before he'd made a complete about face. "Oh, and about Fionn…"

"What about him?"

"I'd mind him, were I you. He's too old for ye, too worldly."

186

Emily's backbone stiffened in response, and while she didn't want to make a scene in front of customers, she couldn't let that remark go quietly. "Actually, he's been very nice to me, not that it's any concern of yours. After all, ye haven't been my da for the last eighteen years, why start now?"

"Look, Em, it wasn't my fault."

"Maybe not, but Henry and Siobhan have been my parents, and Henry's been father enough. I don't need another one."

"Not even a real one?" As if realizing what he'd just said, he apologized immediately. "I hadn't meant it to come out like that. It's not what I meant at all."

"Never mind," she said, seeing the customers looking about for help with something. "It's best if ye just go now."

Dylan returned her look, then seemed to be aware of the small crowd in the store. "Right. Later then."

He hung his head as he left the shop, looking a little like a side character in one of Uncle Liam's films, having been chastised and now more than a little embarrassed rather than the respected chemist who owned the shop next door.

Taking a deep breath, Emily tucked both purse and order book beneath the counter and went to greet the customers who had been patiently waiting.

"Could we see that little vase up there?" asked one of the customers, and Emily nodded and went to fetch the footstool.

Dylan watched her from the window, pondering the fact that he'd just been bested by a teenager. He still couldn't get over the fact that she was his daughter, even though no DNA test had been given. And then he realized that they'd been sidetracked and she hadn't said she'd even go for one, except to say she didn't think it was needed. Instead, she'd taken control of the discussion and he'd had to leave, feeling like he was ten years old again and just been given a good tongue-lashing.

It was time to go back into the pharmacy and sweat out the rest of the day.

* * *

Emily met Fionn briefly before walking back to Gran's. As she walked, she recalled their discussion and his invitation to visit after dinner. He'd be off at ten, he'd said.

She thought about it. Ten was a little late to be going out when you had to work in the morning, but maybe it wouldn't be so bad. They'd exchanged mobile numbers and she'd walked home to Gran's, opening the door to the sound of Damian and Gran in the kitchen, cooking up a storm. Like her, she realized, Damian loved to cook. She only hoped Dylan wasn't coming over. He'd made her feel uncomfortable, falling just short of saying he didn't want her seeing Fionn.

Fionn, on the other hand, was looking better every day. She quite fancied herself head over heels in love with the fella, and he hadn't been put off by her youth after all. They still hadn't fully discussed it, hadn't really even mentioned it, but she'd be eighteen in another week and she'd make sure that evening was going to be spent with Fionn. Emily had already made up her mind there'd be no big family get-together, at least, not without Fionn.

She called hello to Gran and Damian...she still couldn't think of him as her grandda...and went upstairs. Moments later, she heard Henry's voice and then Mam's, and quickly changing into something more casual than what she'd worn to work, raced down the stairs to see them hugging Gran. Or was Gran hugging Mam?

It didn't matter, because, suddenly, Emily had thrown herself into their arms, only realizing as she was engulfed by

Mam's hugs that there was indeed a baby bump in the way.

"It's true!" she squealed in delight.

"Ye think I lied to ye?" laughed Henry, ruffling her hair like he always did.

"No, of course not, it's just, I haven't seen ye since ye told me and I'm ever so excited about it."

"Ye'll want to come home then," said Siobhan, not having released Emily yet.

Emily opened her mouth to speak but nothing came out. What did she want? A part of her longed to be back at home with the people she knew as mam and da, but if that happened, she'd never seen Fionn again.

Oh, Fionn.

"Cat got yer tongue?" asked Siobhan, chuckling. "Well, my sweet girl, ye're growin' up and ye'll always have a home with us. Ye know that." She kissed Emily on the forehead and Emily drew her in closer for a tighter hug.

"I'll be movin' back when ye have the weyan," she vowed.

"Will ye now? And what makes ye think we haven't already done over yer room?" asked Henry, looking serious but with a tightness to his lips that tried to hide his smile.

"Neddy," Emily came back with. "Mam's just said I'll always have a bed there. Besides, she'll need help at first."

"Well, I do appreciate the offer, love, but ye might have plans of yer own at that time. It'll be an early January baby, accordin' to the doctor. Ye might have found some nice young fella to go away somewhere warm with," suggested Siobhan.

"Over my dead body," Henry swore, and Emily knew he wasn't really joking.

"I'll be eighteen next week, Da," she stated, "Ye can't keep me under wraps forever." She tried to hide the fact that she was no longer under those wraps, and feigned innocence as best she could.

"That's true, darlin', but don't think just because ye're eighteen that ye can just run off with any fella. There's some that want only one thing."

"Well, ye'd know, since ye're a man," she replied, and Henry's mouth dropped open.

"The cheek!" he exclaimed, turning to Gran. "Just what is it ye're allowin' her to do? She's a pup, she is."

"Ah, don't get yer shirt in a knot, she's fine. Spirited, is all," said Gran.

Damian hadn't said anything beyond a quick hello, and she was happy that was so. She'd be happier if he wasn't there, but it wasn't her house, and she had to be polite. But this time, he gave her a look that held a different meaning, as if he now had the right to chastise her after all. And however much she loved her gran, if it wasn't for Fionn's sudden appearance in her life, she'd leave with Mam and Da tonight when they returned to Killarney after supper.

Herding everyone into the living room, Kathleen invited them all to have a seat while she offered them something to drink. There was just a hint of nervousness about her, thought Emily. Gran had always held parties and was the consummate hostess, but it looked to Em as if she were trying a bit too hard, or maybe waiting for a cataclysmic fallout. They were waiting on Dylan's arrival, she realized, and maybe Gran's uneasiness could be attributed to that.

Half an hour later, when the tea had grown cold and talk had covered everything from the weather to the latest world news, Dylan was heard, rapping lightly at the door.

"Come in, come in," said Kathleen, opening the door for him. "Ye'll want a cool drink, I expect. I've stout in the refrigerator, or soda if ye choose. I keep stout for yer da, he likes it now and then," she explained.

"Ah, it's no bother. I don't need anything just now. I'm just from the pub. The shop was so hot I needed somethin' to cool me down right away."

Emily fumed. So, Gran kept stout for Damian but wouldn't offer her any, regardless of the fact she would be eighteen next week. She didn't expect Da to be offered any, nor Mam. Da quit years ago, and now Mam was pregnant. She long ago made it a rule never to drink anyway, at least not at home with Da. Emily had seen Mam once at a family gathering, having a small whiskey with dinner. But that had been at a restaurant, and her uncles had ordered it up. One had appeared in front of Gran and rather than foist it off to the highest bidder, she'd joined them in the dram.

Still, Emily made a mental note to check out the stout later.

Dylan walked into the room and bade everyone else a hello. He said the same to Emily and nodded as well, and she noted the challenge in his eyes, the same she recognized from Damian. Well, as far as she was concerned, the only one she'd listen to would be Henry.

As if hearing her thoughts, Henry looked at her with that fatherly stare, saying, "Em, how about lending yer Gran a hand with carrying supper out to the table. Smells like one of her feasts and I'm certain there's more than one or two dishes need to be brought out."

"Sure, Da," she said pointedly, going over to kiss his cheek as if she would normally do that when being asked to help out.

"Pup," he said again, affectionately smacking her bottom as she went into the kitchen.

Emily hadn't missed Dylan's expression, a look that seemed tight with reprimand. She didn't care.

Kathleen had arranged the seating so that Damian sat at one end, herself at the other, with Dylan on her left, Henry on her right, and Siobhan next to Henry, leaving Emily seated between Dylan at one side of her and Damian at the end. Less than happy with the seating arrangements, she knew she'd have to keep silent. As much as she wanted to be out of there, making a scene was not going to help. Da, Henry that was, might just confine her to her room like a recalcitrant child!

As dinner progressed, talk took on a wide range of subjects, everything from the long, hot spell they'd been experiencing to the new additions to the family. Emily joined in at that point.

"I couldn't resist. I sent flowers to Uncle Niall and Uncle Michael as congratulations for their wee girl, and also sent some to Uncle Liam and Auntie Sine for their wee boy. Imagine, born on the same day!"

"Sine's recovering, I hear. She had a mild infection but seems to be doin' better," said Siobhan. "I was down Cahersiveen way to see her a few days ago. They'll be leavin' for home soon."

"That's right," added Henry, and to Emily, said, "and Sine says to say thanks to ye for helpin' me gather her baby things together."

"I'll have to go up to Galway to visit next chance I get. I don't expect she'll be goin' far for the next little while," said Emily.

"What about yer job?" asked Dylan, and Emily felt the muscles in her back and jaw tighten with irritation.

As calmly as she could, she answered his question with, "What about my job?"

As if feigning importance, Dylan took a deep breath and said the obvious. "Well, ye just can't up and go whenever the mood strikes ye."

Take a breath, Emily thought, a deep breath before you strangle him… "In case ye hadn't noticed, I'm a conscientious worker. I'd never just up and leave, as ye say. I'd wait for a couple of days together, maybe add a day if I'm allowed, and then go and see them."

"Or ye could wait for when they pop down to Killarney," suggested Siobhan; words that seemed to relax the sudden tension in the room. "They do that from time to time, and now with the baby, I think Sine will be happier to get out a little more often. We have that spare room, after all," she finished with a laugh.

Emily joined in. "Thanks. First my room is bein' turned into a nursery and next I'll have to make use of the couch so's Uncle Liam and Auntie Sine can have the other spare room."

"It's what happens when fledglings leave the nest," commented Henry in a jovial way.

Then suddenly, Dylan changed the subject. "So, now that ye've flown the coop, what are yer plans after yer gap year? I'll give ye a good recommendation for Dublin University. Ye should go there. It's a good school."

Again, Emily felt her spine stiffen. "That's grand, but I don't know what I want yet. Don't really know if I want to go to university."

"What else would ye do? I'll not have ye tend a shop for the rest of yer days," he said.

The table fell silent and Emily looked to Henry, only to see him shake his head. "Dylan's right. Ye need some sort of higher education these days to get anywhere."

Emily pushed her chair out and stood. "I don't believe

this," she forced between tight lips. "I'm bein' told what to do, where I'm goin' to go, and I haven't even decided yet what it is I want."

"Sit down, Em," said Gran, "no one meant anythin' by it."

But Emily wasn't finished. "No. Let's get this settled here and now." Looking to Henry, she spouted angrily, "Ye've been my da for eight years and I've looked up to ye and listened and been the best daughter I could for ye. I've never regretted the role ye took in my life and I hope ye haven't either."

And before Henry could say anything, she looked at Dylan, saying "It was good we stumbled upon each other. It answered a lot of questions I'd had about my real da, and for you, questions ye'd had about my real mam. Now we know the answers."

"Yes, and as yer real father, I've a right…"

But Emily cut him off. "Ye've no right. None at all. Just because ye…" She had been about to say "fucked" but suddenly thought better of it. "Just because ye lay with my mam doesn't suddenly give ye the right to order me around, tell me what to do, who I can see and so on. I'll be eighteen next week, and I won't have to answer to any of ye's, and especially not you. If anyone has any say over me, it's the parents I've grown up with and call Mam and Da, and not you! Got it?"

With that, she pushed her chair out from the table and went to the front door, gathering her purse off the table as she went. "I'm goin' out. Don't know when I'll be back."

Her hand was on the doorknob when Henry stood. "Wait. Ye're not legal age yet. Ye've one more week, as ye said. I'll know where ye're goin' and when ye plan on bein' back. And if ye aren't in when ye say, I'll go lookin' for ye."

She spun on him, angrier than she'd ever been in her life. "Ye've never said that to me, not like that. And ye know I'll not do anythin' stupid. Ye know that! Ye're only sayin' that because of him," she yelled, pointing at Dylan, "and I'll not stand for it. I may have one week to go before I'm legal, but by heaven, I am not yer prisoner."

She slammed the door, leaving a table of gaping mouths and shocked faces, and didn't care. Hitting the end of the driveway, she set off at a run, hoping Fionn would get home early.

Chapter Sixteen

Emily was breathing hard by the time she reached Fionn's cottage, tears still wet on her cheeks. She'd cried while running most of the way and was pretty much done, but she couldn't help sniffing and feeling even worse when thinking about it.

How could Henry do that to her? How could he play into Dylan's hands like that? Dylan only wanted to control her, as if he'd been her father all her life, but in reality, he was a stranger, and no DNA test was going to alter that relationship anytime soon.

And then there was Henry's admonition to return at an appropriate time. She knew what he meant. She'd had a curfew at home and although Gran had never imposed one, it was expected she wouldn't be late on a work night.

But tonight…if she had her way, tonight would be different. She was on her own, or almost, and she was going to prove to the lot of them that she didn't need anyone hovering over her as if she were still twelve years old and out to the cinema with her first boyfriend.

Fionn's cottage was dark and no vehicle was present so she knew he wasn't home yet. But soon enough, the headlights from his small car could be seen coming up the road, lighting the way past the main house and into his cottage at the back. He stepped out of the car and walked to where she was sitting on his step.

"Emily? I wasn't expectin' to see ye. Has something upset ye?"

She stood, nodding, and Fionn opened the door to his cottage, ushering her inside with a hand to the small of her back. Emily wanted to lean into the pressure of his fingers, but instead, let them guide her to the cool, dark interior.

Shutting the door behind them, Fionn reached for her, pulled her into his embrace, and kissed her. Hard. Emily's arms encircled him, her fingers splayed across his back, pulling his shirt from his trousers to feel the heat of his skin. She could feel the rod of his erection against his pants and had no doubt how the evening would end.

Fionn ended the kiss, his breathing hard as he met Emily's eyes. His hands were on her breasts and she could feel him thumbing her nipples through her clothing. "What's amiss?" he asked again, breathless from the kiss.

Emily could feel his heart thumping in his chest, felt her own beating almost so hard it was difficult to talk without inhaling between words. "It's Dylan," she began.

"Ah, and what's he done now, then?"

They were still cuddled, still holding tight to each other. "I've news about him. About him and Damian both, and I…I just don't know what I feel, how to begin to tell ye."

"Then just begin. It'll sort itself."

Reluctantly, she pulled herself from Fionn's embrace, reluctant because she felt much safer within it. Yet if she stayed there, she'd never be able to tell him. Tears started in her eyes and she sniffed them away. A tissue appeared beneath her gaze, held between two of Fionn's lean, tanned fingers. He'd taken a good tan at the beach the previous weekend and while hers had faded slightly, he'd retained his. But then, she recalled the lone chair he had outside his door and thought he must spend some time there, taking in the sun when not at work.

Taking the tissue, she smiled and said, "Thanks," before making use of it. Gathering her wits, straightening her shoulders, and raising her chin, she began. And once she began, she couldn't seem to stop. Information flowed nonstop, like a pot boiling over.

"It's Dylan. And Damian. Both of them. They're really…I don't know how to tell ye…they're…ah, feckit! They're my da and my grandda. For real. I just found out the other day and it's all I can think on, and now Dylan's tryin' to be my da and Henry's goin' along with it all and I don't know how to handle it. I just want them all to go away and leave me be. If it wasn't for you, Fionn, I'd go back to Killarney, away from all this. But I don't want to leave ye. I want to be here. With you."

Fionn stood openmouthed, unable to speak for a moment, taking everything in. "Dylan is yer da?" At Emily's nod, he continued, "How? I mean, how do ye know? How'd ye find out? I thought Henry was yer da."

Moaning, because Emily knew it was a bit of a long story, she said, "I'd really appreciate it if ye'd sit down so I can tell ye, but I'm not goin' to do it without some of the black stuff ye have in there," she admonished, pointing to his small refrigerator. "And don't give me none of that rubbish about bein' underage. I'm eighteen soon, and last I looked, this was not a licenced establishment. This is yer home."

A grin spread across Fionn's handsome face, the sculpted cheekbones that hollowed his face handsomely, the shadow of a beard caressing his cheeks, his chin, and around his mouth. Moments later, a bottle appeared in Emily's hands and she took a deep drink of the stuff, enjoying the refreshing feeling, relishing the smooth taste.

"Ye know, this is my first bottle since a party at a friend's house when her parents were away. I've always loved it," she said, sighing her appreciation of the drink.

Fionn swallowed his own, saying, "Yeah. It's good stuff. Legendary for Ireland." And then, "But back to Dylan and Damian. What's this about them being related to ye, and how does yer da figure in all of it?"

"Da? As in Henry?"

Fionn nodded.

Emily began her tale, starting with what she knew of her real mam's relationship with Dylan and its ending, and finishing it with how she met Dylan and how they realized he was the one her mother had left. "It was that one discussion that did it. If he hadn't asked about me, we'd still never know." She'd made her way through most of the stout by then and finished it off with a flourish and a small belch.

Fionn laughed, setting down his own bottle, now finished as well. "C'mere to me," he said, standing, reaching for her.

She rose and went into his arms, felt his hands at her back, pressing her to him, and again, that hardened rod against her stomach. A hand left his shoulder where she'd placed it, traveled down his torso to the front of his trousers, fingers molding across the bulge, stroking down the length of him.

"Ah, darlin', ye'll be playin' with fire if ye don't stop."

"I want to play with fire. I want to burn," she answered, seeking his lips, his mouth, with her own.

"Ye're underage."

"Feckit. All the girls at school were underage yet they did it."

"Yer da…"

"Shut up." She had taken his mouth with hers, had made headway, slipping her hands inside his trousers, cupping his nads, stroking his lad until any objection Fionn could have made was swallowed by her mouth on his.

It seemed to be all the impetus Fionn needed and Emily soon felt his hands across her breasts, seeking the nipple tucked within her clothing before finding the zip at the back of her dress and pulling it down, the dress following that direction to puddle on the floor at her feet. Next came her bra and then her knickers, and she still hadn't got his shirt off him.

That was soon remedied and she set to work on his trousers. He gently pushed her hand away when she would have run the zip down and did it himself, dropping both trousers and shorts in one easy movement.

They stood facing each other, nude, aroused, and it was, Emily realized, the beginning of something special. She had never felt this way about anyone before, had never wanted this from anyone before, and if Fionn felt anything close to what she, herself, was feeling, then wasn't this something to cling to?

She went into his arms as if she belonged there, cupped his nads with her fingers, rolled them about and stroked his lad until the moisture beaded at the tip and he hissed his breath in response.

"Easy, ye'll have me shootin' off right now," he laughed, leading her over to the bed. "Let me get a rubber."

She waited as he took a rubber from the drawer, opened the packet, and rolled it on. Their eyes met, and as she lay on his bed and he came over her, all she could see was the future stretched out before her with him by her side. It felt so right.

His hand touched her flange, his thumb encircled her bud, and she began to move beneath him, relishing in his touch.

"Does that feel good?" His voice was a husky whisper in the dark of the room. They hadn't turned any lights on when entering. Hadn't wanted to. It felt cooler, sitting in the dark, and now Emily was happy to have the cover of night, to view Fionn through moonlight streaming in the window combined with the one light over the door outside the cottage still on; a mixture of silver moonlight with golden overtones, bathing his smooth skin in its glow.

"Hmm," she moaned, unable to find the words that could define what she was feeling.

"How about here?" He was moving his hands about, looking for the places she liked best, she supposed.

"Go back. Go back…oh, yeah, there. Ahhh," she breathed out on a sigh.

He took a nipple between his lips, suckled, and Emily's breath hitched.

"Christ, that feels so good." Her hand found Fionn's nads, and since he was sheathed, played with them rather than running her fingers along his erection.

Fionn's breathing was quickening and she could feel his heart pounding in his chest beneath her palm. Running the pad of her thumb across his flat, male nipple, she lifted her head and tongued it, felt rather than heard his chuckle, and knew she was doing something he liked.

"More?" she asked, and then, "Oh, God, what are ye doin'? Don't ever stop!"

"Spread yer legs wider," and then, "is this okay?"

She felt him slide inside, felt the urgency of his movement, his thumb playing with her hard nub, and then the sensation overtaking her, the lights behind her eyes shut tight against the world; the spiralling, whirling feeling she prayed would never stop.

She was coming, was climaxing with Fionn inside her, his body thrusting into her, and as she cried out her release, he stiffened, his arse clenched beneath her hands where she'd grabbed him and held him to her. She hadn't wanted him to fall out accidentally, hadn't wanted him to leave her at all.

They lay together, their bodies recovering from the high they'd been on. Emily's limbs felt boneless, as if she had no will over her body, languid in Fionn's arms. He lifted his head, his fingers stroked her chin and he brought his face to hers, kissed her gently and then more urgently.

"Oh, God, you are so beautiful," he said on a breath, his voice a husky whisper, coated with the roughness of emotion. "No regrets?"

"None," she replied.

She felt rather than saw his head nod in agreement. "Then rest a while. I'll see ye home soon."

"I'd rather stay."

"Emily, ye can't. I mean, I'd love for ye to stay, but yer gran will be worried, don't ye think?"

She sighed into the night. "I guess ye're right. I just don't want to go, though. Not yet, leastwise."

"Then rest a bit. I'd like to make love to ye again before I take ye home."

"That'll be grand," she said, and felt the grin spread across her face, her bottom lip sucked in between her teeth.

"Let me get some sustenance, and we can begin again."

A small light went on in the kitchen, not the main overhead light with its garish, stunning glare, but the softer light of the small lamp Fionn had on the table. A brighter light appeared, then disappeared, as Emily heard him open and then close the refrigerator. There was only a small wall separating the space between the so-called bedroom and the rest of the house. There was no door.

Minutes later, with the lamp still lit on the table, Fionn walked in with a plate of nosh and a Guinness between them.

"What did ye bring?" asked Emily, eyeing the plate with its selection of cheese, some sausage, and a few crisps. "Looks divine," she giggled and helped herself to a few bites.

* * *

Fionn dug in, ravenous since he'd had little at supper. The pub had been busy and he'd no time for more than a quick sandwich, and even then had tossed half of it away after the barmaid soaked it with spilled gin. He'd contemplated eating it, gin and all, but before he could decide, she'd scooped it into the bin with an apology for drowning his meal and wiped the mess clean.

He picked up the last piece of sausage, put it between his teeth, and leaned toward Emily. Watching as she focused on his mouth, he felt the first stirrings of arousal. She seemed to sense what he wanted as she bit the piece he'd left exposed for her and then, when she did, held on to her mouth with his, bringing her down to him in a wild, ravishing tumble of sheets. The plate, now empty of the meal, slid to the floor with a clatter, and Fionn soon had Emily beneath him and wanting him again.

He trailed kisses between her firm young breasts, large yet soft, and she encouraged him to bury his face between them by squishing them together with her hands and then laughing. Lifting his face to plant a kiss on her throat, he moved over one plush mound, took her ruched nipple between his teeth and nibbled gently. Her pelvis arched up against him, and he changed the nibble to a suckle. God, she was so responsive!

Sliding down her torso, feeling her hands in his hair, feeling her belly curve as she tried to kiss him, he fastened onto her flange, tasted the juices between the folds and suckled her bud.

Emily immediately flopped back down, legs splayed, arching toward the source of her pleasure. She was so wet, and Fionn was hard with wanting. He hated to break off now when she was so close but he was so hard, so needy, and she was so ready.

"Now, Fionn, now. Come into me, now!"

"I've no rubber on," he choked out, and went back to feasting on her nectar.

Moments later, he heard her cry out and he thrust his tongue as far up her canal as he could, again, and again, mimicking the moves his lad would do, until she came down from her high.

"Oh, my God, that was good," she sighed.

Fionn grinned and rolled a new rubber down his length. "My turn," he whispered into her mouth before taking her. His lips crushed against hers, his lad slid smoothly inside and he felt his climax mere seconds away.

A banging sounded on the outer door and then the loud voice Emily knew too well.

"Emily, I know ye're in there. Ye've got three seconds to open this door and then I'm callin' the garda."

Emily shot up, dislodging Fionn before he could climax. There was no help for it. Fionn had lost his erection at the first sound of Henry's fist on the door.

Scrambling to throw his trousers and t-shirt on, Fionn said, "I'll go to the door and stall him while ye get dressed." He left her with a backward glance, then wandered slowly to the door, undoing the lock and turning the handle.

But Henry was faster. As soon as the lock was freed, Henry pushed the door open, all but knocking Fionn out of the way.

All Fionn saw was the meaty hand that grabbed at his t-shirt beneath his chin and Henry's face up close and personal as he ground out, "Where is she?"

Emily came running from the direction of the toilet. She'd run there with her dress while Fionn was unlocking the door. "I'm here, Da. Let him go."

"Turn on the light," said Henry, his voice hard and menacing.

Fionn did as directed and the small lamp was soon outshone by the glaring overhead light of the kitchen.

There was no mistaking the anger in Henry's eyes, the tightly drawn lips that moved little when he spoke. His voice, a soft, deadly weapon.

"Emily, get in the car."

Fionn watched with a worried gaze as Henry took in the empty bottles on the table, the mess on the bed, and oh god, the used rubber, lying forgotten on the sheet. He saw a look cross Henry's face that would have spoken volumes if he knew what it meant. The clearest Fionn could make out was "death," and he began to tremble where he stood. Henry O'Farrell was a big man, tall and brawny. He was a stonemason, so Emily had told him, and as such had the built-up muscle the job required. Fionn, lean and somewhat lanky, was no match. Even Henry's reach would prove deadly, and so Fionn remained quiet, knowing he'd be outmatched before he ever began.

"I'm not done with ye yet," Henry ground out between clenched teeth. "I'll be seekin' ye tomorrow. Just be thankful I haven't called in the shades."

At the mention of the garda, Fionn gulped a rough swallow. He was an artist, not a fighter, and feared the rough handling he'd receive at the hands of the garda just as much as he feared what Henry might do when they next met.

"Later," growled Henry, inhaling deeply through widened nostrils.

Fionn could only nod while he held his breath.

Henry took another look around and then, with a last glaring leer at Fionn, turned and left.

Fionn shut the door behind Henry and leaned hard against it. He'd had only a glimpse of Emily in the front seat of Henry's car, her glorious black hair tousled about her, her face pale in the light of the moon and the reflection from the light over the door. He'd closed his door before Henry reached the driver's side, not wanting Henry knowing he'd had another glimpse of Emily, just in case it was one too many.

Leaning back against the solid wood, Fionn realized just how badly he'd been frightened. His legs were like jelly, barely able to hold him up.

He went to the cupboard, pulled out the bottle of whiskey and splashed some into a glass. Downing it in one go, he let the smooth liquor slide down his throat, and only then did he acknowledge that he'd been holding his breath. He let it go, and taking in great gulps of air, cursed himself for being such a wimp.

Chapter Seventeen

Henry gripped the steering wheel with both hands because if he didn't, he'd find one of them around his daughter's neck. What in hell had she thought she was doing, sleeping with some plonker she'd found in a local pub? It sounded so much like Meara's story.

He couldn't remember ever feeling so angry. Or so scared. When she hadn't returned by curfew time, he told Siobhan and his mam to go to bed and he'd go out looking. Dylan had told him where to find Fionn, thinking, and rightly so, that Emily would go there. She didn't really know anyone else in town, hadn't spent any time looking for girlfriends. She'd met Fionn at the pub and that had been it from then on.

One glance at Emily's profile took Henry back to the first time he'd met her with her mam, Meara. She'd looked so much the waif, like a raggle-taggle gypsy, the kind they'd been accused of being. She had the black hair and deep blue eyes he'd recognized as being familiar but it wasn't until they'd figured out the family connection that it made sense.

Meara had been, as Dylan informed them and as Henry had already known, into drugs.

Hard.

She'd leave Emily in a safe place, or safe as far as Meara was concerned, and go seek her drugs. Later, she'd somehow make it back to Emily's side, not always clean.

Sometimes she'd be accosted by a fellow druggie and she'd arrive smelling of cheap liquor and sex and of the hash they'd smoked afterward. She was into it all, was Meara, and it was only time that stood between her and death.

Henry had still had his father's notebook at that time, a book with names, dates, addresses, and phone numbers scrawled in his broad, messy hand, usually for work with how much stone was needed, the weight, color, and all kinds of other information he'd jotted down, just in case.

Well, the just-in-case portion was what Henry found didn't make sense. Not, that is, until meeting Meara. He'd found her name in the book along with Hank's, their address in Killarney, and Hank's mother's name, Ceilidh Mulligan, alongside it. Only he had no idea what it was about. There was no order for stone but there had been a phone number, disconnected long ago, he remembered from his first, futile attempts at ringing it.

And then Meara had shown up, calling him Hank, and suddenly, two plus two didn't add up to four. It went way beyond that, and gradually, all the pieces fell into place, one by one.

The result of all that was the sullen teenager in the passenger seat of his car. A niece who had the O'Farrell look, as did her mam's brother, Hank. He recognized the stubborn set to her chin as she was likely thinking of what to say to him that would put him in his place.

Silly child, there wasn't anything she could come up with. He knew her too well.

Henry pulled into the drive outside his mother's house and stopped the car, turning off the ignition. To Emily, he said very quietly, his voice tightly controlled, "When I finish with ye, we are goin' into the house and ye'll go quietly up to your room and stay there. In the mornin', ye'll be comin' back to Killarney with yer mam and me. Understood?"

No nod, only a downcast movement of her eyes. The stubbornness was still in the set of her chin but Henry had always been able to gain her agreement in matters of behavior and had no reason to doubt his ability now. Except...

"I'm not goin' back to Killarney. There's nothin' for me there."

Henry raised a brow in question, noting that she still hadn't looked his way. "Ye'll come because I'm tellin' ye to."

"No, Da. I have a job here, and I'm stayin'."

"Look at me, Em."

She did, and he noted the chin with its stubborn set, had softened only slightly. Her refusal to do as she was told was not lost on him but it was a night to pick battles, and this wasn't one he needed to worry about. Weyans eventually grew up and defied their parents all the time. While he was willing to give her that concession, he knew there was a deeper problem.

"Em, I've just caught ye sleepin' with a man and ye don't have to tell me what went on. I've eyes. Was that the first time?"

She turned her face away, likely mortified that he'd bring it up.

"No."

Her answer was quiet. Resigned. Truthful.

He heaved a sigh into the night, controlling the maniac inside himself that wanted to rip the door off the car with his bare hands, even though he knew of that impossibility.

"Do ye love him?"

A slight nod and a sniff. He'd hit a nerve.

"Does he love ye, too, or just sayin' he does? Do ye know the difference?"

"Yes. He loves me. I know he does."

"Humph. Fellas say that all the time just to get what they want."

"It wasn't like that."

"Humph."

"Besides, I'm eighteen in a matter of days. I can look after myself."

"Can ye now? Just because ye're turnin' eighteen doesn't mean ye magically know everything."

Now it was her turn to harrumph, and she crossed her arms in front of her, keeping her gaze out the car window. "Why did ye side with Dylan?"

"What?"

"At dinner. Ye went right along with what he said."

Henry squirmed in his seat. She'd gone right for his jugular. He'd known at the time, even as the words left his mouth, that he'd gone a step too far. But it was a damned if you do, damned if you don't scenario. If he'd contradicted Dylan's words, he'd be made to look like an eejit because the man had been correct in what he'd said. Few people ended up well off just because they got lucky. Most had to work, go to university, or learn a trade to make their way. And even then, he mused, recalling that if he hadn't learned from his da's old mentor after Da was killed, he wouldn't have the job and security that he had now. Old Charlie had turned his business over to Henry a bit at a time, and then once Charlie passed on, Henry kept it going.

Emily had yet to make up her mind about her future, but this argument wasn't about that, either.

"Dylan was right. Ye'll need some sort of trade or university to get somewhere if ye don't want to be stuck in a flower shop all day."

"I like the flower shop," she stated defiantly.

"Oh, yeah, ye like it now, but ten years from now, and ye've weyans to look after and the bills are pilin' up, ye'll wonder why ye didn't learn somethin' that would bring in more money."

"I don't care about the money. And I'm still not goin' back to Killarney with ye."

Henry could feel the argument begin to go about in circles and knew, without a doubt, he'd give in. He had no argument big enough against it and had quickly discarded the I'm yer da idea before it could launch itself from his mouth.

Instead, he said, "I don't know if yer gran is goin' to be happy about ye stayin' on."

"I'll move in with Fionn."

Outrage and the words Over my dead body caused his hands to grip the steering wheel with a ferocity that, had it not been made of such stern stuff, would surely have snapped it in two. He hadn't uttered the words, though. They were still stuck behind clenched teeth.

Inhaling deeply, he tried to calm himself inwardly, feeling as if he were sinking in a muddy bog. Struggling was useless.

"Maybe Fionn won't want ye, have ye thought of that? And maybe ye'll have to find yer own place, and maybe ye'll not be able to afford it…"

"And maybe ye're focusin' on all the negative things. I don't care if Fionn doesn't want me to move in. I'll find somethin'. I know I will. And in any case, he's been sweet so far, even offered to stay with me when Dylan came into the store."

That got Henry's attention. "Why? What's Dylan done?"

"Like ye hadn't noticed," she accused. "He's tryin' to play the father role and I'll not have it. He can go…ye know," she finished, as if she'd suddenly run out of steam.

"Fuck himself? Is that what ye wanted to say?" He didn't expect an answer. In fact, her statement was completely in line with his own. "Yeah. I know what ye mean."

"Ye do?"

She was looking at him, the question visible in her beautiful blue eyes. Because she was beautiful, thought Henry. Just as beautiful as Meara had been. Any neddy could see that.

"Yeah. I have to tell ye, when yer gran told me they'd found yer da, and who it was and all that went with it…ye know, with Damian and all…well, I was happy for ye. I thought maybe it might answer some questions ye'd always had. Things I couldn't answer for ye. All Meara's leads were dead ends. Even the photos in that box, at the time, meant nothin'. They could've been anyone, anywhere. But now we know who they are, some of them, anyway. We know that Dylan is the man in that photo with yer mam, just like yer gran said, and it was him she left. But now we know he loved her, and that has to account for somethin'."

"All it accounts for can be summed up in one word. Biology."

"It's deeper than that, Em. He's havin' the same struggle as I am, only in a different way. Ye're my daughter, have been for eight long years, and I'll not trade any one of them for anythin'. Ye've been daughter to both Siobhan and me, and even though we're goin' to have our own child soon, it doesn't diminish how we feel about ye. We love ye the way we always have." He sighed as if the fight had left him, and in a way, it had. They were at least talking, speaking civilly to each other, not in anger but in conversation. "As for Dylan, why, he's just learned he has a daughter; learned of Meara's fate all at once. He's goin' through some turmoil of his own, so if he doesn't know how to react to it all, give him space. He'll figure it out."

"So where does that leave me?" she asked, looking confused and, if he was honest, a little afraid.

He harrumphed through his smile. "Where ye've always been. In here," he patted his heart with his fist.

She left a few breaths in between his heartfelt statement and her question. "Can I still see Fionn?"

He'd swear it was a sticking point. If he said yes, she'd accept it and they'd move on. If he denied her, she'd leave. Of that, he had no doubt. She could leave at any time; she didn't have to be eighteen. Only the upbringing she'd had for the past eight years kept her with them. It had been the only stability she'd experienced, the only comfort and feeling of belonging she'd ever known. And the fact she was even asking spoke volumes.

"Yes. Ye can still see Fionn. But mind, I'll be talkin' to him, eh?"

"Right." A small smile turned the corner of her lips, broadened, and became a cheeky grin.

"C'mere to me," said Henry, leaning across the steering wheel with his arms outstretched as well as he was able, and Emily moved into them. He hugged her as well as he could in the confined space, felt the silky strands of her hair against his face and through his fingers, and thought that if he could be as lucky with the new weyan, whether girl or boy, as he'd been with Emily, then life would truly be grand.

"Let's go inside now. It's late, and we could both use a good kip," he said, kissing the top of her head.

"What'll Mam and Gran say in the mornin'?"

Henry shrugged. "I've no idea. Could be they're still up,

waitin' for ye to come home."

"Feck."

Henry laughed, ruffled her hair, and nodded in the direction of the house, saying, "C'mon."

* * *

Niall scanned the sheet in front of him one more time. He'd come across it when clearing out the drawers, readying everything for the move into their new house in the morning. Everything else had already been packed up, and throwing clothing into a suitcase was the final task. Most had been done already. Michael was busy with the baby and so Niall had gone ahead, said he would do it for him.

Michael hadn't said aye or nay. He'd been focused on Dawn, playing with her toes as he changed her, tickling her ribs lightly and waiting for a response. She was still very young, not into laughing yet, but that didn't stop Michael from trying and it had become a regular nighttime routine after her bath.

So Niall had gone ahead with the packing and found the paper he was now holding, scanning it, wondering what Michael had done this time.

Sensing his husband just behind him, Niall said, "I found this in yer drawer. Ye want to enlighten me?"

Michael took the paper from Niall, curious at first, and then as his brows met in a frown of recognition, scrunched it up to throw it away. "It's nothing." He dismissed the bunched up paper with a toss into the trash bin and was about to walk away when Niall stopped him.

"It's no good, Michael. I've seen it. I know what it is. I can read."

"Well, if you know what it is, then you needn't ask any questions."

214

Niall's temper went from mildly ticked to furious within less than a second. "Y'eejit! Ye think I didn't begin to wonder? Everyone said 'oh, she looks like Michael, isn't that cute,' and I, moron that I am, just thought it was because Farrah has the same background as ye, but that isn't it, is it? It's because ye had Farrah inseminated with yer sperm and ye didn't have the decency to tell me."

"Well, it's not like I took her to bed, is it? We met at the clinic and I tossed off in the loo, gave it to the doctor, who then inseminated her with it. I never touched her. Never had real sex with her, if that's what you're on about."

Niall didn't know what he felt. "I thought she was already pregnant when we found her," he finally choked out, trying to come to grips with Michael's backroom dealings.

Michael had the grace to look ashamed. "I'm sorry, love. I engineered it to happen."

Niall's head shot up at that. "What?"

"Sit down and I'll tell you everything."

Niall sat on the bed, his head still reeling from what he'd learned so far, angry beyond measure but holding it in check. Just.

Michael plunked himself down beside him, steepled his fingers, his elbows resting on his knees, obviously wondering what and how much to tell Niall.

"When did ye meet her? How?" asked Niall. He was so angry he could feel his nostrils flare with every breath he took. It was an effort to speak quietly, to not allow the anger he felt to make its way down the hall to where their child lay sleeping in her crib.

Michael took a deep breath and began. "Farrah was on holiday here with a friend. We struck up a conversation in a pub and she was so easy to talk to. It was like talking to a sister, if I had one, I suppose. Things just started pouring out."

"Michael, people just don't start talkin' about wantin' a baby with someone they just met. That's a load of shite, that is."

Michael turned a sardonic eye to Niall. "Strange, but true."

Niall made a sound of disbelief that came from his throat and through his nose, expelling a great deal of air in a whoosh.

"As I was saying, we met at this pub, she thought I was a prospect, and I soon steered her clear of that notion. We both laughed about it and I said that you and I were married, and were, in fact, looking to adopt so that we could begin our own family. She thought it was wonderful."

"And just like that, the two of ye decided to have it arranged. Yeah. And unicorns fly out of me arse every day."

"Don't get your knickers in a knot," Michael scolded. "As we talked, it became clear we had been thinking along the same lines. Farrah said she wanted to help, and wouldn't it be fabulous if we, you and I, that is, could have a child that one of us had actually fathered. That's when we began to speak about IVF."

"IVF? Oh, in vitro fertilization."

"Yeah. After that, it was just a matter of making an appointment at a clinic, and then later, once we knew she was pregnant, she got in touch with the adoption clinic, the same one you and I registered with, and the rest you know."

"No. I don't know the rest. How does a single woman, with her background no less, decide to become pregnant and donate the child to some fella she just met at a pub?" Niall's stare must have penetrated some part of Michael's brain because he sighed heavily, as if knowing nothing but every detail would satisfy Niall's curiosity.

"That took a while."

"A while. How long is a while? Michael, ye've obviously had a relationship with her for a long time for her to suddenly come up with that idea."

"It was my idea. She thought it over for a few days and decided to do it."

"Why, Michael? Why? What aren't ye tellin' me?"

"For God's sake, Niall, there isn't any subterfuge, I'm not hiding anything," he began.

"Then spill it, Michael. Now!" Niall had tried to keep his voice down for the baby's sake but it was rising nonetheless, and his face felt hot with tightly controlled anger.

Michael stood, hands in pockets, and turned to lean against the dresser where Niall had found the letter and faced his husband. "Right. The sordid truth. Here goes. I've known Farrah for years. We grew up not far from each other, and being from the same background, kind of gravitated toward each other. We even dated for a while, even though I knew I was gay long before we began, and she was so much younger. She once said to me, after I told her I was gay, that if ever she had a child, she wanted it to be mine. She was a little in love with me, I guess, although as much as I like her, I was never in love with her. So we broke up."

"And arranged to meet that day in the pub." Niall supplied the last words.

"No. That was pure accident, that was. I only went in there on a whim and because I was hungry and it was there."

"I feel like there's more to the story." He was a little calmer but the underlying anger was still there. Still angry that Michael carried out his plot secretly, as if to hide it.

"Farrah's parents are very traditional," said Michael.

"Yeah. So I noticed."

Michael quirked a brow and Niall knew they were both remembering his blackened eyes and broken nose, now healed.

"Her father caught us together one day, out on the street in front of her home. We hadn't been doing anything, just talking. But the very fact that she was talking with a fella with no other girls around, and that I kissed her cheek before we parted, just out of friendship, mind," he put in, "made her father go paralytic with anger. I didn't see her for a few days after that. And when I did, she had faint bruising on her cheek and admitted that he had beat her for seeing us together. We were very cautious after that but it started us thinking of a way for her to leave, to get out of their house so she didn't have to follow their rules anymore. She was almost twenty by then."

"But you're so much older than she is. How did ye end up datin'?"

Michael grinned, and Niall tried not to be taken in by his striking golden eyes and engaging smile. Michael could charm the wings off an angel, and no mistake.

"I began noticing her when she was about sixteen, seventeen. She was still pretty girlish at that age, flirting with every young man that walked by. She always went for young men, never boys her age. Maybe it was inevitable."

"So she was…what, when ye began datin'? Eighteen?"

Nodding, Michael said, "Something like that. We dated secretly for a couple of years because we knew her parents wouldn't like me. They didn't want anyone for her they didn't pick out themselves."

"Didn't they have someone in mind when she was pregnant?" asked Niall, attempting to recall something he'd heard in the past but coming up empty.

"I heard they had a friend of theirs who was interested in marrying her. Farrah's mother thought him a catch, some member of the peerage, wealthy as sin, and therefore, despite his being thirty-odd years her senior, a good catch. It would elevate their status in the community."

"That's bollocks, that is," exclaimed Niall.

"I agree, and Farrah wasn't going to go back to her parents after Dawn was born. She was going to assert herself, stay here, and look for a job."

"And?"

"They have her, now, back in London. I'm honestly a little afraid for her, afraid that her father will contact someone from his home country and send her there against her will."

"She's twenty-three, he can't do that," Niall protested.

"Normally, people can't do that. But she's been cowed all her life, made to bend to his will. Even her mother would have no influence over the old man if that's what he wanted."

"But she's had a child. Surely, no one back wherever he's from would want a woman who is not only not virginal but has had a child as well."

"It doesn't bear thinking about but it does worry me."

"So what do ye propose to do? I know ye're thinkin' about it. I can see the wheels turnin'."

Niall's statement brought a quiet eruption of laughter through Michael's closed mouth, spreading his smile as it escaped through his lips. "Humph. Nothing. Nothing, really."

Niall thought it over, knew in his gut that what Michael said was true, even if the full story had yet to be revealed. After all, the evidence was on the piece of paper Michael had thrown away, although why he'd kept it in the first place was still a mystery.

It was that thought that prompted Niall's question.

"So, why did you hang on to that piece of paper? It's pretty incriminatin' evidence."

The rueful smirk on Michael's face broadened. "I know. I kept it because I thought that perhaps, maybe one day if we wanted another child, it could be your turn to father the child, and I could show you that during our discussion."

A nod of acknowledgement from Niall and then, "But why the adoption clinic? Could we not just have paid Farrah as we did and avoid all the other stuff?"

Michael shook his head. "No. I mean, probably. But I wanted to be certain it would all be legal. I didn't want Farrah to come back one day and demand her child back, so I wanted to go through all the right channels, with lawyers and everything, with people who knew how these things worked."

"We could have hired our own lawyer instead of using the one through the clinic," protested Niall.

"Yeah. We could have. But I didn't want to tell you what I'd done. I hadn't talked to you about it beforehand, and frankly, I felt guilty as hell, as if I actually had fucked her. And then afterward, when I thought about it, I thought that I'd approach you one day when we were ready for a second child and tell you what I'd done. Like I said, so you could have a real child, too."

"But Michael, don't ye think I love Dawn just as much as I would if she was my 'real' child, as ye say?"

"No, it isn't that, it's…"

"What, Michael? What? I love her to the depths of my heart. I'll love her no matter what. There isn't anything she can do that will stop that because I'm her da, every bit as much as you are, and biology doesn't matter. Ye think Henry cares that Emily isn't his natural born child? He loves her regardless of anything she might do. He doesn't feckin' care she's not his natural child. She's his. Don't ye get it?"

"You're right. I'm sorry, love, you're right. I had good intentions, that's all."

"The path to hell is paved with good intentions," quoted Niall, but he was losing the anger he initially felt. Taking Michael's hand in his, he asked, "So how did Farrah convince her folks that she was goin' on an extended vacation?"

Holding Niall's hand with both of his own, Michael filled him in. "When she found out she was knocked up, she notified me and I set up a bank account for her. She told her parents she'd been saving and wanted to see more of Ireland, since she'd gotten a taste of it on her first trip. They fell for it since she'd be under the protection of her friend's family, ostensibly."

"But we both know she wasn't."

"Correct. Since her friend's parents were not close friends of Farrah's parents, there was no back and forth, just an admonishment to Farrah to report in every few days. That was why we sent her and her friend around Ireland, so they could appear to be having a grand tour."

"And as we both know, they had good craic on that tour."

"They did," agreed Michael, "especially as it was all-expenses paid." Michael rubbed his thumb across Niall's knuckles. There was a pause as he thought, and Niall knew there was more to come.

He wasn't mistaken as Michael inhaled deeply, his eyes still focused on Niall's knuckles as he rubbed his thumb across the wedding band on his husband's finger. "You know, it seems every time I try to do something for you—for us—I botch it royally. I don't know why that is, don't know how it happens. It just does. I mean, look at how I nearly ruined everything for us when you did that shoot for Liam on the island. It turned out alright in the end, but it nearly went very badly for everyone. And I really did have the best intentions at the outset. It just turned horribly wrong."

"I remember that all too well," mused Niall. "I don't know how Liam didn't take ye out back of somewhere and pulverize ye. Maybe the only thing that saved ye was Liam knowin' how much I love ye."

"Just know that I love you, too, with everything I've got."

Niall met Michael's eyes, took in the deep golden orbs, the dark rim around the lighter gold inside, and knew his lover spoke truly.

Their lips met, and Michael pressed against him, pushing him down on the bed before coming over him. "We've time, maybe," he grinned, before cocking his head toward the hall where the baby's room was silent but for the musical merry-go-round nightlight beside her bed.

Niall's answer was to undo Michael's trousers.

Chapter Eighteen

It was precisely what Henry had imagined while seated in the car outside the house, trying to talk some sense into Emily. They'd walked through the door, and though it was well past midnight, both Siobhan and his mam were waiting, arms crossed, with concerned looks on their faces.

"She's alright, just upset," Henry explained. "We can all go to bed now."

"Emily?" Siobhan said, looking at the girl standing beside Henry.

"I'm fine, Mam," she said, her voice soft and gruff, as if she was spent and needed sleep.

Henry laid a hand across Emily's shoulder in a familiar fashion and hugged her. "Go to bed. All of ye's. We'll talk in the mornin'."

He steered Emily upstairs, watching as she turned the corner at the top and heard her bedroom door click softly closed. Turning to his wife and his mother, he repeated his words. "Let's go to bed."

Siobhan was not to be put off, though. "Henry, where did ye find her?"

He sighed, feeling tired, strung out, and so very thankful Emily was unhurt. It was he, himself, that was hurt. Hurt that his child had given up her virginity. It was new information that had to settle, become a part of him before he could allow it to be a part of her. "She was with Fionn."

"The lad from the pub?" asked his mam, and he nodded.

"As ye can see, she's fine, no harm has come to her, and I told her we would all talk about it in the mornin'. No need to get into it now. It's late, and I need to get some kip. I'm sure ye'll feel the same once yer head hits the pillow," he stated, yawning through his last words.

"Right then, I'm off," Kathleen remarked, "I've got to work tomorrow, but not until the evenin'. I'll meet ye at breakfast and then have a nap, later, like."

Henry nodded and watched as she followed Emily's path up the stairs and into her own room at the end of the hall. Looking into Siobhan's eyes, he saw the tiredness within, and taking her hand, began to pull her toward the stairs. "Let's go."

"Wait," she said, her feet not budging from where she stood. "I need to know what condition she was in when ye found her."

She knew, thought Henry. He wouldn't have to say anything, but he did. "She was in his bed."

Tears came to Siobhan's eyes. "Oh, God."

"It's alright, mo chroi, she wasn't raped, she went willin' like. She fancies herself in love with him."

Nodding, Siobhan dabbed her eyes with a tissue.

"At least," continued Henry, "she waited until she was almost eighteen before havin' sex, and she gave herself to a man she fancies she loves. This wasn't sex in a back alley. It was makin' love in a bed, and I have to think we gave her enough knowledge that she'll be careful. I saw a rubber."

The look Siobhan gave him made him want to laugh.

"Oh, that's so gross to think on, Henry."

His smile turned into a smirk and he hugged her close.

"Ah, that's life, darlin', that's just life. Now come to bed so I can teach ye what it's all about. Seein' ye standin' there in naught but yer nightie has me fair chubbed with wantin' ye."

"If we were home, ye could take me on the couch like ye've done before," she grinned.

"Ah, but I wouldn't be tryin' that in Mam's home. I'd get a scoldin' the likes of which ye've never heard before. Besides, a bed is so much more comfortable, especially now," he said, with a glance toward her bulging belly.

Agreeing with a nod, Siobhan tucked her arm around his. "Let's get some lovin' done before the baby comes too far between us."

"There are ways around that," he said with a grin, and Siobhan's answer was to kiss his cheek and then precede him up the stairs.

He closed the door softly behind him in time to see Siobhan draw the nightie over her head to stand nude before him. Her belly was getting fuller by the day, it seemed, and as she said, it wouldn't be long before her baby bump became a baby mound.

Stripping his shirt and jeans from his body, he quickly divested himself of everything else, freeing his lad to stand erect, waiting for her touch.

They came together, not in a rush, not in any kind of a hurry, but slowly, tenderly, filled with relief from Emily's return, a thankfulness that came from loving, caring, and trusting. Thoughts of their daughter were soon pushed to the back of their minds as their desire for each other, for the nearness and completeness, took over.

And as Henry slid inside his wife's body, he heaved a sigh of comfort, heard Siobhan's sigh mimic his, followed by her throaty chuckle and her saying, "It won't be long and we'll not be facin' each other doin' this."

"That may be true, but as long as ye're willin' and as long as there's no harm, we'll find a way. Ah, ye know just what I like," he whispered, feeling her hands stroking, caressing as he took her plump breast in hand, his fingers drawing the nipple out to suckle on it.

"Now who's doin' what I like?" she asked, meaningfully.

Henry chuckled, releasing her nipple with a slurp. "We've always been good together, haven't we." It wasn't a question, but a statement of what was true. They'd always clicked, from the moment they'd met.

Henry felt himself begin to quicken. They'd been moving, chatting softly, relaxed and not rushing for any ultimate conclusion. Simply being together.

"She'll be alright, won't she?" asked Siobhan on a silky breath.

She was feeling it, too, Henry knew.

"I expect she will. It'll all come right."

Siobhan nodded, and then there were no more words, only the soft sounds of loving in the night and the sounds of summer rain as the first, fat drops hit the window with a static slap-slap.

"I love ye, Siobhan, don't ever question it," he said as he began to move with purpose in and out.

"Hmm," she sighed, and Henry knew she was close.

Through the open window, the sound of rain grew in volume as it picked up in counterpoint to their breathing, their sighs filling the room along with the sound of the rustle of sheets. Moist air outside blew lightly across heated skin, filling the room with its scent, and Henry's deep voice was a whispered grunt in the dark as he came, Siobhan's softer cries, echoing his. And afterward; their panting breaths, the giggles, the kissing, and Henry brushing her hair from her face before taking her mouth with his. The kiss was long, drawn out, their tongues intertwining, loving, just as their bodies had done.

Henry pulled her to him as he slid from her body, wrapping her in a cocoon of love before drifting off to sleep. Siobhan was already exhaling the deep breaths of slumber.

* * *

Emily didn't want to face anyone at breakfast. She came downstairs fully dressed, wanting nothing more than to exit the house before anyone could catch her. It was Fionn's day off, as it was hers, and she wanted to spend it with him.

She got as far as the stairs when Gran's voice hailed her from the kitchen. "Come and get somethin' to eat before ye leave. We've the makin's of a Sunday brunch, though I don't know anyone's goin' to church today."

Relieved of the responsibility of attending the service, Emily followed Gran's voice into the kitchen where Mam and Da were helping with the cooking. Until Gran spoke, Emily hadn't noticed the delightful smells of rashers cooking or the rustle of the utensils as Mam scrambled the eggs in the pan. She'd been so intent on leaving before anyone else was up.

"There's juice on the table, everythin' else is done so come and sit down," Mam said, keeping her eye on the eggs rather than looking at Emily. Emily thought it was a bad sign.

Sitting at the table, the food appeared before her and she felt rather than heard her stomach rumble. "It smells delicious," she said by way of conversation, trying to ignore the twist of her gut, both longing for food and tense with discomfort at the mood in the room.

"Mmm," was all Mam said.

"Here, have some rashers. Gran's got some white puddin'

comin'," Henry said, piling the bacon on her plate.

White pudding was one of Emily's favorites, and so she let her da load her up with breakfast as if it was her last meal. A minute later, the white pudding was ready and appeared on her plate as Gran dished everyone up. Emily met her face but the smile that met her was strained, mournful.

They all knew. It was one thing to admit to having spent the night with your boyfriend; it was entirely another to have the you're not a virgin anymore look from everyone around you, as if you'd made a grave error in life. She hadn't, she knew, because she loved Fionn. It wasn't just sex, and it had been wonderful.

When everyone was seated, Siobhan said to Emily, "We've all done ye a disservice," she began, and Emily looked up to meet her mam's eyes, glassy with unshed tears.

"Mam, it's alright," she began, but Siobhan shushed her.

"No. It's not. We've been treatin' ye like ye're seven, not seventeen. We've ignored the fact that ye've grown up before our eyes, our precious, wee girl no longer a girl, but a woman. And ye've not done anythin' that any of us hasn't done ourselves, and we want ye to know that. We want ye to know that if ye want to be with Fionn, we won't stand in yer way. He'll be welcome here, though I don't know if yer gran will allow him overnight."

Emily felt herself blush as the heat spread through her cheeks. "Oh, Mam…"

Gran spoke up, saying, "I love ye with all my heart and it's goin' to take some time gettin' used to ye bein' a woman. It's like one day ye were a child playin' in the sand on the beach, and the next, ye were grown, lookin' for that someone to build a life with rather than buildin' sandcastles. I can't say as how I'd be comfortable with a man in yer room, but

Damian and I are not married, and ye know he's spent time here. But I must draw the line somewhere. I don't want every young man ye meet stayin' the night, if ye see what I mean."

"Gran, I'd never sleep with just anyone. Fionn is special. And yeah, he's the first fella I've slept with but that's only because none of the others meant anythin' to me. I've never wanted to do that with anyone else before. Only Fionn," she explained, hoping they'd see it had been her choice to remain celibate that determined her actions and not a lack of boyfriends.

"So ye were just bein' choosy?" asked Henry, stuffing a forkful of scrambled egg into his mouth, as if to confirm her thoughts.

"Yeah. It's not like I didn't go on dates, ye know that. It's just that I never liked any of them enough to sleep with them. They were good craic and all, but that was it."

Siobhan harrumphed through her nose. "Wish I'd had yer sensibilities when I was yer age."

"Ye didn't?" asked Henry, and received a swat from Siobhan for his efforts.

"Ye know I was wild 'til I met ye."

"And after," he said with a smirk.

"Humph," Siobhan repeated.

Emily caught her mam's eye just then and they both broke out into laughter.

"Christ, I'm glad that's settled," said Gran rising. "Who's for coffee?"

* * *

"Coffee?" asked Hank, feeling slightly guilty at seeing the lines of a sleepless night, the puffy little mounds beneath Laura's eyes. Normally her sleepless nights displayed minor bruising beneath her eyes but this was different. She'd been

229

crying as well, while he'd slept like the dead.

Laura sat down at the table and nodded as Hank poured a cup and handed it to her.

"Rough night?"

It was the wrong thing for him to say. He knew it as soon as her sleep-deprived eyes met his in an icy glare. He apologized at once. "Sorry. I know Meara wakes a lot at night and I never hear her. It was a senseless thing to say."

"It's not that," she answered as she sipped the hot brew. "It wasn't Meara so much as what you said yesterday. About staying. I couldn't sleep all night because of that, thinking it through, over and over again."

The coffee must be working its magic, he thought, because as she sipped, the strain of the night began to fade, and with it, the animosity she was surely feeling toward him. "Have you come to any conclusions?" he asked, hopeful of an answer he could embrace.

"I have. At least, I think I have."

"And?" he prompted, when she didn't speak right away.

Leaning back in her chair, the fingers of her hand following the pattern on the mug in front of her, she seemed to be mentally putting her words together, thinking of what she would say. Finally, meeting his eyes once more and sighing a sigh that held the tone of one down, but not yet out, said, "I'll agree to another couple of months. That's it. At the end of the summer, I'm going home and I'm taking the kids with me. I'll leave it up to you whether you want to go with us."

Shock ran through Hank, from his head down through his chest, pausing at his heart to pierce it painfully before exiting through his toes. The jolt set him back in his chair, leaving him temporarily speechless. Whatever came out of his mouth next had better be thought through very carefully.

"So," he began, his mind working quickly, "I should call the airlines and re-book for September?"

Nodding, Laura said, "That's conditional."

"Conditional?"

"Conditional. If we can rent a small cottage by the sea for the next couple of months, I'll stay for that long. Otherwise, we leave next week as planned."

Her face was stern. She'd drawn a line in the sand and was daring him to cross it, knowing, just knowing, he'd fail to convince her of anything else.

"Right then. Does it matter where this cottage is? Cahersiveen? Garrettstown? Dingle?"

"Not really. As long as your relatives aren't too far away. The idea is to give you some time to spend with them, forge that bond you seem to need, and to do that, we need to be accessible, both us to them and vice versa."

Hank rose to refill his cup and held up the pot in invitation. Laura finished what she had in her cup and held it out for the refill. The ice in her gaze was beginning to thaw.

He filled her cup, replaced the pot on the hob, and sat back down opposite her, placing his hand over hers and squeezing lightly. "I'll not stay behind and watch you and the weyans leave. I'll go with ye. I'll take what ye propose and be glad of it. Two months with my family is better than none at all, or the little we've had so far. I need more time, I suppose, than just these few weeks have given me. And it's thankful I am that ye've seen to givin' me a few months more."

Laura looked at him, at his hand holding hers, then back to his face. "This is going to come up again, Hank. We can't pretend it's going to go away, just because we're going to stay for a few more months. You will always want to come back. I know it, in here." She tapped her chest over her heart, and continued. "I'm just afraid, really afraid, that one day you'll come back here for good, and be lost to us forever."

He withdrew his hand, but not before another reassuring squeeze. "I can't promise I won't feel that way, but I can promise I'll never leave ye. I love ye too much for that; love them to much for that."

"I don't want you to stay with me just because of the kids. That's no basis for a good relationship."

Feeling like she'd just kicked him in the gut, Hank's voice, choked with emotion and coming out huskier than ever, said, "It's all of us. We're a family. I could never leave any one of ye. It would rip my heart out."

Hank could tell she wasn't convinced, but what more could he promise her? As much as he wanted to stay in Ireland right now, he knew, deep within his soul, that Canada would beckon eventually and he'd long for the wide-open spaces, the mountain refuge they'd carved out for themselves, and want to return. He would be forever pulled between one country and the other.

Sighing heavily, he watched as Laura rose and left the room to answer the baby's wail. Meara was just waking, and true to her nature, woke hungry every time.

Wistfully, he wondered if this tumultuous feeling would ever leave him. Would he ever be satisfied to live in one country, ignoring the tug of his heartstrings for the other? And what was it that pulled those strings? Was he hoping that he could bring back the past, see his mother and sister alive again as if nothing had ever happened? But then, he wouldn't have found his father's other family, like a missing chapter in a book he couldn't finish.

He was still deep in thought when Brandon entered the room, making a beeline for the coffee on the hob.

"Ah, good man, ye've got the important thing goin'," said Brandon, filling his cup and peering into the bottom of the now empty pot. "Hmm, guess I'd best make some more."

"Eh? Oh, yeah, Laura and I already had a couple. She's just off to feed Meara. Ryan is still sleepin'."

"Enjoy these quiet mornin's, boyo. They won't last. Soon the baby will be out of her crib and ye'll have both weyans pouncin' on yer bed to wake ye, whether ye're ready for them or not!"

"Hmm," muttered Hank, causing Brandon to stop midstream of preparing the next pot of coffee.

"Somethin' amiss?" he asked, measuring out the scoops and filling the pot with water.

"Eh? Oh, not really. I've just been thinkin' on some things."

"Such as?" They were alone in the kitchen, no one else was up yet and both men sat unshaven, similarly attired in t-shirts and loose PJ bottoms.

Hank wondered if he should say anything to Brandon. Of all of them, Brandon was most like Hank, the one to suffer the most from their da's death. Again, Hank wondered if his father hadn't died when they were all young, would his mam and sister still be alive and would he have knowledge of his other family?

Meeting Brandon's intense gaze across the table, Hank asked him, "If our da hadn't been killed, would we know each other? What do ye think? Would it have made a difference in our lives?"

Brandon clenched his jaw, his lips tightening as he thought. "I don't know, can't even guess. All I know is we all suffered in different ways, and none of it can be changed. We can only accept what's happened, how we've grown, regardless of what we want."

"I know that," said Hank, but Brandon interrupted.

"No, I don't think ye do. Not really. Ye see, Hank, we've all been shaped and formed by the way life has treated us, some good, some bad. But we've all found women, and Ciara her man, that have pulled us along, made us better, and given us new wind in our sails. We're not adrift any longer. We've purpose, and all of us, even Niall with his Michael, are havin' families. Ye must learn to enjoy what ye have in yer hand, and not look for what ye left behind."

Hank's fingers rotated the mug he was using while the coffeepot burbled its aroma into the kitchen, and Brandon rose to add fresh brew to his own mug.

"Care for more?" he asked, holding the pot aloft.

At Hank's nod, Brandon refilled it, and Hank noticed the drawing on his mug, traced it with his fingers like Laura had done. It reminded him of the Celtic knots he'd carved into the wooden chairs he'd built for his first cabin. They'd been lost in the fire that destroyed the cabin, the only surviving piece being the Claddagh ring he'd given to Laura when he proposed marriage to her that day at Ballycarbery.

"Nice mug," he said absentmindedly. "Where'd ye get it?"

Brandon sat, looked at his own mug with a similar knot carved into it, and replied, "Local potter over in Dingle. We've got a whole set of them, four in all."

"It's true, isn't it, these knots and the things they represent. Life goes on, no beginning. No end. Continuation."

"Ye're waxin' poetic today," Brandon commented, studying Hank with a sympathetic cast to his head. "What's up? Come on. Spill it."

Hank emitted something that sounded like a snort and

a humph put together, accompanied by a smirk. "I think I committed a sin," he said, and at Brandon's raised brow, added, "I asked Laura what she thought about movin' back here for a while, but she'd have none of it. Agreed to extendin' our stay if we could rent our own cottage for the summer, but that's all."

"And what do you want, mo dheartháir? What is it ye're tryin' to recapture?"

"Recapture?" asked Hank, wondering if Brandon had been listening. "I'm not tryin' to recapture anythin'. I want to get to know my extended family, let the weyans get to know each other. Not tryin' to recapture anythin'."

It was Brandon's turn to snort and smirk. "Ye're not? Seems to me ye are. Listen," he continued before Hank could interrupt, "the weyans are too little to really get to know each other yet. That'll come, and we'll make sure of it, we will. But Laura has valid reasons for not wantin' to move here. Just think on this, if ye will. Her life is in Canada, has always been in Canada. And ye moved there, thankful to leave here and relocate there. Ye struggled hard to get where ye are and now ye've three homes, a solid life, both of ye with good jobs, and ye'd leave it all for what? A country that's tryin' to recover from yet another beatin' to its economy and jobs not fallin' from the sky. We're all self-made, we are, except for Niall who works for someone else. But the truth is, ye'd be startin' all over, and what would Laura do? She'd not get the kind of job here that she has there. And the weyans, as much as ye want them to grow up Irish, would be deprived of the magnificent things Canada has to offer them."

"But they'd never get to be Irish if we stayed in Canada," argued Hank.

"Wouldn't they now? There's a great many Irish in that

country and many clubs and organizations that promote Irish culture that would beg to differ with ye. They can learn dancin', music, and all kinds of things. Surely, ye've discovered some sort of organization dedicated to Ireland back there."

Hank shrugged. He really hadn't looked.

But Brandon wasn't done yet. "And another thing. Just think of the other way around. Ye'd be deprivin' us all, the weyans included, of a chance to explore what bein' Canadian means. Ye've only thought one way but there's benefits to both. We'd welcome ye with open arms whenever the need to visit strikes. Ye know that. But the same goes for us. We want to get to know yer neck o' the woods better, to be able to visit and enjoy what yer mountain home has to offer, and more. Don't ye see?"

Leaning back in his chair, Hank ran his hands over his eyes, rubbing the tiredness out of them. Brandon made a lot of sense, and as much as he hated to admit it, he hadn't been wanting to recreate his childhood for his own children as much as he'd been looking for himself. It was time he acknowledged that. "Ye make a lot of sense." He sipped at the coffee, nearly burnt his tongue, and put the cup down again, saying, "Laura and I spoke a bit this mornin', before Meara woke up. She did say as how she'd agree to stay to end of the summer, the caveat bein' that we need our own place. She'd like a cottage by the sea, somewhere close to everyone, for visitin' and the like. Anythin' come to mind?"

"Oh," said Brandon, moving to refill his mug, "I may know of a cottage ye can have for the summer, next to Sam, over near Ballycarbery. It's not quite on the shore but it's close to here and only a drive from everywhere else."

"Doesn't Sam have a neighbor there?"

"He does, but they're leavin' for a few months and rather than shut up the house, they might be interested in havin' an income while they're away. Let me talk to him and see."

A smile spread across Hank's face as he felt a small sense of relief spread through him. It wouldn't be forever. They would leave in September, just as Laura wanted, but it would give him a chance to reconnect to this land, his family, and himself. He turned the smile on Brandon, who smiled back and patted him on the shoulder.

"It'll be alright," said Brandon, as the sounds of other people stirring in the house filtered out to the kitchen.

"Hmm," answered Hank, nodding, and then, "Let's make breakfast for our women. They're much easier to please when they've food made for them."

Brandon's smile turned to a grin. "Now ye're talkin'."

Chapter Nineteen

It was Emily's birthday, and she and Fionn were in a desolate area off the Wild Atlantic Way, at the edge of a low-lying cliff where the sea met the coast in surges of tidal spray, vicious and unrelenting on such a misty, shrouded, gray day. The wind whipped her long, raven locks about, first behind her in a stream, then across her face, the strands invading her mouth as her laughter mixed with the wind. The smell of the sea was in the gale that blew hard, then harder, howling ferociously, only to suddenly fall off to barely a whisper before gusting again.

"Hold still," chided Fionn. "I haven't got ye yet." He held up his sketch pad, gazed from Emily to the Skelligs beyond, faint images, blurred in the unrepentant mist.

The pages were getting damp but Fionn didn't care. It was the image of the moment he wanted to create.

"Ye could just take a photo," said Emily, a wry grin across her face as she pulled her hair from her mouth for the umpteenth time.

"It's not the same," muttered Fionn, intent on his sketch.

"I didn't know ye sketched," she commented, trying to peer over his hands to see the vague image of charcoal lines.

"Don't move," he scolded. "I'm almost done. I just want to get that look…"

"What look?"

"That one. That very one. The look I've now finished. But ye'll have to wait until I've done the painting to see what I'm tryin' to capture."

"I didn't know ye painted, either," she said, and then, "Can I step back from the edge now?"

Fionn looked up from his work. "Eh? Oh, yeah. Sure. Come on, let's get back in the car and go find a chipper or a pub. I'm fair famished and we could use a place to dry off as well."

"I won't argue with that one," agreed Emily, and without waiting for Fionn, ran past him and into the car, slamming the door against the mist that was turning to rain.

Fionn scrambled in beside her, tossing his sketch pad onto the rear seat, the cover wrinkled with dampness, the sketch relatively safe beneath it.

"Will it be alright?" she asked, and he seemed to know what she meant.

"I think so. The paper will dry and the sketch may be a bit skewed, but I know exactly what I want to do with it." He started the car and they drove away from the cliffs, following the Wild Atlantic Way past cottages, stone forts, and hill after rolling hill. A peat bog, partially harvested, took up a small tract of land, its deeply cut trenches a brown so dark as to be almost black in contrast to the variety of green surrounding it. Cottages were few and far between but at the top of each rise in the road, the landscape rolled out before them like the most serene pastoral setting. Only the rain marred the view.

"When did ye learn to sketch and paint?" asked Emily as Fionn steered the car around a cliffside curve and the sea stretched out wild and white-capped along the coast.

"I've always done it. Just now, though, I'm workin', trying to save enough to support myself while goin' to art school. As it is, I'm just makin' enough to take some lessons from a woman down round Garrettstown. She's got a huge home, the likes of which I'd like to own one day. Made her mark through her paintin's, and both locals and tourists buy her work. They're lovely, they are. She does mostly landscapes, so I'm learning what I can from her. But one day soon, I'll have enough set aside and then I can go to art school in Dublin."

"Dublin. It's expensive to live there," Emily commented, and Fionn couldn't disagree.

"That's why I'm savin' most of what I earn. Friends of my folks own the house where I rent the cottage. They charge me little for it, and in return while they're gone—they travel a lot—I play caretaker. Ye know it isn't anythin' fancy, and except for electricity, a bit of water, and gas for the hob, I don't need much. Once I hit Dublin, though, I'll still need to work."

She seemed to let that settle, becoming caught up in the landscape as they drove along. At a junction heading inland, Fionn turned away from the sea, now hidden behind a mountainous rise. They were heading back to Inishannon, keeping an eye out for a pub. Fionn could feel his stomach rumble.

They found one at the edge of the next village, over a narrow bridge whose original, ancient stonework still graced the sides. Majestic trees spread their leafy canopy over much of the road, just where the bakery occupied the end unit, and an inside passage led through to the pub. The smells of freshly baked goods filled the air, tickled their nostrils, and whet their appetites.

"That's a mean temptation, that is," laughed Fionn, eyeing the large Cornish pasties as he strolled past the glass cases filled with mouthwatering treats. "They get ye by showin' all this stuff, knowin' ye can't resist it, nor the pub yonder."

"Mmm, it does smell good. I'll bet there's cottage pie in the pub," she said, her delicate brows raised in expectation. "It's my favorite."

He was holding her hand as he led her through into the pub itself, the dark interior so like every other pub in Ireland, with its polished wood surfaces and tables and chairs waiting to be filled. It was Emily's eighteenth birthday, and they were going to celebrate.

"You've yer ID?" asked Fionn, making sure one more time, although he'd asked three or four times already.

"In my purse," she answered laughingly, patting the bag she carried at her side, the long strap over one shoulder leaving the tiny thing to hang on her opposite hip. Fionn gave it a second glance, and other than holding her identification and maybe a few coins, didn't think it had room for anything else.

They took a seat near the window where the rain of the day continued unabated and the small parking stalls across the road were quickly filling. The barman took their orders as he gave Emily a second look.

"I'll need to see yer ID," he said, looking suspiciously between Emily and Fionn.

"Oh, right, I have it here," she said, handing it over and watching as the man grinned and gave it back to her.

"Well then, yer first drink is on the house, and a happy birthday to ye." He gave the table a quick wipe and walked away, whistling.

Halfway through the meal, a man walked in, his raincoat dripping, and Fionn found himself face to face with Henry O'Farrell, Emily's da. Step-da, he mentally corrected himself, and then, really her uncle, followed by another thought... feck.

Henry gazed back at them, took in the two drinks on the table, and pulled up a chair. Indicating to the barman with a finger in the air, the barman pulled on the tap. Amber liquid filled the glass half way, and after the second pull, was left to sit a moment as it turned eventually to the customary black color.

"Da? What are ye doin'? Ye don't drink," Emily protested. "And why are ye here? Have ye been followin' us?"

Her question mirrored everything that Fionn was thinking, but not knowing Henry very well and being just a little in awe of his stature, those meaty fists in particular, he decided to stay quiet and see where the conversation led before jumping into the fray. This seemed to be more about Emily and Henry than himself.

"No. I'm not followin' ye. I hadn't meant to find ye here. I was repairin' a stone hearth for someone in the village and just finished. I was drivin' by when I saw what looked like Fionn's car with that one door a different color, so I came inside. At any rate, I could use a drink, I'm that thirsty."

Fionn kept his eye on Henry, waiting for whatever that man was about to do. As the barman placed the glass in front of Henry, Henry leaned across the table, his eyes locked with Emily's, and spoke quietly in a low but menacing voice. "If you drink, I drink," then picked up the glass, put it to his lips, and took a deep draught.

It was clear to Fionn that Henry wasn't prepared for the sensation of the drink hitting his gut. Fionn had learned that Henry didn't drink and never thought to question it. But obviously Henry, while he may have done his fair share of drinking at some point, hadn't done so for a long time because

242

he struggled to keep the surprised expression from his face.

"No, Da, ye can't. Mam'll have yer head!" exclaimed Emily, reaching out too late to stop the motion of his hand lifting the glass.

"I told you. If you're goin' to drink, so am I." He plunked the glass down heavily on the table and dared her to do something about it with his look.

Emily was torn, even Fionn could see that. She looked miserable and he felt wretched, knowing he'd ruined her birthday just by taking her to a pub for a drink.

Emily pushed her glass away, a mournful cast to her eyes and lips. A tear filled her eye and rolled down her cheek but was quickly dashed away with a swipe of her youthful fingers.

Henry's expression was, if Fionn was correct, that of a man who'd just done something he deeply regretted. The furrowing of his dark brows, the tightening of the lines around his mouth, all clues that Henry regretted intruding on their day.

"Emily, look at me," said Henry.

"Why? Haven't ye done enough? I'm eighteen, not eight. And this was a drink bought for me to celebrate my day, not turn me into an alcoholic."

Henry shook his head. "Emily, that's what this is about. Don't ye think I knew ye'd had lots of this when ye were a child?"

"So? It never harmed me."

"Ye don't know that. Maybe not physically but in other ways. Ye've always wanted to have some whenever it appeared at family gatherin's. It hadn't escaped my notice, nor yer Mam's. Meara did ye an injustice by feedin' it to ye when ye were so young. Ye never should have tasted it 'til now."

"What difference does it make? I'm eighteen now."

Fionn said nothing, but covered Emily's hand with his, squeezing lightly, hoping to reassure her.

Henry shook his head. "Emily, yer grandfather was an alcoholic. Yer mother was addicted to drugs. Ye don't think that perhaps ye could be addicted to alcohol with just the bit ye've had in yer life? Every chance ye got, ye were asking for some. If that hasn't set up warnin' signs, I don't know what would."

"But Da, doesn't every child ask to taste it?"

Henry couldn't disagree. "Most weyans do want to taste it, but ye already knew what it was like, and I can't help but think that the seed of addiction was planted when ye were but a babe." He pushed his drink away. One deep draught had emptied half the glass.

Fionn swallowed, hard. "I'm sorry, I didn't know. I thought it would be nice to give her a day, to show her how beautiful she is and buy her a treat," he said, taking Emily's cold hand in his, lacing his fingers through hers.

"I appreciate what ye were tryin' to do, Fionn, and I know she's fond of ye. But I'm tryin' to do what's best here and she needs to know she's followin' a slippery slope."

Emily dashed another tear from her eye before retrieving a tissue from her small purse, seemingly reluctant to let go of Fionn's hand to do so.

Henry sighed, appeared to relax a little, and said, "When Siobhan gave me the ultimatum, that it was either her or the drink, the decision was easy to make. I could live without the drink. I couldn't live without her. Or you. And that was what I was facin'. But givin' up the drink was much harder than I thought, harder than I ever could have imagined. And I'm tryin' to save ye from the same fate. That's all."

Henry sat back in his chair, his eyes studying the two of them. Emily had finished wiping her nose, her hand tucked back into Fionn's.

"Mr. O'Farrell, I had no notion of the things ye're sayin'. Em has told me of her real mam, and ye're really her uncle and Dylan is her real da. She told me that story, but nothin' about what her real mam was like." Fionn felt helpless.

Accepting Fionn's words with a nod, Henry said, "Em, I don't know how much ye remember of yer mam. She was a lovely woman when sober. But she was a different person when the drugs were in her system. I saw her steal things so she could get another fix, she didn't care what it was. She was just so desperate to take the edge off the horrible feelin' of needin' somethin' that only the drugs could provide. I was relieved of a few things that went to support her drug habit, but I refused to let it sway me in lookin' out for ye. I could easily have taken ye to the authorities and been done with ye. But once I knew ye were family, especially once I knew, then all bets were off. Ye weren't goin' anywhere without me. I love ye. Ye're mo cailín, a leanbh. Always will be."

Emily sniffed. "But what about Dylan? I'm his child, too. His biological child, and he wants to step into the role of parent. I'll not have it, Da, I won't. And I won't stand for ye to encourage him."

That seemed to make Henry sit up and take notice, his eyes widening. "When did I encourage him?"

Fionn took in Emily's brows, furrowed with emotion, and if daggers could be shot from someone's eyes, then her da would be a dead man. "At dinner that night. Ye said he was right. I should listen to him."

Opening and shutting his mouth, much like a fish on a hook, Henry reached for his drink but, stopping just short of it, drew his hand in as he clasped it with the other. "We went through this last night. I said I was sorry, and I'll say it again. I'm sorry. It was a mistake, tellin' ye to listen to him, sidin' with him if ye will. But what he said was truthful, and I couldn't say it wasn't."

"Look, Da, I know I'll not want to work in a flower shop my entire life. I may eventually figure out what it is I want, and then choose a good school. But in the meantime, I'm happy with what I'm doin', and neither you nor Dylan need to tell me what I already know. I've seen what no education does. I lived with her for nigh on ten years," she said, speaking of her real mam, Fionn knew.

"Right, then. I've said my piece, and I apologize for interruptin' yer lunch." He stood to go, throwing a few euros on the table for his drink. "Will we see ye at dinner?"

"I don't know," said Emily, her eyes downcast, her hand clutching Fionn's as if he were her anchor. Fionn was glad of it and gave her another squeeze of reassurance.

"Right. Well, Fionn, ye'll be welcome to attend. It's Em's birthday, and knowin' my mam, she'll have a good spread on the table. We're expectin' all the relatives. Ye might as well come by and see what ye're in for," he said, following it up with a half smile and a wink to Emily.

Emily didn't respond, and at that, Henry sighed as he shrugged his coat higher on his shoulders before doing it up. "I know it's yer birthday, Em," he said, stepping away from the table, "but there's family countin' on ye to be there. Whatever ye may feel about me, or Dylan and Damian, please don't stay away just to avoid them. Ye'll break yer mam's and yer gran's heart if ye do."

She looked up at him then and gave him a half smile. "I'll think on it," she said quietly.

Henry nodded, pulled up the hood on his rain jacket, and left the pub. It was still raining, still coming down as if there were no end to it, and they watched out the window as he dashed across the road, managing to avoid both puddles and oncoming traffic before climbing into his vehicle and driving away.

Fionn was first to speak. "Are ye alright? Ye're shakin' a wee bit."

Emily nodded. "Yeah, I'm alright. It's just, like…I don't know. Sometimes he can be so dictatorial. It's his way or none at all, and I get what he's sayin'. Maybe he doesn't believe me, but it's true. I know my mam had a problem. Young as I was, I saw other mams and knew the difference. I was jealous of all those other weyans out there because they had what I wanted. My mam wasn't the same as theirs. But then we'd move, I'd make new friends, kind of, and it would begin again."

"And then yer mam met Henry," Fionn finished for her.

"Yeah. He was the best thing that happened to her, only she could never give up the drugs."

"What was Henry like when he was a drinkin' man?"

Emily shrugged. "Okay, like. I was never bothered by it, but I suppose sometimes he'd come home—this was after he and Siobhan got together, mind—and it would be late, and she'd be pissed. Guess it got to be one too many. By that time they were married, and from what I understand, she meant to fight for me. Gran was on her side, so givin' up the drink really was somethin' Da had to do if he wanted to keep me."

Fionn grinned. "I think yer gran and yer mam have nads!"

That made Emily smile and he pulled her close, kissed the top of her head, and turned the closeness into a warm embrace. "Let's go back to my place and I'll show ye my

247

artwork. It's stored at the big house. There's a room at the back they let me use for paintin'."

"Sounds grand," she said, smiling up at him.

Fionn kissed her again, threw his money on the table for their lunch, and taking Emily's hand in his once more, left the pub.

Chapter Twenty

It isn't such a distance from Cahersiveen into Inishannon as I thought it would be," said Laura, craning her head around to view the two sleeping babies in the rear seat of the car.

"No. It's not far into Killarney, and then Inishannon is not as far as Cork, quite close. Actually, almost anywhere in Ireland is close," he joked, pleased to see Laura was settling in with the idea of staying longer in his home country. He was beginning to realize that while he enjoyed driving around the countryside, visiting his old haunts and showing Laura the sights, he was inwardly longing for the wide-open spaces of his mountain home and adopted country. He missed Canada.

They pulled into Kathleen's driveway, where other vehicles were already lined up. They were not the first ones here, thought Hank, and was grateful for that. He didn't know how long the weyans would behave, nor did he know what to expect in the way of provisions for them. Kathleen had said not to worry, she'd have things all set up for them, but Hank was still unsure.

Their knock on the door was answered by a smiling Damian, who welcomed them in, Kathleen directly behind him holding out her arms to take the baby. Ryan, suddenly shy, turned his face into the crook of Hank's neck and shoulder, peering suspiciously at the crowd of people.

249

And there was a crowd. Ciara and Cian were already there as well as Brandon and Aine, who had left Cahersiveen slightly before them.

Also present were Liam and Sine with their new baby, Aedan, a sweet little boy asleep in a homemade cradle on the floor beside the chair she was occupying. She looked good for having had such a rushed delivery and long recovery, thought Hank, noticing the slight lines of tiredness around her eyes. But wasn't tired a typical look for new parents? Even Liam appeared as if he could use a good kip with his growth of beard that made him look like he'd quit shaving altogether.

"It's for the new film," laughed Liam when Hank mentioned it, rubbing his thumb across his half brother's chin and pulling playfully at the stubble.

Liam knocked his hand away good-naturedly, leaving Hank with a feeling of brotherly connection. Of family.

The door opened again and Niall and Michael entered, hefting a small carrier with Dawn asleep inside it. They were both smiling, but there was a strained look to Niall's features, and Hank suddenly had the feeling that not all was as well with them as could be, although he couldn't put his finger on just what it was. Perhaps time would let that information slip, he mused.

With everyone in attendance except for Emily, it was like a cocktail party for adults, the one exception being Ryan who was busily snacking on the cheese tray left at his level.

"Leave him be," laughed Kathleen, as Hank noted another piece of cheese disappear into his son's mouth to join the other two or three pieces already in there.

"He's stuffing his cheeks like a squirrel," commented Laura, going to her son to halt a fourth piece on its way to join the others. Picking him up, she took the cheese tray and moved it out of her son's reach, then quickly grabbed a napkin to wipe his mouth and the residue of half-chewed cheese from his lips.

Another knock on the door and Dylan entered, looking a little unsure of himself. Hank, never having met the man before, thought Dylan had every right to be nervous. From what Henry had told him just last night on the telephone, Dylan had no place in Emily's life. She didn't want him there in any capacity, it seemed.

Hank wasn't sure himself what he thought of Dylan. After all, this was the man his sister had been with before she went off and took a fatal overdose. Henry hadn't said much other than Dylan had tried to get Meara to change. But was that just Dylan's side of the story, hoping to get sympathy, or was he guilty of helping Meara over the edge?

Hank didn't get any time to wonder further because Henry was guiding Dylan toward him and introducing them.

"Hank, this here's Dylan, Emily's biological da, and Meara's fella."

"Hi," said Dylan, holding out his hand for Hank to shake, a small, tentative smile on his face.

Hank looked at Dylan's hand, felt a rush of anger but swallowed it down. This was neither the time nor the place for emotional outbursts. Instead, he grasped the outstretched hand, felt the moist palm and cold fingers, and realized Dylan was just as tense as he himself felt. "Pleased to meet ye," he said, realizing, despite his initial anger, he was pleased to meet him. At least he had an answer to his sister's past, a past that had eluded him until now.

Henry left them before Hank realized he'd gone, and he and Dylan were left staring at one another like blind dates at a dance, wondering what came next.

"Was Meara with ye long?" asked Hank, and if Dylan was surprised at the abrupt start to the questioning, he didn't show it. Instead, he looked relieved, running his hands through what had been perfectly combed hair. It wasn't now, and a stray strand fell over his eyes, ignoring all attempts to paste it back where it belonged.

"Not long enough," Dylan murmured, leaving Hank to wonder on that. "I wanted her to marry me but she wanted drugs more. We'd been together just over a year when she left. I didn't know she was pregnant. God, if I did, I..." He let the sentence trail off, and it didn't take much for Hank to know just how that man felt. It was a feeling of regret so strong as to make a man crazed with grief. He'd felt it after his mam passed and Meara was nowhere to be found. But then he'd met his first Canadian girlfriend, they'd fallen in love, and he'd left Ireland for good, never able to find Meara or know how she fared. And would it have made a difference if he knew she was in trouble, that the drugs she was on would soon take her life? He would never know, and in any case, it was all in the past.

"I guess we need to talk, to fill in the gaps of the story for each other," suggested Hank, and Dylan, nodding, gestured to a less crowded corner of the room where coffee, tea, and an assortment of soft drinks were laid out.

"Jaysus, I could use a whiskey," said Dylan quietly, ruing the absence of any such thing on the tray.

Liam had obviously overheard and was at their side a moment later with a couple of glasses, each with two fingers of amber liquid. Placing a glass in each of their hands, he winked and went back to chatting with Kathleen and Damian.

"Ask and ye shall receive," laughed Hank to Dylan, sipping at the alcohol, letting its smooth aroma engulf him and the warmth of it slide easily down his throat.

Dylan nodded appreciatively. "That's better. I think I'll make it through this now," he said, a wry grin on his face.

"Does it seem such a trial?" asked Hank. They were standing at the half wall next to the drinks, where the dining room was tucked into its own room adjacent to the large kitchen, the sitting room spanned both of the others put together.

Nodding, Dylan said, "To be truthful, I almost didn't come, like. Emily has no wish to see me. I don't know what I did to turn her away. Maybe it was just her finding out we're related as we are that did it. She's had Henry as her da for so long and I don't think she ever thought she'd ever find me. I certainly hadn't ever thought I had a daughter. Never crossed my mind. And as for Meara, well, I'd wondered, over the years if she'd ever return, knowin' in my heart she never would, and likely the reason why."

"I know what ye mean," agreed Hank, nodding as he took another sip. "I left this country wonderin' if I'd ever see my sister again, kind of knowin' inside I never would. But it wasn't until Siobhan got hold of me and lured me back here, saying Emily was my daughter and needed takin' care of, that did it. She pretended she was broke, a single mam who'd lost her job and no money to pay for food and medicine. Could barely cover the rent, she said. Feckin' liar," he grinned. "She told me later she'd put the money I sent for Emily into a bank account for her, so I guess it turned out alright in that respect."

"Why didn't she just tell ye that Emily was yer niece?"

"What, and have to answer all the other questions about her now having a relationship with my half brother, who looks a lot like me but isn't, and who, at the time, I didn't know existed?"

"In a roundabout way, yeah," laughed Dylan.

Sipping again, Hank felt himself relax and silently thanked Liam for the drink. Even Dylan was beginning to lose the tense stance he'd worn when he'd first entered the house. And as Hank observed him, he found he was beginning to like the man, despite his initial anger against him. Anger, he now knew, that was entirely misplaced.

"Let's get wee Ryan fed," said Kathleen, breaking into everyone's conversation. "I'm sure Emily and Fionn will be here presently, but the weyan's gettin' hungry."

"Not by half, he isn't," laughed Hank. "He's full on cheese, he is."

"Well, let's get him started. His aunties can take their own weyans upstairs to either nurse or nap while he eats down here." Then, turning to Niall, she said, "Niall, where's the trunk of yer old toys? The one with the wee cars in it?"

"Ah, I think it's in yer shed. I'll go get it."

By the time Ryan was tucking into his dinner, the box of tiny cars had appeared and though he hadn't quite finished eating, Ryan wanted down, eager to play with the new toys.

Finally, half an hour later, Emily entered the house, a wan smile to her lips, with Fionn close behind her, observing the gathering with a cautious glance.

Immediately Kathleen enveloped Emily in her embrace, then held her out at arm's length to look her in the eye. "Ye've come. That's good. And ye've brought Fionn with ye." To Fionn, she said, "Welcome. As long as it's alright with Em, ye'll always be welcome."

Fionn mumbled his thanks in the breathless room, silent but for the sounds of Ryan, playing with the toy cars.

"Come on, all. Let's get dinner started before it shrivels to nothin' in the oven. All Damian's hard work will be goin' down the drain," she exclaimed.

"Why didn't ye say it was Damian did the cookin'? I thought it was yers so I wasn't in a rush," quipped Brandon, who received a light, backhanded slap up the back of his head for his efforts.

"Ye'll not insult yer mam that way," scolded Aine, to which Brandon only laughed.

"She expects it," he explained, shrugging.

The women automatically went to the kitchen to carry out platters of food. Even though the table was large and held as many as twelve, they'd needed more room and managed to squeeze in extra chairs so that all fifteen of them were elbow-to-elbow around the table.

Kathleen surveyed the group and smiled, taking in each face in turn. "Well, seems as if the weyans are cooperatin' with us today."

"They are," said Liam, his arm laid casually across Sine's shoulder. "That's the blessing of newborns. They sleep a lot."

Hank nodded. "Meara's down for the count, and Ryan finally caved. He's out on the sofa, snoring if I'm not mistaken."

"Ah, then it's good we never shared a room growin' up," laughed Brandon, "I'll be willin' to bet his snores are nothin' like yers!"

No one could argue that, least of all Laura. "It's true," she said, hiding her laughter behind a smile, "but an elbow in his ribs usually cures that."

"Before we start, I'd like to say a wee prayer of thanks," said Kathleen once the laughter had died down. Everyone clasped hands with the person on either side, and with heads bowed, Kathleen began. "Dear Lord, bless us this day for this gatherin' and this bounty, for the children gathered here, and for the goodwill and generosity of spirit so very present. We ask that ye favor us with yer blessing, with patience and understanding, and with the wisdom to see us through our trials. Amen."

"Amen." The murmured replies around the table brought solemn faces from their bowed positions to view each other before Brandon exclaimed, "Dibs on the end piece," and grabbed the long fork lying along the slices of ham, then took the large end piece where the skin had crackled and turned crisp.

"That's bollocks, that is, it was my turn," exclaimed Liam, and the dinner was on, the solemnity broken by the usual bantering of sibling rivalry.

"I foresee a good evenin' ahead," said Ciara, her smile bringing out the dimple in her cheek.

Plate after plate, the group soon made a dent in what had, at first, appeared to be a mountain of food. But with nine men at the table complaining of near starvation an hour before, and with the hearty appetites of the women, the mountain was soon reduced to several empty platters and few leftovers.

"I'm stuffed. That was so good," said Hank, patting his stomach and leaning back in his chair.

"Ah, ye can't be stuffed yet," admonished Kathleen. Then, nodding to Damian, everyone watched as he rose and went into the kitchen, only to return a moment later with a large, frothy confection on a tray with several lit sparklers on top. His great tenor voice began singing, and everyone joined in to sing "Happy Birthday" to Emily.

There was no hope for it, thought Hank, watching his niece, the girl who had been used as bait to lure him home, wait for the sparklers to burn down in order to pluck them out. They'd be hot, and sure enough, the thought had no sooner solidified in his brain than Emily's hand jerked back from the first sparkler, shaking it as she cried out, "Feckin' Christ, that hurt!"

They all laughed, and Henry's admonishment at her language was lost in the din. Hank, seated next to Emily, picked up her fingertips to check them out. A small blister was starting at one tip so he picked up his ice water and plunged her fingers into it, much to the surprise of everyone.

"Any neddy knows if ye burn yerself to stick it in cold water," chuckled Hank.

"And what if it's yer arse on fire?" queried Brandon, a cocky grin blazing across his face.

"Then ye jump in a lake," answered Henry, quick to join in.

Minutes later everyone was extolling the virtues of cold water and burns. Everyone, that was, except the women, who'd helped Emily cut and distribute pieces of cake to everyone.

Ciara reentered the room, having just come from the kitchen with a refilled coffee urn, and slipped behind Emily, affectionately rubbing the girl's shoulder as she passed. Immediately an image appeared, a knowledge so profound that Ciara knew in that instant that her gift had returned. Keeping the knowledge to herself, she walked on past, and after refilling her own cup as well as Cian's and anyone else's that needed it, she sat down, unable to take her eyes from Emily's smiling face. How long the girl would be smiling, she didn't know. And that left her with a quandary of global proportions. At least, it felt like that. Would she tell her niece what she foresaw, or would she keep mum and let the future unfold on its own? She'd never been faced with such a decision before, since almost all of her glimpses into someone else's life had been easily shared with the family. But this…she wasn't sure about sharing this.

Dylan was faced with a decision of his own. He'd been quiet most of the meal, and although the talk had been general, he'd contributed little, nodding in agreement now and then or remaining silent if he had an opposing opinion. He didn't want to be there, would rather have sailed to France or flown off somewhere forever. But no. He'd been dutiful to his father, a man he cursed and blessed, because if it hadn't been for Damian's affection for Kathleen, Dylan would still be ignorant of the daughter he now knew was his.

His daughter, who possessed the haughty air of his estranged mother, though she didn't know it. A woman who, in Dylan's hazy recollection, could put him down with a look that silenced him immediately. And once he'd figured that out, that Emily held such power over him, he knew he could never be the father she deserved. It was like looking at a cherished object in a potter's workshop, knowing he'd created it but having no more say in her life than that of the potter watching his work leave the shop in someone else's hands.

As for Emily, slightly across the table and down a chair from Dylan, she'd rarely looked at him. And when she did, that cool, disdainful expression was there, as if she wished him to disappear from the face of the earth. At those times, Dylan simply averted his gaze, pretending her cool demeanor held no sway over him. Inside, he was that little boy again, abandoned by his mother who cared only for herself.

A shrill cry was heard from upstairs and both Niall and Michael cast their faces toward the baby's wail. "Ah, that would be ours," said Niall, rising. "My turn, I think." He left the dining room, heading up the stairs, leaving Michael to finish his coffee.

258

"Tonight's his night for getting up. I was on shift last night," joked Michael.

"Ah well, ye've neither one of ye's got the right parts to do what the women do, so it's no matter which of ye gets up, does it?" said Brandon, laughing.

"I've the right parts, they just don't work the same," Michael corrected his brother-in-law.

"Now that's the truth," Liam chimed in.

Dylan stayed quiet, wondering if he'd ever be in their shoes. Would he ever find a woman as fine as Meara had been when she wasn't on drugs? She'd been his ideal mate, and for a time after first meeting Emily and before knowing of their connection, had thought he'd found that woman again. Suddenly finding out she was his daughter had been a shock to his sensibilities. He'd been about to ask her out on a date, even as young as she was, because he thought her to be what he was looking for.

And then all hell had broken loose in his guts when the knowledge of their relationship surfaced. He'd been disgusted with himself, hated himself for where his mind had gone, and hadn't yet forgiven himself for his carnal thoughts. Because if he was honest with himself, those thoughts still lingered. He still thought of her as very fine, and what kind of a man did that make him? He didn't deserve such a child as Emily.

One by one, the weyans were brought downstairs as they woke and needed feeding or coddling. They were all babes, all except wee Ryan, who, having woken from a prolonged nap, was guaranteed to run his parents ragged until strapped into his car seat for the long ride home. His sister, Meara, was once again asleep, tucked into her car seat after having her meal. Laura was beginning to show signs of wanting to sleep as well, and Hank thought it the perfect time to give

Emily her gift. Other presents were stacked on the table and she'd begun opening them slowly, oohing and aahing over each one. Slipping his hand inside the diaper bag where he'd placed the envelope, he pulled it out now and handed it to her, saying, "Happy birthday, mo chroi."

Smiling, she took the envelope and opened it, drawing out the notice and scanning it quickly before jumping up and throwing her arms around Hank's neck. With her face buried into his shoulder, Hank felt her tears and knew he was choking up himself.

"Thank ye, Uncle Hank, oh, thank ye!" she exclaimed, seeming to ignore the pleas of the gathering to share her knowledge.

Stepping back and wiping her eyes, she said through a broad grin, "It's a paid flight to Canada to visit, any time I want!"

Brandon, the cheekiest of them all, was not to be kept quiet. "Ah, so that'll get ye there…how will ye get home?"

"Neddy," said Emily with a laugh, "it's for both ways."

"Ye're just jealous," Liam accused Brandon. "Ye had so much fun when ye were there before, ye were hopin' to do it again."

Brandon nodded, "That may be truer than ye know."

"This time next year, in Canada," cried Hank, and the O'Farrell brothers joined in with cries of "alright!" and "can't wait!"

Fionn, noted Hank, like Dylan was very quiet. If anyone felt out of place in the room, it would be those two, looking like interlopers the way they held themselves apart, and it was Hank's sense of family, of bringing people together, that prompted him to say, "I'd like to invite everyone, including you, Fionn, if Emily wants ye, and you Dylan, as part of the family. We're all here because of Emily, and I think we should recognize that."

Hank noted the sullen expression on Emily's face directed Dylan's way but he also couldn't deny seeing Fionn's face break into a broad smile and a wink to Emily as he squeezed her hand affectionately. It was Dylan, uncomfortable and fidgeting, who Hank knew would take some time to resolve.

"Laura and I would like to stay longer but it's time we had the weyans in the car and were on our way," said Hank, standing. With goodnights all around, Hank, Laura, and the two children were soon rolling down the driveway for the long drive back to Cahersiveen.

"We should go, too," said Brandon with a nod to Aine, who didn't disagree.

"It's been a lovely time and dinner was grand, thanks," said Aine, her gaze on Emily as she continued, "Emily, if ever a young lady looked perfect to be eighteen, it's you. God bless ye, my dear, and a happy birthday to ye, once again." Aine hugged Emily close, kissed her on both cheeks, then waited at the door as Brandon came up to do the same. And as quickly as Hank and his crew had left, Brandon and Aine were gone, too.

Michael glanced at Niall, but before he could utter a word, Niall said, "Michael and I need to tell ye somethin', so if ye don't mind stayin' a bit, we'd appreciate it. Should've said it before the others left, but, well…"

Michael gave Niall a look that questioned his motives, though Niall was certain his husband knew exactly what was about to be said.

"I found somethin' out earlier that I think ye'll all find interestin', and we want ye to know it's how we mean to go on."

261

"Niall," Michael broke in, "this isn't the time…"

Niall ignored him. "If not now, Michael, then never, and it'll come out eventually. Why not now?"

"Why wait until Hank and Brandon had left? Why not keep them here so everyone hears at once how stupid I was, how self-serving?" Michael cried.

"I just said…" Niall began, but his mam shushed the argument before it could begin.

"What's amiss?" she asked, leaning forward in her chair.

"Nothin', Mam," said Niall, struggling to keep calm. "It was a sore point between Michael and me, but we're through it now. Least, I think we are."

Michael sighed heavily and sat back with a look that admitted defeat.

"Right, then," Niall continued. "It's about Dawn."

"She's alright? Surely?"

"Yes, Mam, she's fit as a fiddle." There was a hesitation as he took in his husband's countenance, at the tight lips and downcast eyes, and said, more softly and with a tenderness to his words, "She's also Michael's natural child."

Exclamations of "what?" went round the room but were quickly silenced by Kathleen's admonitions of, "Whisht, everyone! Let him speak."

Nodding his thanks as everyone quieted down, Niall began the explanation of Dawn's similarity in looks to Michael. "Even I began to notice the similarity and it was confirmed when I found that invoice in the drawer," he finished.

"So what's this, then, the way ye mean to go forward?" asked Liam.

Michael picked up the story and continued. "Niall's right. We had words over what I'd done, and I was very sorry I'd kept things from him but my intentions were honorable. I'd wanted to surprise him with a gift, as rare and as precious as any gem could be. And when Farrah agreed, she and I got together and that was that. She told me once, when she was about six months along, she was enjoying pregnancy, and if we ever wanted a second child, she'd be up for it."

"But what about her folks?" asked Henry. "Aren't they the traditional kind? The kind that keep their daughters under lock and key until a suitable marriage can be made?"

Michael nodded his agreement. "That's true. But I think she's doing okay. We haven't heard from her for a bit, but hadn't expected to, either."

Kathleen was still looking perplexed and, if Niall wasn't mistaken, worried as well.

"It's okay, Mam," he said, "We've time. Dawn is only a few weeks old. She won't need a sibling for a couple of years." Niall grinned, hoping his relaxed attitude would put his mam at ease.

"Well, I'm gobsmacked by it all," said Henry, shaking his head. "I thought the adoption was one thing, now it turns out it's another. But in this case, I suppose the end has justified the means, as they say. It's grand. She's a beautiful baby and ye're both very lucky. And Niall, when it's yer turn, ye'll maybe have Michael help ye out."

Niall turned the color of the crimson cushion he was leaning against, while Michael, true to form, guffawed.

"Ah, feckit," said Niall, "that was too personal and if it was told to a woman, ye'd be the first one there to redeem her honor."

"That may be so, but ye're no woman and I've always enjoyed gettin' the better of ye," Henry finished, laughing. "Fine, then. I apologize. It was a wee bit below the belt," he said, then laughed all the harder for his double entendre.

"There's young'uns present," admonished Kathleen. "Mind yer tongues."

Emily and Fionn, both listening with keen ears, merely grinned at each other, clearly enjoying the discomfort of her uncles. Despite the subject matter, the easy banter had relaxed the crowd, and even Dylan had begun to ease up. He'd had another whiskey, compliments of Henry, and was feeling genuinely mellow. So much so that he addressed Emily directly, something he hadn't done all evening long.

"Emily, if I may say a few words?" he asked her, and was met with the look he was quickly growing accustomed to.

But then her face softened as if she reconsidered. "Sure. What is it ye have to say?"

Dylan licked his lips nervously, looking at his hands fiddling with the paper napkin in his lap. He'd finished his drink and had wiped his lips but now his mouth felt dry, as dry as the napkin he was crinkling and smoothing, crinkling and smoothing. Forcing himself to move as naturally and steadily as possible, he placed the crinkled napkin in the empty glass. Any more whiskey and he wouldn't be worth talking to at all.

"I haven't handled our relationship at all well," he began, and heard Emily's muttered words of, "Got that one right," but ignored them and carried on. "I hadn't meant to intrude in the relationship ye have with those ye call Mam and Da. I know I will never take their place in yer heart, and never intend to. I only would like a relationship with a young woman whose mother I loved so very much. But I didn't know how to go about it. I was gobsmacked at finding I had a daughter in the first place. In all honesty, I didn't know what to say, how to act, and in the doin', came across badly. So if ye'll forgive me, I'd like to try again."

At the mention of Emily's true mam, tears started in her eyes, and if anyone there couldn't guess why, they would have to be made of stone.

"Em," said Henry, taking her suddenly cold hands in his big, warm clasp, "I can tell ye're missin' yer mam just now, and that's as it should be. But though ye've lost her, ye've gained the knowin' of who yer real da is, and that's worth somethin'. Siobhan and I are here for ye and always will be as long as we are able. We're proud to have ye call us Mam and Da, proud to say ye're our daughter. But ye're also Dylan's daughter, and another father figure to look out for ye, not interferin', mind," this said with a sideways glance at Dylan, "isn't a terrible thing. Give it some time. Give him a chance as he's asked. We all love ye so much, we only want what's best for ye."

Emily withdrew her hands from Henry's clasp, taking the tissue Fionn held out for her, and wiping her eyes and nose, said, "Yeah, I'm missin' my real mam, though I haven't for so many years. Don't know why I'm doin' it now," she exclaimed, laughing despite her tears.

"This is a milestone for ye," said Siobhan, who had been quiet for most of the evening, letting the night be Emily's alone.

"I suppose," Emily agreed. Then turning to Dylan, said, "I'm sorry, too, Dylan, for the way I acted. It was a shock, learnin' I had a real, biological da. To me, that was like a fairytale, somethin' that couldn't exist in real life. Yet here ye are, as real as anythin'. Da's right. Uncle Henry, that is, is right. I'm lucky to have not one but two das, and if the both of ye can get along, then so can I. But there's one thing ye'll need to turn a blind eye to," she said, looking sternly at Dylan as if to pin him to the chair he was molded into.

"And what would that be?" he asked tentatively.

"Ye'll pay no mind when I walk into the pharmacy and pick up my pills."

"Pills?" asked Liam, and got an elbow in his ribs from Sine for his efforts.

"Birth control," Sine hissed, unfortunately, loud enough for everyone to hear.

No one said anything for the space of a few heartbeats and Dylan's crimson face became darker if it was at all possible.

The room vibrated with an audible gasp, and Siobhan, a portrait of incredulity, ground out, "But ye're a good, Catholic girl!"

Unwilling to be limited by the bonds of a religion she only lightly catered to, Emily put on a brave face. "Mam, ye know I love ye, and ye know I'd never do anythin' to hurt anyone, but this is the twenty-first century, and I'll not bring an unwanted child into it. I know what it's like to be dragged around by a parent unprepared for the role they must now play. I won't have it. Gran got me an appointment with a specialist who'll write me a script for them."

"But the Pope has sanctioned rubbers. Why don't ye use them?" Siobhan asked, ignoring Kathleen's complicity in the scheme.

"They don't always work," Emily said. "I'll not end up like my mam, dead too early and leavin' a child behind." She felt the tears begin again, but not before Dylan's hand reached out to cover hers.

"I promise," he eventually got out, "not to say a thing, not to give ye any kind of look with a hidden meaning when ye come in for the pills. In fact, if my coworker is there, I'll let her handle it all. Ye have my solemn word on it."

He sat back into the chair, a little straighter, and the flush on his face began to fade.

"Ye're certain?" Emily queried him, her nose in the air.

"Absolutely," said Dylan.

"Fine…" she began.

"Ah, there's that word," exclaimed Liam. "When a woman says 'fine,' ye'd all best watch out." Again he got the jab in his ribs for his efforts but the tension in the room had broken, and Fionn stepped up, holding out his hand for Emily.

"We're off," she said, as some hidden communication flitted between them. "I want to thank everyone for comin', for givin' me a birthday celebration I'll not forget. And thanks, Gran and Damian…or should I say Grandda…for a lovely dinner. It really was grand and I'm glad I came."

Emily and Fionn moved to the door, waving goodbye amid admonishments to drive safely, when Henry's voice boomed through all the rest. "And be home by midnight," he called.

Emily turned around, gave him the look every teenager from every country knew by heart, saying only, "Humph," before Fionn closed the door behind them, leaving the group with a grin and a wink.

"Cheeky pup," said Henry, but no one took him seriously.

Ciara, who had been quiet the entire time, said, "Just to let everyone know, she's goin' to be fine, she is. It's the in between that'll get rough." The more she'd thought about it, the more she thought her premonition was something she could share.

All heads turned to her in question.

"What the hell is that supposed to mean?" asked Henry. "I thought ye'd lost the sight."

"I had," agreed Ciara, "but tonight, I felt somethin' as I brushed past Emily at the table, and although it isn't clear

267

exactly what it is, at least, not yet, it is clear that somethin' is goin' to happen."

"Is it bad?" asked Kathleen.

"I suppose it depends on yer definition of bad. I look at it as life. Sometimes it's good and sometimes it isn't, but we all get through it."

"Feckit, Ciara, that doesn't tell us anythin'," swore Henry.

Ciara only shrugged. "It's all I can give ye for now."

Niall and Michael stood, the rounded bundle of the baby perched on Michael's shoulder, sound asleep.

"We need to go to bed, get the weyan tucked in," said Niall as Michael patted Dawn's well-padded rump. The baby snuggled farther into his neck and the sound of her sucking her fist could be heard in the quiet of the room.

Henry and Siobhan rose to leave for their ride back to Killarney. "Thanks for the supper, Mam, ye outdid yerself once again," said Henry, and no one could argue that point except Kathleen.

"Well, a lot of it was Damian, wasn't it, love," she said, winking at Damian as he stood beside her, his arm around her ample waist.

"No matter," continued Henry, "it was all good and ever so fillin'. Can't say that about my own cookin'."

Siobhan laughed. "I won't argue with that, although ye do try."

Henry merely shook his head as he allowed her to precede him out the door and then they were gone.

After saying their farewells, the room seemed suddenly larger, infinitely quieter, leaving only Liam and Sine, Ciara and Cian, and the lads in the room with Kathleen, Damian, and Dylan. As their homes were a greater distance, the three couples had been invited to stay the night.

"Anyone for coffee or tea?" asked Damian, getting up to take some dishes into the kitchen.

"Not for me, da," said Dylan, rising. "It's been an interestin' evenin', and I'm thankful to have been invited and glad I came. Havin' Emily accept me, even just a little, was more than I could have asked for."

"Ye'll always be welcome here," said Kathleen, while Damian, his arm still around her waist, agreed.

"It was good ye came," he said to his son, and as Dylan thanked them again and left, they all breathed a light sigh of relief that the evening had gone so well.

"It could all have backfired," observed Liam.

"It could," agreed Kathleen, "but I know my granddaughter. She's strong-willed but sensible. And she hates to go against anything Henry says."

"Did he tell her she had to come?" asked Liam.

"Not really. He only told her she'd be disappointin' a lot of people if she didn't show. I guess she listened. Now, about that tea?"

Chapter Twenty-One

Dylan had just opened the pharmacy the following day when a woman walked in, looking a little lost the way she was scanning the shelves. Appearing undecided, she merely stood, looking around the pharmacy as if it held all the answers.

Taking in her stature, Dylan knew he'd never seen her before. She was dark-haired, a lovely tanned complexion that he realized was not a tan but her true skin tone. Her figure, a little thick around the waist, didn't detract from her beauty, for beautiful she was. Especially her eyes. They weren't brown but a deep moss green, and so striking with her black lashes that Dylan had to stop himself from staring. Instead, he came out from behind the counter, down the two steps to the main floor of the pharmacy, and approached her, smiling.

"Can I help ye? Is there somethin' ye're lookin' for?"

The woman smiled back. She was not tall, Dylan noted, and thought she couldn't be more than a hundred and sixty centimeters, give or take. Her smile lit up her eyes and Dylan's heart thudded.

"Not something, really," came the heavy London accent, "but a someone. I'm looking for an address but I can't seem to find it and as it's early yet, this is the first place I've seen that's open. I was hoping you could help."

"Ah, yeah, I do open early and stay late. Lots of folks

travel through here, needin' all kinds of things at an hour where there's no other help."

"Well, I for one, am certainly glad you're here, then," she replied, rolling her eyes in a semblance of relief.

"So, who is it ye're tryin' to find?"

She looked confused, as if she wasn't certain, and her words said as much. "Actually, I'm not sure if I have the name right. I understand there's a woman by the name of Kathleen O'Farrell who lives somewhere in this area, but I don't have her address. And in any case, I'm not really looking for her, but for her son."

"Mrs. O'Farrell? Yes, I know her well." Dylan silently excused himself because he didn't know Kathleen all that well, but having had dinner at her home the night before, felt he was permitted to say so. "And which son would ye be lookin' for?"

"Which son?"

"Well, she's got four and a stepson, and as some are in town and some aren't, ye'll need to be specific."

"Oh, I hadn't realized," she began and then said, "Niall. It's Niall and his partner, Michael. They're who I would like to see."

A smile split Dylan's lips as the door chime went off, indicating someone entering the store. He acknowledged the person with a nod, saying, "That's my coworker. Now that she's here, I can show ye to the house if ye'd like, it's not hard to find. Do ye have a car? A map?"

"I do," said the woman, "both a car and a map. Only, I have no idea where I'm supposed to go, only that Niall and Michael are here, visiting their mother."

"Well then, let's have a look at yer map."

She took him out to the car and pulled out the map of

271

Ireland and Dylan laughed. "Ye'll never find it on there," he said jovially. "Give us a moment, I'll be right back."

He dashed back into the shop and was out again in minutes, a small pamphlet in his hand. Opening it up, he pulled out his pen and began to draw on the local map inside it. "We are here," he said, indicating the shop with an X on the paper. Then, drawing the line along the road she needed to follow, said, "And when ye come to the crossroads here, ye carry on straight and it's a wee bit up here. Not far. I can walk it in twenty minutes."

"Oh, I see," she said, and looking at him, grinned a heart-stopping expression of thankful relief. "Thank you so much," she exclaimed, and holding out her hand to shake, said, "and whom shall I say helped me out?"

"Dylan's the name. Dylan Lynch."

"Oh, you're the pharmacy owner?" she asked, looking up at the sign on the window that read "Lynch's Pharmacy."

"Yes, that's me," replied Dylan proudly.

"I'm Farrah. Farrah Nassar."

If Dylan's smile could broaden any more it would have split his face in two. As it was, it was ear to ear and he was reluctant to let her hand go. "I don't know how long ye're plannin' to stay, but if ye find yer way back here anytime soon, I'd be pleased to buy ye coffee or lunch if ye've a mind," he said, hoping she wouldn't find him too forward.

"Thank you, that's a lovely invitation. I don't know how long I'm staying, though. But if I do end up back here, I'll be sure to stop in."

Nodding, Dylan realized it was as good as he was going to get by way of a reply, and reluctantly letting her hand go, waved her on her way.

* * *

Farrah checked the rearview mirror as the man on the road grew smaller and then retreated back inside the pharmacy. She wondered if she would have the nerve to go back, remind him of his invitation, and maybe enjoy his company for a while. She liked him, thought him cute, and felt comfortable with him, even though they'd only just met. Then turning her attention back to the road, followed the directions he'd sketched on the small map inside the pamphlet until she came to the house she sought.

It was a grand house on a bit of a rise, the driveway curving slightly upward. The hedge surrounding the front garden needed trimming but other than that, the home was in good order. And as early as it was, the draperies in one of the main rooms were pulled back and she could see someone moving about. At least she wouldn't be waking anyone, she thought as she parked her car and went up to the door.

Her knock was answered by a middle-aged woman, blonde and slightly rotund. The face, however, was as familiar as if she'd known her all along. Niall bore the same look, the same intense gaze and broad cheekbones, for all his hair was black.

"Mrs. O'Farrell?" she asked timidly, and the when the woman replied in the affirmative, she introduced herself. "I'm Farrah Nassar. I was hoping to find Niall and Michael. Are they here?"

Instantly, Niall's face appeared behind his mother's and Farrah breathed a sigh of relief, felt tears come to her eyes, and before she could comprehend what was happening, was ushered into the room as the outer door closed tightly behind her.

"Farrah, my God. What's amiss?" asked Niall.

Farrah took in the cloth on his shoulder and the mewling

of the baby in the bassinette and felt new tears erupt. Impulsively, she put her arms around Niall and cried into his shoulder, letting out the trials of the last few weeks with every tear she shed.

Eventually, the tears slowed and she gradually gained control of herself.

"I didn't know what else to do," she sniffed, gratefully accepting the tissue from Niall's mother. "Thank you," and blew her nose and wiped at a tear that rolled down her cheek. "I'm sorry to be a bother, I just didn't know where else to go."

"Damian, will ye put the kettle on the hob, please. I think we need some fresh tea." Kathleen led her to a settee and helped her settle in. "Now, how's yer health? Are ye healed from the birth?" she asked, and Farrah was surprised at her question.

"The birth? Oh, yes. I am. At least, I think everything is fine, thank you for asking."

Niall sat on the hassock in front of her and took both her hands in his. "So, what's amiss? Ye look like ye've had a rough time of it and I'm all for makin' ye feel more at ease. So what can we do to help?"

Tears began again. Farrah couldn't help them as they trickled down her cheek, and grabbed at a tissue from the box that magically appeared beside her.

"It's my father. He tried to make me a prisoner inside the house but I escaped. I drove up to Wales to take the ferry across, thinking to find you in Dublin, but no one answered my knock and I had no choice but to try to find you. All I remembered was you once telling me your mother's name and that you had lived in Inishannon before moving to Dublin. It was just lucky I found someone who knew how to reach you."

Niall looked nonplussed but Farrah was too keyed up to stop talking. "I got the night ferry from Holyhead, thinking that if I went up that way my father wouldn't know where to look. No doubt he'd think I took a plane over here, and I would have if I thought for one minute he wouldn't concoct some scheme to stop me. So I headed to Wales and took the ferry instead."

"I'm glad ye did. I can't imagine havin' parents like that, interested only in keepin' ye under lock and key. It's not right."

Niall's mother brought in the tea on a small tray, a creamer and sugar container standing next to a teapot, the empty cup and saucer with the spoon alongside. "Here ye go, luv," she said to Farrah, and Farrah heaved a choked sigh.

"Thanks so much, Mrs. O'Farrell…"

"It's Kathleen. I'm not one to stand on ceremony here. None of us are."

"Kathleen, then. Thank you. I didn't know what to expect…"

"Never ye mind. Ye've been through a lot and we've room here. I can put ye in with Emily for a time until the others leave, which will be tomorrow. Em didn't come home last night, guess she stayed with Fionn, so we can have ye settled in no time at all."

Farrah didn't know who Kathleen was talking about but the fact that she didn't need to go anywhere else suited her just fine.

"Good heavens, Farrah!" exclaimed Michael as he came down the stairs looking slightly sleep-tousled and handsome as ever.

"Hi," she said, feeling suddenly unsure. She'd known Michael for so long, had no idea if anyone knew the truth of what they'd done to conceive the baby, and now that she was here, hoped no one would think she was looking for a relationship with him.

"Are you alright, luv? You've been crying." He approached her with sympathy and concern marring his features, creating a frown between his brows.

Niall poured some tea for her.

"Any more of that?" asked Michael, pointing at the pot.

"There's lots of tea in the pot, and coffee in the kitchen if ye'd prefer. I'll get ye another cup," said Damian.

"I think tea, that's brilliant, Damian. Thanks," he said, sitting down beside Niall, making him scoot over on the hassock after pouring Farrah's tea.

"Why are you here?" asked Michael.

Niall broke in before Farrah could speak. "She's run away from her tyrant of a father who wants to keep her prisoner in his house."

"Actually, I think he wanted to send me to Egypt, to live with his brother's family and be their servant. He said that's all I'm good for now."

The astonished looks on everyone's faces didn't come as a surprise but Niall's next question did.

"Did he say anythin' about the baby? About wantin' her or wantin' to take her?'

"What? No," she said, shaking her head. "No. He never mentioned the baby at all, only that I was a slut and not good for marriage or anything other than being a servant."

"And what about yer mam?" asked Damian. At least, she thought that was his name. Kathleen had called him that.

"My mother doesn't have a say. She has to follow everything he says or it'll go worse for her. I really think my father is losing his mind. He never used to be like this," she explained. How could she tell them the kind of man he used to be, so loving, so caring, and then suddenly, as if a switch had been flicked, overnight he'd turned into something very different.

"Has he been this way long?" asked Kathleen.

"He's always been overly protective of me," she began, remembering how he'd badgered her for simply speaking with Michael, "but he's been getting steadily worse over the past couple of years. It got really bad a year ago last Christmas. We, that is, my mother and I, were in the kitchen Christmas Eve, getting a head start on Christmas dinner for the next day. Mum wanted to go to church that night, and I did, too. It had been a while since we'd attended the midnight service, and while Daddy would never go, he'd always wave us off cheerfully and look for some sports to watch on the telly until we returned. Only it never happened that night. He stood at the doorway, forbidding us to leave the house, and told us to go to bed. He refused to let us make any further preparations and forbade us from cooking up a Christmas dinner. From then on, we ate only traditional dishes. He absolutely forbade everything else."

"Was there no clue, no indication he was goin' to flip like that?" asked Kathleen.

Farrah shook her head. There had been none until she recalled a heated argument he'd had over the phone. "It was his older brother," she stated, "the one he wanted to send me to. I think his brother is jealous because Daddy has the good life in England, and his brother isn't enjoying the same thing in Egypt. Anyway, I don't know if that's what started it but it's become intolerable, and I don't know how long my mother can take being there, either. I just knew I had to get out while I could."

"What about the fella of the peerage that yer da wanted ye to wed?" asked Niall.

"I want to know why or how you ended up back at home when we'd set you up here?" put in Michael, casting his gaze back and forth between Farrah and Niall.

"I'm sorry, I seem to have left some things out," Farrah apologized.

"Never ye mind, dear, just take it easy, like," said Kathleen, looking concerned and more than a little maternal.

Farrah swallowed some of the tea, closed her eyes, and gathered herself to begin. "I hadn't intended to go back with them to England after the baby was born, but Mum was so insistent and Daddy apologized, said it was just the shock at finding I'd given birth and the circumstances and everything. I thought he'd had a change of heart and they were both ever so nice on the way home. But once there, I was locked in my bedroom, literally confined to my room. Mum brought meals up on a tray and that was the only contact I had with anyone since the baby's birth. I couldn't ring anyone because I'd left my phone downstairs when I first got in. But then as soon as I got upstairs to my room, they locked the door behind me, and I couldn't get out."

"That's unconscionable!" Michael's raised voice was quickly hushed as the sounds of a crying baby and footsteps could be heard above. In a quieter voice, he said, "And what about the old codger? The one they wanted you to marry?"

Shaking her head, Farrah said, "I don't know. Perhaps the deal fell through because I think Daddy's brother was putting pressure on him again. The phone seemed to ring a lot and whenever Mum opened my door, I could hear Daddy downstairs, talking to someone. I asked Mum, but she wouldn't tell me anything."

Ever the mother looking after her children and any others that had tagged along, Kathleen asked, "Have ye had anythin' to eat yet? We've just put breakfast on the table, Damian and I, and there's lots here," she suggested, the invitation with a wave of her hand indicating the laden table.

Feeling her stomach grumble in hunger, Farrah smiled and said, "I would be delighted to share whatever you have. I haven't eaten since leaving home. I've been driving like a maniac since arriving in Dublin to get here. I didn't want to stop anywhere, just in case my father was tracking my movements."

"Hmm," mused Kathleen. "Well, come and eat, all of ye. The rest will be down shortly. I can hear them stirrin'."

By the time everyone had arrived downstairs—at least, Farrah thought it was everyone—the table was full and a breakfast fit for a king had been laid out on platters of various sizes.

"I had five children in all," explained Kathleen when Farrah remarked on the size of the table, "and enjoyed entertainin', so we bought this table years ago, and ever so glad we did. It's come in handy, it has, especially now when everyone is wed, and young Emily havin' a boyfriend."

"Speakin' of Emily, is she home?" asked Liam, not having been present earlier when his mam had mentioned where she was.

"No. Stayed with Fionn is my guess, now the cat's out of the bag," she joked.

"It's good Henry's not here, then," said Liam, but there was a smile on his face and Farrah got a glimpse of what Niall would look like if he ever chanced one. It seemed Niall didn't smile much, but Michael had explained his personality to her one day while they were discussing her situation, early on. Of Niall, he'd said only that while his smiles were rare, they were all gold, meaning, Farrah supposed, that his smiles were genuine and heartwarming and given only when special circumstances rose. She hoped to be the recipient of one at some point.

They were at the end of the meal, and as meals went, this one had taken a long time, with people lingering at the table, coming and going, and the endless pots of coffee and tea. Farrah couldn't remember having felt so full, both physically and emotionally. If ever she could meet a man whose family encompassed this kind of warmth, she'd snatch him up immediately.

But that didn't seem possible, especially not now, not when she'd just given birth to a baby she'd given up for adoption. As if her thoughts called to her daughter, the baby began to mewl, squirming in her carrier, hungry again for the next feeding.

Michael excused himself to check on his child, and Farrah suddenly felt as if she were intruding. It wasn't a good idea for her to be here, so close to the child she'd birthed only weeks ago. It tugged at her heartstrings, brought a heaviness to her breasts where her milk flow had not quite abated, and brought her close to tears. Choking them back, she took what she hoped was an invisible deep breath and resumed the conversation at the table while Michael carried the baby upstairs. So, perhaps he knew it was difficult for her. He was perceptive that way, she knew.

A knock on the door, and at Kathleen's cry to "come in," Dylan strode through, his eyes immediately alighting on Farrah.

"Ah, good, ye found the place, I see," he said.

Farrah felt her face grow warm as she caught his eye.

"Yes. I've been invited to stay. You never said how welcome they would make me feel," she explained, encompassing the table with a wave of her hand, taking in those present and the remnants of food.

"Coffee or tea?" offered Damian, and at Dylan's nod toward the coffeepot, poured out for him.

"Ah, grand, Da, that's grand." The chair next to Farrah was vacant and Dylan wasted no time in sitting down beside her.

"Ye two have met, then, have ye?" asked Niall, casting a raised brow to Liam, who was eyeing Dylan and Farrah outright.

"Oh, yeah. I suppose she never said. She came into the pharmacy this mornin', looking for directions. And as I knew the both of ye were here, Niall, I was able to help her out."

"We're very glad ye did, Dylan. Seems Farrah's got some difficulties in England she needs to steer clear of," explained Kathleen.

"Oh?" asked Dylan, looking at Farrah.

Again, Farrah felt herself blush under his gaze but was glad of his presence, and without confusing him with too much detail, regaled him with her story.

"Good God," Dylan swore after hearing the tale, "has the man not entered the twenty-first century yet?"

"She'll stay with us until we can find her a place of her own," said Kathleen, "It's no bother, none at all."

Dylan seemed to think a moment and then offered a different solution, one Farrah thought she might enjoy.

"If her da is lookin' for her in Ireland, sure he'll look up every O'Farrell in the book and land here eventually. But I've an extra room and my cottage is tucked away, like, not near any main road, and there's a wee river behind it with lots of trees. It's a place to make any heart heal and I'd be very pleased to have ye stay as long as ye'd like," he said.

Farrah couldn't believe her luck and tried to hide it behind a hesitant smile. "That's lovely, but Mrs. O'Farrell, I mean Kathleen, has offered me a room here."

Kathleen put her hand on Farrah's arm, a soft, reassuring squeeze. "What Dylan says, though, is believable; and from what I've heard of yer da so far, he'll likely come lookin', and if not himself, then he'll send someone else. No. Dylan's got the right of it. Ye'll still be welcome here if that's what ye want, but I'd rather see ye safe, at least until this is all over."

"But will it ever be over?" asked Niall.

Farrah hung her head, felt tears start in her eyes, and once again choked them away. "No. Never. Not until he's laid in the ground. He'll never stop."

"What if ye were to wed?" Niall continued. "If ye were wed, then he'd have to listen to yer husband because that's the way his culture works, isn't it?"

"Yes and no. I'd be my husband's property, but, in Daddy's mind, only if it was a husband he chose for me, and that's not likely to happen."

"But he can't get to ye here, surely," remarked Damian.

Farrah could only shrug. "Dylan's right. It's possible he'd look up every O'Farrell in Ireland in order to find me."

"Never ye mind, luv," said Kathleen in her soothing, mother's voice. "We'll think of somethin'."

"So," said Dylan, "ye'll come stay with me, then?"

"If you don't mind," answered Farrah, "I think I'd like that a lot."

Liam and Niall exchanged glances once more, Farrah noted, but didn't care. She'd already had a child. Her father already thought she'd had sex with someone and hadn't listened when she'd said it had been through in vitro fertilization. He couldn't understand how any woman could become pregnant just to help fulfill a wish for a man she didn't know all that well. She had refrained from telling him more about Michael, that he was the one her father had forbidden her to see when she was much younger. No wonder he'd gone ballistic when he saw Michael in her hospital room. But still, it hadn't seemed as if he'd put two and two together. He'd been too enraged.

Now she really would be pushing the boundaries of his culture, staying with a single man in his home, even though she would have her own room. If this was spreading one's wings, then she was hoping to spread them wide. Very wide.

Chapter Twenty-Two

Niall and Michael arrived home shortly before the supper hour, having left Inishannon not long after noon. They'd stopped a few times along the way to tend to Dawn's needs and once just to enjoy the view, taking a photograph of each of them holding their baby in turn. And now, with the late afternoon sun falling slowly in a cloudless sky, they pulled into their driveway, the now familiar landscape welcoming them home.

"I never knew what we were missing by living in a flat," said Michael as Niall pulled the car to a halt just before the garage door. "It's brilliant that we own this."

Niall agreed. "I know. I can't imagine it sometimes, either. Although I will say as how glad I am we don't always have to make the trek into Dublin. That home office was a grand stroke of luck," he exclaimed.

As they entered the large foyer and placed both Dawn and their bags down, Niall asked, "What do ye think of Farrah stayin' with Dylan?"

A grin split Michael's face and Niall was certain they were thinking the same thing. "I hear wedding bells, if I'm not mistaken," he said laughingly.

"That's what I thought. Only, it seems rather sudden for Dylan, doesn't it? I mean, I know we don't know him all that well, but..." His voice trailed off uncertainly and Michael picked up the thread of the conversation.

"But nothing. He's been looking for a partner all his life, thought he had one in your half sister, Meara, and now, seeing a woman in dire straights once again, he's determined not to let her go."

"Ye think so?"

"Pretty sure. Listen, Meara was a troubled young woman when they met, only she had a drug problem that took her away. Who knows, maybe if she hadn't been an addict, they would be together today and all this might or might not occur. But she did, and here we are. Farrah is in a similar way, only not an addict. But she does have a tyrant after her, and needs some protection. It's the same scenario. A woman needing to be looked after. Just a different player."

Shrugging, Niall couldn't disagree. "Ye think she likes him enough to wed him?"

"Well, not right now, maybe. But they've all the time in the world in which to connect. I'd say that's long enough, especially since they'll be virtually living together. It's not for us to speculate whether or not that means sharing a room."

"Sleepin' together, ye mean."

"Yeah," answered Michael with a wink. "Which reminds me, we haven't done that for a few nights. Yon child is still out and, I believe, since she was just fed an hour ago, we still have a bit of time if you're willing."

They both cast a glance at Dawn, sound asleep and comfortable in her carrier.

"Let's attach it to the swing. That'll ensure her cooperation," laughed Niall.

Michael wholeheartedly agreed, and minutes later, they were in the bedroom, kicking off their shoes and setting the baby monitor.

"Wait," said Michael when Niall began to unbutton his shirt, "let me do that for you, dear."

The first button came undone easily, as did the next. Methodically, Michael went down the shirt, a button at a time, until he reached the top of Niall's jeans. Pulling the shirt out, he undid the remaining buttons before pushing it off Niall's shoulders and stepped closer to place a kiss on his lover's lips.

Niall took the kiss and more, taking Michael's t-shirt and pulling it over his head, breaking the kiss only for the moment it took to remove the shirt altogether. Then it was Michael's hands on Niall's skin, pushing his jeans down, while Niall did the same for Michael, thinking how crazy it was they could read each other's minds, know exactly what was wanted and expected. They were true partners in every sense of the word, and when Michael slid down Niall's body to engulf his erection in the warmth of his mouth, Niall knew he wouldn't last long.

It was too soon, and pulling himself away from the heat of his lover's mouth, Niall dragged Michael with him to the bed, pulling back the covers to lie on crisp, clean sheets, so cool after the heat of the day. Michael laid on the bed, arse end exposed, ready for his lover, and Niall took only enough time to lubricate them both before spreading Michael's cheeks wide and pressing in.

Michael sighed at his lover's touch, grabbed at the t-shirt that had been deposited on the bed, and placed it beneath him. And while Niall pressed into him from behind, Michael took himself in hand, a culmination of sensation and Niall's intensifying grunts as he came closer to completion.

A shriek, followed by a wail, rent the air through the baby monitor and Niall heard Michael swear and felt him begin to move off.

"Wait, no…ah, feckit, Michael, I was nearly there."

A quiver reverberated through Michael's body as his laughter, buried deep in the sheets beneath him, infiltrated Niall's hearing.

Another wail and then another came through the monitor, and Niall grabbed the t-shirt from Michael's lean hand, held up for him to clean himself with.

"Nothing like fatherhood to put a damper on impromptu lovemaking sessions," said Michael, still chuckling beneath Niall's weight.

"Humph," muttered Niall, but he knew there would be time later. Now that he and Michael could work from home, there was no saying they couldn't take a midmorning break or a midafternoon break for a little personal time.

"I'll go see what the problem is," said Michael, the first one to don jeans and a clean t-shirt from the drawer.

"Right behind ye," said Niall, buttoning his shirt as he went.

* * *

"And this will be yer room, if it ye like it. There's another just there," said Dylan, pointing to one across the hall, "but this one faces the garden at the rear. A much lovelier view and more feminine."

Farrah took in the view from the second-floor window, a dormer with a deep window seat, all decorated in light mauve and perfect for looking out over the expanse of the garden. A meandering path led toward the river, just out of sight beyond the row of yew trees and willows, and a fringe of flowers bordering the expanse of lawn on all sides. A large fuchsia grew against the side of a shed that had a look of newness to it.

"It's lovely," she exclaimed, breathless in her wonderment. The last thing she expected was a house as large as this, especially since he'd described it as a cottage.

"Ye've yer own facilities, just there," Dylan pointed to the bathroom and toilet through a connecting doorway. "I did a few renovations when I bought the place, and since there was already a bathroom connected to the master suite, I thought this second bedroom deserved at least as good."

"That was a brilliant move," said Farrah, still trying to take everything in. "Looks like there's another bedroom down the end, just there?"

"Yeah," answered Dylan, "mostly it collects dust. But there's a study on the main floor, next to the living room if ye remember?"

"I do. So that means this other spare room can be for other guests, or your guests' children, since your family seems to be growing."

"Oh, they aren't my family," Dylan was quick to correct.

"No? Oh, I do apologize, with your father and Niall's mother together there, I just assumed…"

"They aren't together. At least, not married, if that's what ye're thinkin'." A moment's pause, and then, "It's complicated," he finished with a shrug.

"So it seems," she said half-apologetically, and wondered suddenly exactly what it was she'd stepped into.

They finished the tour and Dylan brought her lone bag up to the bedroom and then retreated.

As she unpacked the few things she was able to stuff into the bag, her mind went over her flight. Her father had finally gone to bed and Farrah had crept around her room, careful to avoid any squeaking floor joists, and packed whatever she could into the only bag available, the sports bag she took to the gym. Her bedroom door was locked and her father had the only key. So as quietly as she could, she leaned out her bedroom window and gauged the distance to the ground. Having seen enough movies where sheets became ropes, she wasted no time in fabricating a way down the side of the house with what she had at hand. Her bedsheet would not be enough to deliver her safely to the ground but the light duvet could be used as well. The sheet torn in half, even with the duvet, was not enough. Her homemade rope needed to be longer.

Spying her manicure scissors, she had an idea and managed to start a small cut down the center of her duvet, then tore with all her might until the material gave and a flurry of feathers flew into the air and scattered, floating like softly falling snow when the two sides finally came apart. It would be enough to give her the extra length she needed.

After that, she laid her desk chair on its side, figuring that in that position it would be impossible to drag it through the narrow window once her weight was pulling on it. It was a simple kitchen-style chair, and she'd made a knot with the sheet through the legs and the cross beams, praying it would hold.

Searching the room, she located her purse where she'd placed it before coming upstairs to bed. It held her spare car keys, her wallet with her driver's licence, everything she'd need on her journey. Except her phone, which was still downstairs. Her father had taken it away, along with her computer. He hadn't wanted her to be able to reach the outside world. It was just a lucky quirk that her spare car keys had been forgotten in the depths of her purse. And while her mother had driven one car home, her father had driven the second one, Farrah's car, with her inside it. And once home, he had kept the keys to himself and promptly ushered her upstairs to lock her in her room.

Having secured her purse across her shoulders and under her arm, it was a simple thing to pick up her sport bag, now stuffed with essentials, and fling it to the ground. Her parents' bedroom was toward the front of the house and on the opposite side, so she wasn't worried about the bag's fall making too much noise. In fact, she thought it had made only as much noise as the neighbor's cat when it jumped into the bushes to play below her window.

Stealthily, she worked her way down the side of the house, her hands on the homemade rope with a white-knuckled grip, her purse hanging from her shoulder. Gaining the ground safely with a soft thump as she dropped the last few feet, she crept along the side of the house, safely making her way to her car. Her heart was beating madly and the feeling of someone standing, ready to grab her, was so great that she felt her breath hitch as she looked quickly about. Relief! No one was there, and obviously her father hadn't thought her capable of escaping because her vehicle remained where he'd last parked it, on the street in front of the house. Should he wake just now, she felt she could still make it, and as she gained the car and started the engine, she noticed the curtains to his bedroom fling back. But by then, she was speeding away in the direction of the motorway and he'd have a devil of a time knowing where she'd gone from there.

It had been that close, her heart slamming against her chest in remembrance, that she'd felt the blood rush through her veins creating a headache of huge proportions. Yet once she was on the M40 and heading north, the moment of indecision was gone and she opted to make for Wales and the crossing at Holyhead, only a few hours away through nearly deserted roads at this time of night, rather than the airport, so much closer.

Her ID in her handbag, she'd made her way through the night, arriving at the ferry in time for the final night sailing. She'd been driving at breakneck speed for nearly five hours. And as her escape from the house had been charmed, so had her drive through the night—evading any speed traps and reaching the Holyhead ferry terminal scant minutes before it was due to pull away. They'd drawn up the gangway and begun to pull away before she had time to realize she'd actually made it. She couldn't stop the shaking that seemed to have set in her bones and settle in for the trip that would have her in Dublin in less than two hours. The water was calm, the ship fairly glided across the waves, and she laid her head back, allowing her eyes to close.

The rest of the trip had been uneventful, and for the first time in twenty-four hours, she'd felt a semblance of safety.

She came back to herself, realizing that Dylan had poked his head in her door and asked her something.

"Sorry, I was woolgathering," she laughed.

"Would ye care for some tea or anythin'? An iced glass of somethin'?"

For the first time, Farrah noted the warmth of the room with the afternoon sun pouring in. "A cool drink would be lovely, if you have any."

"It's no bother," and then looking around the room, added, "I guess that's the one drawback of this room is the sun pouring in all afternoon. It's grand, it is, but sometimes too warm. I'll have to invest in some sort of cooling system for the house. We usually don't need it," he ended on a laugh.

"I'm sure, if it gets too warm, a simple fan will do. I can pick one up tomorrow."

She had finished unpacking and was stuffing the now empty bag in the closet, a shelf just a bit too high for her to easily reach. As she tried to place it on the shelf, it fell, caught in Dylan's hands before it could entangle itself in her long hair or hit her.

"It's fine, I have it," said Dylan, glancing down at Farrah as she pulled a length of hair from her face and tucked it behind her ear.

It was a moment in time, barely a second before she looked away. But his eyes had been locked with hers and she didn't think she'd mistaken the look of wanting in his expression.

He pushed the bag onto the shelf and stepped back, breaking the spell, and she wondered if it was just her imagination or if Dylan really did want to kiss her. Instead, he scanned the near empty closet and commented on it. "Ye've hardly anythin' to wear. I'll take ye shoppin', buy a few things for ye so ye've a decent selection."

"Oh, you needn't buy things for me, although I appreciate the offer," she said. "I've my own bank account."

"Right then, but if yer da is as bent on findin' ye as ye say, do ye not think he'd be monitorin' where ye're spendin' yer money?"

"Hmm, perhaps you're right. He has friends, you know?" Dylan shrugged through a half smile, and she knew he caught her meaning. "Although if I just transferred it to my Irish bank, he'd never know where exactly I was. He'd only know I moved it."

"Sounds reasonable. I'll show ye where everythin' is tomorrow. In the meantime, I'll get that cold drink. Would ye like some beer?"

Farrah took the tiniest of pauses before she broke out into

a wide grin as a bead of sweat made it down between her breasts. "Oh, a beer sounds delightful!"

"Beer it is, then," said Dylan, grinning as he left her to finish up.

Dylan turned to go downstairs to the kitchen, leaving Farrah to wonder how they were going to deny the pull of electricity between them. She watched Dylan leave from beneath her lashes while pretending to sort out a tangled necklace. It was definitely tangled, but it was also an excuse to busy herself in something because she wasn't sure what else to do. She had, she realized, two problems.

The first was the most urgent. She had to find a way to stay hidden in Ireland. It was the only way she could ensure absolute safety from her father's clutches and his ultimate scheme. It had something to do with him saving face with his elder brother, a man she had never met and sincerely hoped never to do so. At least, not through her father's machinations. She'd be no one's slave! And if she stayed in Ireland, found a job, and was happy here, then nothing short of kidnapping could force her to leave.

The other problem was a little more complex but it held an appeal that lingered and popped into her head at odd times, like now, when Dylan had pushed the bag back onto the shelf. She was certain he'd wanted to kiss her, but he hadn't. And that had thrown her next move off. If he had kissed her, would she have let whatever happened next to continue on its own? Would it have led to another kiss? Would he have wanted more? Would she? She didn't think so, at least, not at this stage. It had only been a month since the baby's birth, and she still couldn't give voice to the child's name; it brought it too close. So the child was "it" and nameless, and like her heart, her body had yet to heal completely inside.

She should have taken Niall's and Michael's offer of staying on in Ireland for another three months, in case anything went wrong with either her or the baby. But Farrah couldn't bring herself to stay. She'd needed her mother just then, a woman who seemed to want to help, who had been angry and upset that Farrah would give up a child, depriving her mother of grandparenthood. And Daddy had seemed to suddenly mellow, his rash behavior quite tempered as he told her they would be good grandparents and visit the child when the two men allowed it. Otherwise, they'd miss so much, the sight of their grandchild as she grew up.

Farrah had never thought of it that way, that her parents would be deprived of a grandchild. It had been her decision alone to give Michael and Niall a child, and it gave her a taste of freedom she'd rarely enjoyed, especially over the past two years of her father's newly found fanaticism. Of that she had no opinion, other than he was no longer the kind father she'd grown up with. Perhaps he was mentally ill, she thought, making an excuse when no other reasonable answer could be found.

Her mind wandered back to Dylan. He was nice looking and had a gentle, caring streak that she thought endearing. His eyes were kind, twinkling when he smiled, and he seemed to smile a lot. It was as if the stars had suddenly aligned, and although she'd thought herself in love with Michael for the longest time, she now knew that it had only been infatuation and the attention of an older man that had brought about those feelings in a teenaged girl.

But Dylan…he was older as well, a good ten years or so if her guess was correct. But that didn't seem to faze her, nor did her twenty-three years seem to bother him. And although she'd been sheltered, she was mature for her years.

Motherhood and running for your life, your freedom, did that to you, she mused.

The necklace, finally losing its stubborn knot, dangled freely in her hand, and she looked at the symbol of the Hand of Fatima palming the delicate lace-like silver in her hand. Khamsa, her father had told her when he gave it to her, a symbol of protection, good luck, good health, and also faith, applicable to many religions.

She placed the necklace on the small dresser opposite the bed. She had no jewellery case, no place to tuck it away except an empty drawer, and for the first time since fleeing, she felt like crying for herself, for what she had left behind, for the mother she would never see again.

Standing at the side of the bed, she put her face in her hands and let the tears come, quietly sobbing the loss of the only home she'd known and the life she'd left behind; her mother, her friends, her possessions. All that had seemed to matter.

A tissue was pressed into her hand and she took it, felt Dylan's arms go about her, the kiss that was bestowed on the top of her head as he held her close and let her cry. And then, as she looked up and he gazed upon her face, there was only a momentary pause as his lips came down, touched hers tentatively, and then, when she didn't shy off, touched again and deepened.

Farrah welcomed the warmth of his lips, the solidity of his embrace, and felt her worries fade. The ache was still there but it was tempered by the knowledge that Dylan would keep her safe, that she would have a home for as long as she needed it and, maybe, much longer than that.

His tongue touched hers and she followed suit, meeting his kiss with her own before drawing slowly away.

"Ye're alright now?" he asked, still holding her close but allowing her to withdraw.

She noted his ragged breathing, the desire in his expression, and the rapid beating of his heart. It matched her own.

Nodding, she answered, "Yes, better now, thanks. I'm sorry, I…"

"Don't be sorry, sweetheart. Ye've nothin' to apologize for. Ye've been through a lot, childbirth, givin' up yer babe, and now this, havin' to flee from yer da. It's enough to make even the strongest person crumble."

"I've really done it, though, haven't I? I've really left my home for good."

"Yeah. Looks that way. But things can change. Could be he'll have a change of heart one day."

She shook her head vehemently. "No. That will never happen. And if it does, it would only be to lure me into complacency so that he can ship me off to Egypt." She popped the tissue into the bin, only then noticing the two glasses of beer on the top of the dresser. "Oh, thank you," she sighed, picking up one glass. "Beer never looked so good!"

Grinning, Dylan picked up the other, and nodding in the direction of her doorway, said, "C'mon, let's take these down to the garden. The sun is warm out there and I've a couple of chairs set up to enjoy the view."

Feeling slightly better for having a bit of a cry, Farrah followed Dylan down the stairs to the garden at the rear of the house and was delighted by what she saw. It was a scene she hadn't expected. A small patio, unnoticed by her view from the bedroom window, was tucked beneath an overhang and the small rose garden at the opposite corner of the house. It was only a few bushes but they were in full bloom, partially shaded by the yew tree that grew meters away. They sat on the two chairs, a patio table between them, and Farrah felt herself begin to relax.

It was going to be okay.

Chapter Twenty-Three

Why does it have to be such a warm summer?" asked Siobhan, her now very obvious baby bump supporting the iced fruit tea she was sipping. Sweat beaded up on her forehead even though she was sitting in the shade.

"At least ye're not near the end when ye'd be big as a house and suffering more than ye are now from the heat," said Henry, downing the last of his coffee.

"If this continues all summer long, I'll be miserable by the time I give birth."

"Ah, it'll be alright, ye'll see. We'll make sure there's fans galore, or I'll put a cooling unit in the bedroom to keep ye comfortable."

"It's good ye're handy that way," she smiled.

"I'm handy in all kinds of ways," grinned Henry, winking at her with a meaning she couldn't misunderstand.

"Away with ye now," she scolded in fun. And then, "When's Hank arrivin'?"

Henry glanced at his watch. "Should be here soon."

"Ye think he'll work out okay with ye? He's never worked with stone before."

Nodding, Henry said, "It'll be fine. He may never have worked as a stonemason before but everyone starts somewhere. And he's handy as well, built that mountain home of his by himself. So, no, I have no worries about his ability. He'll learn, and then maybe Laura will feel better about them stayin' on for a while."

Siobhan seemed to mull it over before commenting. "Hmm, I got the feelin' that she wasn't too pleased about stayin' a couple of extra months. She was a bit short with the weyans and didn't say much at dinner the other night."

"No, she didn't, that's true." Henry was going through the ratty notebook he carried with him on workdays, jotting down items as he thought of them, crossing other things off as being done.

"Do ye think they'll stay longer?"

His concentration, such that he wasn't really listening, caused Siobhan to repeat her question.

"Eh? Oh, I doubt it. From what I gather through Brandon, the two had words and Laura won. Seems her condition was they'd stay until September and not a moment longer."

"She's likely missing her friends and her life there," observed Siobhan, absentmindedly rubbing her belly.

"That may be so. But I can't help think that Hank is enjoyin' the feelin' of bein' part of a family again. Must have been hard, losing his mam and then findin' out his sister was dead, too. He'd no one else."

"And now he's got you. Us. And all the rest. I wonder that Laura isn't pleased for him."

Henry looked up at that, met Siobhan's eyes, and disagreed. "I think she's happy for him. Why wouldn't she be? But this isn't her home, and until ye lured Hank back here with yer tale, it wasn't his home, either."

"Are ye sayin' I shouldn't have done it?"

She suddenly looked upset, and the last thing Henry wanted on his hands was his pregnant wife upset just before he was due to leave for work. "Ah, no, my darlin', not sayin' that at all. I think it's grand what ye did. Ye brought all Da's offspring, at least the ones we know of, together. And that has turned out to be the best for everyone. Young Emily, especially."

Siobhan seemed to be thinking about something while Henry spoke. She had a far-off expression that told him her mind was working. She sighed deeply, her eyes focusing on her tea as she asked, "Ye think there may be others?" with a voice that held more than a hint of speculation.

A feeling like the bottom of his stomach suddenly giving way hit Henry. Christ, that's all we need, he thought. "Humph, wouldn't put it past the bastard, but there's no sign of any others." He stood to go, noting that Siobhan still held a worried look. She was frowning slightly and chewing at her bottom lip.

"What's amiss?"

"Hmm? Oh, just thinkin', and wonderin'…no, never mind. It's alright."

Henry knew his wife too well to leave it at that. "No, it isn't alright. Spill it."

Putting down her tea, she sighed heavily and stood, shaking out her dress before meeting his eyes. "Ye've been true to me, haven't ye Henry?"

He'd swear she was close to tears, but then, she was pregnant after all. "Ah, feckit, Siobhan, ye know I'd never step out on ye. I've never even looked at another woman since you." He closed the distance between them to draw her into his embrace. "Feckit, darlin', I don't know what I'd do without ye, so let's not even discuss it." He finished his statement with a kiss, not a light peck but pouring everything he felt for her into it, a prelude to much more if time allowed.

Time didn't allow, if the knock on the front door was anything to go by, and Henry released her with a wink, saying, "If ye're up to it later, I'd like to continue that."

Siobhan smiled. "It's nice ye still want me, even though I'm growin' fat."

"Fat, shmat. Ye've my child in there and that's a grand thing," he exclaimed, heading to the front door where he knew Hank was waiting. "I'll see ye at dinner," he called, waving goodbye.

"Henry," she called, and he turned at the opened door, "don't forget yer lunch."

Smacking his forehead with the heel of his hand, he laughed. "Right."

Hank waved his hello and goodbye as Henry retrieved his lunch and then the two were off.

"Where's the job?" asked Hank when they were underway.

"Just over near Firies. A fella's chimney needs rebuildin' and I'm partway through it. Should be an easy job for ye to begin with."

Hank nodded and gazed out at the countryside between Killarney and Firies. It was a busy road, though they were soon heading down a narrow lane off the main road, bordered by thick trees on either side. "I appreciate what ye're doin', Henry," said Hank. "I wasn't sure where else I'd get work for only a couple of months."

"And how is Laura takin' it all?" He thought he understood how Hank must be feeling, being unsure of himself like a boy fresh from school and trying to fit into a culture he'd abandoned so many years before. Henry had noticed the differences, the expressions Hank sometimes used, the way he approached things, more typically what he thought of as

Canadian rather than Irish. But as time was wearing on, Hank was reverting to his Irish ways, fitting in more easily, as if he'd never left, and Henry wondered how Laura was taking it, if she was happy to stay a little longer knowing she had a firm exit date.

"It would likely be better for her if she had a job as well. She might be happier, but with the two weyans so young it would be tough, Meara not yet a year. Still, with Aine close by, and Sine and Ciara popping down every so often, she's faring okay. Especially when Sine comes by, since she's American and has gone through a similar adjustment."

"But Laura doesn't want to stay?"

"No. And I don't think I'll ever change her mind on that."

Hank had a crooked smile on his face and Henry wondered what it meant. "Are ye fine with her wantin' to go back? Are ye fine goin' back yerself?"

Hank's smile broadened. "Ye know, at first I was angry. Really angry. I wanted to stay, to remain a part of everyone's lives. I mean, it's been hard, not havin' a family anywhere until Laura became mine. She's very independent. Her own folks are across the country. We hear precious little from them and she's okay with that. Don't know that I would be but she's quite fine with it all. And as for me not stayin'... well, to be honest, Henry, I'm fine with goin' back to Canada. Whatever family connections I have here will always exist. I'm not losin' anyone by returnin' home. Just the opposite. People will come and visit and it's grand we have the space for everyone there. And another thing," he said, just as Henry dodged a cyclist on the road, carefully maneuvering his vehicle between the fella on the bike in his lane and a lorry carrying silage in the oncoming lane. "I'm missing the wide open spaces of Canada, not to mention the wider roads. There they have shoulders on almost every road, even country lanes. There's room to dodge things without hittin' a wall or a fence. Or runnin' over a cyclist," he laughed.

Henry joined in the laughter, "And where's the fun in that, then?"

"The fun, dear brother, is in the beauty of the land, the wide open spaces, the mountains that are filled with waterfalls and giant trees. And lakes. Lots of lakes."

"Hmm, sounds grand, but we have that here, too."

"Ireland has mountains and lakes, and beautiful trees, too," admitted Hank, "but not the same. Not the same at all. I guess I've just learned to love where I'm at as much as where I came from."

Henry cast a quick glance at his brother and smiled to himself. It seemed Hank was realizing just what he had at home and would be content to leave when September came. In the meantime, he'd keep him busy with odd jobs, ensuring his brother had some extra coin to keep Laura happy. It was the least he could do because, although he'd resented Hank's presence in his life at first, he was thankful for it now, for the closure it provided Emily in her search for her own roots. No one had known Meara as well as Hank. Not even himself, although she'd lived with him for a time.

"Right then, this is the place," he said, turning his truck off the road and into a short driveway, bordered on either side by a well-maintained wooden rail fence. They both got out of the truck and Henry patted his brother's shoulders, saying, "Ye're about to get yer first lesson in professional stonemasonry."

Hank grinned his response and followed, looking eager to begin.

* * *

Laura was feeling less at ease than Hank, with things as they stood. She was bored and hadn't been feeling up to her normal, energetic self. She was stuck in the middle of nowhere with a toddler and a baby, and unable to go anywhere. Hank had taken the car, the only form of transportation they had, to meet up with Henry this morning, leaving her stranded in the cottage next to Ballycarbery Castle. It was a comfortable place, though small, situated next to Brandon's friend Sam and a five-minute car ride away from Cahersiveen where Brandon and Aine lived. It had been Sam who had talked to the owners and secured the cottage for them for the next few months.

She glanced out the window at the great stone edifice, letting her mind wander. The castle had since lost its appeal as something wonderful. She saw it every day. It was no longer new and exciting.

She sighed and turned her attention to the dishes in the sink. There was no dishwasher. Meara had just been fed and Ryan was playing quietly with the homemade play dough. A quick glance showed he was getting it in his hair and her heart sank in dismay. Now he'd need a bath because she hadn't been watching him as closely as she should have. At least he wasn't eating it, she said to herself, then quickly amended her thought as he placed a chunk in his mouth.

She was just easing the now slobbery mass from where it was lodged inside his cheek as the door was opened following a light rap, and Sine entered.

"Hi, how're things?" she asked.

Laura looked up, feeling near tears with frustration and loneliness, but suddenly happier now that she had good company. "Wow, are you a sight for sore eyes," she laughed, successfully retrieving the play dough from Ryan's mouth.

Sine plunked the baby carrier on the floor and Ryan, wriggling away from Laura's grasp, ran to peek over the light blanket covering the baby.

"Mind your fingers," said Laura, taking Ryan's pudgy toddler hand away from the baby's eyes.

"I wonder why they always do that?" mused Sine. "My cousin's little boy did exactly the same thing when his sister was born. Went right for the eyes."

"Maybe it's just boys," laughed Laura. "How's Aedan doing? Are you still continuing with breast feeding?"

"Hit and miss," said Sine with a tone of regret. "It would be so easy if he'd just be satisfied with what I've got, but the truth is, he isn't. They all tell me to persevere but it isn't working out. He goes more and more for the bottle."

"I guess I've been lucky," said Laura, filling the kettle and putting it on the hob to boil while Sine unpacked a bottle from the diaper bag, "Ryan had no trouble breast feeding, and Meara has been the same. It's been lucky for me that she's a good feeder and this trip hasn't put her off at all. So no formula to worry about or anything like that."

"That is lucky for you. In a way, I wish it could be the same for me but I'm okay with this. When Liam is home, he gets to feed and cuddle and I get to do things like have a leisurely bath without interruption for any reason, especially not feeding," Sine exclaimed, and Laura couldn't disagree.

"That is definitely a perk. I've had instances where my milk has let down while I was in the tub and the water got murky, just because I heard Meara cry. She didn't need me, she just needed changing, but it ruined my bath time anyway."

"I think that's the fate of all mothers," said Sine.

Moments later, another rap could be heard and as the door opened, Aine's cheery face appeared. "Hello!" And then seeing Sine as well, said, "Good to see ye here, too, Sine. Too bad Ciara's not here to join in, though. I don't have any clients today and I thought it would be a grand day to go for a picnic, maybe take in Rossbeigh? Wee Ryan can run on the sand and wet his toes in the water."

"Oh, that sounds lovely, Aine," said Laura, "but I don't have the car seats for the kids. Hank took the car to Killarney to meet up with Henry for work."

"Oh. Hmm. Give me a minute. I've the new car seat at home for my weyan, whenever it arrives," she added with a roll to her eyes, "that Meara can use, and I may be able to borrow one from a friend for Ryan. Let me see what I can do."

"How about some tea in the meantime?" Laura offered. It was the least she could do to return the gesture. As Aine went to work on locating another car seat, Laura made tea and they all sat down to chat.

"You're looking a bit glum this morning," commented Sine while Aine chatted on the phone.

"Yeah. Just feeling a little isolated without the car and no one about that I can visit, which is why I'm so glad you two are here," she exclaimed, brightening a bit.

"Ireland not your thing?"

Laura's smile faded as she thought. "I wouldn't say that exactly. It's beautiful and I love visiting, I just don't think I could live here. We have so much at home that I'm missing, you know?"

Now it was Sine's turn to look serious. "I get it. I missed home a lot when I first came here, even though I've got relatives all over the place. But I kind of got to like it, mostly because I was able to work again, and that made the difference for me. And now, with Aedan and Liam, I couldn't

306

imagine being anywhere else. But I can see how it would be different for you with no job and no close friends. I don't know what I'd do without Liam's family because other than a few actresses I know and some people from Galway I've become acquaintances with, I really don't have any close friends either. That'll come though, especially now I'm doing a mom-and-tot group thing. There are a couple of women in that group that I seem to have connected with."

"Success!" cried Aine with a grin, breaking into the other conversation. "My neighbor's got a seat she's not using just now. Her weyan just outgrew it so he's now in a booster seat. I can run over and get it whenever we decide to leave," she said, coming to join them at the table.

"Perfect," said Laura as she poured the tea, hoping that her day would improve now that her friends were here.

"Ye know, feeling isolated is certainly a new-mother experience," commented Aine when they were nibbling on biscuits and chatting. "I don't think there's a new mother out there that hasn't felt it at one time or another, and being in a different country, away from home, doesn't help."

"Thanks for your support. I can't tell you how much it means to me that you understand, and I know I'll miss you guys when we leave. But for now, all I want is to be back home," and before she could stop them, the tears started in her eyes.

Immediately, tissues appeared from both Sine's and Aine's hands, and Laura took them both. "That's not all, though," she said, dabbing at her eyes and sniffing loudly. "I haven't even told Hank yet."

At her hesitation and as if on cue, the other women leaned in closer with curious expressions across their faces.

Gathering herself and sitting a little taller, Laura

announced, "I'm pregnant again," and then burst into tears once more.

Chapter Twenty-Four

What?" Both women looked aghast at Laura, who had broken into tears and, placing her face in her hands, wept out her anguish.

Aine was first to react, her background as a counselor switching into gear. "Alright, so ye've found out ye're pregnant. How far along are ye?"

Sniffing, and taking another tissue from Sine with a nod of thanks, Laura answered Aine's question. "About six weeks. I've even begun to get the baby bump since it hasn't been so long since I've given birth. Guys, what am I gonna do? I won't even have a chance to go back to work before I have baby number three!" she wailed.

It was clear neither Aine nor Sine had much to add. Facts were facts, and nothing anyone could say could or would make a difference.

"You've got to tell Hank," said Sine in her matter-of-fact way. "And you aren't crazy about staying in Ireland any longer than you have to. You've said so yourself. So why not tell him you're pregnant and that you have to go home?"

"Because for some crazy reason, I love being here," came Laura's quiet reply.

Neither of the other women were quite ready for her remark and again, their expressions and exchanged looks said it all.

"I know, I know," said Laura, taking in their unasked questions and seeing the confusion in their expressions. "I'm being contrary. Contrary to everything. I like it. I hate it. I want to go, I want to stay. I don't know what the hell I want."

"Sounds to me like you're pregnant," said Sine, a kindly smile spreading across her face.

"It sounds to me like ye're also afraid of the unknown," suggested Aine. "It happens when we're faced with a situation we can't see our way through. And here, Hank has asked ye for more time in Ireland, and not just until September, if I'm right?" At Laura's nod, she continued. "So, as far as I can see, the situation is that Hank wants to stay, to solidify the bonds of family he's so recently discovered, and ye've negotiated it to a couple more months instead, to which he agreed, albeit reluctantly. Then the other item in the mix, besides the fact ye've not quite got used to the idea, is suddenly ye're slammed with the knowledge that ye're pregnant. Either of those two situations is huge and neither one can be dismissed out of hand. They're both reasons to feel the way ye do."

"When did you learn you're pregnant?" asked Sine.

Laura took in a deep breath, running her hand through her long hair and tucking it behind her ear as she did so. Sniffing and wiping her nose before speaking, she said, "Last week, after we moved in here. I hadn't been feeling well and it suddenly occurred to me that I hadn't had a period for a while. I wasn't worried at first, because with breastfeeding, it can often be off. At least, with me it can. So I didn't worry. But then my pants started to feel tight and anything I wore around my waist felt tight and the last thing was the craving for cola. I never drink cola unless I'm pregnant. So I picked up a test kit and bingo, there it was, plain as the nose on my face. It even said more than three weeks."

"So how do ye know it's six weeks? If it's only a month or less, ye've lots of time before ye need to be back home; and September isn't too long to wait before seein' a doctor if ye don't want to find one here," said Aine.

Laura's wan smile seemed a feeble effort to acknowledge her friend's attempt at being helpful. "I've craved cola for almost two months. I figure that I probably got pregnant the night we celebrated my hitting the six-week mark after Meara's birth. I was feeling good, and for once, I wanted sex. Hank would never turn me down, although he did ask if I was ready, which was nice of him."

"Hmm, so ye had sex and then…did ye use any protection?"

Bowing her head, Laura answered with a grimace, "Kind of. I mean, we used a condom, or rubber johnny, or whatever you want to call it, but there was an 'oops' with it."

"Oops?" asked Sine, chewing her bottom lip thoughtfully.

"Yeah. Oops. It slipped off while he was withdrawing, and I think not everything stayed in the condom."

"Doesn't take much," agreed Aine.

"Nope," added Sine. "Not much at all."

"Yup. Just one little slipup. I mean, Hank just has to look at me and I get pregnant. When we wanted another child after Ryan, it took no time at all to happen. Like this, it was probably the first time we tried."

"Well, so let's say ye're as ye say. Ye're six weeks along. Ye'll still be in the first trimester when ye get home. It'll just make life that much more interestin'," said Aine, smiling encouragingly.

"But, here's the thing," explained Laura, "part of me wants to have this baby in Ireland. I'd like to be home where everything is familiar, but in a way, I'd like our Irish connection to continue, be reinforced."

"I think that's a talk you and Hank need to have," Aine said in a motherly fashion, albeit tinged with her clinician's point of view. "He needs to be a part of the conversation and I've no doubt between the two of ye, ye'll find the right answer."

"You think so?" asked Laura, afraid to hope.

Laughing, Aine added, "Well ye don't think he'll be upset, do ye?"

Joining in the laughter, Laura said, "No. Definitely not. He loves kids and another one, even so close to Meara, would be welcome. I'm quite certain of that."

"Then it sounds like you've got every reason to trust you'll both be okay, whatever happens," added Sine.

Pulling herself together, Laura stood, clearing up the cups and teapot and plate of biscuits. "Okay, let's get going. Ryan's starting to get edgy. In fact, I'm surprised he hasn't bugged me in the last ten minutes."

"Could be because he found the contents of my diaper bag," said Sine, and sure enough, Ryan had pulled nearly everything out of the bag and was lining it up on the floor to play.

"Right. If ye can give me about twenty minutes, I'll be back with the other car seats," said Aine on her way out the door.

Laura waved her off and said to Sine, "Boy, am I ever glad you guys are here. I don't know what I'd do without you."

"It's no big deal," said Sine. "I remember my first few weeks in Ireland. I felt a bit lost even though I had cousins here. But they were cousins I'd never met before, and despite sharing family stories, I still felt like a foreigner. I sometimes still do, but not so much when Liam is around."

"What's it like to be married to such a charismatic person? You guys are both famous, you turn heads everywhere you go. How do you manage to keep it all real?"

"Real, as in ordinary life?" At Laura's nod, Sine replied, "It gets tough sometimes. Sometimes he's the actor, all full of himself and walking the I-can-do-no-wrong road. Occasionally I have to drag him back down to earth. That's when it gets tough. But the other stuff, the adoration of fans and such, is just stuff I've become used to. He doesn't seek them out, doesn't pay them any more attention than if someone had asked him what time it was. He really is pretty good about handling them without making me feel like an extra wheel. In fact, he often pulls me in closer, physically, I mean, so that the fans, usually women, can see that I'm the one in his life. And now that Aedan is here, he's so obviously the daddy that people are generally pretty good about leaving us alone. They can see we're together."

"Hmm. Hank isn't famous, but he does resemble his half brothers quite a bit, especially Henry. Liam and Niall look more like their mom, but with the same hair and blue eyes as Henry and Hank. Even Brandon and Hank look quite a bit alike. It's uncanny, isn't it?"

"Yeah, sure is. The first time I saw Hank, I did a doubletake. And then once Brandon stepped beside them, there was no doubt they were related."

"And here we all are, all part of an amazing family and I have to confess, it's a little overwhelming at times. Maybe that's part of my fear. I'm afraid I won't fit in and will always feel like the extra wheel you mentioned."

"Maybe that's just being women and being the ones new to the family. I imagine Cian feels a little bit of an outsider,

313

being Danish," Sine put in while reassembling her diaper bag.

"I suppose," mused Laura. And then the door opened and Aine was back, announcing the fact that the two car seats were now installed and they could leave at any time.

"Great," smiled Sine. "Laura, do you have anything to throw in for snacks for Ryan? We can put them in my diaper bag, I've got lots of room."

"Let me put together a PB&J for him," she said, heading into the kitchen area, open to the rest of the house.

"PB&J?" asked Aine.

"Peanut butter and jelly sandwich," answered Sine and Laura at once, and then laughed.

"Mmm, that does sound good. Maybe we should make one for each of us. Do ye have enough?" asked Aine.

Holding up the loaf, Laura said, "Lots. And I've got other stuff here we can throw in for a picnic, too."

Half an hour later, a picnic had been assembled and the children tucked into their respective car seats. The two vehicles pulled away from the cottage, heading down the narrow lane to enjoy a sunny afternoon at Rossbeigh.

* * *

It was sunny in Inishannon as well, the heat that had warmed them all in June continuing through humid, lightly breezy days in July. Farrah was in the rear garden, enjoying the atmosphere, listening to the silence accompanied only by the tweet of birds in the trees and the ruffle of the wind, sloughing through the leaves. The river—not much more than a creek, she now knew—burbled its way past the end of the garden but could neither be seen nor heard from where she was sitting.

Dylan approached, a tray of cool drinks and a plate of egg sandwiches in his hands. Two small bowls of strawberries, a thick dollop of Devonshire cream crowning the top of each one, sat beside the plate of sandwiches, and he grinned, obviously proud of himself, as he placed the tray on the small table beside her.

"Thought ye could use a bite, since it's after noon," he said, giving her a wink as he turned the tray so the sandwiches were closer to her.

"Oh, Dylan, that's so lovely. Did you make these all yourself?" she asked.

"Yeah. Cookin' seems to run in the family. Da's always been grand with doin' up meals. Don't know where he learned, but he taught me and, well, I rather fancy myself a good cook as well."

"Mmm, it's delicious," observed Farrah, taking a bite of the sandwich and tasting the blend of mayonnaise, seasoning, and hard-boiled egg all together. "Mmm, it really is good. I was beginning to feel rather peckish," she admitted with a grin.

They'd become closer in the days since she'd moved in, and her opinion of the quiet, unassuming man had altered somewhat. She'd grown to like him even more. And this, this display of caring for her, of providing more than the mere necessities of life, moved him up yet another notch. When he walked into a room, a little something inside her gave a jump of joy, and when she saw him off to work each morning, she looked forward to the kiss he afforded her, a promise of more to come.

Only nothing more had come. Not yet, and Farrah hadn't quite decided what she would do when the time came. She wanted him but didn't want to seem eager. It wasn't in her nature. And although she had given birth, she was technically still a virgin; she had never had sex and was more than curious about that. And, if she was honest with herself, just a little bit scared.

And now Dylan had taken a few days off to make sure she felt at home and to enjoy the rare stretch of warm weather with her. It sometimes rained at night but the days dawned clear and warm and heated up to humid, hot afternoons. The rear garden, with its sheltered patio, was the perfect place to be, catching the bit of a breeze while providing shade from the overhead sun.

They ate their lunch in silence, enjoying the somnolence of the day, the buzzing of the occasional insect, the sleepy fluttering of a butterfly as it flitted from plant to plant. It too, looked like it was willing to take a nap.

"Mmm," Farrah inhaled the warm air, leaning her head back, enjoying the feel of the day. "That was perfect, Dylan, thank you."

"Ye're more than welcome, ye know that," he said quietly, as if talking any louder would break the spell.

"I could just go to sleep, right here," she said, eyes still closed against the brightness of the day.

Her eyes startled open as she felt something touch her lips and then she smiled, allowed Dylan to deepen the kiss. She hadn't heard him get up from his chair.

"Sorry, couldn't resist," he murmured, not moving from her mouth.

"Mmm, don't stop," she mumbled back, placing her arms about his neck, and for the first time, she wanted him in a way that a woman wanted a man. She wanted to be completed by him, and crazy as it seemed, acknowledged that she had loved him from the moment she had met him in his pharmacy that not so long-ago morning.

As if reading her mind, Dylan slid his hands beneath her

bum, picked her up out of the chair, and carried her to the grass where it was thick and cool, even in the heat of the day. Setting her down on her back beneath the shade of the giant yew tree, he asked, "Is this alright?"

"Lovely. Oh, don't stop whatever it is you're doing," she objected as he pulled away.

He'd half risen and was peering at her. "I just thought I'd get a blanket for us to lie on. Much better than lying on blades of grass."

"Indulge my fantasy," she giggled out. "I've imagined a scene like this since I was a child reading medieval romance novels where the hero takes the heroine in an open field."

"Ah, but they never tell ye about the creepy crawlies, nor the fact that the ground beneath can be hard. Stoney, even."

"I'm willing to take my chances. Aren't you?"

"Farrah, I won't lie to ye. I want to be in ye, not just with ye. So ye'd best tell me now if ye want that, or if it's too early, or ye want me to just feck off and not bother ye at all."

Laughing, she pulled him back over her, "Make love to me, Dylan, only please know I've never done this before."

That stopped him cold. "But ye've had a child," he protested.

"Yes, but like the holy virgin, I've never had a man. I was artificially inseminated. In a clinic."

Dawning seemed to light in his eyes. "I thought…no, never mind. It makes sense, now."

"No. I never had sex with Michael, although the baby is his natural child," she explained.

"Whew," said Dylan, and then apologized. "I shouldn't have said anythin'. I've other things on my mind."

"Oh, please don't worry. I've something else on my mind, too."

The light dress she was wearing was easily accessed from the row of tiny buttons down the front, opening the dress like a shirt, exposing her body beneath, covered in sturdy knickers and bra. She hadn't transitioned into anything lacy yet since her body shape had yet to return.

Dylan didn't seem to mind, and easily undid the clasp of her bra to slide his hands beneath the sturdy cotton, molding his fingers around her raised nipples.

Farrah sighed, closing her eyes, feeling the sensation build in her groin, and rocking her hips toward him. She felt the warm air turn cool as he lifted his lips from her nipple, having suckled and teased it to a peak before moving over to the next one. He lifted his head abruptly, remarking, "There's milk there," and then lapped around her nipple, cleaning it off.

"Maybe don't suckle too hard, I don't want to start lactating now that I've pretty well finished."

"Hmm," muttered Dylan, engrossed with what he was doing.

"Wait a minute," she said, half rising to slide her arms from both the dress and her bra. "I feel a little tangled."

Dylan helped her shrug off her dress and then removed the t-shirt he'd been wearing. His shorts had an elastic waist and when Farrah had settled again, he took her hand and slid it past the waistband where his lad was hard with need. Farrah gasped as she touched him, felt the silkiness of the head and the bit of moisture at the tip. He was thick around and a moment of fear made her hesitate.

"It's alright, I'll fit. Ye'll see," he said, as if reading her mind.

"Take off your shorts. I want to see you." She felt bold and wanton, everything her father had accused her of being.

He did as she asked, standing nude before her, his lad upright with wanting, while she slid her knickers off, thanking all the stars in heaven for the thick foliage and remote location hiding them from everyone's view. It was as effective as being inside in a bed. Farrah hadn't been joking about her fantasy, and now she was about to live it. "Come to me, please. Now."

"No, not yet, my darlin'. It's too soon, ye're not quite ready. Give me a moment and I'll make it so it's the best experience of yer life."

Farrah could only nod. "Just tell me what you want me to do for you."

"Whatever ye want," he breathed, turning back to her breasts to knead, to lick, to roll her hardened nipples between his thumb and fingers while he kissed his way down her body to the midnight black hair that lined her crotch.

Dylan couldn't believe his luck. He'd felt a connection with this woman from the moment he met her, only he hadn't known it would happen this way. Time with her made things better as they got to know each other. Their likes and dislikes were similar, they thought along the same lines, and Dylan had no second thoughts about marrying her as soon as he could convince her. This step, making love to her like this, was only the beginning, and what a beginning!

Her warm skin was a beautiful dusky color, her scent slightly exotic, likely from the bath oil she used. He could smell it on her skin, everywhere he touched her, a slightly floral scent. Tropical. Intoxicatingly mysterious, just like her. And then, as he worked his way down her body, the scent of her juices tickled his nostrils and if he'd ever felt randy before, it was nothing like now. It was all he could do to refrain from taking her immediately, cautioning himself that she was still

319

raw from childbirth and not experienced in any way.

His mind had quit working once her tang hit his brain. He slid down between her legs, opened them wide, and gently spread the folds of her sex, exposing the gleaming lips, the channel that his body would follow. Kissing her curls, he tasted her with his tongue and groaned out his desire.

Farrah gasped her surprise and then began moaning her pleasure as he plunged his tongue inside her. His one hand was still attached to a nipple, the other had slid beneath her bum to place her jewel at the perfect height.

She squirmed, gasping as he flicked his tongue across her bud.

He flicked harder, faster, and Farrah responded, her cries of impending climax a signal that if ever the time was right, this was it. Dylan thrust his tongue in, sucked at her juices, and Farrah's channel quivered in spasms as she came, crying out her completion, bucking in his hands.

Holding her as her climax subsided, he sighed and kissed her, pressing his tongue into her mouth much as he had done below. She accepted it, sucked on it, and seemed not to notice that he'd slowly slid into her, and as her pelvis began to move in rhythm to his, Dylan felt the moist heat of her body engulf him, her juices coating him, her body encouraging him.

Belated, he realized he had no rubber. There was just him and her, skin to skin, and he hoped with every fiber of his being this would only be the beginning of many more trysts like this.

Farrah didn't seem bothered by it, likely hadn't thought of it, he mused, but only briefly, because his body had taken over, and moments later, he was on his way to his own climax. As he came, his body rigid above her, his only thought was how right it felt.

They lay silently together, waiting for their breathing to return to normal, Dylan still covering her body with his. And as his lad shrank and slipped from her sheath, he felt her giggle beneath him.

"What's funny?" he asked, smiling.

"It's an odd sensation, that's all," she said.

Dylan pressed a kiss to her lips, and then another. "It's a sensation I hope ye'll enjoy with me again."

A broad smile crossed Farrah's features and she bit her lip, saying shyly, "I was hoping you would say something like that."

"Only one thing," said Dylan, unable to stop from running his hand along her hip and across her breasts. "I should be using a rubber. What if I've got ye pregnant?"

"Shouldn't be a problem," said Farrah. "I've just had a flow."

"Hmm, well, I was thinkin' that maybe I should make an honest woman of ye. Maybe, since we've had unprotected sex, I should marry ye. What would ye say to that? Could ye become Mrs. Dylan Lynch?"

"Hmm, Farrah Lynch. I like the sound of that, so yes, Mr. Lynch, I will become your missus."

Her answer was so sudden and so direct that Dylan nearly fell off her. "What? Ye really will?"

Farrah giggled. "Dylan, I've wanted you from the moment I first saw you, so yes, I believe I'm quite serious."

"Well then, we should celebrate some more."

She cupped his cheeks with her hands and brought his face down to hers to return his kiss.

He broke the kiss, slowly, and gazed at her as if he couldn't believe his luck. She was like a fairytale come true. "One question."

321

She looked up at him with a query in her wide, moss-green eyes.

"Did I fulfill yer fantasy?"

Her answer was to grin and take his mouth again.

Chapter Twenty-Five

Marry me, Kathleen," said Damian, holding her in his arms after loving her. She was due to go back to work tomorrow and he was suddenly aware he didn't want to be apart from her, separated in any way. He wanted to spend all his tomorrows with her and wished he could have had his yesterdays as well.

Kathleen's eyes softened as did the smile across her face. "Ye're daft, ye are," she said lovingly. "It's just sex that's addled yer mind."

"No. I love ye, Kathleen O'Farrell, and if it takes the rest of my days, I'm goin' to convince ye to marry me."

"Why? Why ruin a good thing, Damian? We've done well so far. Let's not spoil it with a weddin'."

"Spoil it? Is that what ye think marriage to me would do? Spoil what we have now?" He sat up, suddenly wary of the woman he had just made love to. Maybe he didn't know her as well as he thought.

"No, don't misunderstand, love." Kathleen looked flustered, ashamed that she had broken the atmosphere of loving that had engulfed them. The peace had fractured, and Damian moved off.

"Well then, maybe ye'd better explain, because I never thought of our relationship as a part-time thing. To me, it's been all or nothin', and ye seemed to be in agreement."

To her credit, Kathleen blushed. And then teared up.

Whipping the covers from her sex-warmed body, she stood and made her way to the en suite bathroom to wash her face and cool herself down. She still had hot flashes, and Damian was used to seeing the heat that spread along her torso, up her breasts and chin, to finish on her cheeks. He often teased her of nipping at some rum when that happened because that's what it looked like.

She came back from the bathroom, more in control, looking less pink. More like the woman he loved.

"Damian, I love ye in my way, I just don't know if I can stand a man around full-time, like. I've tried it before and it's never worked out, so what do ye think makes this different, that I'll be able to stand the sight of ye day after day?"

Her words could have hurt a less confident man, but Damian was not a coward. He loved her with a passion and knew she loved him. The difficulty was to convince her of that.

"Kathleen, ye're all I've ever wanted in a woman. I love yer independence, yer fortitude. And I love the way ye ride herd on yer family and don't take any nonsense from them. I wish I could tell ye all the ways I love ye but I'm hopin' we can stay together long enough that ye'll eventually learn them all for yerself."

Kathleen sat on the edge of the bed, her back to him. He looked at the long column of her back, at her waist that rolled out rather than in, at the thickness of her arse as it widened to her thighs. He could feel himself chub up at the sight and refused to compare her to his first wife, whose body was thin as a reed, all hard angles and bony protrusions. He much preferred Kathleen's softer body and cared not one whit that she had a little extra padding.

"I don't know, Damian. Can we not just stay this way for a while longer? I'm not used to havin' ye around so much, like, and I'm feelin' a little trapped…"

"Trapped? How am I makin' ye feel trapped? Because I'm here more than at my own place?"

"Maybe. It'll take some gettin' used to, so I can't answer ye right now. I've retirement comin' up and this doesn't fit in with what I'd envisioned for myself."

He slid across the bed to place his head beside her thigh, to look up at her from his prone position. Laying his arm across her lap and rubbing her opposite thigh with his hand, he said, "Retirement will give us all the time we need to figure this out. It's a big adjustment, and if ye don't want to do anythin' formal just now, I can see that. For me, I believe I've got everythin' I need here with ye. I don't need anythin' else. I can help Dylan at the store, do errands, fix things. I'm willin' to do whatever ye need in order to make ye happy. And if that includes some time away, I can always bunk in with Dylan."

Her green eyes met his brown ones, then looked away, her arms cradling the limb he was stroking her with. "What about yer place in Cork City?"

"I thought I'd sell it. I've no use for it now, but if ye want, I'll keep it and we can use it, or it'll be there if ye pull a late shift and don't want to come home afterward."

She smiled at that, saying, "Ye realize, do ye not, that ye've given me ample excuse to avoid ye? I only have to say I'm still workin' and then go there instead of here to be away from ye."

"If that's what it takes to please ye."

Sighing heavily, she twisted to face him as his hand moved up to cup her very ample breast. The nipple sprang to life beneath his touch and she sighed again as her lips came down to meet his.

"Come around and let me love ye," he said, urging her to lie down lengthwise on the bed. She followed his direction and he spread her legs, placed them over his shoulders exposing her box to his gaze, and leaned in.

"Damian, ye're insatiable for an old man," she laughed.

"Am I not? It's a terrible thing I'm afflicted with, but lucky for me, it only occurs with yerself."

"Hmm," she murmured as he went to work on her. And then, "Damian?"

"Hmm?" It came out more of guttural grunt, given he was busy with his tongue.

"Ah, feckit, Damian!"

Damian's answer was a chuckle as he continued his ministrations.

A quietness came over her, her body moving rhythmically in time with his tongue that was dipping, lapping, swirling as her breaths came faster, harder. Moaning out her climax, her juices flowing fast and wet, Damian feasted, swallowing all he could. And before she had finished her high, Damian slid into her, his lad hard and eager as he thrust to completion before she had a chance to think.

His nads had tightened to little rocks, his body straining inside hers, the cheeks of his arse in knots of muscle for all his advancing age. Damian at sixty-eight was more fit than many at forty. He worked out regularly and was physically active so that he hadn't yet acquired the effects of advancing age. His body was still that of a man much younger, and he wondered if Kathleen's knowledge that she'd not looked after herself in quite the same way was part of what kept her single. It didn't matter to him, he mused, but he'd sometimes wondered if his physical prowess was intimidating to her; if she saw him as someone who might see a woman in better shape and want to chase after her instead of being saddled with a slightly overweight female.

Kathleen needn't worry, he knew. It wasn't about her body, although he was ever so pleased with it. It was about her entire being, the way she looked at the world, the way she connected with him. It was an emotional connection that heightened the physical. In short, he loved her for who she was, not the way she looked nor anything else. She was, to him, a perfect match.

"Damian?"

"Mmm?" He was still enjoying the postcoital effects and hadn't quite recovered his normal rate of breathing.

"That was good craic."

* * *

As lover's quarrels went, it wasn't horrible, thought Emily as she went about the shop, methodically watering the plants tucked away in various nooks and crannies. Some were on large display items, such as an antique Welsh dresser that had been there for the last ten years, or so she was told. Its well-worn surface was still in good form, the few scratches and gouges it had received over a lifetime of use not detracting from its majestic presence in light of other, lesser pieces. Emily loved dusting it off, and hoped one day to have such an item in a place of her own.

Her mind replayed the argument she and Fionn had engaged in; she couldn't believe he wouldn't see her point of view. He'd avoided it. Whenever she brought it up, he changed the subject, and she was beginning to get the feeling that Fionn was tiring of her. But then she'd go to walk away and he'd grab her, kiss her hard, and make love to her; and she, silly girl that she was, allowed it.

Still, he hadn't addressed her proposition. Had refused to talk about it.

Turning after emptying the watering can, she nearly bumped straight into her boss, who'd come to see how she was making out.

"Are ye enjoying the job, Emily?" asked Dharia.

Emily smiled, "Yeah, it's interestin', learnin' about all the different types of plants and plant care. I had no idea about most of them."

"Well, I can tell ye're intelligent, and ye've learned a lot and been a big help to me. Can ye put that down for a bit and come and sit? I think we should talk."

It was a quiet morning and the shop hadn't had many customers yet as it was still early. Sitting down behind the counter with Emily, in plain view of the door should anyone walk in, Dharia said, "I've noticed ye seem a little distracted lately. Is everythin' okay?"

Feeling tears prick at the back of her eyes, Emily quickly blinked them back and sucked in a deep, calming breath. "It's that obvious, is it?"

Dharia nodded. "I'm afraid so. Care to get it off yer shoulders?"

It seemed to be what Emily needed just then. Unable to go to her gran or her mam, and especially not her da with such a problem, Emily was relieved to have a girlfriend of sorts to open up to. Looking at her boss, a woman in her mid forties, slightly older than her mam, Emily began. "It's Fionn. He won't discuss what'll happen with us when he goes to art school this September. I want to go with him, to work and be with him while he attends, but he refuses to discuss it. It's as if he doesn't want me there. It's as if he doesn't want me at all," she explained, trying valiantly to keep the emotion from her words. But her voice wobbled, and she swallowed hard over the lump in her throat.

"Are ye livin' with him now, then?"

"No. Just the odd night I stay with him, when we've been out and it's too late to go home. Gran's been good about it, although I can see it in her face she's none too pleased. I feel guilty, but then, I'm eighteen. I shouldn't have to explain myself to anyone."

"Eighteen. And that's a ripe old age, isn't it!" Dharia exclaimed, laughing. Sobering quickly, she said, "At eighteen, ye're right, ye shouldn't have to explain things to anyone, but ye're also just feelin' yer way in life. Ye're bound to make mistakes. It's how we learn, how we all learn. Yer gran just doesn't want ye to make a mistake. She wants things to be smooth for ye."

"And how would ye know that? Ye don't know my gran," Emily said, but the look on her boss's face gave her pause for thought. "Do ye?"

"No, no more than to say hello. But I've eyes and ears and a daughter a wee bit older than yerself. She's moved up to County Meath, so I don't see her often, but we're still in touch."

"And her da?" Emily wasn't sure if she should ask. It wasn't really any of her business but she was curious because Dharia had never mentioned a husband before.

"Well, that's a long story, and since ye've asked, and since I know a little of yer own background, I'll tell ye. I never married."

The statement put an O of surprise on Emily's lips, and she sucked in her gasp as wicked thoughts raced through her mind.

Dharia laughed. "I can see I've surprised ye. It's true, though. I never married the man who fathered my child. In fact, after I got to know him and even though I was pregnant, I realized I didn't want him in my life. He wasn't interested in the baby, never cared much about me, either, so I left. It hurt for a long time, especially once I came to grips with knowin' he didn't love me and never had. I was a body for him to cuddle at night and take his pleasure. I hadn't intended to become pregnant. But I did. We fought, and rather than him throw me out, I left and raised my child on my own. Believe me, it wasn't easy in those days. People frowned on unmarried women with children and I was looked at for the longest time as a hussy. But that was years ago, and it's different now. People are more acceptin'. I eventually found my way here, began to work in this shop, just like you. But then the owner wanted to sell, and even though I had only a little in the bank, we worked out a way for me to buy her out. And here I am, a self-made woman, and happier than I've been all my life."

"Does yer daughter not want to know her da?" asked Emily, scrunching her nose in thought.

"No. She's no use for someone who never wanted her. I offered to find him so she could meet him, and I did look for a while. But then she came to me one day and said she wanted me to stop. We had words. I thought I was doin' her a kindness, but I was interferin', she said. After that, I started to pay attention to what she wanted and needed from me and it turned out she truly had no desire to meet the man who sired her. She was quite content without him and without knowing him. So I let it be. She has his name and his last known address if she wants to find him. As far as I know, she hasn't, but that's her story, her life. It's not up to me any longer."

"Ye know Dylan is my father?" There, Emily had said it, it was now out in the open.

Dharia's reaction wasn't the surprise Emily thought it might be and she answered the girl's question easily. "Yes, he mentioned it. Oh, not the details, mind," at which Emily breathed a sigh of relief. "Ye see, I've known Dylan a long time. He's a very nice man, once ye get to know him. Just a bit shy, and abrupt at times because of his shyness. But he really is a sweetheart."

"Humph," mumbled Emily, clearly not sharing her boss's impressions of the man. "I guess I'll have to wait and see. I suppose I don't know him so well and shouldn't form an opinion. But I once thought that if I ever did find my da, I'd know him instantly and love him like I knew he'd love me. But it didn't turn out like that, not at all."

"Give him time. He's a lot on his plate just now. Look at the nice young woman he's got now. They seem so happy together. It's the first time I've seen Dylan this happy since I've known him." She paused, cocking her head slightly as if gauging how much she should impart. "Did ye know his mother left him and his da when he was just a child?"

Emily shook her head, hoping Dharia would enlighten her.

She wasn't disappointed.

"It's true. I think he's always felt insecure and unloved because of that one act. She was terrible to him, cut him off, wouldn't even write. Never sent birthday or Christmas gifts. Not even a note. It was as if, in her mind, he didn't exist."

"That's terrible," exclaimed Emily. "Who could do that to a child?"

"My old boyfriend could, and so, apparently, could Dylan's mam. And his da has now found a wonderful

331

companion in yer gran. So maybe ye should sit down with Fionn and make him talk. Have that conversation and find out what it is he wants. Some things in life are tough and if ye want the truth, ye might have to pull it out of him, like. And ye know what?" At Emily's questioning gaze, she continued, "If he doesn't want to talk, then leave. Ye're not so far into this that ye can't back out."

"But I love him," Emily exclaimed, tears starting in her eyes again.

"That's a load, that is," Dharia admonished, but her tone was gentle, albeit chiding. "Ye think ye're in love but it's really just infatuation. He's yer first love, yer first crack at life. Those almost never work out. Take what this relationship can give ye and move on. He's a nice boy, but there's much nicer out there."

"Humph," Emily mumbled again. "I've been here over two months and he's the only one I've met. I haven't met any other fella at all."

"Inishannon isn't the biggest place on the map," Dharia offered kindly. "Ye've really only just begun lookin'. If ye go to school in September rather than stayin' on here, ye'll find someone more suited to yerself."

"But ye need me here," she protested.

"That I do. But I'll find someone who can help out. I always do." A twinkle appeared in her eye as she met Emily's gaze. "I found you, didn't I?"

Emily had to laugh at that because it was true. She'd walked into the store, looking for work at just the right time. "I don't know what I want to do at school, though. I haven't a clue."

"Time will tell. Just don't place all yer hopes with Fionn. Like I said, he's a nice boy, but he has his own agenda, and it doesn't sound like it's matchin' yer own, at least not right now. However, all that aside," she rose from her chair and smoothed out the imaginary wrinkles in her skirt, "we need to get on with our day. I've a new shipment of flowers comin' soon, so we'll be busy."

Nodding, Emily rose also, retrieved the watering can from where she left it, and went to refill it. She'd planned to have lunch with Fionn but maybe she'd run up to Gran's and get something there instead. Gran was working today, but that didn't mean there wouldn't be leftovers in the refrigerator to scrounge.

* * *

Fionn wiped down the counter, not bothering to look up when the door opened. It was nearly the lunch hour and people had already begun to file in. The kitchen was busy putting together the special today, and the smell of the oil heating up for the fish and chips was rapidly being taken over by the aroma of the ale being poured.

His mind returned to the argument he and Emily had the night before. She had become a complication in his life he hadn't expected, and now she wanted to go to Dublin with him, to keep house and look after him while he was at school. It wasn't something he wanted. As an artist, he was used to getting up at all hours to work on his paintings and sketches. He honed his craft seriously and while Emily had been a wonderful diversion, her constant presence was beginning to chafe.

Avoiding her probing questions last night hadn't been easy and he'd changed the subject more than once. Tried to, he amended. She'd been persistent, wanting to have his feedback on ideas and questions she had for going to Dublin. Where would they live? Did he think she'd be able to find work there? The list seemed endless, and Fionn, who already had a part-time job lined up at the pub he'd worked at previously, didn't want Emily there; hadn't thought she'd ever really want to move to Dublin when she'd only recently come to live with her gran.

They'd argued and she'd left, but not before he'd kissed her and made love to her again. It was the only way he knew to shut her up, and it had worked. They were once again in harmony when he dropped her at her gran's around midnight.

He couldn't keep doing that, he knew. They had to break it off, he couldn't keep up a relationship with a woman who wanted his body morning, noon, and night. It had kept him from his artwork, and even though he'd tried to paint her, he found himself dragged away from the work, and often it was because his mind wasn't on it. As lovely as she was, and he thought her body to be as gorgeous a thing as ever he had seen, Fionn was tiring of her. Or rather, her constant presence. If he had put his foot down in the first place, disallowed her to stay overnight, he wouldn't be in the pickle he now found himself in. He'd be in control of the situation and see her only when he wanted to. It hadn't worked out that way, though, and now he was paying the price of having a beautiful woman in his bed when he'd rather be alone.

This was all too much, and suddenly, in front of him while he'd been daydreaming, stood her da, or rather, her uncle, looking to be in a mood as black as his hair.

"Mr. O'Farrell," nodded Fionn.

Henry nodded and sat down. "Coffee, if ye don't mind," he said, but Fionn was certain it wasn't coffee he wanted. In fact, he'd swear the man wanted the black stuff. Or maybe whiskey. But certainly not coffee.

"Would ye like anythin' else?" he asked, and was relieved

to see Henry shake his head in the negative.

"Just stoppin' in for a break," said Henry, taking a sip of the strong brew.

It was strong, thought Fionn, watching Henry's face react to the bitterness. "We're tryin' a new brand. What's yer opinion of it?"

"Humph," said Henry, swallowing. "I've had worse. It's the first one I can honestly say has a kick to it."

There was almost a sparkle in his eye and he almost smiled, Fionn noticed, and quickly took another order while Henry sat with his coffee.

After twenty minutes, Henry stood to go. "Got a minute for a break?" he asked, and Fionn, looking around in a rapid assessment, nodded.

"Is this about the other night?" asked Fionn as they stood outside. The man hadn't come around the day after he and Emily were caught together, and in truth, Fionn had been expecting him at any time. Maybe that was part of the man's tactics; keep your opponent guessing.

Henry faced Fionn, hands in pockets. Once again, Fionn was aware of the size of those hands, of the capability of the man, and thought it was just another reason why he and Emily should part ways.

"Partly," he shrugged. "Em's been harpin' about wantin' to go to Dublin with ye. Says ye're goin' to school there and she wants to go, too. I was just wonderin' yer take on it."

Feckit, thought Fionn. The man was as perceptive as a wizard with a crystal ball. "It's true," he answered. "I'm startin' my second year. I've a job lined up and leave here in another month."

"And what about Emily?"

If Fionn thought this was going to be easy, he was

beginning to realize he was sadly mistaken. "We haven't really talked about it, like," he replied, knowing he'd been evading the issue.

"Well, maybe ye need to. I know she's eighteen. She thinks she's old enough to make her own decisions but I don't think she's ready for Dublin yet, at least, not this way."

"And what way would that be?" It rankled that Henry seemed to think Fionn was incapable of watching out for Emily. He stretched as much as he could but Henry was taller and he couldn't meet the man's eyes without looking up.

"I think ye know exactly what I'm sayin'," said Henry, his very deep blue eyes looking black in the shadow of the pub sign overhead.

Fionn sighed, wondering what to say that would appease Emily's da. "Mr. O'Farrell, I'd like to tell ye it's between Emily and me, but I also think if I said that, ye'd be callin' me out. Maybe not now, but sometime." He took a moment to assess Henry's reaction and knew he wasn't wrong. "The truth is, I can't take Emily with me. It wouldn't work. I'm goin' to art school, did she tell ye?" At the shake of Henry's head, he continued, "Well, it's art school. And I can't paint when she's around. I—I can't do anythin'," he stammered.

"Except take her to bed," finished Henry.

Fionn hadn't expected to feel so enraged. Henry's words had hit home because as crass as they were, it was the truth. So instead of hitting the man, which was his first instinct, he stood taller, shaking with anger, trying to calm his breathing and get himself under control. "I won't apologize for that," said Fionn through tight lips. "It's her as much as me."

"Are ye sayin' she's a sex-crazed ráicleach?" Henry's black gaze grew even darker, daring Fionn to answer.

"Enough. I don't have to listen to this," muttered Fionn,

turning to go back into the pub.

Henry stopped him with a hand on his shoulder. "Do us all a favor," he said quietly, the threat in his words clear, "Tell her the truth. Ye don't love her and don't want her. It's easier than bein' cowardly and draggin' her along. I've no wish to see my daughter dragged through the mud by the likes o' ye."

Fionn, frozen on the spot, watched as Henry stalked off, got into his vehicle, and drove away. He was shaking, but whether from anger or indignation, he couldn't have said. Stuffing his hands into his pockets to stop the trembling, he recognized that what Henry had said was exactly what Fionn had been feeling. Emily was always horned up, always looking for a piece of Fionn, and was often the one to initiate sex. It was exactly what Henry described, but he wouldn't say she was a slut. Far from it.

But Henry had been absolutely correct when he said that Fionn was being a coward. The knowledge didn't sit well.

"Fionn!"

The call from inside brought him back to where he was, to the pub, to the spot on the street, and briefly, to the flower shop down the road. Emily was in there now, but there was no time to come clean to her, to tell her what she needed to know. He didn't love her, and especially didn't have time for her now. In fact, if he was smart, he'd go to Dublin now, give up some of the wages to pay rent instead of staying in Inishannon nearly rent free, and get on with life. She was a complication he didn't need.

"Fionn!"

The call came again, more insistent this time, and Fionn shook off the feeling of Henry's unspoken threat and went inside.

* * *

337

Lunch time came and went, with no sign of Emily. They were to have met up at the pub, and even though Fionn didn't take any kind of a lunch, she would sit at the bar and he'd serve her whatever she ordered. When he wasn't busy with other customers, they would talk and laugh together.

But she hadn't come, and Fionn wondered if it was because of her father. Emily had a lot to deal with just now, he knew. She'd recently met the woman who had fallen in love with the pharmacist and moved in with him. So was that woman to be another mother figure for Emily? It was confusing, Fionn thought, and if it was confusing for himself, it must be doubly confusing for Emily.

When his own break came near the end of Emily's work day, Fionn wondered if he should go up to the flower shop and see if she was alright. But something made him hesitate, as if Henry's words were penetrating his skull, urging him to tell her. But tell her what? That he didn't love her?

Did he, or didn't he? Henry had been right in calling him a coward. He was a coward. He didn't want to see the hurt in Emily's eyes, didn't want her accusations of him playing her to leave her lips. Because inside, he felt they were true.

Lots of women loved Fionn. He was cute, or so he was told, and he knew how to make a lady feel good. He knew it because he wasn't a selfish lover, and had been told that, too. Yet there was something special about Emily that he couldn't quite shake. Finding out that the chemist was her real father was both a surprise and a complication he hadn't counted on. Dylan Lynch seemed an alright fella most days, and was certainly easier to deal with than Henry O'Farrell. That man scared the bejaysus out of him, what with his grand height and meaty fists. A fighter if ever he'd seen one.

Dylan, however, was another matter. Calm on the surface,

he seemed a loose cannon underneath, as if you never knew how he would react to something. At least with Henry, he knew and could either outrun the man or duck the punches before they came.

There was also the business of Emily's true lineage. Trying to unwind her actual family history was as bad as straightening the pub after a royal brawl. Not impossible, but feckin' difficult. It was, in short, a lot of hard work.

It would take a lot of hard work to understand Emily, or more to the point, get her family onside. And at this point in his life, he didn't have the internal resources to manage it all. Her gran had made him feel welcome and he thought things had gone well at Emily's birthday dinner. Yet Henry O'Farrell had not been moved. Either that, or he was still pissed at Fionn for taking his daughter's virginity, and before she'd turned eighteen, no less.

No, it wasn't so much himself being a coward, thought Fionn as he finished his break and went back inside, as it was he couldn't break her heart. He knew she had feelings for him, although he didn't know how deep they went. Maybe they were such that she'd get over his leaving for school easily. Maybe she already had. After all, she hadn't shown at lunch and it wasn't like her to break a date. If anything, she was always eager to see him and wanting to plan their next get-together before the current one had ended.

Two more hours. He had two more hours left in his shift. Maybe then he'd give her a call. Maybe.

Chapter Twenty-Six

It was Kathleen's final shift, or at least, her final shift as a full-time nurse. She'd agreed to be on-call and smiled ruefully at the thought because on-call was sometimes more frequent than full-time. There were always staff shortages and Kathleen had more than her fair share of extra hours to her credit. She'd worked all her life. It had been a veritable lifeline after her husband was killed, and even before that when she'd found out about his infidelity; about the other family he'd kept secret from herself and their own brood.

As she closed her locker door for the last time and turned to leave, she hadn't been expecting the crowd that had formed to wish her well on her way with flowers and a gift. They'd taken her out to lunch at the cafeteria—no one had a great deal of time, especially when their pagers could go off at any moment—and that had been lovely, thought Kathleen. But now the tears came as she was overcome with emotion, and as everyone gathered round, it finally hit home that she would not be coming back tomorrow, nor the day after that. She was well and truly retiring.

Loading up Damian's car with her flowers, the lovely gift of a Belleek china vase from her coworkers, and the contents of the now empty locker, she scanned the angry sky overhead. Emily had taken to driving Kathleen's car to and from work since the weather had turned rainy, and as Damian was helping at Dylan's pharmacy this week, he'd offered her the use of his car.

Dodging fat raindrops, she hustled herself into the driver's seat and started the car. She sat, looking at the clouds overhead and wondering if this rain was trying to make up for all the sunshine they'd had. It had been a lovely stretch of weather, and though everyone was glad for a day of rain, the gladness dimmed after it had continued for a solid week with no letup in sight. Well, it was Ireland, after all, and there was a reason it was so green. She only wished for a small break. A half day of sunshine would be nice, just to let things dry out a little.

As she steered her way toward Inishannon, her mind drifted over Damian's proposal. She was tempted, so tempted to take him up on it, but she just couldn't see herself as a married woman. It had been too long. She'd been self-sufficient long before Henry's accident. Henry-the-senior, she reminded herself, as if to say his name without that addition would bring bad luck to her son.

They'd managed well for all the family had gone through after the accident. Young Henry had taken matters into his own hands, had begun playing father to the rest of the weyans, and Kathleen, feeling lost and at sea herself, hadn't objected.

She should have. She should have taken the mantle of responsibility from Henry's young shoulders, but he was so capable and seemed to take it all in stride. It had simply been easier, took less of her energy, to let him do it.

Life had gone on from there; she at work with as many shifts as she could pull, and young Henry watching out for the weyans, riding herd on the boys, looking out for wee Ciara. Between young Henry and herself, the family grew up, and only Brandon seemed the worse for it all. She hadn't realized, until Aine came along, how troubled Brandon had been. It was as if he'd been running from something all his life. And then he met Aine, and while things were very bad for a while, they eventually sorted themselves out, and now Brandon and Aine were to be parents.

Grandchildren! Oh, how she loved them, all of them, even Hank's two weyans. Although no blood relation to herself, she couldn't deny the love she felt for them—not just the two children, but Hank and Laura, too. They were a blessing, just as each of her other children and grandchildren were. Hank had suffered just as much as the rest of them with Henry-the-senior's death. Perhaps more. He'd lost his sister, his mam. And until the pieces of the puzzle were put together, the niece he never knew about. The poor boy had been set adrift with no one to lean on, and yet he'd fared well in the end. Like Brandon, Hank had gone through hell before finding Laura, and through Siobhan, the rest of his family. How they had all suffered!

That was life, Kathleen ruminated.

The rain began falling heavier, forcing her thoughts back to the road. N71 was a busy stretch and she really needed to pay more attention. The wipers were going as fast as possible, but still the rain came down in sheets, making it a challenge to see clearly. She'd have to remind Damian to purchase new wiper blades, she cursed, as the torrent on her windscreen turned oily. To add to the stress, it was dark, and headlights glared at her from the opposite direction.

* * *

Emily stood at the door of the pub, wondering if she should go in or just go home. Dharia's words lay heavy on her heart, repeating with every beat, "leave-Fionn, leave-Fionn."

Then suddenly, her mind made up on a different course of action, she turned on her heel and returned to where she'd parked Gran's car that morning. She was ever so glad of it, since the darkening sky was a good indication there'd be rain before she got home. And true enough, she felt the first light spatters before she closed the car door.

Instead of going home, she went to the grocery store, picked up a few items, and headed up to Fionn's cottage. She knew where he kept the key, even though there was hardly anything in the place to steal. He had little in the way of personal possessions. He was, as he had told her, a student, and lived his life accordingly.

But for now, she was going to cook for him. She wanted him to see that she could provide for him, give him sustenance after a long day at classes, or hours at the easel, his back sore from standing or sitting too long. As she unloaded the groceries, enough to make a hearty stew on a chilly summer day, she imagined him coming home, her fingers kneading the sore muscles of his neck as he sat down to tuck into a wholesome meal.

Opening the door to the little cottage, she was thankful for its solid warmth on this not-so-warm day. The light came on with a flick of the switch and putting the bag of groceries on the table, she abandoned them only long enough to remove her raincoat and get to work.

Emily was a good cook, Siobhan had seen to that. Siobhan, ever the health-nut, had begun teaching Emily the tricks to cooking simply and with wholesome ingredients as soon as they had become a family. In time, Emily became adept at throwing a good meal on the table, often accompanied by homemade bread. So while the vegetables and the meat in the stew simmered away, she threw together ingredients for a quick soda bread. Everything would be ready when Fionn got home.

* * *

By the time Fionn pulled into his driveway, the rain was coming down in wind-driven sheets, more like the winter storms that plundered the coast in January than a summer squall. The reflection of his headlights on the vehicle parked by the door could not be ignored. He recognized the car, realizing just then that the lights were on inside the cottage as well as the one single light over the stoop. Emily must be inside.

He turned the car off and sat for a moment, wondering what he should say to her. Examining his feelings as he'd done all day had amounted to little in the way of solutions. Yes, he was guilty of everything her da had said about him, and he wondered if he truly did love her enough to want to marry her, would that make a difference with Henry? They'd gotten off on the wrong foot, surely, but did he have to pay for that mistake over and over? Was an apology, an allowance that he hadn't realized she was underage and still a virgin, enough? Would that not account for something?

Again, he thought not. Henry would hate and make trouble for anyone who took an interest in Emily.

So where did that leave him? The answer was clear— somewhere between a desire to keep on seeing her and the need to break it off. Neither spot was comfortable because he had no doubt that if he kept on seeing her, wedding bells would chime. And for Fionn, it was too early for that. He hadn't finished art school yet, hadn't settled himself on a path in life with a wage with which to pay his own way. It was too soon to be saddled with a wife and family.

Yet, if he broke off their relationship as Henry wanted,

Fionn had no doubt he'd break Emily's heart. Part of him acknowledged that her feelings for him were likely because he was her first lover. Girls were sentimental that way.

He didn't get a chance to examine his feelings beyond that, as the door to his cottage opened slightly and Emily poked her head outside. The small overhang did little to shield her from the rain, so he got out of his car, slamming it shut behind him as he ran, enduring his fair share of rain in the process.

Stepping inside and shaking the water from his hair, the first thing that hit him was the smell of something hearty, wholesome. Something that made his stomach rumble with hunger. The sandwich he'd had during his break hadn't been much, but they'd been busy, and he hadn't had time to eat more.

Before he knew it, Emily was guiding him to sit at the table before a steaming bowl of stew, a loaf of soda bread still warm from the oven and wrapped in a tea towel, sliced and ready to butter. As Fionn began to eat, Emily served herself up and sat down to join him at the table, their knees touching beneath the scarred wooden surface that sported what appeared to be new placemats of a colorful printed design beneath their bowls, and next to the wall, a small bunch of summer flowers were sitting in a jar with a bit of water. She'd even put a bright yellow bow around the jar in an artful attempt at brightening his small space. It worked.

Sighing as he ate, Fionn reflected that he could get used to this, and his emotions, already conflicted where Emily stood, were confused further by her attentions to his needs. She'd known better than he just what it was he'd needed on this day.

They spoke little during the meal, and for that Fionn

was grateful. He didn't know what to say, but when it was done and Emily cleared the dishes away, she stood behind his chair before he could rise and began to knead the muscles of his neck, his upper back, her thumbs digging into the knots created by hard work.

Fionn moaned his appreciation, closing his eyes as his head lolled forward. "Where the feck did ye learn to do that?" he asked.

Giggling, she answered, "I'd watch mam do it for da when he came in after working all day. Ye could tell his back was sore and she'd start at his neck and work down. Course, after a bit, some secret would pass between them and they'd end up upstairs, but at the time I only knew that he was enjoyin' whatever she was doin'." Continuing her ministrations, she asked, "Are ye likin' it?"

Fionn didn't even hesitate. "Oh, yeah."

A few minutes later, as Emily began to move down his back, he said with a laugh, "I think I know why yer folks went upstairs."

"Oh?" asked Emily, a giggle in her voice.

Spinning out of his chair with a fluid ease, Fionn faced her to pull her close, ignoring all his previous thoughts of breaking it off. He couldn't think while she was with him.

Immediately, his hands went beneath her top to tug it off and expose her body to his gaze. Her clothing had no sooner hit the floor than his followed suit, and they stood, naked before each other beneath the glare of the overhead light.

"Let's make this more romantic," said Fionn, reaching over to turn off the light, allowing the darkness to engulf them as he took her hand and led her to the bed. Flicking on the small bedside lamp, he faced her, pulled her to him, and wondered why he'd ever thought he could live without her.

"I've not finished yer massage, yet," she said into his mouth.

Fionn's hands were roaming the length of her body, cupping her arse one minute, playing with the nipples of her large breasts the next. His mouth moved down, kissing her breasts as he went, then her abdomen, and taking a moment to tickle her belly button, he nibbled at her belly, making her giggle before settling at the mound between her legs. Spreading her crease, exposing her jewel to his tongue, he was rewarded with her sigh and felt her fingers part the strands of his hair before cupping his nape.

"Ah, Fionn," she breathed on another sigh. "I was supposed to be massaging ye. Ye've totally taken over."

"Mm-hmm," he mumbled, not willing to give up what he was doing, not even for a massage. Her body's nectar was his dessert and he would be hard pressed to give that up willingly.

"Lie down," he said, indicating the bed with a nod, and with a smile as broad as could be, Emily did so, her long, black waves like a curtain around her breasts. Brushing those silky tresses aside, he came over her and began his ministrations once again.

They'd made good headway, Emily's breathing was quickening as she lay beneath him, her hands roamed his body, encouraging him on. Fionn placed his lad at her entrance and then he slid inside, felt her warmth engulf him, and quit thinking. From then on, it was pure pleasure, Emily's young body moved beneath him, her insides clenched his lad as he slid in and out, each movement bringing them both closer to fulfillment. As Emily's breathing became faster, she began to moan her climax, and Fionn was right there with her, thrusting for all he was worth until she cried out with pleasure, his own body growing rigid as his own sounds of completion echoed around the silent room.

He opened his eyes to the glare of the lamp and turned his head into her neck, curtained by those silky waves of her hair. Ever since she'd started on the pill, they'd done away with rubbers, and it was ever so nice a feeling, he reflected, lying there in the aftermath of lovemaking, his lad still deep inside her.

Emily moved beneath him and Fionn came back to himself. Christ, he thought, I shouldn't have done that, shouldn't have made love to her. But it was too late, and as she opened love-drenched eyes, he couldn't help but smile and feel as if he could lose himself in their depths. She had eyes like a summer pool, dark blue, tinged with the lighter blue of the sky. Sometimes the ocean was like that, he knew, and sometimes it would turn angry and gray…and why was he suddenly thinking like this?

Heaving a sigh, he brushed a wayward lock of her midnight black hair from her eyes, met her gaze, and said, "Em, we have to talk."

"No. I don't want to talk."

She was stubbornly refusing as if she knew what it was he wanted to say. No, he amended, what he needed to say.

"Em, ye know I care for ye?"

"Yeah. I care for ye, too. Maybe even more than just care."

"I know," he agreed. And he did know. Emily wore her heart on her sleeve, so the saying went, and in this case, it was all too true. "Ye couldn't lie to me if ye wanted to. There isn't a false bone in yer body." Women could be shifty, he knew, when they wanted something. Scheming even, and he had no doubt Emily could do both. But lie to him? Never.

"Then what is it ye want to talk about?"

She was running her fingers along his shoulder and down the length of his arm, following it with her eyes, avoiding his gaze.

"Em, look at me."

Her eyes met his, wide open in an innocent expression. "What?"

"As nice as this is, as lovely as supper was and the massage…"

"Ye never let me finish the massage," she interrupted.

"What I had of it was nice."

"Then let me finish it," she said, trying to move out from beneath him.

His lad slipped from her body and he softly cursed. "Em, please listen."

A big sigh and then, "Fine."

"I can't have ye come with me to school. It won't work." There. It was out. He'd said it. Again. How many times would they need to have this talk?

"Fionn, I can help ye through it. I can cook for ye, be there to do all the things ye won't have time for. I can ease yer…"

"Em, ye aren't listenin'. I can't have ye there because I can't think when ye're around. I can't work, I can't paint. I can't bloody do anythin' with you in the room. Feckit, I can't even hardly breathe when I'm with ye!"

A grin spread across her face. "That's a good thing then, eh?"

Fionn pushed himself off her body, grabbed some tissues out of the box, and handed her a couple. "Here. Ye may need them."

"No, wait. Don't go yet."

"Go? Where would I go?"

349

"No, I mean, come back to me. Let me make love to ye, finish the massage."

The pleading look he received was almost too much for him. He could feel his body quicken at her suggestion.

Sitting beside her he pointed to his lad, threatening to rise. "Ye see? This is why we can't be together. I'd never get anythin' done except make love to ye. I have no control where ye're concerned and I don't know what to do about it."

"Then why fight it?"

Frustrating. This whole argument was frustrating. And pointless. She was not going to be convinced they had to part. He stood and she followed him, wouldn't give him the space to leave. Yet where would he go?

"Em, I need to go alone. Can't ye just accept that?"

"No. I get that it'll be a hard year for ye, but that's why I can make it better. I can go to work, make the money to keep us both so ye don't have to work. Ye'll be able to concentrate on yer studies."

"But that's just it," he yelled in frustration, his hands fisted at his sides, his voice ringing through the tiny cottage. "I can't concentrate when ye're around!"

"Why are ye bein' so bull-headed about this?" Her voice was rising in volume along with his, her fingers splayed wide in question. "It's a simple solution, and I won't bother ye when ye're workin'. I'll stay away while ye need to paint. I'll do all those things so ye can do yer paintin', and studyin', and anythin' else."

"Bull-headed? Me? What about yerself, standin' there, lookin' like the thing I want most in life but can't have because I can't feckin' work while ye're around! How can I make ye understand?"

"And I say ye can. Ye just have to get used to me bein'

here," she retorted in the same tone he'd just used.

He took her shoulders in his hands, was about to say more when she closed the gap between them and took his mouth with hers.

"Ah, feckit. I have no argument against that," he said as her mouth claimed his again.

They moved back to the bed, Emily pushing him down so she could sit atop him to then begin her ministrations once again.

"It's all about the sex with ye," he said, breathing hard as she moved her way down his abdomen and began licking at the tip of his lad.

A giggle of a response came and then silence as she engulfed him with her mouth.

She had him, he knew. He could no more deny her this than he could deny himself, and all arguments aside, she was a habit that was going to be tough to give up.

"Em, what are ye doin' to me? What are ye turnin' me into?" he sighed, fully enjoying the feelings she aroused in him.

And then he couldn't take it anymore and pulled her from him to roll her beneath his body and enter her swiftly, not waiting for her this time, unable to stem the need he felt in his nads. He was pumping, Emily's giggles had turned to sighs, and as he felt himself tighten and begin to climax, Emily's mobile rang.

"I have to get that," she breathed.

"In a minute. Ye can ring them back," grunted Fionn, unwilling to stop now.

"No, Fionn, I really mean it. It's da's ring tone."

She was pushing at him, and despite his close proximity to completion, Fionn felt himself dwindle to nothing.

Emily scrambled from beneath him, running to the kitchen and only a step away to get her phone from her bag when the ringing stopped. "Feckit," she mumbled, having missed the call, and hitting the re-dial button, cast Fionn a glance that said he was to blame and now all hell would break loose.

It had already, he thought. Henry would blame him for Emily not answering immediately.

His thoughts were stopped by Emily's scream and her sudden tears. It was alarming, and then he realized the time. It was after midnight. Why would Henry be calling so late?

"I have to go," cried Emily, scrambling to get dressed, retrieving her clothing from the floor where they'd ended up.

A frisson of fear streaked up Fionn's spine. "Em, what's happened?" It had to be something terrible for her to react like this.

"It's Gran, she's been in an accident," she cried. "Da's at the hospital, says I better come quick!" Having thrown her clothing on, she grabbed for the car keys, dropping them from shaking fingers.

"Feckit, ye're not goin' alone," said Fionn, taking the keys and placing them on the table. "I'm parked behind ye, we'll take my car." He was scrambling himself, throwing on his own clothing and pulling on socks and shoes as fast as possible while Emily finished dressing.

The rain was still pouring down, still an onslaught of water as they made their way through the dark night to the hospital, the very one Kathleen had walked out of earlier that evening.

Chapter Twenty-Seven

They were all here, thought Henry as he gazed about at his siblings, their spouses, and even the weyans. All had come to Cork to be at his mother's bedside from the accident that nearly claimed her life two nights ago.

She was still in a coma, still had not so much as fluttered an eyelid.

He cast a glance at Emily, his beloved daughter, asleep against Fionn's shoulder. As much as he wanted to hate the fella, Henry was grateful for his presence, for the fact that Fionn hadn't allowed Emily to drive to the hospital, as distraught as she was. He'd been nothing if not attentive to her needs, bringing her coffee, sandwiches, whatever he thought she might want, and never asking for anything for himself. That spoke volumes to Henry, especially when he found out that Fionn had asked his employer at the pub if he could take a few days because of a family emergency. The lad hadn't just abandoned his job, as some might have done. Nor had he abandoned Emily. Henry was going to have to give the fella some leeway. Whatever anger he had felt at finding Emily in Fionn's bed was dwindling, the more he saw of them together. There was closeness there, a real connection of sorts.

Siobhan returned just then with a coffee and a pastry for herself and Henry. No one else had wanted anything but

Henry knew he had to have something or his emotions would run rampant. As it was, he wanted to kill the plonker that smashed through the barrier of the oncoming lane. He'd been going too fast for the conditions, the car had swerved and then flipped, landing exactly in front of Kathleen's vehicle. There had been no way she could have avoided it and it was only luck that had kept her from being killed outright. Killed like the fella that hit her.

Even more alarming, she hadn't come to yet, hadn't given anyone a sign that she'd make it, although the doctors were quite certain she'd pull out of it eventually. These things take time, they'd said. The brain needed time to rest. But Henry knew from what his mam had told him that the longer people stayed in a coma, the less likely it was they'd come out of it. He hoped to God she was wrong about this time.

Damian was sitting with her. The family had given everyone a chance to sit with her, talk to her, anchor her to this world, because the last thing to go in a person was their hearing. People in comas could hear what was said, Mam had told them once upon a time. So they'd taken turns, kept up a cycle of conversation for her, following the advice she'd given her brood off and on over the years, and when they ran out of things to say, they would read to her.

Ciara looked miserable, thought Henry, blaming herself for not foreseeing this, for not being able to tell Mam to stay in Cork that night. And then Henry remembered that Damian had just sold his flat to move in with Dylan and Farrah, so she'd had no choice. She'd had to go home.

Thinking of Damian brought to mind a whole other dynamic in this crazy family. Damian, his daughter's true grandda, and Dylan, her true father. Henry didn't like to think of Dylan in that way, but there was no denying biology. Like it or not, everyone here was linked, in some way or another, to Kathleen.

And what would Da have thought of all this? Henry mused. His da might not have been the most faithful of husbands but he'd loved Mam, although he'd also loved Hank's mam. Mam had said that his da once told her he couldn't leave Ceilidh any more than he could leave her. He loved them both.

What a feckin' legacy, said Henry to himself. All these folk like a feckin' meltin' pot, sittin' in one room, all of them together, yet separate. There was Hank and Laura and the two weyans. They were the most distant relations. Hank was no relation to Mam at all, and yet here he was, supporting his half siblings, doing what he could to help. And Laura, bless her, takin' all the weyans under her wing whenever anyone went in to see Mam or needed a break away. All the women were doin' that, but Laura had stepped in most of all.

Ciara was rubbing her belly. Cian had brought her down from Galway following Liam and Sine, meeting up with Brandon and Aine at the hospital's entrance. And as Henry watched Ciara rub her belly as if there was great discomfort there, he wondered if she wouldn't give birth early because of the stress they were all surely feeling. Especially Ciara. Her features bore the guilt she felt at her failure to see the accident as much as the worry they all felt.

Brandon was too quiet, off in a corner brooding, looking ready to kill whoever dared approach him. It was typical of his brother, thought Henry, for once at a loss as to what to say or do to bring him out of it. But then he didn't have to because Aine was there, taking Brandon's hand and gazing up at her husband. Just that reassuring touch softened Brandon's features, and Henry gave in to the relief he felt that he wouldn't have Brandon to contend with as well as Mam's condition.

The lift doors opened and Dylan and Farrah entered, their arms laden with things the others might need: cold drinks, bags of sandwiches, sweets for wee Ryan. Dylan hadn't said anything, at least nothing that Henry had heard, about him and Farrah getting together but by the looks of them, they'd already sealed their bargain.

Henry was glad of that, if nothing more than it would take Dylan's focus off Emily, although Dylan had calmed down since those first, early days of finding out he was her father. Henry didn't suppose a leopard could change its spots, but if Dylan was a leopard, the spots had definitely changed, morphed into something else, something nicer. Kinder. Less domineering than he'd seemed at first. Or maybe it was just not knowing how to behave and letting his insecurities guide him rather than just accepting things as they were.

He didn't have time to ponder more as, from the corner of his eye, he saw Ciara wince and somehow knew it wasn't a trifling thing.

Instantly by her side along with Cian, they were crouching down in front of her as she keeled over into Cian's arms, the only words Henry heard were, "It's comin'."

Aine sprang into action, and moments later a wheelchair appeared. "Here, get her on here," said Aine, applying the brake and helping Ciara to sit. Then having settled her, the brake came off and she was moving as quickly as possible, Cian following.

Henry watched them disappear into the maws of the lift and wondered how long it would be before they saw any of them again.

* * *

Ciara vaguely felt them lift her onto a bed, was only partially aware of someone stripping her down, baring her so they could check how far into labor she was. A gush of liquid could be felt, someone cursed softly and then chuckled. It was the best that could happen, the breaking of her waters, they said.

The room spun and circled in whirling patterns and then she was outside of herself, floating above her body, seeing Cian pushed out of the room and Aine's anxious face. Her power animal, the merlin, appeared, guiding her off to some ethereal realm where she was surrounded by featherlike clouds in a roiling mist.

And then Mam before her, smiling, and Ciara pleading with her, "It's not yer time yet. Ye must go back!"

And Mam just smiling, brushing Ciara's golden locks away from her face, wiping the tears that seemed to be falling uncontrolled down her cheeks.

"Mam, Mam!" and then the merlin, taking her away as she heard people call her name. The calling was so insistent, "Ciara! Ciara!"

A pain ripped through her abdomen, jolting Ciara upright.

"She's with us, praise be to God," said someone nearby.

"Push, Ciara, push. That's a good girl. Give it all ye've got now."

Who spoke? Ciara didn't know but she was suddenly aware of the need to push, of someone's arms around her, behind her, helping her to sit, just like Liam had done with Sine that day at Ballycarbery.

"One more, I just need ye to give it one more."

Oh, it was the doctor at her feet that spoke, the one with her hands between Ciara's legs, doing something. Ciara didn't know what.

And then another push, as if she'd just had the biggest relief of all after a Christmas dinner. And then blessed calm, descending, threatening to engulf her.

And like an echo in her mind, Mam saying, "It's alright, mo cáilin, it'll be alright."

* * *

Cian walked back into the waiting area where the family was still gathered, still keeping watch, only this time, their faces looked a little hopeful.

"Well?" asked Henry, stepping up to Cian, acting like the head of the family Cian knew him to be.

"We have a son," said Cian, still not over the euphoria, the surprise of an early birth. And in a louder voice, steadier this time, he said, "It's going to be alright. Ciara said her mother told her it'll be alright."

Immediate silence and looks of awe covered the faces of those gathered, and only Dylan and Farrah appeared confused. The family began to breathe a sigh of relief.

Henry felt as if someone had just run a pointer down his spine and he shook off the feeling with a quick glance to his mother's room before turning back to Cian. "I don't know how Ciara knows that but I'll not question it. Ye've a son, and I'm happy for ye."

"Thought of a name yet?" asked Liam, shaking Cian's hand and giving him a brotherly hug.

Nodding, Cian answered, "Christian. She wants to call him Christian, and I can't have an objection to that. After all…"

He didn't have to finish. The family knew all about it, of the child they'd had in their past life who had grown to become a man and taken on his father's mantle. His name had been Christian.

A noise came from Kathleen's room, and Brandon, being the closest in proximity, was inside first, watching as his mother's eyes began to flutter and hearing her croak out, "Damian…Damian?"

Brandon stuck his head through the door and beckoned Damian over, saying, "It's you, mate. Ye're the one she's askin' for. Ye'd best get in here."

The look of thankfulness on Damian's features could not be misinterpreted. He was more than grateful.

Sliding in beside the bed, among the machines and the lines she was hooked up to, he saw her eyes open, focus on his face, and drift closed again.

"Damian."

"I'm here, love. I'm here." He took her hand, rubbing it between his own, softly caressing it.

"Damian."

"Yes, love."

"Damian, I've an awful itch, just by my nose. Just can't seem to make anythin' work…"

It was clear that even that little speech had taken all her effort, and Damian, chuckling through his tears, took a finger and scratched the upper part of her lip, just below her nose. "Is that it, my darlin'?"

"Mm-hmm," she mumbled, too weak to move or say much more.

And then she was asleep again and Damian sat down beside her bed, still holding her hand in his while a flood of nurses entered the area, suddenly busy. The smiles on their faces and the cheery nods conveyed what they all wanted to hear. As Ciara said, it would be alright.

Henry left them there, feeling the weight of the world lift from his shoulders. His mam was coming around. It would take a while for her to recover, for her strength to rebuild, and even the doctor said that once she came around, she'd have a long way to go. He hadn't enlarged on that, and Henry hoped that whatever he'd thought would eventually be alright.

"I'm goin' back to see Ciara," said Cian, looking suddenly as tired as everyone seemed to be feeling, as if a great weight had been lifted. And indeed, it had.

Nodding, Henry saw him off with his blessing.

Emily was standing just outside the room, watching Damian with her gran. Henry saw Fionn go to stand beside her, to lay his arm across her shoulder and pull her into a warm hug. He leaned his head to touch hers, and as their eyes met, Fionn kissed her—not deeply, but a kiss of reassurance. A kiss to say he'd be there for her always.

Henry felt like an arse. There'd been a closeness there he'd missed, simply because he was overly protective of his child.

No, he amended. Dylan's child. But she would always be his little girl, no matter who sired her. He wouldn't let a little thing like DNA come between them. Besides, she was as much related to himself as she was to anyone else, except perhaps Dylan. And Damian. He couldn't forget Damian.

Family. Once again, his da's legacy had borne through. They were a mish-mash of folk, all come together in this one instance, for one purpose. And now there was a new weyan in the bunch, wee Christian. He'd have to go visit Ciara later, to make certain for himself that all was well.

And from the background, he could hear Hank saying to Laura, "Coke? Ye're drinkin' coke? Laura, ye never touch that stuff unless…"

Henry turned just in time to see Laura nod and everyone else begin to cheer.

Hank's expression said it all. Henry didn't have to be told, although Laura's next words confirmed it.

"In about six months," she said, grinning from ear to ear.

"But ye'll be goin' back to work then," objected Hank, and Henry could see the confusion on his half brother's face.

"No, I won't," answered Laura, seeming quite pleased with herself.

"I think Hank needs to sit down," said Henry, walking over to his half brother and pushing on his shoulders.

"I don't want to sit," said Hank, still not having taken his eyes off Laura.

"Ye're in shock," said Henry. "Ye'll sit if I tell ye to. I'm yer big brother, after all."

His statement brought out grins all around, and even Dylan, who'd sported a look of concern when Henry first put his hands on Hank's shoulders, relaxed and joined in.

"Well," said Siobhan, "I guess the two of ye will need to head home sooner than expected."

"No," said Laura. "I want to have the baby here."

If Hank's jaw could have hit the floor, it would have, thought Henry.

"Here? But we've only got the house until September," Hank pointed out.

"We'll find something else," said Laura, sounding all too sure of herself.

Henry was about to interject when he spied the figures of his gran and grandda approach. They looked worried, and he'd need to put their minds at ease as soon as possible. They'd been away when his mam had her accident and were only now coming to see her for the first time.

"Is everythin' alright?" asked Grandda.

"It is," said Henry, hugging them both and helping

them to the room where Kathleen lay sleeping. "She's come around. Still weak, mind, but goin' to be okay."

Gran wiped a tear from her eye and gratefully took the chair Damian offered her. Looking up at Damian, she asked, "Has she accepted yer offer yet? I'll have to have words with her if she hasn't."

Damian could only shrug. "I don't know."

"I think she has," chuckled Henry. "Damian's the only one she's called for so far."

"Ah, that's good then," smiled his gran as she turned her attention back to her daughter.

Henry merely smiled.

Chapter Twenty-Eight

It was yerself who wanted to stay until the baby was born," observed Hank as they gazed outside at the driving sleet and cold, January wind. Ballycarbery Castle was a hazy shadow, engulfed by the storm that raged around the tiny cottage but not within. Inside was a vision of peace and warmth, with a small fire burning merrily in the grate. The cottage was blessed with electric heat but the fireplace was a nice touch, thought Hank.

"Hmm," mumbled Laura, sleepy-eyed and drowsy. She hadn't had much rest the past few nights and was sitting on the sofa, her head against the cushions at her back, eyes half closed, legs stretched along its length.

Any day now, he mused. Laura was due any day now, and then they'd be able to make their way back to Canada. He longed for the comforts of their cabin in the mountains for weekend jaunts, of their home in the city during the week, and of course, the place Hank had always called home, his own bit of Ireland in the woods. The original cabin that had burnt down and was now rebuilt.

Laura's boss, Kerry Gallagher, had guffawed his laughter through the telephone when Laura broke the news of her pregnancy to him. Hank could hear him from the other side of the room. And as the conversation continued, he knew Laura would be welcomed back whenever she was ready. It would be at least another year, and even then, Hank wondered if she'd want to return. Financially, they were doing fine—not wealthy, but able to keep their heads above water, as his mam used to say during one of their good spells. The good times when his da was around and Mam was happy. It wasn't often.

But his own life was different, and they were doing just fine.

His two weyans were playing on the floor, and now Meara took a toy that Ryan was busy with and the battle was on. Picking up his feisty one-year-old daughter, Hank said, "C'mon, mo chroi, time for a nap," and took her, screaming her objections, to her bed.

He met Laura's gaze when he returned, the last muffled cries of Meara fading as she fell asleep. "Are ye still glad we stayed?" he asked.

Laura, looking calm despite Ryan insisting on using her legs as a race track for his toy cars, met his question with a half-crazed grin. "Yeah, when all is said and done, I'm glad we stayed. However nasty it is outside right now, next week could see fair skies. And no snow," she added with a so there kind of nod.

"There is certainly snow at home," he replied, remembering their meeting three years before, the avalanche that knocked his truck on its side and nearly imprisoned him in an icy grave. He'd escaped from his would-be coffin and made his way to the nearest shelter, Laura's cabin, where they'd discovered each other.

Those few days of being stranded on the mountain together had led to so much more than the little fling Laura had seemed to prefer. She hadn't taken easily to his proposal of marriage but Hank hadn't been dissuaded by her stubborn refusal. He'd simply waited until she was ready.

"Hank, I know you've just put Meara down, but do you think we could take a drive?"

Hank's eyes widened, watching her rub her belly and swore he could see it tighten beneath his gaze. "Now?"

"Yeah. I think now."

"How much time?"

"I think enough time to get both kids in their winter coats and into the car. Not much more than that, though. This is number three, after all." She let the rest hang in the air, the look in her eye that recalled Meara's birth and how she'd been warned to come early next time. Meara had nearly been born in the car.

Hank lifted Ryan's winter coat from the peg by the door and retrieved his boots, mittens and hat, and throwing them to Laura to catch, went to retrieve Meara. His daughter was none too pleased about being woken up so soon after falling asleep, but Hank had no choice. It would be faster than waiting for Aine to arrive to watch the weyans. She'd have to pack up her own babe, and that took time he didn't think they had.

Instead, less than ten minutes later, they were on their way to the hospital in Cahersiveen. Laura's time had come.

Hank was still waiting for the blessed event an hour later, but not alone. Henry had arrived from Killarney, and Aine had come to take Ryan and Meara home with her until the nanny they had employed could pick them up and then return with them to the cottage, leaving Hank to stay by Laura's side unencumbered.

"How's yer wee man?" asked Hank, seeing the fatigue lining Henry's eyes and knowing he would look the same very soon, if he didn't already.

"Ah, grand, he is," answered Henry of his one-month-old

365

son, the pride in his voice evident in the grin spread across his features. "Siobhan's doin' well, getting' lots of sleep. I don't know how she does it, but as soon as wee Ronan is out, she falls asleep as well."

"She doesn't try to play super-mam?"

"Oh, ye mean do all the housework and such while he's sleepin'?"

"Yeah. Laura always tries to do too much. Thinks the house will fall down if laundry's not done and put away immediately."

Henry laughed. "I love Siobhan, but I can honestly say that has never been a fault of hers."

Hank only shook his head, chuckling because he knew it to be true. Henry's house always had that lived-in look. "I'd best get back in there, see how she's doin'," he said, indicating, with a nod of his head, the door to Laura's room.

"I'll be here if ye need anythin'," said Henry, "I'm sure others will be stoppin' in. Brandon's just finishin' some paperwork, he says, so he'll be round soon, although Liam won't be by for a while. He's on a new film and they're in Scotland doin' some work. Just left home yesterday," he finished.

"Scotland? Oh, I'd forgotten about that one. Bad timin' on our part," remarked Hank.

"I've talked to him, though, and to Sine as well. She's called Ciara…ye know how these things work between the women," Henry chuckled.

"A veritable network," agreed Hank. "I'm assuming it'll be a while before we get to see the lads and their wee girl."

"As soon as they can arrange it, they'll come by. Likely on the weekend when they can get away more easily. I've said they can have our spare room—ye know, Emily's old room—since she and Fionn are in Dublin."

"Emily's goin' to be upset at not bein' here just now."

"Won't she just!" said Henry, but there was laughter in his voice. "But she's so intent on lookin' after Fionn, seein' that all goes well for his schoolin' so he'll succeed. He's takin' commercial art, and from what she's told me, he's already got a few job prospects lined up."

"That'll suit Emily, havin' him work in commercial art rather than the pub. She's his biggest fan."

"Ah, the boy has talent, to be sure."

"Henry, are ye alright with them together?" asked Hank, suddenly wondering how his half brother was really feeling over his daughter's situation. He'd wanted her to stay in Inishannon at her gran's and at the flower shop where she'd worked all summer. But Emily would have none of it, and after Kathleen's near fatal accident, life changed.

"I wasn't at first," he admitted, "but since the accident, and as big as the house in Inishannon is, it got crowded right quick if ye get my drift."

"Ah, the weddin', yer mam and Damian."

"Hard to believe her name's not O'Farrell any longer, but Lynch."

"That was a spectacular weddin'," smiled Hank, remembering the two couples—Kathleen and Damian, and Dylan and Farrah—walking down the aisle, both couples side by side, so reminiscent of the twins' weddings at the cabin in Canada.

"I'm glad ye were here to see it." A mused look crossed Henry's features. "What changed Laura's mind on leavin'?"

Hank could only shrug. "I don't know. All I know is that if she had any second thoughts after that, it was too late." He couldn't help grinning his pleasure.

"It helped that Sam's neighbors decided to stay in Spain for the winter. Seems they were only too happy to have ye stay at their cottage and keep it up in their absence."

"It's a bit small for us with the two weyans, but we enjoyed their garden and that's a fact," said Hank, remembering the fresh produce they'd happily consumed, right up until the first frost that killed even the heartiest plants.

Henry fiddled with a pen, clicking it open, clicking it shut, then laid it back down again where he'd found it. "Hank, I don't think I ever mentioned how grateful I was to ye for takin' over my work to the extent ye did when Siobhan gave birth to Ronan. Ye did more than I'd asked, stepped up to the plate like a good brother would."

Hank waved it off. "It's no bother. Brandon helped, too."

Henry acknowledged that with a nod. "He did. And I've told him. But I thought it important that ye knew, too. As I said, I don't know that I told ye."

Hank began to chuckle. "Henry, ye didn't know much that day, I can tell ye. And havin' ye describe the birth was a little more than anyone needed to hear. If Siobhan knew what ye'd said, she'd have beaten ye within an inch of yer life and ye'd have deserved it."

"I'd never seen anyone bein' born before, nor anythin', when I think on it. That tuft of black hair comin' through…"

Hank clamped his hand on Henry's shoulder to stop the reminiscing. "I know. I witnessed my own two, and if I don't get back in there soon, I may miss the third."

Nodding, Henry agreed. "Off ye go, then, and I'll see ye directly."

The afternoon faded into night, the weather worsened, and the wind howled its progress in a true Atlantic gale. Laura's contractions were close now, the midwife assured them that all was proceeding; but she didn't look convinced and Hank knew this was different from the first two weyans. They'd come quickly and easily, and he didn't know why this one should be different.

Taking up the cloth, he dipped it under the tap, wrung out the cold water, and went to wipe Laura's sweat-covered brow. They'd wanted to have the baby at home, have the midwife come to them, but the cottage was too small. There was barely enough room for the four of them as it was. And although there hadn't been complications in the first two births, Laura had indicated a preference for a hospital birth. She'd consulted Ciara, whose talent now seemed hit-and-miss and who could only say the hospital was the safer bet.

Hank wondered if she'd seen trouble but was unable to define it.

A moment later, the midwife appeared again, this time frowning as she checked Laura's progress. "Ye're just not dilatin'," she said. "I thought stretchin' yer cervix would have got things goin', but ye're still nowhere."

Hank took in Laura's drawn expression, the pain of another contraction, and the controlled breathing she'd begun. He tried to help her through it but though she grabbed onto his hands and squeezed for all she was worth, it seemed that it was all for naught.

A half hour later confirmed no further progress, and the midwife called in the anaesthetist. "Time for a little intervention," she explained. "We'll give her an epidural, see if that doesn't let her relax and open up."

Laura had been stoic up until then, breathing through each contraction and maintaining a near silent cry with each one, but this time, as her abdomen turned to stone beneath Hank's hand, she let loose a sound that sent chills up his spine.

He'd never felt so helpless in his life.

Henry heard the cry from the hallway. He'd talked to Siobhan, who'd called him once an hour asking for another update, but there hadn't been any news. And now he watched with concern as a second doctor entered the room just as Laura's cry died away. He was alone in the waiting area, Brandon having gone home to relieve Aine for the next couple of hours with their own child, just weeks older than Henry and Siobhan's, and as Henry paced the floor, Aine arrived, greeting him with a worried look.

"Well?" she asked, brow raised in question.

Shaking his head, Henry replied simply, "I don't know. There's another doctor just gone in. The midwife's been there for the last hour, and someone else went in about fifteen minutes ago. I don't know what's goin' on."

As he spoke, the door opened and the doctor that had just entered left. Aine quickly caught up with him, calling, "Tom! Tom, can ye tell me what's happenin' in there."

The doctor seemed to recognize her, and although Henry couldn't hear what was being said, he knew Aine would tell him. And sure enough, she spun on her heel, returning to Henry's side, saying, "They've given her an epidural. If that doesn't work, they may have to section."

Henry blinked. "What the hell's an epidural?"

"Oh, it's a kind of anaesthetic where the patient is awake but doesn't feel anything. It's also called a spinal block. They put the needle in the spine with a drip line…" she began.

At the mention of needle, Henry felt his stomach turn. He was no good around hospitals, and especially not when the word needle was implied. "It's okay, I don't need to know more," he said, choking down his words on a lump of bile.

Aine must have realized she was talking to someone who

didn't understand medical lingo, and furthermore, had a fear of needles. Apologizing, her words tinged with laughter, she said, "I would have thought with yer mam bein' a nurse and all, ye'd automatically know what I was talkin' about."

"No. I knew enough to bind wounds, staunch blood flow, do anythin' I had to if one of the others were hurt, providin' no one came with a needle. Blood never bothered me. I've seen enough to last a lifetime, but needles are somethin' else." He shivered as if a cold breeze had just blown in through the hallway.

"Hmm, I'm a bit gobsmacked but I understand. Let me just poke my head in, see how things are goin'."

She didn't get a chance, though. Hank emerged just as Aine was about to enter.

One look at his face, and Henry knew it wasn't good. "Well?" he asked in a hopeful manner.

Hank was only silent, looking pale and, if Henry wasn't mistaken, ready to cry.

"Hank?"

Hank looked at Henry, swallowed visibly, and said, "They're goin' to take the baby by section. She's showin' signs of distress."

A chill seemed to settle over them, and Aine, ever the nurse, asked, "Hank, do ye want to be there when she's born?" They all knew it was a girl, had known for some months.

"No. I'd faint dead away. I was barely good for a natural birth, I don't know what I'd be like at a section."

"It's for the best," she advised. "If there's a problem, it's best they get her out now, as quickly as possible."

Agreeing with a nod, Hank sat down in the chair only to stand as the door to the room opened and Laura's bed was propelled in a rapid fashion down the hall. Hank followed, holding Laura's hand as far as he was able until the swinging doors to the operating theaters closed before him with Laura on the other side.

Henry stood watching as a nurse approached Hank, said something, saw Hank shake his head and return to where he and Aine were waiting.

"God forgive me, I didn't want to go in there," said Hank, crumbling into the seat, defeated.

"It's alright, mo dheartháir. No one expects ye to handle this easily. We're here, waitin' with ye."

Hank could only sit and stare into the distance at some unknown object.

Henry sat down to wait with him and Aine went to procure some coffee. That done, the three sat together. A silence of sorts filled the waiting room and only the normal sounds of a hospital interrupted the quiet with announcements through the address system, the sound of gurneys rolling down the hall, the custodian's mop being rinsed in the bucket as he cleaned the floor along the corridor where they waited.

After what seemed like days, and was in reality only an hour later, the doctor emerged from the swinging doors, removing his surgical cap as he approached. At least he's smiling, thought Henry, feeling that if the news was bad, the doctor would not look happy at all.

"Congratulations, Mr. Mulligan, ye've a fine wee daughter. They're just cleanin' her up, weighin' her, and makin' sure all's well, and then ye'll be able to see her."

"And Laura? What about my wife?"

"She did well. Came through it all easily enough. She'll be taken back to her room soon, and then ye can see her as well."

As the doctor retreated down the hall the way he'd come,

the threesome looked at each other, at the signs of relief on their faces, and sighed audibly together. Laughter broke out at their timing, and Aine stood, saying, "I think we could all use another coffee."

"Got anythin' stronger?" asked Hank.

Henry smiled and pulled a small flask from his back pocket. "I thought ye might want somethin', so I brought ye this. Aine," he turned to his sister-in-law, "when ye get the coffee, make certain there's room in it for a wee bit o' this, only not in mine, right?" He held up the flask, and Aine grinned.

"Too right!" she exclaimed, and went off to refill their cups.

Chapter Twenty-Nine

Farrah wasn't prepared when she answered the knock on the door. Opening it wide, she stood in shock for the space of one heartbeat before trying to slam it closed it again. The intruder blocked her move, knocking over the umbrella stand in the melee. Fear catching in her throat, she spun on her heel to run for the back door. Dylan was at work, and not due home for lunch for another half hour. There was no one around for miles, and her father had found her.

She hadn't run more than the depth of the sitting room before he'd caught up to her, grabbed onto her arm, and forced her to turn and meet him.

"Let me go," she said, her voice wavering as her mind rapidly scanned her options. There weren't many, although she thought she might be able to lure him into complacency and then outrun him through the woods or across the wide lea to a neighbor's house to seek refuge.

But he didn't give her a chance. His hand around her upper arm gripped hard, bruising her flesh, and she cried out in pain.

"You will come with me," he ordered.

Farrah knew she had to stand her ground. It was now or never. "No!" she protested, lifting her arm and pulling it back sharply in order to dislodge it from his iron-like grip.

It didn't work, he only gripped it harder.

Dylan, she prayed, oh Dylan, please hurry home!

Anwar pulled Farrah toward the door, but she wasn't going to go willingly. Going suddenly slack in his grasp making her body a dead weight, she noted him stagger under the sudden pull of almost nine stone on his arm. Farrah dropped and rolled, breaking his manic grip, and as he lunged for her, swiftly evaded his clutches and headed for the door that hadn't quite latched.

Grasping the knob, she'd nearly succeeded in escaping the house, had nearly broken free of the menace her father had become. But just when she thought freedom was hers, he managed to grab at her clothing in a last desperate lunge, and Farrah, thrown off balance, went down hard, her arm outstretched as if in supplication. But supplication for what? There would be no salvation for her, she knew.

"No, Daddy, please, no," she cried, feeling his hands clawing at her, attempting to secure his hold.

A final effort, a final strategy in her battle for freedom and perhaps her life, came in the way of the umbrella stand, a short column of old brass that had stood with three umbrellas inside. It had been knocked over as Anwar had blazoned his way inside the house. Reaching, she grasped at one of the umbrellas that had tumbled free, and as her father dragged her by her feet toward the door, she on her belly, her outstretched hand grasped the handle, and held. Flipping to her back, she was close enough to lunge forward using the umbrella as a lance.

It was a large umbrella, the kind used on a golf course. Dylan had said it was much easier to fit the two of them beneath one big one when walking in the rain, and she had agreed. She liked its bright colors, and while it was a little ungainly, when Dylan held it she merely snuggled next to him and they were both sheltered beneath its broad canopy.

Now she used it as a weapon, and as she sat up and lunged forward, Anwar leaned over as if to take it from her, shortening the distance between them. He hadn't anticipated her move, she thought as the exposed tip penetrated his abdomen. Not stopping to think on what she was doing, she pressed harder, sitting up and putting her full weight behind her as best she could and pushing.

Blood began to flow and a look of disbelief crossed Anwar's features. She pushed again, and as he let go of her foot, she slid backward, beginning to tremble violently as she watched him take in the injury she had done him.

Anwar dropped to his knees, the umbrella firmly stuck in his middle until he grabbed at it, and she stared, transfixed, as he pulled it from his gut in a growl of rage and pain before dropping the rest of the way to the floor, open-eyed still. He'd stopped moving.

It was a bad move. Blood flowed freely, soiling the ancient and worn Aubusson carpet, ruining the floral pattern with streaks of ill-placed crimson.

By now, Farrah's mind had caught up with what had happened, and she began gasping out her fear. She hadn't had time to be truly afraid before now, hadn't had time to think, so busy was she on trying to escape. And survive. And now, as she looked on in horror, her father's blood oozed steadily out, a growing pool of scarlet marring the carpet and leaking onto the floor.

A crunching sound of tires on the gravel drive signaled the arrival of a vehicle, the sound only just penetrating Farrah's hearing. She was concentrating on her father's raspy sounds as his life-blood left him.

And then Dylan was there, pulling her to him, away from

the sight of her father, dying on their floor.

Dimly, she felt Dylan's hands lead her to the couch, place her there, and then bring her a dram of whiskey. She heard him say, "Drink this. Ye're in shock. It'll smarten ye up." And as he glanced quickly at the figure on the floor before meeting her eyes again, he said, "I want ye to know, ye're my only concern right now. I don't care if he dies there. It'll be less than what he deserves."

Mechanically Farrah nodded, downing the dram in one great gulp, while from a far-away place she could hear Dylan's voice calling for the garda and perhaps an ambulance.

In short order, sirens were heard as emergency personnel arrived. First the garda and then the ambulance, although one look at her father and she knew there was no hope of him surviving. And sure enough, once the ambulance attendant leant down to check his pulse, he only gave a shake of his head to the garda officer, who hadn't seemed surprised.

* * *

It was over. The Aubusson carpet had been removed, the reminder of her father's death lingering only in the walls around them. Dylan couldn't change the room but he had made it over into something unrecognizable as the space where her father had determined his own fate. The room, he told her as the old wallpaper came down and new paint went up, had been in dire need of updating. It turned from the haphazardly decorated space with outdated furniture that didn't match to a cozy cottage room, one with new furnishings and an upbeat modern feel. Farrah seemed to like it, and if she remembered the exact spot where her father died, she didn't show it.

Sylvia walked into the room just then, carrying the tea tray, laden with fresh scones and clotted cream. "Come and have some tea," she invited, and Farrah met her mother's gaze, a look of love on her face as well as the sadness of losing a loved one, no matter how deranged he'd become. They would eventually heal, and life would go on.

"Have ye thought what ye'd like to do?" asked Dylan, helping himself to a scone and ladling a huge spoon of cream over it. "Ye know ye're welcome to stay," he finished.

Suddenly unsettled, Sylvia exhaled deeply as she sat beside her daughter on the sofa. Dylan was seated adjacent to Farrah in the newly re-covered wingback chair, the only bit of furniture that had survived the renovation.

"I've not wanted to think about it," she said. "Anwar had always eschewed fanaticism, and suddenly he became the worst fanatic of all. It had happened quickly, almost overnight. We were suddenly no better than his kept prisoners for the last two, nearly three years, and I don't know if I can go back there yet. Still, it was our home, a loving home, for more than twenty years before that. I've tried to maintain a positive attitude, to think everything will work out, given time. But I'm still at sea with my feelings. I don't know which way to turn."

There wasn't much that could be added. They'd all felt at sixes and sevens with Anwar's behavior and subsequent death; with the horror of that day and the relief that followed. Relief at finally banishing the threat he'd become to Farrah.

Farrah was still overwhelmed with emotion at losing her father, and by her own hand, no less. Everyone had said she'd had no choice. It was self-defence. Yet Dylan knew it would haunt her forever and only time and understanding would diminish its ravaging effects.

Sylvia had similar wounds. She'd lost a husband who at one time had been her loving partner. The autopsy had discovered a growing lesion in his brain; one, the doctors had said, that could very well be responsible for his sudden change in personality. It would have eventually taken over and killed him.

Instead, his death had come from the end of the golf umbrella, whose protective, plastic tip had broken off the very first day they'd had it, leaving an exposed, machined end of metal with an extremely sharp edge to it. Dylan had meant to file it down but, as the weather had been dry, had forgotten about it, and the umbrella stayed innocently in the stand until Farrah's ultimate attempt to free herself from her father once and for all. If not for that still sharp tip, it would not have broken skin; would not have penetrated his organs the way it had. And if Anwar had not pulled it out, further damaging himself in the process, he might have survived. He'd inadvertently sliced through his descending aorta, the rough, exposed metal tip as sharp and deadly as a wicked blade.

They'd given the umbrella to the garda as evidence. Neither Dylan nor Farrah ever wanted to see it again.

"Mummy, you can stay here with us. It would please us so much if you did," said Farrah, her hand covering her mother's with a reassuring squeeze.

"Yes, please," echoed Dylan. "My own mam left when I was a weyan. I've never experienced a mam's touch. I only had my da's way of growin' up, and I think he did a fine job, but our house was always a man's house, not a feminine touch anywhere. Unlike now, where Farrah has so obviously had input," he grinned.

That seemed to bring a smile to Sylvia's grief-worn features. "You're very kind. Of course I shall be delighted to stay, for a while, at least. Although, with two women in the household, I think we may clash eventually."

"Yes, but eventually I would want you here anyway, because at some point, Dylan and I would like to have children of our own." Farrah's moss-green eyes swam with unshed tears, and a grin split her features as she bit her bottom lip laughingly.

"Are you?" asked Sylvia, the O of her mouth gaping open in a most unwomanly manner. She would have been shocked to see herself that way, thought Dylan with a smile of his own.

Shaking her head, Farrah chuckled. "Not yet. I'm not ready to carry another child yet. Perhaps in a year or so. My body needs a break!"

"Are you alright with that, Dylan? That's she's given up a child to those two young men?" Sylvia asked, suddenly bringing up the adoption of Farrah's child.

"Ah, it's no bother. We're related after all, however lightly, and so we'll see her grow up."

"Oh, that's right. I'd forgotten. You're their niece's father. Gosh, what a tangled web it appears!" she exclaimed, and both Dylan and Farrah laughed.

"It could get worse," said Farrah, and Dylan wondered if she'd tell her mother about Michael.

He didn't have to worry. It was soon evident that Sylvia knew all about him.

"Oh, you mean because Dawn really is his child as well as yours?"

"Partly that," answered Farrah. "It may be that they will want a second one, a child of Niall's who would be a true half sibling to Dawn."

"What?" If Sylvia seemed aghast before, now she appeared completely blown out of the water.

"It's true," added Dylan. "We haven't fully discussed the

possibility yet because, of course, Farrah and I would like our own. But we haven't completely discounted it yet, either."

Abruptly standing, as if she didn't know what else to do, Sylvia plunked herself down again in her agitation and faced them. "I don't understand. How could you? It's not up to you to populate the world," she said to Farrah.

"No," her daughter agreed. "But Niall and Michael are both so sweet, and Dawn deserves a sibling. And wouldn't it be nice if that sibling could be a least a half sibling in reality? I would have happily done it for them if not for meeting Dylan. And this way, I still get to see Dawn grow and become a young woman, as well as another child if things fall in line."

Looking extremely vexed, Sylvia picked up her tea with slightly shaking hands, murmuring, "I don't know. I just don't know."

"Well, it's nothing that's going to be decided just now. It's something we've all agreed to discuss later on, keeping our options open. It may be that the lads will truly be happy with just one child, and it may be that Dylan and I want our own family at the same time, so I wouldn't be available to have a child for them."

"And it may be that we'll decide she's had enough," put in Dylan, eyeing Farrah with one brow raised.

That seemed to settle Sylvia somewhat. "So it isn't a fait accompli, in other words?"

"No, not at all, Mummy. And I'm sorry if we've upset you."

"I'm not upset. It's just…well, it's just something I'll have to get used to, especially knowing that Dawn is really your child and Michael's. He is the one your father forbid you to see, isn't he?"

"Yes. But that was a long time ago. It's all water under

381

the bridge, so to speak, and we're all friends. Just friends, but good ones."

"Well, I think you are going above the call of duty for just a friend," huffed Sylvia into her tea.

"Yes, Mummy," grinned Farrah, winking at Dylan.

"Delicious scones, Mam," mumbled Dylan through his mouthful of pastry and cream.

"Mmm," acknowledged Sylvia, before a smile crept across her features.

Dylan had known he'd get to her if he called her Mam.

"More tea?" asked Farrah, and the afternoon settled down into a congenial sitting.

Epilogue

It had been dubbed The Irish Manse, looking every bit the stately abode of some of the more newly built homes that spotted the countryside throughout the south of Ireland. Only it was Hank's mountain home in British Columbia, Canada, finished at last, and glowing with a newness in the late July sun. The last of the family had arrived from Ireland, and everyone had managed to be there for a week-long celebration, farmed out between his and Laura's two homes on the mountain.

Hank shook his head, wondering how he could ever have thought himself alone in the world when he'd had such a family as this at his fingertips all along. And what would the old man think of it all, he'd wondered more than once, of the two families he'd begun, one in Cork and one in Kerry? They were unknown to each other until well past his death.

One of Ciara's friends, as fey as Ciara herself had been, had suggested that their father was pulling strings from the other side, getting the two families together. Hank didn't know if he believed that or not, but stranger things had occurred, and he wouldn't put it past the old bastard to do just that. Certainly, the way the siblings had found out about each other had been highly coincidental. Yet it had begun a search for answers that had touched every last family member, and then some.

Ryan went racing past his da, in hot pursuit of the puppy they'd adopted. The mongrel came from the animal shelter in town and although anyone would be hard pressed to identify the different breeds that made it up, they'd all agreed it was the perfect dog for Ryan.

Ryan, the second eldest of Henry-the-senior's grandchildren—Emily being the eldest—was nearly four, and they went down in age from there. Meara, next in line, was two and a half.

Then came Niall and Michael's wee girl, Dawn. She was a year-old toddler now, and born on the same day as Liam and Sine's baby, Aedan.

Brandon and Aine's baby, wee Katy, was only a few months older than Ciara and Cian's child, Christian. As Brandon had said, almost everyone else seemed to be named for someone, except Dawn and Aedan, so he wanted to strengthen that tradition by naming his daughter after his mam.

Henry and Siobhan's baby had been born at Christmastime, a healthy, strapping boy, looking much like his father. They'd called him Ronan, an Irish name meaning little seal. Henry had laughed, so giddy with happiness when the child burst forth from his mother to Henry's outstretched hands, hands that nearly failed to catch the baby, slick and wriggly. The doctor, close behind had said, "He's like a rónán, all slippery and such." And that was how the child got his name. It was one of the secrets Henry had shared with Hank. Hank shared that story with Laura, but no other, having promised Henry. Eventually, though, Siobhan herself had spread the tale, and now everyone knew how Ronan had come by his name.

Hank's third child, Ceilidh, named for his own mother, was the youngest at six months of age. But they were all doing well, all thriving, growing, happy children. Hank was as gobsmacked as the rest, seeing how everyone mingled and related, just like the family they were.

Not be left out, Kathleen's elderly parents were in attendance, as spry and alert as they could be although they were both closing in on their ninth decade.

Emily had made the trek from Ireland by herself, abandoning Fionn to his studies and his summer job. He'd been unable to get away, and Emily seemed fine with that.

"How are things between you and Fionn, anyway?" asked Hank of his niece.

Emily shrugged. "Alright, I suppose, like any couple."

Hank took a sidelong glance at her, caught the resemblance to his sister, and smiled to himself, grateful for that one glimpse. She was special to him, was Emily, and so he offered up his opinion. "Ye know, if ye aren't happy, if things aren't goin' the way ye want, ye need to acknowledge that now, and if ye can't make it better, then leave."

Nodding her agreement, all Emily said was, "This is a time for me to think on it, Uncle Hank. I'd like to say Fionn and I will be together always, but I don't think we will. As much as I love him, I don't think he feels quite the same; and though he was grand when Gran was hurt, I can't help feelin' that he thinks he needs to protect me and that's why he let me go to Dublin with him. Besides, I think I know what I want to do, and it doesn't involve Fionn."

"And that would be...?" he let his voice trail off, the question hanging.

"I'm goin' to go to culinary school. Haven't decided which one, yet. But the more I think on it, the more I think that's what I'd like."

Hank laughed and ruffled her long, wavy hair, that mop

so much like Meara's. "Ah, takin' after yer grandda and his cookin'. Damian must be pleased and I can tell ye sure that we're all appreciatin' what ye've done here, cookin' up a storm as if we're all starvin' all the time. I think we'll all gain a few pounds from yer delicious fare."

"Speakin' of," said Emily, "I think it's time to start the barbecue for supper. I've got a rare surprise for everyone and I'll need to get started if it's to be done in time."

Hank watched her walk away as the sound of a car approaching up the road could be heard. Recognizing it as it pulled into view, he saw Kerry and Sarah Gallagher arrive to join the party. Kerry was Laura's old boss, and Sarah was Laura's neighbor from the condo. The two had finally wed after much speculation and a very long courtship. Kerry had been nothing if not persistent, against Sarah's highly fought independence and resistance to having anyone tell her what to do. Her belly sported an obvious baby bump, as Hank had learned to call them, and he wondered if that hadn't been the final tactic that had brought the two together.

Kathleen and Damian took charge of Ceilidh, cooing at her new technique of blowing bubbles, and Dylan and Farrah, newly expecting themselves, went to greet the newcomers, having met them for the first time a few days before.

Hank turned around just as Laura's arms went about his neck, pulling him into a full-blown kiss, drawing him down to her height, Hank going willingly.

"Now?" asked Hank, a sultry gleam in his eye.

"Any time you want, fella," she laughed, and then added, "but no. Not now. Kerry's brought his camera and is obliging me by doing a group photo. Come on, let's get everyone together."

As the sun blazed through the leafy canopy of trees around

them, Kerry directed them to stand before an especially picturesque bower, yelling, "Say cheese!" while Sarah held out squeaky toys that brought a smile to the youngsters in the group and laughs to the adults' faces.

So many gathered all together, and all because of one man, however misguided his intentions had been, observed Henry. There was a legacy here, from the old man himself down to the newest member. And, as Henry knew, they were all okay with that.

THE END

A letter to my readers:

It feels like a life-time has gone by since I began this series, but in actuality, it has been only slightly less than four years. The words have flowed onto the page as if of their own accord, and while I stumbled and sometimes fought with my craft, I believe the intent of the stories comes across loud and clear. The O'Farrells, including Hank and Laura, are a family. A family with all the same inner struggles and imperfections of families everywhere. They make mistakes, go down the wrong roads and generally act as people in love do, especially when they fight it or seek too hard for it.

Yet their very weaknesses are their strengths. Coming from a rather large family, at least by today's standards, I can honestly say that, given time and the right circumstances, we all face down our own devils, with or without each other's help. I have allowed the siblings in this family to explore their relationship with one other, hate it, resist it, and come to terms with it. And in the end, embracing it and each other.

In attempting to give the novels the character of speech so prevalent when listening to an Irish person speaking English, I have dropped the 'g' of the 'ing' suffix in many places and used 'ye' instead of 'you'. Please note that the Irish accent is differs greatly across the country, from the light lilt in Dublin, to the very strong accent, quickly spoken, in Dingle. It is impossible to encompass the entirety so I have chosen to take the middle ground. In one instance, I have Laura acknowledging the way Hank says 'place', like 'pless'. It is this kind of thing that makes attempting to mimic the accent so difficult. Were I to change each word according to the way it truly is spoken, no one would understand what was written.

Lastly, I acknowledge that I am not a native Gaelic

speaker. I have tried to stay close to the Munster dialect in words and meaning, but interpretation can be varied in some cases. Again, the intent is there, but if I have erred in its usage, please forgive me.

If you would like to write to me, I invite you to do so through my website at www.smcross.net. I look forward to hearing from you!

Thank you for your interest.

S. M. Cross

ABOUT THE AUTHOR

The daughter of an Air Force family, and therefore an extensive world traveler, Ms. Cross has been writing since the age of fifteen, creating stories around the places she has lived and visited. After writing an editorial column for a newspaper for fifteen years, she is now retired and living in Canada's north with her children, grandchildren and an assortment of cats and dogs.

BOOKS BY THE AUTHOR:

THE O'FARRELL LEGACY SERIES
Mulligan's Dream – Book One
Double Take – Book Two
Brandon: Bad Boy of Kinsale – Book Three
A Winter Sky – Book Four
C'mere To Me – Book Five

COMING SOON
A Regency Series:
A Quality Woman
Duchess Incognito
The Daunting Duchess
Monique

GUIDE TO IRISH SLANG
AND PRONUNCIATION

The following is a list to help the reader understand and pronounce the words and phrases used in the books. Please note that as there are three dialects in Ireland (Munster, Connaught, Ulster) pronunciations are approximate. For those curious readers, the books use the Munster dialect.

NAMES OF PEOPLE AND PLACES:

Aghadhoe—Aha-doe
Aibreann—AW-bren
Aine—AHN-ya
Carrauntoohill—CARE-an-TOO-hill
Ceilidh—KAY-lee – Hank's mother's name; also a traditional social gathering
Cian—SEE-an
Ciara—KEER-a
Cliffs of Mohr—Cliffs of Mor
Daithi—DAW-hee
Dierdre—DEER-dra
Grainne—GRAN-ya
Lough Leane—Lock Lane
Sine—SHE-na
Siobhan—She-VAUGHN

SLANG/EXPRESSIONS:

An bpósfaidh tú mé—(un BAWS-hee too mey) Will you marry me

banjaxed—broken, usually irreparable

bean sidhe—(BAN-shee) – In Irish folklore, the bean sidhe (woman of the hills) is a spirit or fairy who presages a death by wailing

black stuff—Guinness

bollocks—nonsense, balderdash

bowsie—thug, scumbag, wife-beater

box—vagina

boyo—boy, lad

chipper—a place for burgers or fish 'n chips

chubbed—erection

Claddagh ring—Irish ring showing hands cradling a heart with a crown on top

cop on—smarten up, leave off, settle down, etc.

craic—fun

eejit—idiot

fáilte—(FAHL-cheh) welcome; also the name of the National Tourism Development Authority

fella—your guy, partner/husband/boyfriend

flange, fanny—women's genitals

gabh transna ort fhéin—(gave tras orth hayn) go fuck yourself (Literal translation: Go sideways on yourself)

gonch—underwear

gligeen—stupid person

gobsmacked—surprised

gráim thú—(GRAW-im hoo)I love you

horned up—horny

is tú mo ghrá—(iss too muh yraw) I love you

jarvey (jarveys)—men who drive the jaunting cars (horse drawn carts)

kip—sleep

lack—girlfriend

langer—multiple meanings – here it is used as a term for penis, as are "lad" and "flute"

leanbh—(LAN-uv) child

mhac—(mock) son, also buddy, dude, mate

manky—dirty, filthy, disgusting

mo cáilin—(muh colleen) my girl

mo chroi—(muh khree) my heart

mo chuisle, mo chroi—(muh KUSH-la, muh khree) darling/ sweetheart – literally pulse of my heart

mo dheartháir—(muh ghrih-hawr) my brother

nads—gonads; balls

neddy—idiot, fool

Oiche mhaith agus codladh sámh—(EE-hyeh WY(h) ogg-uss KOLL-oo SAA-oo) good night and sleep safe

plonke—country bumpkin, slow on the uptake

ráicleach—(raaklochk) slut

shandy—beer mixed with another drink - lemonade, ginger ale, etc.

skank—untrustworthy, low-life criminal type

sláinte—(SLAWN-chuh) health

Táim I ngrá leat—(TAW-iming-RAW lyat) I'm in love with you

Tá tú go h-álainn—(taw too guh HALL-in) you are beautiful

thick—extremely stupid ("brick" is also used)

wankers—idiots

weyans—(WAY-uns) wee ones, children

wisht—(weesht) hush, be quiet, etc.